The Shepherds

also by
Hallie Lee

The Shady Gully Series
Paint Me Fearless
Wolfheart
Shades of Violet

For a list of Who's Who in Shady Gully? visit
https://www.hallielee.com/whos-who-in-shady-gully

The Shepherds

The Shady Gully Series
Book 4

HALLIE LEE

WordCrafts Press

The Shepherds
Copyright © 2024
Hallie Lee

ISBN: 978-1-962218-37-5

Cover concept and design by Mike Parker
Original art ©Yafit Art/Adobe Stock

Published by WordCrafts Press
Cody, Wyoming 82414
www.wordcrafts.net

For Tammy Lynne,

My forever bestie, my sister in Christ, and one very
intuitive and treasured shepherd…

I love you!

Prologue

"Watch out for false prophets. They come to you in sheep's clothing, but inwardly they are ferocious wolves."

~Matthew 7:15

Timothy

Where was I? The Garden of Eden? Heaven?

I hadn't a clue, but life was beautiful here…inside the gates.

Everywhere I looked I was met with a kaleidoscope of images, shapes, and colors. Oh, the colors! While orange—yes, orange—had never been one of my favorites, here the varying hues of carrot were simply mind-boggling!

Surrounded by similar visual presentations at every turn, my psyche bounced from one breathtaking stage to another. Exquisite culinary delights. Cascades of breathtaking flowers. Landscapes, plant life, and insects, all nothing short of spectacular.

And the creatures! Simply magnificent! Some were so microscopic and purposefully designed they made me weep with wonder, while others towered so high, I was sure they could reach the heavens. I marveled at the soulful tenderness lurking behind the giant animals' eyes, apparently designed—masterfully, I might add—to offset the sheer scale of their bulk.

But it wasn't just the scenery inside the gates that evoked a sense of well-being and joy, the atmosphere itself aroused a sense of rightness. Truth. Purity.

Security. Safety.

So why then was I drawn to the gate's edge, desperate to see, to experience, what was beyond? I blinked repeatedly, determined to clear my vision so I could identify what beckoned to me in the darkness.

The moon hovered, teasing me with a hazy film that left me frustrated.

What was that?

A voice. A cry for help. A need.

I shook the iron rungs on the gate. "Who's out there?"

A lamb bleated in return. And then another. "Baaaaa."

I could see their shadows now, writhing in the gloom. Poor creatures, they needed me!

"Baaaaaaaa!" The innocents cried out again, increasingly frantic.

"I'm coming." I shook the bars. "I'll help you!" And then something miraculous happened. The iron rungs melted away before my eyes, just enough so that I could squeeze through the restrictive bars.

As I made my way to the shadows in the dark, I pronounced gallantly to the frightened lambs, "Here I am. I've come to save you."

All at once, the mounting flock surrounded me, and I discovered, to my horror, that they weren't the grateful lambs I'd expected. In fact, I found myself in front of a pack of snarling wolves! With their heads lowered, they moved in on me with their bloody tongues lolling.

A particularly daunting beast approached me then, a crooked grin spread across his nasty face. "Fooled ya."

"You're no better than us," another feral wolf snarled. "Face it."

"You're a fraud," another chimed, foaming at the mouth.

"Fake. Faker," they heckled as their sphere tightened around me.

I wheeled, wildly searching for a way out, for a path back inside the gates, but the pack had now multiplied, and I was completely trapped.

It was then that a particularly grotesque wolf, whose blue eyes matched my own, advanced. Her wretched voice was painfully familiar. "I knew you'd come," the She-Wolf croaked hoarsely. "You'd do anything for me, wouldn't you?"

"No," I gasped, recognizing the voice at once, recalling its brokenness—and cruelty. My breathing came in sharp, panicked hiccups. "No."

As she circled me, I spotted the familiar poison-filled needles dangling from her tangled fur, and the cloudiness in her dull, blue eyes. "You're a charlatan," she hissed.

"A flimflam man," the others chanted. Their shabby, whiskered wolf faces morphed into a series of men I'd spent years trying to forget. Men who meant to use, mistreat, and torment me...

I wheezed, gulping for breath, the usual panic settling in and making itself at home. Ashamed now, I pined for the cascading flowers inside the gates, the mammoth creatures with soft, kind eyes, and the bursts of sunny orange that had brought joy to my heart.

"Go now!" The wretched wolves nipped at my heels and chased me back toward the gate. "Do what you do best. Trick them. Deceive them. And bring them back to us."

"Be a fisherman," the She-Wolf teased. "Isn't that what you call yourself when you're feeling especially proud?"

Drooping in a puddle of tears, sweat, and God knew what else, I crawled toward the gates, praying I could get through the melted bars. The wolves jeered at me as I covered my ears and returned to safety.

"No," I cried, shooing her away, terrified now that this abominable creature would threaten the sanctity inside the gates. "You can't come in here."

Fueled by bitterness, she swiftly slipped her distorted head through the rungs of the gate. "Of course, I can. Through you." Before she turned and skulked back to her mangy friends, her watery blue eyes met mine. "You shouldn't have broken your promise."

†††

I woke in a fit of sweat, my heart hammering inside my chest. I gulped, pleading for air, ever grateful when it came, and even more grateful when I placed my bare feet against the floor... and steadied myself.

I cupped my face into my hands, only half-surprised when my fingers came back wet.

Tears. Snot. Sweat.

Just another night, I lamented, standing to face my day. I wistfully fondled the framed photograph perched on my nightstand.

Meadow.

We'd met three years ago at a wedding in Shady Gully…and with one disagreeable scowl, she'd changed everything. Unknowingly, her begrudging vulnerability had stirred a flood of deeply rooted wounds inside me, and her bewitching, irreverent temperament dared me to confront the ones that were soon to come.

I smacked the frame down hard against the nightstand, and the glass cracked and splintered into jagged daggers that punctured her beautiful face.

But it wouldn't end well for us.

And I knew what I had to do.

Chapter One

Shimmering Lights
Timothy

Normally, Sunday mornings in downtown Lexington were quiet, even after a huge University of Kentucky Wildcats win, and last night's victory had been especially exciting as it was their first home basketball game of the season.

Because of the particularly gorgeous daybreak, I took a moment to appreciate the fog rising amid the skyscrapers of the city's epicenter. I imagined the same fuzzy fog currently hovering over black horse fences all around Jessamine and Fayette counties as stock horses and Triple Crown winners alike scampered in anticipation of their morning hay.

After clicking my blinker, I waited patiently for the light to turn green. That's not true. I wasn't at all patient as my fingers tapped along the steering wheel of my Toyota Corolla. Agitated. No, unsettled was more like it, and definitely anxious.

I let out an exasperated sigh and turned left, entering the Northlake Christian Church campus at the center entrance, the one directly under the formidable—and quite large—cross.

The campus itself sprawled over three blocks of downtown Lexington, with entrances on the north and the south, and of course, the center. The main building held a Worship Auditorium with enough seating for nearly three thousand people and several "spill-over" theaters live streaming the Sunday service. Over time, folks acclimated to their favorite service time—there were three—but occasionally latecomers still couldn't find a seat, which is why the local TV station aired the sermons on Sunday mornings. As Northlake's following had spread to other states and even other countries, the service was streamed on Northlake's website as well.

The Fellowship Center was also in the main building and featured a variety of coffees and donuts for congregants to enjoy as they lounged on chairs, cushy couches, or around café tables. The Children's Ministry and Daycare Centers expanded into the north and south buildings, as did the administrative offices, Outreach Center, and the Music and Creative Departments.

The landscape behind Northlake Christian Church included a concrete basketball court outlined in Kentucky Wildcat blue, as well as a grassy field deep enough to play football, baseball, or soccer. Naturally, there was a pond for fishing—and baptisms.

Finally, a grand shed big enough to house donations sat on a hill at the edge of the property. Clothing, furniture, and even vehicles came in weekly from all across Kentucky. Northlake had a solid reputation and was known for "walking-the-talk" as they say, and givers gave generously. And often.

Every time I parked my well-used Corolla in the massive parking lot, the sheer scale of the property sent a thrill up my spine. Conversely, the impact of the ministry itself never failed to ramp up my anxiety, as sometimes the responsibility of tending to the fold seemed too much to bear. Once in a blue moon, I felt I was in my element, but most days I felt like a feckless imposter.

After gathering my Bible and my notes, some of which I'd added only late last night, I took a deep breath and closed my eyes. *Holy Spirit, lead me today. Help me help people. I need you—*

"Morning, Timothy." Luther, Northlake's head of security and the jolliest man I'd ever known, opened the door of my Corolla. "You ready to light it up today?"

I couldn't help but smile, always so touched by Luther's ingrained southern politeness and unconditional faith in me, even as I glimpsed my haunted eyes ringed with dark circles in the rear-view mirror. "How about that game last night, Luther?"

I pivoted, hoping to avoid scrutiny. "Wasn't that buzzer shot at the end something?"

His face, the color of dark cocoa, flushed with pleasure. As he collected my duffel bag and folders, I noted the way he took special care with my Bible as he chatted. "True that, my pastor, true that. Me and my cousin sure appreciated the tickets."

"I'll let you know when we get more." Donors didn't just donate clothes and groceries, some of the wealthier movers and shakers of Lexington frequently gifted the staff with courtside seats.

"That'd be great, Timothy." His wide grin stretched up to his ears. "But feel free to give them to the less fortunate, like usual. The thrill of last night's winning shot will last me a lifetime." He let out a hearty chuckle. "My grandma baked you some of those lemon cookies you like. I put them on your desk."

"What? She shouldn't have done that. She was feeling faint the other day."

"She was, that's true. But your visit perked her right up. She'll be watching from her recliner today, along with my contrary Uncle Herman, who she's determined to see baptized before… well…"

Visiting Luther's grandma was always the highlight of my week. A slight woman with terminal cancer, we usually prayed together and pored over the Bible, trying to make sense of why bad things happened to good people. Unlike most folks, Grandma Tallulah never looked at me for answers to what was surely the hardest question pastors were asked. Instead, we combed the Bible together, making notes and highlighting scripture like pioneers exploring for treasure.

Sometimes I read to her, and sometimes, on really good days, we played gin rummy. Our tournament had extended over several months, its weekly tally haphazardly scribbled on the worn pages of a Steno pad. She often teased—especially on days when she'd taken the lead—that she planned to leave me the Steno pad in her will. *Something to remember me by,* she'd say.

As if I could ever forget such a fine woman.

"Pretty quiet in there right now," Luther said as he shut my car door. He dipped his head toward the street. "But in a couple of hours, I expect the traffic cops will arrive for the first service."

"Bring 'em on."

Luther hooted as he led me to the door. "And Miss Meadow? Will she be joining us today? She's a nice lady. For an LSU fan, anyway."

My heart lurched at the sound of Meadow's name.

Although I knew the proper response would be a chuckle followed by a witty, slightly playful remark, I quite literally couldn't make my mouth work. Nor could I catch my breath or control my heartbeat, which seemed to fluctuate between a NASCAR pace and the putt-putt tempo of an elderly driver on a Sunday afternoon. Even more alarming was the way my heart skipped like a jump rope.

"Are you alright?" I felt Luther's large hand against my back. "You're as pale as a ghost."

As I attempted to nod in the affirmative, the concrete steps rushed up toward my face, or vice versa, and I felt Luther's big, burly arms scoop me up in a timely rescue.

While I insisted that I was fine, the tinny sound of my voice sounded unnatural. "Whoa."

"Let's get you to your office," he said. "Sit you down. Get you a drink." Being such a good, empathetic man, Luther discreetly glanced in both directions of the corridor before leading me to my office and plopping me into my chair. "Don't move," he ordered, more sternly than I'd ever heard. "I'll be right back."

Once I was finally alone, I raked my hands through my hair in frustration. *Holy Spirit, please help me.* I prayed the Lord's prayer, then recited the scriptures that usually reassured me, but I felt…nothing.

I opened my folder, thinking a brief perusal of my notes would help, but the paper in front of me appeared blurry and incoherent. I snapped the folder closed, frantically rubbing my face. When

I sensed the heaviness behind my eyes building to a crescendo, anger flashed through me. *This is ridiculous! I cannot fall apart now.* I had a sermon to do in just over an hour.

"Here." Luther burst through the doorway with a cup of water and a Coke drowned in crushed ice. "Drink this first." When he shoved the water in my face, I looked at him in disbelief. Well aware of my weakness for icy sodas, he sighed and handed me the Coke. "Okay, but at least alternate it with water."

After he watched me like a hawk for several minutes, I met his eyes. "Thanks, Luther. I'm fine—"

"Should I call Miss Meadow? Or Miss Robin?"

"No," I said firmly. "I just need a minute. I've been a little tired lately, but I'll be okay." I glanced at the clock, realizing the service was fast approaching. I reached again for my notes, hopefully encouraging Luther along.

"Alright then, I'll check on you in a bit." He moved toward the door, hesitating.

I looked up expectantly.

"You're not God, you know?" His expression was solemn. "I'm just saying, sometimes we all need a little help."

When he closed the door behind him, I welcomed the quiet as it gently curled around me. I knew I didn't have long before the Creative Team started tuning their instruments in preparation for the service, and soon after that the lights and special effects would begin.

Sometimes we all need a little help.

With my elbows propped on my desk, I let my head fall into my hands. *Defeated. Lost. Broken.* Eventually, I pulled out my phone and opened the text message app. My fingers hovered over the keys, typing, then deleting, then retyping…

I stared at the message for a long, long time. Was I really ready to do this?

There was a knock on my door, and Bob, a long, tall drink of water and Northlake's associate pastor, peeked his head in. "Game time."

Struck by the passage of time, I used the edge of my desk to push myself into a wobbly stand.

Bob frowned in concern. "Are you—?"

"I'm fine." I picked up my phone and hit send before locking it in my desk like always. And then I made my way to the stage of Kentucky's biggest megachurch to deliver a message that would go out to countless people around the world.

†††

I moved mechanically through the long corridor that led to the auditorium, a smile plastered on my damp, pasty face. Because I was aware that congregants and staff lined either side of the pathway, I did my best to present a strong, robust front, despite a growing sense of light-headedness.

A short, stocky man pushed himself from the wall, offering me his hand. "Timothy."

"Hey, Trent, how's your wife?" I took his hands into mine.

"The MRI came back good. Totally clear," he nearly sobbed. "Thank you, Timothy."

"Don't thank me." I shook my head. "That's all God. I'll continue to pray for Candy, and you as well."

"Slow down." Tina from the Technical Department trotted alongside me, forcing me to slow my pace, which admittedly helped temper my increasing dizziness. She looked at me strangely as she clipped a microphone to my shirt. "Remember to click it when you get on stage."

"Got it." I flashed her a smile, squinting as the strobe lights from the stage sparred with my vision. The music was in full swing now, the pulse so loud I could feel vibrations pound through the floor and into my belly as I moved closer.

A large, energetic presence flitted past me, all smiles and dreadlocks, as Billy from Lexington's most renowned Hospice Group brought his hands together in prayer. "Praise." He winked at me and pointed upward before racing to claim his seat. Still in his scrubs, he'd undoubtedly just finished a shift.

"Your nephew sounds good on stage!" I hollered back at him, and he shot me a thumbs up over his shoulder.

I ducked into what we called the Passage Room, which was essentially a hallway leading to the bright lights of the stage. Like magic, Bob appeared and handed me my Bible and my notes, while handing a podium stand to the young student who would carry it out for me.

"I read the copy you emailed me last night." Bob indicated the sermon. "What a fantastic message."

I thanked him, but suddenly couldn't remember anything about today's message. Or even the first lines of my sermon.

I massaged my temples, desperately trying to recall, but all that came to me were the blurry words I'd seen on my desk earlier.

A tremor rushed through me as the heavy thumps of the band's song swelled in conclusion. The audience clapped and cheered, lifting their hands in appreciation. As the multi-talented collection of Nashville-worthy singers and musicians exited the stage, their faces lit up at the sight of me. I was bombarded with thumbs up, prayerful hands, fist bumps, hugs, and pats on the back.

"He makes a way when there's no way," Millie, the lead female vocalist said in passing, her face rosy with the gospel.

I crossed paths with Sterling; guitarist, lead male vocalist, and Robin's son. He tipped his head, seemingly distracted.

"Praise." Billy's nephew winked at me, repeating his uncle's mantra as he hurried backstage.

The lights dimmed. "Praise," I said in a shaky voice.

Just as the opening video for the series reflected off center stage and appeared on the four jumbotrons positioned throughout the auditorium, the student carrying the podium walked with me onto the stage.

"My aunt and her family are visiting from Derby, Kansas," the kid whispered as he neatly placed my notes on the podium. "They're in the audience today."

The sandy-haired, blue-eyed kid's unadulterated adoration

shook me to the core. It seemed like the final straw. "I got a tattoo just like yours. See." He exposed the underside of his right wrist, revealing a scripture from Philippians glistening in the stage's shimmering lights.

"No," I said hoarsely, just as the lights came on.

As the boy slipped off stage, I turned to the audience. They smiled expectantly, sat up straighter, and leaned forward in their seats. I searched the faces in the crowd, finding only adoration, hope, and trust…

And then I saw *her* face. Beautiful, dark-haired Meadow, who'd traveled all the way from Shady Gully, Louisiana, to be with me here in Kentucky. Full of adoration, hope…

And trust.

Which is why I had to end our relationship immediately. For her own good.

I smiled for the cameras, and at the congregation, and then held my arms wide in supplication…

And immediately collapsed into darkness and despair.

Chapter Two

Whippersnapper Goes Rogue
Fireman

The gravel crunched under my boots as I made my way to my car. That's right, *my* car. The 2014 Chevy Impala sitting under the bright lights of the Shady Gully Fire Station might not look like much by normal-people-standards, but to me, it was a dream come true.

Unbeknownst to me, Bubba and Daryl, employees at Luke's Auto Body Shop at the four-way stop, had conspired with nearly the whole town to get the Impala in working order for my fifteenth birthday. Destined for the junkyard, Bubba had envisioned it with a fresh coat of paint, while Daryl imagined it with a working engine.

Together, they schemed and drummed up business—and funding—in the back of the auto body shop. Even Granny Lacey had been in on it, serving as tie breaker when Daryl and Bubba couldn't decide between paint colors Berry Red or Blue Velvet Mystique. Praise the heavens above she went with Daryl's choice of Blue Velvet Mystique rather than Bubba's favorite, Berry Red. While Bubba's heart was in the right place, he was also colorblind, and Berry Red looked very much like very plum, as in, very, *very* purple.

Since Granny Lacey's mental faculties had started to wander and now hovered in the trenches with her rock bottom rankings in cooking skills, I was grateful she'd been able to take part in my birthday surprise back in February. Now, just nine months later, she dithered in a state of constant confusion and spent most of her time doodling in her cookbooks rather than actually cooking for the residents of The Creek and Shady Gully. For this, they were all eternally grateful.

Because of her declining health, I'd gotten into the habit of cutting off the gas to the oven and stove before going to school or to my various part-time jobs, just in case she got an *envie*—or a Cajun hankering—to whip something up. This usually happened after lunching with her gang of old ladies—Beth, Linda, Debra, Melissa, and Michelle—who mistakenly saw no harm in encouraging Granny's passion for cooking.

Meanwhile, Brad Wolfheart, who served as The Creek's leader in every sense of the word—including as city council member, herbal medicine specialist, and overall champion of all things related to life on The Creek—checked in on Granny daily. He also provided us with a variety of herbal potions to ease Granny's arthritis pain as well as her trademark crabbiness. For this, *I* was grateful.

Wolfheart was also responsible for my getting my Louisiana learner's permit, which meant he'd carted me to driver's ed for weeks and made sure I passed a vision and a knowledge test. And since I was underage and couldn't technically own a car, or get car insurance, he took care of all the logistics, including putting the title in his name and keeping it under lock and key—in case Granny tried to cook it or something—until I turned eighteen.

Unfortunately, he and Sheriff Rick were both sticklers for rules and safety. One of them was always nagging me about something. "You can't drive at night," Wolfheart reminded me constantly, "even with a licensed driver."

The sheriff liked to rant while smacking his taffy. "It's illegal for you to drive alone." Cue the handcuffs jiggling against his belt. "I'd hate to have to lock you up."

Whatever. They weren't here now.

A puff of unexpectedly cool air erupted on my sigh as I glanced at my watch. It was almost daybreak now, and I needed to get moving.

After I'd finished my shift as "assistant to the firemen" last night—or technically, early this morning—I'd bunked at the station with the rest of the team. The plan was for someone—likely either Deputy Quietdove or Deputy Max—to pick me up later this morning and ride home with me. Either that or Wolfheart would meet me here and drag me to church with him.

But I had a situation that needed takin' care of *now*. You might even say it was an emergency. So, I hiked the rest of the way across the gravel parking lot of the Shady Gully Fire Station and quietly slipped into my 2014 Blue Velvet Mystique Chevy Impala. I pulled out, turned left, and waited until I'd passed the four-way stop before turning on my headlights.

I figured since the sheriff was in Kentucky and Wolfheart was asleep across the creek, what they didn't know wouldn't hurt them.

†††

I dimmed my headlights as I closed in on Sacred Heart Catholic Church. Not much need for illumination though, seeing as how every light in the modest little house beside the church was blazing.

I parked a distance from the driveway of the home, concealing my car behind a row of hedges so it wouldn't be seen from the main road. After trekking to the side door, I raised my hand to knock but thought better of it. Instead, I fished through the pocket of my jeans and pulled out a bobby pin. *Just like in the movies*, I thought, working the pin into the lock and wiggling it.

Again, not necessary, as the door pushed right open. Certainly not locked, barely even closed. No alarm. No dog. Just a sparkling beacon of light beckoning one and all to come on in and help themselves.

I entered through the kitchen, which looked like a war zone with an obstacle course of dirty dishes, empty TV dinner boxes, Post-it notes, and piles of mail. Because of the simple ranch-style floor plan, I merely had to look over the bar to find the man of the hour slumped in his recliner, snoring like a freight train, and completely oblivious to the way the blaring light of the lamp on the end table reflected his circumstances.

I padded across the ceramic tile until it met the carpeted living room, and then not so gently grabbed the toe of his slipper and shook it like a rattlesnake.

"Wh…Wha…What?" He came alive like a banshee, squealing in shock, and then immediately grabbed his back like he'd pulled something. "What's going on?" Father Patrick blinked at me. Grimaced. "Ah, what time is it?"

"Almost time for Mass. You're going to be late. People are depending on you."

"What? No!" He fumbled for the side handles on his recliner but failed to hoist the bulk of his weight out of the chair. "That can't be! We simply mustn't have that."

I shook my head, bewildered. "I sent you a hundred texts."

He at least had the courtesy to look sheepish as he glanced about for his phone.

A crusted bowl of pasta, a stained wine glass, and an Alka-Seltzer glass caked with salt littered the end table. "It looks like you enjoyed another five-star meal last night."

"Hey," he balked, his reddish-gray hair spiking in wild, cartoonish directions.

Like a forensic scientist, I waded cautiously through the debris on his end table to gather the dirty dishes. When I picked up his Bible, which burst at the edges with scribbled notes, passages, and index cards marked heavily in the general area of Proverbs 23, I wisecracked, "Can't wait to hear Mass today."

"Ah! Now wouldn't that be a miracle?" he mumbled in agitation. "The whole congregation would likely keel over at the sight of you."

Very few people knew Shady Gully's beloved Father Patrick like I did, and with that intimacy came the gift of sparring. "You need to lose weight."

"That's no way to talk to a priest, young man," he growled as he tried once again to heave himself out of the recliner. "Come help me out of this thing, would ya, Little Fire?"

I snorted, finding his reference to my given name amusing. I gently positioned the insides of my elbows under his armpits and helped him up. "Geez, that's some rancid morning breath you've got there, Padre." I maintained a light grip along his shoulders until I was certain he'd found his balance.

"I was working," he huffed, searching for his breath, "and I fell asleep. Is that a crime?"

"When's the last time you went to a doctor? And do you always leave your house unlocked? You need to be more careful."

Ignoring me, he plodded into the kitchen and fumbled around trying to put on a pot of coffee. I followed, carrying the bowl and glasses and taking the coffee carafe from his trembling hands. "Let's see if I can find a clean mug." I opened a cabinet. "Nope, not there."

"You sure are a cheeky one today."

I opened another cabinet. "Not there either."

"You know," he started, "I've never quite understood the significance of the male names on The Creek, but I find them simply delightful. So manly and rugged, many of them a tribute to the earth and to nature." He huffed. "Unless, of course, some young whippersnapper goes rogue and decides to rename himself after an entire profession." He choked between wheezing coughs. "Albeit, a noble one, but—"

"Seriously," I pestered. "When's the last time you've been to a doctor? You're probably a diabetic. Or have high blood pressure. I could drive you in my car—"

"And the irony is," he went on, his voice rising to drown out my nagging, "you named yourself Fireman after you singlehandedly burnt down a church. What chutzpah!"

"It was an accident," I clarified before asking, "and what's that mean? That word you just said?" After turning the coffee pot on, I ran a sink full of hot, soapy water and began washing dishes.

"Aha! So, you don't know everything after all."

"Hard to believe, I know, but back to that word. What does—?"

"It's a Yiddish word meaning unbelievable gall, audacity, insolence—"

"Got it, thanks." I rinsed a bowl and placed it on the dish rack to drain. "And by the way, I didn't name myself anything. People started calling me Fireman because I wanted to be a fireman. And that was long before—"

"—I know, I know. Long before Jesse set fire to James's church because you set fire to his—"

"—accidentally. And did you know the kids used to call me Little Fry? That's another reason I changed my name. Isn't that mean?"

"Aha! So, you admit it, you changed your name." He stared at the coffee pot, mug at the ready. "And don't try to distract me by making me sympathetic. You bounced back just fine. You're the only fifteen-year-old I know who has his own car."

"And aren't you glad? Otherwise, you'd have missed Mass, and your worried parishioners would have marched over here to find you snoring over there in your house-bed."

He sputtered in mock outrage as the coffee pot gurgled. "Oh, praise the heavens. The caffeine has arrived." Father Patrick slumped at the table and drank his coffee while I finished the dishes. "You know, those fires five years ago are why we don't have a protestant church at the four-way stop anymore."

"And what's wrong with that?" I wiped down the bar with a hot rag. "The four-way stop is a better place for Violet's Veterinary Hospital anyway. And the church Petey built near the Unity Bridge is doing great. Wait." I stopped cold. "Are you jealous because of how popular Petey's church is?" I teased. "Is that why you're spiraling lately?"

"Ah, the sun has risen." Ignoring me, he dipped his head toward the window. "I suspect I need a shower."

"I'd say. And you didn't answer my question."

"I'm not spiraling, young Fireman. And frankly, it wounds me that you'd think I'd be envious. You know how hard I fought for Petey, and how much it bothered me that those charlatans, Jesse and James, held the town hostage for years with all their bickering. And frankly, having a church near The Creek that unites them and Shady Gully proper—"

"—especially one so popular and widely attended—"

"The success of Unity Christian Church is one of my biggest delights. A feather in my cap, as they say."

"Even if it's protestant?"

"*Especially* because it's protestant. I have my Catholic faithful, trust me, but the people of Shady Gully deserve a choice, and as I always like to say, there's plenty of God—"

"—to go around. Yes, I know."

He eyed me suddenly. "Thank you for checking in on me." His voice thickened with forced gruffness. "Even if only to fuss at me. What would I do without you?"

"I shudder to think." I folded the washcloth.

Father Patrick's belly rolled as he laughed, which made me laugh.

"Seriously, where's your phone? I texted you a hundred times. I had to sneak out of the fire station to drive here. Wolfheart is going to kill me. And you know the sheriff would love to throw me in the slammer."

"Oh, heavens." Father Patrick looked horrified, setting his mug down and using his hands to push himself to a stand. "It's around here somewhere." He frowned. "I probably silenced it so I could concentrate."

"So you could sleep, more like it." I padded behind him, lest he wobble like a giant Weeble and fall down. "I don't see it."

"Check between the cushions on the recliner."

I shut my eyes in dread as I stuck my hand under the cushion and rummaged. "Gross!" I found nothing but a series of questionable crumbs I'd missed while tidying up. "Have you got any latex gloves?"

"Amusing. Try on the other side."

"Found it!" I held my breath as I rescued the phone from the underbelly of the recliner. "Yep, it's on silent." My eyes widened as I saw the screen roll with dozens of messages, mostly from me, but one from—

The phone literally vibrated in my hands. "Whoa…"

Father Patrick shuffled over, curious.

I forced my gaze onto Father Patrick, probably because I was embarrassed by the stunning text I'd just read. "I think you'd better sit down."

The priest paled, nearly dropping to the edge of the couch. "What's happened? Not a car accident? Or, God forbid, a murder, and while the sheriff is away—"

"No, it's from that fancy preacher in Kentucky."

"Timothy? Well, I do declare. Now there's someone to aspire to, a stellar example for me…" His words slowed. "No extra weight on him." He sighed. "Ah, gluttony is a sin, isn't it? I know that, but I…"

"Father."

"Yes, yes, I'm sorry. What does it say? I can't read without my glasses, so I suppose you'll have to go digging for those next."

I brought the phone over and sat next to him on the edge of the couch. "It says: *I'm in trouble. I need your counsel.*"

"Oh, my word. That can't be. Timothy? Needing *me?*"

"We all do, Father."

"Oh, well…" His eyes darted away from me, landing on the chaos of the disorderly living room, bouncing off the recliner imprinted with his large derriere, the stain marks that looked almost unseemly on the end table, his sermon notes haphazardly scattered across the coffee table. "This won't do," he fretted. "I simply must get myself together." He looked at me, his eyes wide with panic.

I nudged him, brushed my shoulder against the mountain of him. "I'll help you."

When his blue eyes pooled with tears, I looked away, embarrassed. "But we need to text the fancy preacher back. He doesn't sound too good."

Father Patrick cleared his throat. "Quite." He thought for a moment. "You'll have to do it. My clumsy fingers don't get along well with that tiny keyboard. "Tell him…"

I waited.

"Tell him to come at once."

Chapter Three

Thank You for your Consideration
Sterling

Now that the opening music set was done, I could relax and sink into the service. God knew I needed my weekly infusion of faith, especially after the hellacious disappointment of the last few days. Or months. Heck, who was I kidding? I was deep in the quarries of the valley lately. I'd skimmed past Timothy after the final number, hoping beyond hope that the distraction of his imminent sermon would quell his usually gregarious nature. Luckily, I managed to duck my head into my collar and avoid eye contact. I just couldn't face him yet…not after what happened.

Just as the lights dimmed and the series music erupted along with graphics that spotlighted the auditorium with gyrating blues, greens, and purples, I took a seat between Mom and Meadow. Thank God I didn't have to sit next to Sheriff Rick. Honestly, I'd had about all I could take of his country-come-to-town routine.

How long was he staying, anyway? Would he ever leave?

I might not want to know the answer to that, considering how increasingly cozy he and my mom had become.

Now I knew how my fraternal twin sister, Violet, had felt three years ago when the sheriff stepped up his game in pursuit of our mom. She'd been unhappy, unwilling to accept that he was alive, chasing our mom, while cancer had stolen our dad at forty-three years of age. *Not fair, not having it, no way.*

Her antipathy had put me in the unenviable position of

peacekeeper, which regrettably endeared me to the sheriff. Now he was under the impression we were best buds.

"I'll be, Sterling." He leaned across my mother, his twang echoing three aisles in each direction as he complimented my musical number. "I reckon that's the finest performance I've ever seen. You sure know how to play that guitar." *Geet-tarrr.*

"Thanks, Sheriff," I whispered.

"Ricky, call me Ricky." He patted me vigorously on the leg. Numerous times.

I wondered if I'd have a bruise in the morning.

Meadow nudged me from the other side, tilting in with a quiet remark. "Hang in there. He grows on you after a while."

I nearly snorted with doubt, but if Meadow, the most disagreeable, sarcastic, aloof, and stunningly beautiful woman I'd even seen in my life could warm up to Dudley Do-Right, I reckon I could too. Of course, ever since she and Timothy had become attached at the hip, to her, all was right with the world.

Timothy had that effect on people, me included, which made me feel guilty for sorta kinda lusting after his girlfriend, who happened to be fifteen years older than me.

"If you say so," I responded, noting the way she watched the stage in anticipation of Timothy's entrance. *Ah, maybe in another life,* I thought.

Honestly, the whole exchange made me miss Tammy Jo, my on-again-off-again girlfriend who'd lost interest in me about the time all my dreams crashed and burned. Coincidence? Maybe. Maybe not. Either way, the relationship had apparently run its course, so I might as well suck it up.

If only I could be more like my sister, who on the surface seemed meek and agreeable, but in reality, owned a fiery spirit that ignited a trail in the direction of her choosing. After nearly seven years of collecting medical degrees with acronyms I couldn't even pronounce, my sister veered from her dreams of curing cancer in memory of our dad, and instead, redirected her efforts to embrace her true calling. While becoming a veterinarian was also medically inspired, it seemed more suitable for my outwardly shy, no-nonsense, twin sister.

While she was in Baton Rouge at LSU's School of Veterinary Medicine working hard to accomplish this goal in quick measure, her besotted husband, Petey, was building her the grandest animal hospital the little town of Shady Gully had ever seen. When she graduated just over two months ago, the doors to Violet's Veterinary Hospital were ready to open on the hottest piece of real estate Shady Gully had to offer, aka the four-way stop.

Go, Violet, go!

I was proud of my sister, who was truly my favorite person in the world, but sometimes her discipline and unadulterated success discouraged me. Just once, I'd like to get the win. Or *a* win. Or even a tie.

Nevertheless, I'd been so inspired by my sister's bold change of course and decision to enter veterinary school three years ago, I decided to pursue my own secret aspirations. While I made good money as a member of Northlake's Creative Team and loved performing, I couldn't help but think I was meant to change course as well.

When my dad was sick, I became obsessed with the reading he did in the weeks leading up to his death, so much so that I reread all the whodunits he and Billy, his hospice nurse, had yacked about all the time. Because I missed him so, I'd been trying to get inside his head and connect with him on some divine level, but I found that the books were really, really good. I loved the mystery, suspense, and the procedural aspects of legal thrillers, but I also loved the way the authors weaved words together to build worlds and evoke feelings.

So, despite my disdain for academics, I enrolled as a part-time student at the University of Kentucky. Not ideal, of course, because I was considered an "older" student at twenty-five, but my mom encouraged me, and because I didn't have gobs of scholarships like Violet, she helped me financially. I signed up for a creative writing class and a pre-law class, and it went well. I daydreamed about plots in the pre-law class, and I spit-balled with the aspiring writers in the creative writing class. I felt included, and I was engaged.

When the literary professor announced that half of our grade would be determined by the quality of the novella we wrote during the semester, I was psyched. I'd already worked out a killer plot, and my story was going to be gold!

For four months I bounced from class to class, researching in the evenings, singing on Sundays, and writing every chance I got. I was on fire, and by the end of the semester my novella rocked. It had everything—romance, intrigue, suspense, a super twist, and finally, a courtroom drama.

I knew my professor was going to be amazed. I imagined he'd reach out to all of his publisher and literary friends and tell them about me and my talent. Undoubtedly, I'd get a huge contract with a Big Five publisher, and agents would clamor to represent my work, and because the story was so relevant, I was sure Hollywood would come calling next. But did I really want to hand my hard work over to some screenwriter? It was my story after all. Maybe I'd write the screenplay as well. I had a lot to consider, to be sure, but one thing was certain, I'd created something smart, edgy, and immensely entertaining.

Only I hadn't. And the professor certainly hadn't winked at me with barely contained awe when he passed out the results. Instead, he'd massacred my masterpiece with garish red marks and passage upon passage of harsh notes. The hoity-toity professor said my characters were flat and the plot was contrived. He said my pacing was terrible and my grammar atrocious. Finally, at the end of my novella, he added in red: *I'd like to say that this was a decent **attempt** at a novella, but unfortunately, I can't.*

I flunked both the creative writing class and the pre-law class, and shortly thereafter returned full-time to Northlake with my tail between my legs. Of course, because Timothy was Timothy, he reached out to a friend in publishing. One day after rehearsal he'd handed me an email address. "I talked to this guy and he really, really wants to read your novella."

Thrilled, my hopes pounding in my chest, I once again imagined my dreams coming true. I sent the publisher my book and checked my email daily. Perhaps he'd just call and offer me a contract. I mean, when they were serious, they probably wouldn't waste time with an email. Right?

But he never called, and while I vacillated between self-pity and rampant despair, Violet was trucking along diagnosing lethargic pups, acing difficult tests, and maintaining her position in the top percentile of her class.

In time I picked up my novella and considered the professor's notes. Admittedly, my plot *was* contrived, and my characters *could* have been better developed. Although still committed to giving up my silly dreams, I eventually circled back to my ragged novella and made an effort. I even worked on a proposal and submitted a query letter to a number of other publishers and agents. A glutton for punishment? Probably.

But as a man of faith, who sang songs with conviction on Sundays about our God making a way when there was no way, I remained hopeful.

Until a few days ago. Nearly two years after I sent the novella, I got a rejection letter from Timothy's publisher friend. Unbelievable, and discouraging, but even worse, he mentioned that he'd emailed Timothy as well, thanking him for thinking of him, etc. What worried me was the *etcetera*. I imagined it was full of ridicule and unflattering words about my writing, and maybe even a snarky request that Timothy not give any more aspiring writers his email address.

I was mortified. Humiliated. And I didn't know how I would ever face Timothy again.

And yet, as the music and graphics faded, and Timothy lumbered onto center stage and surveyed the crowd, I knew I couldn't avoid him forever. Blue-eyed, tall, and lanky with tattoos lining his arms, Timothy's down-to-earth, shaggy-haired presence won over everyone he met. Including me.

But just as my mom halted the sheriff's hands to keep him from clapping, a hush fell over the crowd. And then Meadow, seeing something the rest of us hadn't, gasped when Timothy raised his arms…and promptly crumpled into a heap on the stage.

†††

Pandemonium set in as the entirety of Northlake's church family made for the stage at once. Not a great situation considering there were at least three thousand people in the audience.

To his credit, Sheriff Rick immediately placed himself on deck and herded people away from the stage. He competently assigned anyone with a blue staff shirt to, "go yonder way and position yourself at the head of each aisle." Within seconds, the staff and security had successfully prevented a dangerous stampede.

"I called 911!" someone shouted. "Medics are on their way."

"Medical personnel coming through." Dad's hospice nurse, Billy, jumped onto the stage and proceeded to check Timothy's vitals. Meadow, who was kneeling beside Timothy, flicked her gaze at Billy imploringly. I could see him nodding at her but couldn't hear anything above the roar of the crowd.

I hopped on stage and snatched a microphone from the keyboard's sound equipment. "Northlake community, listen up." The roar immediately lowered a decimal. "Everything is under control. Unless you're a doctor or a medical professional, the best thing to do is to go home…and pray."

The quiet that swept over the audience then was nearly as deafening as the mayhem only seconds before. Finally, urgent whispers increased, followed by light, concerned chatter, and then folks began to file somberly toward the exits.

"This way, this way." Luther, Northlake's head of security, directed the paramedics toward the stage. Once they converged around Timothy, Billy stepped aside, urging Meadow along as well.

"Sterling." Mom appeared out of nowhere, wrapping her arm around my waist.

I enveloped her in what was hopefully a reassuring hug. Still beautiful, my mom was trim and, as always, put together. A chic bob with blonde highlights framed her face, and bold purple eyeglasses magnified her eyes. Sometimes I felt such an overwhelming rush of love for my mom I had to resist the urge to squeeze her with all my might.

"Billy." She turned her attention to one of her favorites as he approached. "How is he?"

Billy affectionately folded my mom's small frame into his giant one. "He's gonna be fine, Robin. Don't you worry."

"Thank God," I muttered while we quietly watched the paramedics put Timothy on a stretcher as Meadow trailed behind, looking concerned.

"They'll take him to the hospital, monitor him carefully, and run some tests," Billy said. "He was starting to come to, so I think he just fainted."

About that time, Sheriff Rick meandered over. "Y'all wanna follow them to the hospital?"

My mom linked her arm neatly with the tall sheriff's, who sometimes reminded me of Tom Selleck. "If only we were in Shady Gully, you could use your siren," she remarked.

Billy and I watched as they joined the caravan headed toward Saint Joseph Hospital. Once they were out of sight, he offered me a light slap on the back. "I know, I know," he said perceptively, "but it's been ten years, Sterling."

I sputtered in denial. "Hey, it's not me who has a problem. It's my evil twin."

✝✝✝

The mood in the waiting room was relaxed and grateful, if not a tad punch-drunk. "I need to text Desi," Mom said. "They're an hour behind in Louisiana. I wonder if—"

"She's up," Sheriff Rick said with a glint in his eye. "I just texted Lenny. He told her about Timothy."

"You beat me to it." She pursed her lips, pretending to be annoyed.

I had to look away. It was just too much. I turned to Meadow. "So, who are you texting?" Immediately regretting my pertness, I flinched over my gaffe. She was beautiful, but a little scary. "Sorry," I said. "Too much caffeine."

Pastor Bob carried in pastries along with another tray of coffee. I automatically reached for another coffee, reasoning that if I was going to eat one of those delicious pastries, I'd need to wash it down with something.

"No thanks." Meadow sort of smiled at Bob while simultaneously tapping on her phone. She turned to me. "I texted Uncle Wolf and Bella. They're both very relieved with the doctor's report."

"Me too." The doctor had confirmed that Timothy's collapse had been caused by a lack of oxygen to the brain, likely brought on by dehydration, too much stress, and not enough rest.

"I miss them," she said suddenly. "Especially Bella. Have you talked to Luke lately?"

I wolfed down a blueberry cream cheese Danish as my thoughts drifted to my "cousin" Luke, who was married to Bella, Meadow's daughter. "Every day. I swear, he's so anal I think he calls everyone he knows and tells them goodnight."

Meadow laughed unabashedly, and since I liked the sound of her laughter, I went on. "Petey told him he oughta do a conference call at night, and we could be like the Waltons and call out good night to everyone in one session."

"It would save some time." Her words slowed, ringing suddenly with melancholy. Meadow had had a difficult, rather cheerless life, but I had a feeling a big, cozy family was in her future whether she wanted it or not.

Our giant, non-conventional family had erupted many years ago when my mom and Aunt Desi became best friends in high school. Because their bond was so strong and only deepened over the years, their future families would forever be related. Aunt

Desi and Uncle Lenny's children, Luke, Petey, and Micah, were the best cousins Violet and I could ever have.

The twist is that somewhere along the way, Violet and Petey started crushing on each other, and it was a whole thing convincing them that was okay…and legal.

In other ground-breaking romances, Luke fell head over heels in love with Bella, Meadow's daughter, at a time when Shady Gully proper and the folks on The Creek weren't as united as they were now. In fact, many say their love story was the catalyst to unification and jump-started the building of the Unity Bridge itself. Shortly thereafter, Luke was elected mayor in a landslide, and he and his lovely bride, Bella, were beloved in the community. Side note: Bella was every bit as beautiful as her mother but way friendlier.

The merger—for lack of a better word—between The Creek and Shady Gully proper was complete when Petey raised a church smack dab in the middle of both communities.

Evidently, Micah and I were the wingnuts because it seemed neither of us could decide what we wanted, career-wise or partner-wise. The more I thought about it, I missed the whole lot of them down there in Shady Gully.

"Maybe Timothy ought to take a retreat to Shady Gully?" I whispered to Meadow.

While Meadow had apparently returned to her texting, my mother overheard my remark. "I think that's a great idea. Don't you, Ricky?"

"What? What did I miss?" It was hard to take him seriously with cream cheese smeared across his mustache.

Mom turned to Bob. "What's on Timothy's schedule? Maybe he needs a little sabbatical down south."

About that time Luther walked in with more donuts. I said nothing, just stuck my hand toward the box. He shook his head, "How can you eat so much and stay so ripped?" He patted his own slight belly. "It's not fair."

"Ripped?" the sheriff asked.

"It means muscular and in good shape," Mom told him, leaning into me affectionately. "And that he is, my handsome boy."

While I puffed up from her flattery, I was disappointed that an age-appropriate female hadn't been around to hear the compliment. "Here, Mom." I offered her the pastry box. "Have a donut." Even though she declined, I winked mischievously at the sheriff.

"Do you know where Timothy's phone is?" Bob asked Luther. "I bet he'd have his schedule on his calendar app."

Luther reached for his second pastry. "He locks it in his desk drawer before he preaches. But seems to me," he appeared thoughtful, "a sabbatical is exactly what he needs."

✝✝✝

Because he was resting, no one, other than Meadow, had been able to spend much time with Timothy that day, but since the doctor had given him the all-clear, it was with hopeful hearts that we filed into our respective places of rest that evening. Meadow retreated into the basement of my parents' extravagant home, while the sheriff retired to his bedroom suite upstairs. I hung out in the theatre room where I'd probably watch a movie, read, or play video games until I fell asleep.

Because I was feeling especially aimless, I scrolled distractedly through my messages and emails. Unfortunately, nothing of note popped up, except for another arbitrary email from Pippa, a girl I'd met in Santa Fe several months ago at a writer's conference. A little *extra*, as they say, but a friendship worth maintaining as we often exchanged our writing and offered each other notes and editing suggestions.

A small lamp was all that illuminated the room, so when a sudden crack of light sloped across the floor, I was surprised. My mom's freshly washed face peeked at me through the angle in the door.

"May I come in?"

"Of course," I answered softly, loving the sight of her face without make-up, looking snug in her night clothes, complete with fluffy robe and slippers.

"Hey." She sat next to me on the cushy couch. "How's my sweet boy?"

"I'm twenty-eight, Mom."

"You'll always be my sweet boy, no matter how big you get."

"I'm okay. Just relieved that there's nothing serious going on with Timothy."

"I'm not talking about Timothy. I mean you." She stalled. "May I ask you something?" When I nodded, she seemed to rouse a measure of courage. "Are you…okay with my dating Ricky?"

I chuckled. "I'm good with Sheriff Rick. I mean, Ricky." As she scrutinized me, I put an expression of sincerity on my face.

"As you know, my relationship with Violet has always been … complicated. She and Dean always had their special bond, and that was okay because you and I had ours."

"We still do," I said, my throat thickening.

"It's just that Violet seems to finally be coming around—and I know that's only because she's happy with her own life right now and doesn't have room to be angry with me—but I couldn't bear it if you were unhappy with me also."

"I'm not, Mom, I swear."

"Because you've always been on my side, and I really, really, need you to be on my side now." When I reached for her hand, she clutched mine with a ferocity I'd never felt. "I loved your father, and I miss him every day. And I know Ricky is very different from Dean, but…" she shrugged, "maybe that's why I like him, because nothing could compare really…"

"He's crazy about you," I told her, adding, "and even though he's a little over-the-top sometimes, I was impressed with how he handled himself today when Timothy fainted."

She shook her head, her expression off somewhere, to a place and a time I wasn't privy to. "He was always like that. Lenny was the star because he was so solid and so good, and Brad Wolfheart was a star because he was so irreverent and so bad…but Ricky was always…how'd you say it? Over-the-top, yes, but *present*."

She giggled. "And apparently, he always had a crush on me."

I laughed, growing genuinely tickled, and soon she was cackling beside me. When we finally recovered from our hilarity, I tried to reassure her, channeling Billy's words from this morning. "Seriously, Mom, it's been ten years now, and I want you to be happy."

After a long pause she said, "Life is funny. You just never know when something from your past might circle back out of nowhere and bring you happiness…or opportunity." She kissed the top of my head and padded toward the door. "What is that saying about not burning bridges?" She winked. "Don't stay up too late."

"Yes, ma'am." I rolled my eyes playfully.

For a long time after she was gone, I thought about our family, about Violet and Dad, and me and Mom. It occurred to me that Violet was just like Dad. She was a doer, extremely capable, and very accomplished. Both of them were forces of nature, captains of their own fates, as the poem goes.

But I was more like my mom, and our destinies always seemed to be dependent on the whims of others.

I opened my laptop and pulled up the email from Timothy's friend. All day I'd been wavering between two responses. One desperate, explaining that I'd rewritten the novella and improved it immensely, and perhaps he'd like to take another look at it or one of my recent short stories. Or I could go with a snarky response, sarcastically referencing the obscene amount of time that had passed since I'd sent him the work.

I hit reply, and watched my cursor palpitate on the screen for several moments. Finally, I typed: *Thank you for your consideration.*

Mom was right, best not to burn a bridge.

Chapter Four

A God Wink
Timothy

Come at once.

I reread Father Patrick's text for the hundredth time. No hesitation, no questions asked, just *come at once*. Now there was a true man of God. An admirable man dedicated to the service of others. A noble man who believed in the healing powers of the Lord. Father Patrick was an inspiration during troubled waters and a beacon of hope when one stumbled. And for those of us who were called to bring others to Christ, he was the ideal.

A faithful man with a robust personality, the seasoned, red-headed priest of Irish descent was my only hope. My crisis of faith would require a mountain of conviction, an innate understanding of the cultures and people at play, and above all, discretion.

The fact that Father Patrick had ended up in Shady Gully, Louisiana, just when my life was on the verge of imploding, was divine intervention. Or, as I liked to say, *a God wink*.

Despite my hard work, my obsessive precautions, and my careful shedding of the past, it had now reemerged like a cancer and offered no mercy. It had settled in for the long haul and bellied like a snake, robbing me of peace as I waited for the inevitable strike. Worse still, my vulnerabilities had started to present physically as my mental, spiritual, and emotional stamina stalled.

My anxiety was suddenly interrupted when a raucous round of the zoomies developed between two of Sam and Ellie's thoroughbreds in the pasture behind Robin's home. In an effort to help me convalesce, she and Meadow had propped me up in an expensive gravity chair in the backyard of Robin's extravagant estate. Like an invalid I eased deeper into the comfortable chair, absently rubbed my thumb along the condensation on the glass of iced tea in my hands, and settled in for the show.

The game of chase was on, and while Juicy Fruit, a light bronze mare with a streak of white between her eyes, raced past a younger filly named Bubblicious, the upstart changed course and made for the water trough where a bright red ball bobbed. I chuckled as Bubblicious used her snout to maneuver the ball out of the water and proceeded to bounce it up in the air. An annoyed whinny sparked from the far end of the pasture as Juicy Fruit begrudgingly trotted over so she could partake in the fun.

Point one to Bubblicious for creativity. Or trickery, depending on how you looked at it.

I raised the zipper on my windbreaker against the increasing chill in the air, studying the wind as it carried the last of the narrow leaves of a willow tree over my head. Over the last several years Robin's luxurious home had become a retreat to me as it sat in an exclusive, but blessedly rural, area of Lexington. Other than Juicy Fruit, Bubblicious, and whatever assorted horses Sam and Ellie invited into their kingdom, I had the entire place to myself. I thrived in the quiet setting and found the isolation restorative.

And yet, despite the serene setting and the after-effects of the meds, I couldn't help but scroll through my phone, perusing messages and emails that I'd missed while in the hospital. Thankfully, it had been locked in my desk, safely tucked away from random—and innocent—eyes. I clicked an email from Northlake's partners in Haiti, wonderful missionaries who'd hosted many trips for the staff and community members who wanted to serve. I smiled as I read the well wishes and prayers for my health.

Another email from Uganda and our team there, this one with a photo of a giant banner painted by a joyful class of second graders who were finally getting the opportunity to learn to read. *Get well, Timothy!* Big smiles and thumbs pointing upward cheered my heart…and reminded me that everything I did, and anything that happened to me, would affect a lot of people.

Despair flashed in my lower belly, catching fire. After a greedy gulp of fresh, crisp air. I vigorously shook my head, thinking—hoping—I could chase the panic away.

With a sigh, I returned to my messages, eager to stumble onto something that would quell my anxiety. I opened an email from Mark Cerrillos, a friend and faith-based publisher who had been pushing me for years to write a book. A stab of concern pierced through my tranquility. *Had he heard rumors?* But as I read the missive, I realized the subject was Sterling and his submission of a few years ago.

Just then I heard the screen door on Robin's back patio slap against its hinges. Out she came with a Thermos of some kind while Ricky—he insisted I call him Ricky—lugged a large tray piled with food. Sterling trailed behind, carrying a bag of peppermints and looking preoccupied.

A tall, handsome young man with dark, affecting eyes and sable hair cut stylishly around his face, Sterling was a bit of an enigma. An immensely talented vocalist and musician, Sterling was the star of the creative team. He and Millie set the pace at rehearsals, as both were excellent at navigating the deep bench of creatives on Northlake's staff. Together they managed to inspire a group of highly imaginative people, consistently producing stunning performances week after week.

Sterling's ability and talent simmered just below the surface, and occasionally, when he was able to break through the anguish that he carried with him like a backpack, fragments of brilliance sparked around him like humming fireflies.

All thoughts of music, fireflies, and art vanished as soon as Meadow came into view behind Sterling. Reflexively, my lips curved upward in a goofy grin while my mind scrambled for witticisms that might tease a smile from her singularly ornery disposition. Amused, I watched as she scowled at something awkward Sterling had said, and then predictably, desperate to make up for his apparent blunder, Sterling responded with an injured—probably incoherent—comeback.

I understood, of course.

Meadow was a spectacular creature. Tall and lithe with coal-black hair that fell in a wave along her back, she possessed the striking green eyes that were prevalent among those from The Creek. Recently, I'd been close enough to discover that those mesmerizing jade eyes flickered with shimmering gold specks. Sadly, Sterling would never get close enough to explore those bedazzling jewels, as Meadow's off-putting demeanor struck fear in the majority of men.

I understood that as well.

When I'd first met Meadow three years ago in Shady Gully, she'd been standing in her bedroom with her hair soaking wet, completely naked except for a short, flimsy robe.

As I recall, I'd done a lot of babbling myself that day.

"Got your cure-all right here," Ricky hollered, distracting me from my reverie as he balanced a tray laden with deli sandwiches, potato salad, and zucchini bread. Even with his hands full, he managed to dig in his pocket and toss me a sprinkling of taffy. "Coconut is my personal favorite, but the grape will make you wanna slap your mama."

I flinched. "Thanks." I tilted my chair so I could pick up the candy I'd missed.

"There's a watermelon in there." Ricky set the tray on the picnic table as Robin and Meadow organized the food under the shade of the willow tree. "It's real hard to get, but Lenny special orders it for me at his hardware store."

I nodded as I stuffed the grape taffy into my mouth. Meadow, seemingly disinterested, eventually strolled over to me and shielded her eyes with her hand as she watched Sterling feed peppermints to the horses at the fence. When I turned to follow her gaze, her mouth covered mine. Although it was a quick, very chaste brushing of the lips, the effect was the same, perhaps even heightened because it was covert.

"How are you feeling?" she asked softly, licking grape sugar from her lips.

"I'm okay," I said hoarsely, "just a little tired."

At last satisfied with the spread on her picnic table, Robin moseyed over, joining our conversation. "The doctor said that was normal. Would you like me to fix you a plate?"

Even though I wasn't hungry, I knew there was no point in protesting. "I'd love a sandwich and some potato salad."

Meadow unfolded a lawn chair beside mine, and we watched in silence as Ricky and Robin dilly-dallied around the table. I couldn't help but think of Dean, a fine man and successful executive who'd provided a life of affluence for his family. Sadly, it had taken a cancer diagnosis to revive his and Robin's marriage, and yet, the quality of those last few months together had seemed to restore a lifetime of misunderstanding, doubt, and uncertainty between them.

When Ricky threw his head back in raucous laughter, I glanced at Robin's ring finger. Still naked. I felt a pang of worry for the small-town sheriff. It seemed he was madly in love with a woman who still grieved for her husband.

As if reading my mind, Meadow whispered, "She's in love with him." She looked a little baffled. "I don't get it."

I looked at her curiously, as the idea of Robin and Meadow sharing girl talk seemed preposterous. "She told you this?"

"Good lord, no, but I can tell. She's afraid of the kids' reactions."

"Oh."

"Mayo or mustard?" Robin called out to me from the willow tree.

"Both, please." I turned once again to Meadow. "How are things at the art gallery? Robin mentioned how appreciative she was to have your help."

Meadow looked at me over a cloak of dark lashes. "You know that's just a ruse so I could come see you, right?"

God, I loved her irreverence, her refusal to put on airs, even for the sake of civilized society. "I know that, but I still want to know, how is it? Are you having any fun?"

When Desi's mother, Sunny, died several years ago from an overdose, Robin used her vast wealth to buy back all of Sunny's paintings, specifically the ones Desi had to hock to make ends meet while Lenny had been out of work. Even better, Robin used her influence to showcase Sunny's paintings at exclusive art studios across the country, and Desi never had to part with an original painting because they sold only Giclee prints, which were digital prints made on canvas with an inkjet printer.

Before long, Robin and Desi became known as movers and shakers in the art world and opened their own gallery in downtown Lexington. The goal? To feature unknown talent—people like Sunny—and give them an opportunity to break into the very cliquish world of art.

"Actually," Meadow said, "I'm going to try to hook Robin up with this woman from The Creek. I've never actually met her, but I've seen her pottery, and it's amazing. Like, really incredible."

"I believe you," I kidded. "Would she be open to showing her work?"

She lifted her shoulders doubtfully. "Not sure. Maybe I can get Uncle Wolf to help me persuade her, although I don't know if he even knows her because she's kind of a recluse. She does wonderful paintings as well, mostly animals like wolves, foxes, raccoons, hawks…you get the idea."

"Nice," I said in response as Robin walked over and handed me an obscene amount of food on a plate. "Wow, Sterling, you want half of this?" I lifted my plate, calling out to him over my shoulder.

"Naw, that's just a snack for me." He pulled himself away from the horses and made his way to the picnic table. As he proceeded to shovel food onto his plate, he asked, "So, are we going to Shady Gully or not?"

"What?" I perked.

Ricky didn't utter a peep. Instead, he busied himself folding out a chair for Robin before finally settling into one of his own.

"Well, we wanted to talk to you about that." Robin sat down.

"We know you're busy, Timothy, and have a hundred things on your schedule, but we think it would be good for you to get away for a while."

When I glanced at Meadow she smiled.

"I've got to head back soon," Ricky said between bites of potato salad. "I've been grooming Quietdove for sheriff—for when I retire—but he ain't quite ready yet, so…"

"We thought we could all travel together," Robin added in an eager tone. "Sterling is going to come as well."

"I don't know," I protested halfheartedly, "if I don't preach next Sunday, folks might start to wonder if I'm losing it."

"The tall guy said he could handle it." Meadow shrugged.

"Bob? I don't know—"

"He can handle it," Sterling insisted. "Plus, he deserves a chance to take center stage, and you know the Northlake staff will rally so you can get a break."

"I've got to get back as well." Meadow tagged me with those captivating green eyes. "I have a job, and I need to check on Bella."

"What's wrong with Bella?" Robin asked in concern. "Is she okay?"

"It's probably nothing, but her texts have been cryptic lately, and the mail isn't going to deliver itself in Shady Gully. At least that's what Claire says."

Ricky chuckled as he assaulted his zucchini bread. "And here I thought Cruella Claire would help you out and deliver it while you were on vacation."

Meadow smirked before turning back to me. "I think it's a good idea." She patted her thighs definitively. "It's decided."

I managed to swallow a large bite of sandwich without choking. *Was this really happening?*

"What do you think?" Robin pressed me.

"Well, I have been wanting to check on Petey, to see how the Unity Church is coming along." *And Father Patrick.*

"Yes!" Robin balled up her fists in excitement. "I cannot wait to see Desi." She lowered her voice conspiratorially. "We've been working on a little something…" When Ricky looked at her curiously, she 'zipped her lips.' "Patience, Sheriff." She jostled him.

Sterling's expression brightened. "We haven't seen Violet's new veterinary hospital yet either. That would be cool."

"Excellent!" Robin's tiny body seemed about to burst with frenetic anticipation. "I'll go schedule the flights now."

Yes, this was really happening.

If only they'd known, they hadn't needed to work so hard to convince me.

†††

Once Robin had snagged first-class airline tickets for the whole lot of us—including her cat, Buford—we whiled the afternoon away making plans for our trip to Shady Gully. Robin spoke to her daughter, Violet, and then she and Ricky Facetimed Desi and Lenny.

Undoubtedly, by sunset, word of our upcoming trip would be swinging on the backwoods grapevine. Charlie Wayne, the town curmudgeon who owned the Cozy Corner, Shady Gully's favorite eatery, would be stocking his freezers in expectation of increased revenue, while Cruella Claire, the town's post office manager, would be making the news viral from behind her bully pulpit of *Forever* stamps.

Even though I hadn't had a moment alone to text Father Patrick, spending time with Meadow had done wonders. Especially when Sterling gravitated to his man cave in the theatre room and Ricky and Robin were—

Well, they were somewhere inside that big ole mansion.

Finally, just the two of us sat in front of a fire pit in Robin's backyard, nothing but the sound of frolicking horses and buzzing fireflies in the background. I stoked the fire, trying to keep it going as long as possible, because the very tone of the day had soothed my soul.

"Did you talk to your uncle?" I asked.

"Yes, and Bella, and even Luke, who she put on the phone during our conversation."

She didn't look particularly pleased, but that was Meadow's way, so I chuckled. "What have you got against Shady Gully's mayor?"

"Meh," she sighed. "I'm working on it."

I used my free hand to test the space over her thigh, which proved worthwhile as she entwined her fingers into mine. I moved our hands to my mouth and lightly brushed the top of hers with a kiss, and for my trouble, I was rewarded with a few of those golden flecks twinkling inside those green irises I loved so much.

"Everybody in Shady Gully is freaking out because you're coming."

"They shouldn't." I stared into the fire. "I'm not who they think I am."

"What does that mean?"

My heart plunged when I realized I'd actually said the words aloud. "Just, you know…" I recovered. "It's impossible to live up to the image, to the expectations…"

She scrutinized me for such a long moment I feared she'd detected something—a flaw, a crack...the *truth*. But thankfully, she moved closer and leaned her forehead against mine. I sank into that moment like a thirsty man rescued from the desert. Our lips mere inches away, I closed my eyes and just parked there, our heads touching, our lips so close we could feel one another's breath.

And during the kiss that finally came, my anxiety lifted, swept up in flight with the fireflies, as if their twinkling lights cele-brated the moment along with us.

In that instant, everything seemed right. Doable. Hopeful. Sustainable.

But eventually, the fire turned to smoking embers, and Meadow said goodnight. "I'd better go in," she said huskily. "Robin and I have a lot to do at the gallery tomorrow to get ready for the trip."

"I understand." I kissed her again. "I have things to do in preparation as well. I want to go by Northlake tomorrow to reassure everyone I'm alive." I glanced at my Corolla reflecting against the landscape lights. "I'll let myself out."

She laughed noisily, which made my heart do a little flip. I watched her stroll back to the house, trying to memorize the elegant lines of her back, her long hair swishing back and forth, and her almost pugnacious stride.

Just as she walked inside and disappeared from my view, my phone vibrated, followed by the ding of a text.

`Time is running out.`

And right behind the ominous script a photo emerged. A grotesque and painfully compromising one…of me.

Chapter Five

My Best Girl
Fireman

My fingers had become wrinkly from swishing my hands back and forth in the bucket of cleaning solution. The Fire Chief, Redflyer, a Creek man who oversaw the fire stations in both Shady Gully and The Creek, insisted that the only way to get the trucks to that perfect cherry shine was with Lenny's secret blend of—

Not sure exactly what was in the concoction Lenny and Redflyer brewed up at Lenny's hardware store, but whatever it was, it left my hands red and blistered.

And I had to admit, it made the truck look dynamite. I admired the "cherry shine" Redflyer went on and on about as I tugged my rubber gloves off. Impressive. Once I dumped the soapy water down the drain of the large tub in the utility room, I pulled a load of freshly dried towels out of the industrial dryer. Now, for my favorite part, drying off that bad boy. I circled the awesome, forty-foot beauty in anticipation.

"Looking sweet." Moonpipe, another man from The Creek, admired my job as he showed up for his shift.

I acknowledged his compliment by lifting my head half an inch. I was pretty sure I'd nailed the expression, the one they did in cop shows after the good guys caught the bad guys, and the team exchanged a look that said, *yeah, we know we're tough and total bad*—

"Fireman!" Big Al hollered from the kitchen like there was a fire or something. "Fireman!"

"Coming." I set down the towels and raced toward the kitchen in case there really was a fire. But it was only Big Al pulling stromboli out of the industrial oven. "What?"

"You want one? I put Italian sausage and spinach in these."

"I do." Moonpipe sat at the bar. Looked at me mischievously as he tickled his chin. "Is that a little peach fuzz I see?"

I grinned, heat flashing across my face.

Big Al smirked as he scooped a bowl of marinara on the plate for Moonpipe's dipping pleasure. "Won't be long before the ladies start lining up for your attention."

"Whatever," I mumbled behind a smile.

"I'm telling ya. You're tall and you have green eyes and a thick head of dark hair." Big Al rubbed his scant hairline nostalgically.

"Don't worry," Moonpipe bantered with his friend, "you've still got a few strands left. I count at least four…or wait, maybe that's just three."

I watched as the two of them laughed easily together, still confounded that five years ago they were ready to rumble at the four-way stop. Not a good chapter in Shady Gully's history, that's for sure. That was the year that Wolfheart's sister, Peony, had been murdered, I'd burned down a church, and everyone on The Creek had been mad at the sheriff. Lots of distrust to go around back then.

But then Luke became mayor, the Unity Bridge was built, and shortly after that, The Creek had its very own fire station. Today both stations were manned with the likes of Big Al and Redflyer, as well as Thaddeus, and Creeks like Moonpipe and Youngdeer.

Even more amazing, able-bodied men from *both* communities made up the volunteer fire department.

When I turned to attend to my truck, Big Al stopped me. "Hold up. The other thing is Micah called, and they need you at the vet. ASAP."

"Again?" Moonpipe quipped. "What is he? The good Samaritan? He's got more jobs, floater positions, and do-a-favor gigs than I've had my whole life."

"Well, that's no surprise," Big Al volleyed and then turned back to me. "We need at least two of us here in case we get a call, but if you want to drive your car, I can call Quietdove or Max at the sheriff's office to ride with you."

"Yeah, I doubt they're doing much." Moonpipe bit into his stromboli. "What with the sheriff in Kentucky on vacation and all." He flapped his eyes with pleasure, giving Big Al the thumbs up of approval. "Delicious."

"No, I'll walk. It's just right there. What's going on?"

"Heck if I know. It's Micah, so it could be anything."

I left them laughing over Micah's revolving daily special of theatrics and headed to my locker to pick up my phone. After scrolling through numerous texts from Shady Gully's very own drama queen, I figured it would be good to hurry, but not necessary to rush in with sirens ablaze.

While at my locker, I peeked inside the crisp envelope containing the previous week's pay. Since I didn't have a bank account, I was paid in cash, so on the way out I stopped at my car and stuffed the bills into the secret partition I'd sewn into my glove compartment. I made a mental note to stash it soon since the mound of cash was getting fat enough to be noticeable.

Just over a hundred yards beyond the fire station, I walked past the sheriff's office and then Sprite's Quick Stop, Shady Gully's catch-all store where people could buy gas, ice cream, or fishing lures, all in one shot. I only had to look diagonally then to see Violet's Vet, a brand-new building with a crisp, modern design. The small pasture next to it was even neater, as it landed right at the four-way stop. To me, it was the coolest thing ever to reside there, as folks could take a gander at the recuperating goats, donkeys, or even calves while waiting at the stop sign. Before long the community had started to feel invested in the animals' recovery, and soon updates on a goat or a miniature donkey became normal topics of conversation all around town.

"Hey! Hey, Fireman!" *Bella. Beautiful Bella.* I'd recognize her exquisite voice anywhere. Even though I was trying really hard to get over my not-so-secret crush, the sound of her voice always made me tremble.

She and her husband were walking their Shiba Inus. I bent to pet the dogs after giving the Mayor of Shady Gully the evil eye.

"Look at that," Bella said. "Duke loves you."

The tan, black, and white Shiba Inu loved everyone. He was easy-going and very affectionate. Thick-furred with dense undercoats, Shiba Inus were known for their giant personalities. They were also known for being mischief makers. The hope was that Duke would be the calm to Duchess's crazy, but when the rambunctious princess herself presented him with a ragged golf ball lodged within her toothy smile, it seemed they had a way to go.

"What? How did you…?" Luke bent to wrestle the filthy ball out of Duchess's mouth. "Where do you find these things?"

Luke and Bella lived in one of the fancy units in the duplex Luke bought five years ago, just across from Sprite's. He also owned Luke's Auto Body Shop right next to it, where Bubba and Daryl worked. I begrudgingly gave him credit for being a savvy businessman, which undoubtedly had helped him get elected as mayor, but his buttoned up, nerdy look didn't seem right for Bella, who was smoking hot.

"Where's your car?" Bella asked me. "It's so pretty."

"At the fire station. I'm on my way to see what kind of trouble Micah got herself into at the vet." I screwed up my eyes at Luke. "You'd think she'd call her own brother."

Luke snorted. "Not likely. When it comes to Micah's jams, my track record isn't great." He frowned, glancing at Violet's Vet. "But I guess we could head that way," he said to Bella, "just in case."

Great. Should have kept my big mouth shut.

When Bella tugged Duke's leash, the black-faced pup with white eyebrows obediently scampered beside her, whereas Luke wrestled with the ginger, fox-faced Duchess as she seemed inclined to go in the opposite direction.

"How's that going?" I asked Bella wryly, referring to both her lame husband and the chemistry between the dogs.

"Good. Duke isn't the brightest bulb in the pack, but he does seem to temper some of Duchess's rowdiness."

"I can see that," I deadpanned, and Bella laughed because she always got my humor.

"Is that…is that Father Patrick?" She squinted in the direction of Lenny's Tool Shed and the Post Office. "Is he…exercising or something? And what is that he's wearing?"

"It appears to be some sort of…warm-up suit." I shook my head, bewildered by the sight of walking aluminum foil.

"Wow." Luke, breathless, had finally caught up with Duchess. "Is that a headband he's wearing?"

My pocket vibrated with a new text from Micah, this one in all caps.

WHERE ARE YOU???

"Hey, did you hear that Robin and Sterling are coming back with Mama and Sheriff Rick tomorrow?" Bella's beautiful face lit up. "Even Timothy is coming."

I grunted, feigning ignorance.

When we turned right at the four-way, we were disconcerted by the sight of Quietdove's cruiser in the parking lot of Violet's Vet. "Humph," Luke mumbled, a sense of responsibility hurrying his pace.

Reaching the entrance to the animal hospital seconds before Luke did, I opened the door to what could only be described as pandemonium. Bubba, previously of the Berry Red paint camp, would be considered chunky regardless of what color he wore. Currently, he was on his hands and knees peeking under the chairs in the waiting room. "He's got to be around here somewhere." He crawled to another chair and ducked under it in search. "Pierre, come here, my man. Pierre!"

Micah, who had clearly been crying as black mascara traced down her cheeks like Raggedy Ann, shivered and squealed simultaneously. Quietdove, a shade paler than his usual olive-toned Creek complexion, waved his arms up and down and all around, guarding Micah from…something.

"What is it?" Luke asked.

Good question.

"It's…it's…it's…" Micah babbled incoherently.

"It's just Pierre," Bubba said lightly, thankfully pulling his jeans up a notch before bending down again to surveil beneath a chair. "He's harmless."

"Who's Pierre?" I asked, just as Duke backed his way to the door in fear and Duchess jerked Luke's arm forward in curiosity.

"There!" Quietdove pointed behind a shelf loaded with twenty-pound bags of dog food. His eyes widened. "Okay everybody, let's calmly back our way to the door. Slowly now." He turned to Micah, apparently set on escorting her to safety.

"What the…" I stalked to the dog food shelf just as Duchess broke free of Luke's grip. Keen on adventure, the rowdy dog panted beside me, her well-muscled bottom prancing as she sniffed the lower shelves. I bent to look closer.

Just as Bella and Micah screamed in perfect soprano harmony, I came face to face with a twenty-foot reticulated python that flitted its tongue at me like I was a prized guinea pig.

✝✝✝

Screaming ensued. Bella's, Micah's, and honestly, maybe even mine. Even Duke let out a nervous yelp. But one scream rose above the rest, and that was because it contained no fear. The Boss-Lady had emerged from the surgery room, wearing scrubs with a little blood dotted here and there, and annoyance plastered all over her porcelain face.

"For the love of God, what is going on here?" Violet, blonde, tall, and tough—with a commanding presence I was sure even the snake took note of—stood before us in disbelief.

In principle, since they were employees of Shady Gully proper, Deputy Quietdove or Mayor Luke should have been the ones to step up with an answer, but because they didn't, that fell to Micah. "It's…Bubba's snake," she said, calmer now that her take charge sister-in-law was present.

"He has a name." Bubba's face was flushed as he pulled himself up and gave his jeans a tug. "It's Pierre. And he ain't doing too good. I think he got himself burnt, Violet. He tried to crawl in the oven this morning. I was making those little French toast bites, you know the kind that crisp up real nice—"

Violet raised her hands, and Bubba immediately zipped his lips.

She walked to the shelf and said, "Help me pull him out." After she and Bubba wrangled the nearly one-hundred-pound python from around the shelf, Violet turned to Micah. "Let's get Pierre checked in. You'll need to weigh him."

"How…how?" Micah stuttered.

"The oven was only on preheat." Bubba berated himself. "But he's got a blister the size of a brick."

"Bubba," Violet swiveled, "I assume you brought a tote for Pierre. I know you didn't just carry him into my hospital like this."

"Yeah, yeah," he said. "But he escaped. Like Houdini."

Micah shivered.

"Use zip ties next time." She turned her gaze onto Micah. "Be creative, get him weighed and checked in." And then to Bubba, "When Pierre is checked in bring him into exam room one." When both started to speak, she raised her hands. "I have a Saint Bernard on my operating table who is almost neutered. I say almost because his surgery was interrupted." Violet's eyes flitted over me. "Pierre isn't dangerous. Somebody get this done."

The weight of Violet's gaze made me shrivel a little. I wasn't sure if it was because of the mental image of the Saint Bernard, the fear of her wrath, or the implication that she was looking to me to be the adult in the room.

Once she disappeared behind the swinging doors, we all looked at one another, a little shell-shocked. Duchess's low growl snapped us out of our daze. Bubba sighed elaborately as he held the front end of the snake along his right arm. "Can I get some help here?" He directed his gaze to the men in the room. I wasn't sure if that meant me or not, since technically, I wasn't eighteen.

"What were you thinking?" Micah hissed at Bubba. "Why did you even get that…thing?"

"What? Women dig snakes. They're chick magnets."

Micah positioned herself safely behind the counter. "You've been misinformed, and"—she lowered her voice—"I'm not touching it."

"Somebody just needs to get on the scale," Luke suggested, "weigh themselves, and then…weigh again with the snake." But he didn't move.

"Good idea," Quietdove echoed, but he didn't move either.

Bubba frowned, sucking in his gut. "I wouldn't really feel comfortable doing that in front of y'all."

Geez.

"Okay." I got on the scale. "Now, if I can get Pierre around my shoulders…"

†††

After we got Pierre checked in and back into his tote, we hauled him into exam room number one. I washed my hands and caught my breath, and everyone except Bubba gathered around Micah's counter in the lobby of the waiting room. She'd just put on a fresh pot of coffee when Father Patrick appeared in the doorway like an illuminated angel of mercy.

I blinked as my eyelids felt seared from the reflection sparking off his aluminum foil warm-up suit. "What's that in your hands?"

"What a flushed and youthful bunch you are," he pronounced. "I took the liberty of stopping for some pastries."

Quietdove looked doubtful as he peered into the box. "Those are Twinkies."

"Quite." Father Patrick removed the handkerchief from the pocket of his glossy ensemble. "Unfortunately, Sprite had neither the Little Debbie Glazed Donut Sticks or the Zebra Cakes."

"I'll take one." Duchess perked up at Luke's feet as he reached for one.

"Pass," Bella and Micah said in unison.

I scarfed one down before Luke removed the wrapper on his.

"I was hoping I could see the doctor today," Father Patrick said with his uniquely sophisticated, Irish politeness. "If she could squeeze me in."

"Where's your pet?" Micah peered over the counter. "Did you adopt a puppy?"

"Uh, no, uh…" he stammered, "but a friend of mine did, and he wanted me to ask the doctor about some of the things he's, or I should say, his puppy, is experiencing."

As everyone turned, momentarily distracted by a large, almost behemoth shadow as it stretched past the window, I pulled Father Patrick aside. "This is an animal hospital, Father. It doesn't count," I whispered. "You promised me you were going to get an appointment with a real doctor."

"I'll have you know that veterinarians are indeed real doctors. Can you imagine diagnosing a patient who can't even answer your questions? They're very likely smarter than people doctors." He scoffed at me. "Besides, Violet *was* a people doctor before she became an animal doctor, so she's doubly as smart…"

I tuned him out as the entrance chime announced the arrival of the one and only Hoot Wheeler. Originally from Toulouse, Louisiana, the six-foot-tall, muscled owner of Wheeler's Construction carried a teeny-tiny carrier.

"Oh no." Micah rolled her eyes in dramatic fashion. "Not you again."

The brawny, blue-eyed Hoot grinned as he brushed his fingers along his dark, neatly trimmed beard. "Hello, all." He glanced around the room, momentarily tripped up by the sight of Quiet-dove. He pivoted back to Micah. "Why such a brusque greeting, Micah? What have I ever done to you?"

A giant sigh erupted from Micah's tiny frame. "You're everywhere I go. I can't seem to get away from you." She daintily tucked her highlighted blonde hair behind her ear. "You should get a life."

"Well, maybe *you're* everywhere *I* go," he returned. "You ever think about that? You're at your dad's hardware store every time I go get lumber—"

"I work there."

"You're at my dentist's office every time I go get my teeth cleaned."

"I work there. I'm a dental hygienist, you know?"

The two of them had been doing this dance for nearly three years now, much to poor Quietdove's dismay. As Luke and Bella seemed to be enjoying the back and forth, Quietdove grew vexed. "Is there a problem, Micah?" he asked in a commanding tone. Deputy to the rescue. After all, he'd just tamed a python.

"I'm confused." Hoot leaned on the counter, flirting as he positioned his face only inches from Micah's. "Where exactly do you work?"

"A lot of places." Frustrated now, especially as someone dared to raise the subject of her slightly aimless career path, Micah nearly toppled her coffee. "Throw me one of those Twinkies, Luke."

Her brother simpered as he unwrapped a Twinkie and placed it next to her wobbly coffee.

"What's your business, Hoot?" Quietdove moved closer. "There's a lot going on today. Do you have an appointment?"

"Yes." Micah chewed defiantly. "What's in that itty-bitty carrier of yours?"

When the carrier jiggled, Hoot placed his giant hand gently against the side. "I just need a minute of Violet's time—"

"No can do." Micah arched her eyebrow. "Until we get"—she peered at the carrier— "until we get whatever that is checked in."

"Rules are rules," echoed Quietdove, clearly no fan of Mr. Brawny.

"Fine," Hoot acquiesced in a low tone. "This is Tootsie. She weighs four pounds, and she's not feeling well."

Bella approached the carrier, lightly brushing her hand against the netting. "She's adorable. Is she…oh my goodness…is she a Pomeranian?

"She is," replied Hoot. "And she's my best girl." He pushed himself away from the counter and glanced around the room, his steely gaze landing squarely on Quietdove. "Anybody got a problem with that?"

Chapter Six

Mass Castrations
Sterling

The Dallas Fort Worth International Airport, or DFW, as it was called, was located halfway between Dallas and Fort Worth, Texas, and sprawled across twenty-seven square miles. It spilled into the cities of Grapevine, Irving, Euless, and Coppell. It also happened to be the third busiest airport in the world.

What it wasn't, was Sheriff Rick's favorite place. "This is obscene." His mustache twitched as we fast-walked toward the terminal for Alexandria, Louisiana.

"Bluegrass Airport in Lexington was quaint," he told my mother. "They give you bourbon balls when you arrive, and the speaker booms with a bugler playing "First Call" when the luggage comes out. You know, like at the Kentucky Derby? But this," he exhaled loudly, "this is madness."

Because it took my mom two steps to cover our one as we rushed to make it to the Skylink—a light rail train connecting all the terminals—she used up twice the energy. And yet, she still found the breath in her lungs to fret. "I should have given Buford his anxiety treats earlier. I can feel him getting rumbly."

"Let me take him." Although I half expected a howl and a hiss when I reached for the sleek designer cat carrier, I instead received a disinterested yawn and a judgmental blink. "He looks pretty chill to me, Mom. Don't worry."

Now free of the two-pound carrier and the ten-pound cat, she rallied to grab the sheriff's arm and slow him down. "Did you remember to pack the chargers—"

"Look at that!" Ricky gasped. "Did you see that, Robin? That guy was in such a hurry, he nearly ran right over that poor woman."

I glanced over my shoulder, unsurprised to find Timothy doing his thing, dazzling the "poor woman" with his kind sincerity as he stopped to gather her carry-on and purse from the floor. Meadow stood by, watching patiently, a hint of amusement flashing in her otherwise flat expression.

When we finally made it to the Skylink, we quickly hopped aboard and flew across multiple terminals at the speed of light. Well, maybe not that fast, but enough to make the sheriff apoplectic. "This ain't right," he huffed. "We're crammed in here like sardines." To his credit, he folded his tall body around my mom's as he was determined to buttress her slip of a frame lest it flew off "this gliding monstrosity."

At last, we made it to Terminal B, which was much more to the sheriff's liking. Quieter, and dotted with easier, less hurried travelers, Ricky had finally found the quaintness he so desired. And even more importantly, there were several available seats. Even the pilots relaxed in comfortable spaces, sharing coffee and conversation as they waited along with the passengers.

Once I was sure Ricky wasn't planning to strike up a conversation with the aviators, I was able to settle into a cozy chair of my own, a respectable distance from him and my mom, as well as Timothy and Meadow, who'd gravitated to seats overlooking the runway.

I sank into isolation, coveting it, needing it, even as I scrolled through my messages, desperate for interaction. For something… life-changing, for anything…earth-shattering, but there was nothing of the sort in my inbox. Not even a rejection of one of my query letters or a mundane email from Pippa.

I sighed, glanced around the terminal, and realized I was surrounded by couples.

When I caught my mother observing me, I quickly turned my focus to my phone and began a text. Without thinking, I typed

Tammy Jo's name in the "To" box. My fingers pumped the tiny keyboard with intent. I was going for the friendly, casual, *hey, we're going to be in Louisiana, it would be great to see you,* kind of vibe.

Originally from Naryville, Louisiana, Tammy Jo was a nurse who'd taken care of Uncle Lenny when he'd had back surgery some time ago. Ironically, she'd dated Petey, Violet's husband, for a while, but even that hadn't bothered me because the attraction that had sparked between us at Luke and Bella's wedding three years ago had been a game-changer. Curvy, with raven hair, Tammy Jo was totally my cup of tea. And for a while, I'd been hers.

Because of our hopeful beginning, she'd seized the opportunity to become a travel nurse, which not only doubled her salary but allowed us a chance to rendezvous occasionally. She'd even enjoyed a stint in Lexington for a time. Or maybe *I'd* enjoyed it. Either way, our long-distance relationship got complicated, and she returned to Louisiana.

After sending the text, I waited for several minutes, but not even the dancing dots of promise appeared on my phone.

I hurriedly texted my sister then, for fear Mama Bear's radar would go up again. Surprisingly, the dots gyrated, then stopped completely. My phone rang. *Typical Violet.*

"Hey, what's up, Dr. V?" I grinned.

"You texted me," she teased. "You know I don't have time to type."

"Why? Are you neutering some poor kitten?"

"No. The mass castrations happened yesterday. Are y'all at the airport?"

I surveyed the collection of passengers surrounding me, most of whom were scrolling, reading, or asleep. "Yeah. You wouldn't believe how jazzed folks are about coming to Louisiana."

"I bet," she said, missing my sarcasm. "Aunt Desi is planning a party, Petey is planning a sermon, and let's see, what else? Oh, Charlie Wayne bought Cozy Corner T-shirts for him and his new employee. Or partner, depending on who you talk to."

I chuckled. "Oh yeah? How's that going? I still can't believe he and JJ Wheeler came to an understanding."

"Tentative, at best." Buttons beeped in the background. "How's Mama? And the sheriff?"

I cocked my head. While Meadow and Timothy canoodled near the window, Mom and Ricky continued to flap their gums, no doubt bonding over the outrageous airport and Buford's rumbly condition. "He wants me to call him Ricky," I told her, "but in my mind, he'll always be Sheriff Rick."

Violet snorted but didn't bite. Most likely trying to be a better person now that she'd married a man of the cloth. I heard the muffled sound of barking, followed by an entrance chime. "I can't wait to see your place. How's business?"

"Great." I could tell she was smiling over the phone. "Speaking of which, I'd better go. Things are hopping."

"Hey, Violet," I butted in, "did you ever have a chance to read the short story I sent you a few months ago? It's something new. Something I thought you'd like—"

"Huh? Oh, it's been crazy busy here, Sterling, but I will. I promise."

"Yeah. Okay."

"Love you. See you soon."

As we ended the call, I was unable to conceal my frustration. *No hurry*, I thought, *it's just my life.* Disgusted with myself, I tried to shake it off. *How pathetic am I? So desperate for approval, for a single compliment, from anyone…*

"Hey, sweet boy." My mom sat beside me. "Was that your sister?" Her radar was state of the art, no doubt about it.

"Yeah. She said everybody's excited to see us." I forced levity into my voice.

Her purple eyeglasses fixated on me. "Sterling."

My irritation flared. "What? Seriously, would you just stop? I'm way too old to have a helicopter mom." But then she upped her mom-game and waited me out, infuriating me all the more. "Look, I can't wait to see everyone. I'm just dreading all the questions." I parroted a mocking tone, "Oh, Sterling, how is law school going? How's the writing?"

"People care—"

"—and the cursed answers that unfortunately have to follow. Well," I mimed the tone again, "I flunked out of the one pre-law class I took, so law school is definitely not in my future."

"If you want to try again, you know I'll help you."

"No," I grunted. "I didn't even like it that much."

"Well, maybe you should focus on the writing then."

I lowered my voice as Timothy and Meadow had come from the window and were chatting with Ricky. "Apparently, I'm not good at that either. I can never seem to make the plot come together or the mystery believable like the suspense authors I like. Like the ones Dad liked."

Mom's mouth formed an O as she sat back in her seat and looked blankly around the terminal. The airline employees behind the counter lifted the rope to the jetway and waved to the pilots, who rose and tossed their coffee cups in the trash. Mom and I watched in silence as they headed that way with a group of flight attendants who'd just arrived.

"Maybe, Sterling," Mom said with deliberation, "*maybe* suspense isn't your thing. Did you ever think about that?" Her gaze intensified. "Maybe that's simply not your genre."

"Flight 115 for Alexandria, Louisiana, will begin boarding in twenty minutes." As the announcement blared from the intercom, passengers scrambled for last-minute snack runs and bathroom visits.

Mom rose and headed toward the sheriff, to Ricky, and I swear the man stood a little taller at the very sight of her. They huddled with Meadow as Timothy moved toward me. "Hey, man, do you smell that?"

"Yeah, it's impossible to think of much else." I stood, stuffing my iPad and electronics into my backpack.

Timothy grinned like an eleven-year-old boy. "Let's go get us one."

We followed our noses and our bellies to the place with the tasty cinnamon rolls. "My treat," Timothy said as he paid. We ate the delicious, sticky pastries standing up, with only the sound of our groans of satisfaction filling the silence. "So good," Timothy declared as he balled up his napkin.

I concurred, washing the pastry down with bottled water from my backpack while Timothy sipped coffee. After the fractious conversation I'd had with my mom, I figured maybe I could redeem myself by coming clean with Timothy.

"So, uh," I started, "as crazy as it sounds, I finally got a response from Mark Cerrillos."

Timothy paled, and for a second, I thought he was going to faint again. Reflexively, I raised my arm to break his fall, even as mortification filled me. Perhaps it wasn't a fainting spell at all. Maybe he was rebuking himself for going to bat for me in the first place. In doing that, he'd lost credibility with a powerful man, and why? Because of *my* failure.

"Are you okay?" I maintained my grip while speaking in a reassuring voice. "Do you want to sit down?" His eyes darted frantically over my head, and I wondered if I should call for medical assistance. "Timothy?"

"Excuse me, sugar," a ragged voice blew behind me.

While I wanted to turn around to see who—or what—had unnerved Timothy so, I hesitated. He appeared as if he might topple over at any moment. I maintained my grip, swinging my free arm around his waist, and I half-pulled, half-carried him over to a seat.

"Flight 115 for Alexandria, Louisiana, is now ready to board passengers." I cut my eyes in the direction of the travelers, searching for any sign of Meadow or my mom. Or better yet, the sheriff.

"Sugar?" The gravelly voice persisted.

When I finally turned, I saw that the grating voice belonged to a haggard, rough-looking woman, thinner even than my mom on her thinnest of days. The aged woman crouched on the floor below our chairs, and the stench that emanated from her hit me in a wave so foul I nearly lost my cinnamon roll. Her hair hung in clumps around her shoulders, and the bones in her chest appeared concave and brittle. She tapped my knee impatiently with her open hand.

"Got any spare change, Sugar?"

Having slightly reclaimed his composure, Timothy leaned on one haunch and dug into his jeans pocket. He pulled out several bills and handed the woman the money.

"Thank ya, kind sir," she croaked, and when she smiled, I realized she was missing more than half her teeth, and the yellow ones dangling from her mouth weren't long for this world.

Her cloudy gaze lingered on Timothy longer than necessary, and when he turned away from her, I realized I'd just witnessed something few, if any, ever would. For if the tattooed, charismatic pastor of Northlake Christian Church in Lexington, Kentucky, was known for anything, it was for his fierce need, his insatiable drive even, to search the world over for dirty feet to wash.

But this woman had truly unsettled him.

He actually flinched when she used his knee to push herself up from the floor. We both watched as she hobbled away, finally disappearing out of sight when Terminal B morphed into Terminal C.

I studied Timothy. "Are you alright?"

"Yeah, yeah." He raked his hands across his jeans. "I just…that was upsetting. Seeing someone like that."

I stared off into the space where the ghostly woman had disappeared, shaking my head. "How did she even get in here? I mean, she was clearly on drugs. How would she even get past security like that?"

"I don't know." Timothy cleared his throat. "Maybe she works somewhere in the airport."

I handed him my water, noting the way his eyes flitted nervously in every direction. Eventually, his panic seemed to subside, and he regained his usual aplomb.

"Hey!" Meadow waved from the end of the boarding line.

Instead of asking nicely, she threw up her arms in a big, fat *what the heck are y'all doing?* gesture.

"We're coming," I mouthed, pivoting to Timothy. "Aren't we?"

"Yeah, yeah." He stood on his own, and we walked together toward the other stragglers and late passengers. "Hey, what were you saying? Before the old lady?"

"Oh, nothing." Definitely not the time, I thought, embarrassed now. "It can wait."

I pulled up my ticket's bar code on my phone and showed it to the airline employee so she could scan it, while Timothy, characteristically old school, handed her his paper ticket with a smile.

She chuckled, pointing. "Right that way, gentleman."

We were the last to board Flight 115 headed to Alexandria, and as we waded through the jetway toward the plane's door, our voices echoed. "I remember," Timothy said, "what you were saying. It was about Mark Cerrillos. And your novella."

"Yeah," I said mournfully, trying hard to appear nonchalant. "He rejected me, but it's no big deal, and at least he was nice about it."

"No," Timothy replied, "he didn't reject you, Sterling. Far from it."

Chapter Seven

A Plaintive Howl of Want
Timothy

Because of the miracle of modern aviation, we arrived at the Alexandria International Airport shortly after noon. Somehow, through the grace of God, I'd managed to evade Meadow's questions about my wonky behavior and subsequent boarding delay. Actually, because it was Meadow, there were no questions at all, only the slightly judgmental tilt of her beautiful eyebrow.

It hurt, sure, but it was better than the alternative. I can't imagine what I'd have done with any woman other than Meadow, who would have—expectedly so—interrogated me until I'd come up with a reasonable explanation.

As always, Meadow proved thoroughly unique in that she refused to ask questions, make demands, or meddle. Nevertheless, I feigned sleep during the flight—just in case.

Desi, Lenny, and Wolfheart were waiting for us with signs, balloons, and cookies, much to Ricky's delight since DFW had traumatized him—and there were no bourbon balls in Louisiana.

Desi and Robin embraced for a long moment, and while they giggled and carried on with their usual gaiety, I sensed something lingering just below the surface. A few urgent whispers followed by flashes of concern signaled a language all their own, a language the rest of us weren't privy to, especially us men.

As I marveled at their skill to keep the rest of us out of the loop, I pondered Meadow's ability to appear aloof and indifferent, even when I knew that wasn't the case. I watched her now, standing on the outer circle of Desi and Robin's closeness, looking both uncomfortable and intrigued. The notion of such a long, intimate friendship such as theirs must seem unimaginable to her.

Meadow didn't have friends. Not only was her relationship with her own daughter, Bella, strained, but according to Wolfheart, her mother, Peony, had also struggled to penetrate Meadow's glum nature.

The only one who came close was her Uncle Wolfheart, or as she called him, her Uncle Wolf. I watched as he tugged her into his chest now, prompting an even deeper snuggle after speaking into her ear affectionately. But even his ferocity hadn't been enough to protect her years ago when a predator, posing as a school counselor, preyed on her youth, her uncertainty, and her loneliness. The result had been Bella and a lifetime of shame for Meadow, who grew even more isolated, more closed off, and most distrustful.

And yet here I was now, leading her astray even though I loved her deeply. When she fumbled for my hand, I took it and moved to greet her uncle, who was not only an honorable man but one I'd had the privilege of baptizing three years ago.

Meanwhile, I heard Lenny, the most gracious and considerate of men, razz Meadow as he enveloped her in a warm hug. "How was Kentucky? Did you meet some horses? Drink some bourbon?" He took her bag, something I should have done if I'd been paying better attention.

She smiled generously for Lenny since his genuine kindness had a way of disarming people, even those who'd been severely broken like Meadow. "Actually, I had both. I prefer the horses."

"You got that right. We used to feed them peppermints whenever we'd go visit Robin."

Sterling perked at the sound of his uncle's voice. "I gave them extra candy for you, Uncle Lenny." I watched as they embraced, a young man who'd lost his father and a grown man who'd lost his friend—a growing bond that would serve them well and would have pleased Dean immensely.

I shook Lenny's hand when he turned to me.

"Good to see you, Timothy. How are you feeling? You sure had us worried."

"I'm good." I shook my head. "Just an elaborate stunt to earn a vacation in Shady Gully." Lenny threw his head back in laughter, his paunch thicker than the last time I'd seen him, his hair thinner.

When he moved on to embrace Ricky, Sterling flicked his eyes at me. "Hey, we had to board so quickly, I never got to ask you about what Mark said." He moved the cat carrier—with Buford inside it—to his other hand. "When you said he didn't reject me…"

Sterling and I had ended up on opposite sides of the plane, and I imagined he'd spent the whole flight analyzing my comments. "He absolutely didn't reject you." I led him aside. "Don't think of someone passing on your work as a rejection of you personally."

He waited, expecting more. Needing more.

"He was impressed, Sterling. He said your work had merit, but it just wasn't what he was looking for now. He had concerns about marketing it."

"Marketing?"

Desi, a firecracker who put the *pizz* in pizzazz, rounded on us then, giving Sterling a fierce hug and a kiss on the cheek. "It's a business, honey." Having heard part of our conversation, she added, "Don't be discouraged."

With some effort, Sterling yanked his gaze away from me and embraced his aunt. He seemed to fall into Desi's curvy frame and rest there for a moment. "Hey, Aunt Desi," he said brusquely. "You look good." He ruffled her hair, which had probably been especially coiffed for the occasion. A beautiful woman, petite like Robin but shapelier, Desi had dark eyes and chin-length hair with frosty highlights. She jested with Sterling for mussing her hair, and he chuckled as he gave her another kiss on the cheek.

"Alright." Lenny grabbed someone's bag as Sterling and Wolfheart exchanged an enthusiastic man hug. "I think we can all fit in Desi's minivan." He slyly eyed Ricky, Sterling, Wolfheart, and me. "I wanted to bring y'all for a ride in my truck and show you the sights, but Desi wouldn't let me."

"Absolutely not," Desi scoffed, moving easily into the center of Sterling and Wolfheart's space for another quick embrace. "There'll be plenty of time for that later." She linked arms with Meadow and led her to the vehicle. "Robin said you were enjoying your time at the art gallery in Lexington."

Meadow glanced back at her Uncle Wolf and me as she reluctantly fell into pace with Desi. "I wouldn't go that far, but I didn't hate it as much as I thought I would."

Desi cackled as Robin bookended Meadow's other side. "Ricky," she instructed over her shoulder, "we'll need to get Buford settled in with Gerty at your place before we go to Desi's."

"Yes," Desi squealed, "we're having a party. Did I tell y'all? Everyone is coming, and Lenny is barbequing ribs."

"Sounds good," Ricky quipped, "but I'm starving now."

Lenny winked at his buddy. "We'll stop at the Cozy Corner on the way."

When Desi and Robin hooted, I couldn't help but grin as the tiniest of smiles escaped Meadow's lips.

Sterling handed the pet carrier to Ricky. "You're responsible for Buford. I'm sitting with the cool chicks in the back."

✝✝✝

As expected, all the usual suspects—and characters—dropped in at the Cozy Corner—which was literally on the corner of the four-way stop. No doubt they wanted to get the skinny on the pastor of the megachurch who'd fallen flat on his face on live television. Cruella Claire, as the locals called the nosy, pierced, and bespectacled post office manager, sat next to me and looked deeply into my eyes. Her cohort in gossip, ole man Chester, stood over her shoulder and mirrored her manner.

"Are you sure it wasn't a stroke?" Claire remarked. "Same thing happened to my Aunt Noreen, and now she's in a nursing home."

"*Humph*." I replied, "Well, so far, so good, I guess."

When Claire reluctantly dragged her eyes away from me, she glanced at Meadow. "Will you be back at work tomorrow?"

"Nope." Meadow stood next to me with her arms folded across her chest. "Sorry, Claire, but I'm still on vacation."

Bubba and Daryl rambled over from across the four-way stop where Luke's Auto Body Shop sat. They gave Meadow a giant hug and asked about the bourbon. She told them about the horses—and the art—which I could tell greatly pleased Robin. Daryl was the skinny to Bubba's hefty, and when they both barreled in on tiny Robin, I feared for her frail frame. She eventually popped up between them, laughing at their antics.

A honk sounded as a snazzy red car passed the stop sign at the four-way. A slender, tanned, and very female arm waved from the window. "Welcome home!" Dolly, the owner of Dolly's Diva Dome, called. Everyone waved back, despite the hairdresser's less-than-stellar history with a few in the group.

"Well, I've got to bid my farewell, folks," the wiry Wolfheart announced in an understated tone. "I've got some counsel business to attend to on The Creek and a few check-ins to do." After a quick, somewhat serious word with Desi, Lenny, and Robin, one that rang with the same tone of disquiet I'd noted at the airport, he made his exit. A hearty round of whoops and hollers followed him as he climbed into his ancient black truck and disappeared toward The Creek.

Sometimes I forgot that they'd all gone to school together— Lenny, Desi, Robin, Ricky, Bubba, Daryl, Dolly, Claire, and sadly, Dean, who rested just across the road at the cemetery beyond Violet's Vet. Not only did these graduates of Shady Gully High stay in touch, but they lived in the same town! Incredible as that notion was, it said something about small town life, about the beautiful rewards that came from holding true to your roots.

Just then, Charlie Wayne, the owner of the Cozy Corner, sauntered over with his new business partner, JJ Wheeler. They both wore blue Cozy Corner T-shirts, although Charlie Wayne's distinguished him as boss. It actually said BOSS. They fluttered around the picnic table, placing platters of pizza rolls, sliders, and nachos in front of us.

Everyone except Bubba swooned appropriately, and that was only because he dove directly into the pizza rolls, using those three seconds of distraction to his advantage. "Delicious," he said between bites.

"They're elevated," JJ Wheeler proclaimed as he stood with his hands precisely folded, every strand in his man bun perfectly contained. "I used fresh herbs and a twist of lemon." While everyone *oohed* and *aahed*, I caught the cross look that flickered just beneath Charlie Wayne's coke-bottle glasses.

While JJ Wheeler had undergone quite the transformation from the wild-haired bohemian I'd met at Luke and Bella's wedding three years ago, the partnership with Charlie Wayne seemed to be working, testy looks notwithstanding.

Everyone turned as a siren sounded in a melodic fashion. When Deputies Quietdove and Max pulled their cruiser to a stop in front of the Cozy Corner, Quietdove opened the door, and Micah climbed out of the backseat.

"Oh hell," Bubba said through a mouthful of pizza roll, "Micah's done got herself arrested."

"I did not," she scoffed, dashing over to Robin and Sterling and embracing them affectionately. "Some of us just get special escorts to big events." Although she seemed oblivious, the blush on Quietdove's cheeks was front and center.

Ricky shook his deputies' hands and asked after his town. "Did we lose anybody?"

"Hi, Timothy," Micah swept by me, giving my shoulders a squeeze. "Glad to see you looking better."

"No, they're all accounted for," Quietdove answered the sheriff while watching Micah through a curtain of dark eyelashes. Tall, olive-skinned, and handsome, with the mesmerizing green eyes of his Creek heritage, the thirty-three-year-old Quietdove seemed a perfect match for Micah, but I sensed that she, like her cousin, Sterling, still had some self-exploration to do.

Max's handcuffs flapped against his hip as he pulled his sister into a deep embrace. "Robin, you look good, girl." He then playfully boxed with the sheriff. "I figured she'd keep you in Kentucky longer." He side-eyed her. "Unless she's moving back home to Shady Gully."

One could almost hear the collection of eyeballs swinging in the direction of Robin's ring finger, followed by a barely audible breath of disappointment. Ricky cleared his throat. "So, no problems while I was gone?"

"Well," Quietdove confessed, "there was a little brush-up at the vet yesterday."

"Brush-up?" Bubba pinched his face in objection. "Come on, QD, I'd hardly call it that."

"We got a call," Quietdove explained. "We had to log it."

"What happened?" Ricky asked.

"His python got loose," Quietdove said.

"His what?" Sterling made a face.

"My snake. It was a tiny incident," Bubba argued. "Everything turned out fine."

Micah shot Bubba a look of annoyance and then grabbed Sterling's hand. "Come on, let's go see Violet. I'll show you around her place."

"Is the snake still there?" Sterling wanted to know.

"No, thank God." She speared Bubba with her heavily mascaraed eyes. "Pierre was discharged."

"Well, he ain't in the clear yet," Bubba said, "and frankly, I'm still worried—"

"Who wants to come?" Micah asked. "Violet is booked back-to-back but said she'd peek out to say hi, and of course, she'll see everybody tonight. And Petey won't get to see everyone until later either. He was doing some counseling on The Creek or something."

"That sounds great, Micah," Robin said, glancing at Ricky, "but let's drop in with Buford and get him and Gerty squared away."

I chuckled. "Do the cats get along?"

"They do, but they haven't seen each other in a while"

Meadow brushed her hand along my shoulder. "Bella is in Belle Maison, but she said we could go over and let the dogs out, and she'd be back soon."

"Sounds good." I rose, following her lead. While I very much enjoyed the lively personalities in Shady Gully, the disturbing scene at the airport had left me uneasy. I also craved some quiet time with Meadow.

And I needed to text Father Patrick to let him know I'd arrived.

"I'll be dang." Max put his sunglasses on. "There goes Fireman again." Everyone turned toward the four-way stop, watching as the blue Impala rolled to a stop and then headed straight, moving past the post office, Lenny's Tool Shed, and beyond. "He's been to Sprite's Quick Stop at least three times already, buying up bags of…something…and then heading out again in that same direction."

"Tell me he's not driving alone." Ricky frowned, his mustache twitching.

"Damn." Bubba shook his head. "I knew somebody was getting arrested today."

✝✝✝

Meadow and I walked to Luke's Duplex along with Ricky and Robin, while Buford the cat squirmed inside the pet carrier hanging from the sheriff's shoulder. We were feeling especially pleased that we'd convinced the sheriff not to arrest Fireman.

"Ah, he's a good kid," the sheriff conceded, "but Wolfheart can't be with him every minute of the day, and I worry about him."

"It was good to see your Uncle Wolf," I told Meadow. "He looks good."

"He stays busy," Ricky chimed as he switched the carrier to his other shoulder. "He looks out for the folks on The Creek, that's for sure."

"That sounds like Brad." Robin smiled fondly. "I hope to see him later."

"He'll be at Desi's," Meadow said. "He's looking forward to it."

"Good." Robin waved as our paths diverged. "After we get the cats settled, we're going to go see Violet, but we'll see y'all tonight."

I turned to Meadow. "Is everything okay with Bella? Why was she in town?"

Meadow's lips lifted in a nearly imperceptible smile. "What's the one thing we don't have in Shady Gully? Even after the surge of new businesses in the last five years?"

I thought as she found a housekey under a rug in front of the neat, brick duplex. "A doctor's office?"

"Unless you're a cat or a dog, or apparently, a snake, you still have to go to Belle Maison to go to the doctor. What do you make of that?"

"I don't know." I was clueless. Until Meadow grinned.

"I could be wrong," she said. "Lord knows they have their hands full." She put the key into the lock. "Brace yourself." In a flash, two Shiba Inus presented as a flying swirl of red, ginger, black, tan, and white, and nosed through the door with such force and enthusiasm, I really did have to brace myself.

"Whoa." I laughed. "Look at them go." I watched as they ran around and around the perimeters of the fence, stopping only to pee and romp on one another. At first, they barely seemed to notice us, so intent on freedom and the joy of zoomies. But then as they relieved themselves and became more comfortable, they began to prance and explore their environment. "I remember Duchess. Violet saved her life."

"She did. The black one is Duke. He's much more my style."

"Let me guess. More reserved and serious."

"Exactly. They were hoping he would rub off on Duchess, but I don't know." Meadow gawked as Duke eyed a large oak tree in the middle of the yard. "He does have one very bad habit though. Duke, no!"

Duke launched across the yard with a quick, excited bark, and then rooted his front paws on the massive tree, letting out a plaintive howl of want as he stared up into the highest of branches.

When the leaves fluttered, I noticed the flicker of a bushy tail. "Squirrel."

"He's obsessed. He'll stay like that all day. Or night. Like seriously obsessed." When she looked at me with a delighted grin, my heart flipped. Just like at the airport when amusement had settled across her face after Desi and Robin buttressed her with their own joy, I sensed more simmering beneath the surface now.

"Well, as the sheriff would say, I reckon we ought to pull up a chair and sit a spell." I took her hand and led her to the bench swing Luke had situated with a bird's eye view of the tree, and to Duke, who gazed up at the flashy squirrel with longing.

I put my arm around her, and she rested her head on my shoulder. The tips of our feet lightly grazed the grass just enough to keep the swing going. I closed my eyes, wishing with everything in me, with every prayer I'd ever prayed, that life could be as simple, as glorious, as easy, as this...

"What more does anybody really need?" Once again, I surprised myself when the words tumbled from my mouth.

"Nothing," Meadow whispered, and to my absolute shock she brushed a tear from her eyes.

"Meadow." I caressed her hair from her face, nicked her chin up so she'd look at me. "What's the matter?"

"Nothing. I'm just agreeing with you, that's all."

"Tell me," I teased. "What is it about this moment that you love so much?" When she blushed, I threw my hard-core girlfriend a rope. "The brisk, fall weather? The rambunctious dogs? The ill-fated squirrel?"

She laughed, freeing her chin and burrowing her head into my chest, keeping me from seeing her face.

"—or maybe knowing you'll see Bella soon?"

"All of it," she finally said. "And you being here."

"On the swing?" I joked.

"On the swing. In Shady Gully." She scrubbed another tear

away. "I've wasted a lot of time being…how did you say it? Reserved. Serious." She managed a wobbly grin. "But really I've been angry and bitter. And now I just want to be happy."

I cradled her head with my free hand and let my fingers roam through her luxurious, dark hair. And then I kissed her deeply, thoroughly, in a way that left no question about the way I felt about her.

I loved her more than I'd ever loved anyone in my life. And I needed her desperately…

But our story wouldn't have a happy ending…

The slam of a car door pulled us apart. "Bella's here," I said hoarsely.

✝✝✝

As we enjoyed a wonderful visit with Bella, I found it impossible to tell if Meadow's hunch was correct. As always, Meadow's daughter seemed warm, friendly, and especially joyful, but perhaps women's intuition, or mother's intuition, had sparked Meadow's suspicion.

Bella was enchanting, mysterious, inscrutable, and stunningly beautiful—an absolute clone of her mother—except for her warm, approachable disposition…and her striking blue eyes, so different from her mother's extraordinary green ones.

"Luke hated that he couldn't be here this afternoon, but he'll be at Desi's tonight." Bella sat between the dogs, her hands resting lightly on each's head. Thankfully, she'd been able to lure Duke away from the tree, at which point the squirrel barked his appreciation and skittered from the tree to the fence, and from there to freedom.

Sensing that enough time had passed and that their mother-daughter time might require a little privacy, I managed to discreetly text Father Patrick a quick,

    I'm here, at Luke and Bella's.
Within seconds I got a,

        Splendid! I'll send my driver
        to you now.

He'd added a few fire emojis and one of a blue car.

The shared moment of intimacy with Meadow had rattled me, and my moment of truth was at hand as I geared to come clean with Father Patrick. I didn't have much time to fret as within five minutes there was a honk, followed by a quick tap on the door.

"Don't get up," I told Bella as I stood. "It's for me." I lowered my head to Meadow's and gave her a chaste kiss on the cheek. "While you two catch up I'm going to have a visit with Father Patrick."

"Oh, I adore him," Bella exclaimed. "Tell him I said hello, and I hope to see him tonight at Desi and Lenny's."

Meadow tilted her head, clearly curious, but for now it seemed her desire for time with Bella trumped my mysterious date with the spirited, red-headed priest. I let myself out, finding young Fireman at the wheel of the blue Chevy Impala parked in the driveway.

"Nice ride," I said, sliding into the passenger seat. When a pungent wave of bleach and cleaning fluid immediately hit my nostrils and eyes, I sneezed and reached for a tissue in my jeans pocket. "Wow," I said thickly. "Really, nice ride."

"Yeah," he beamed, "I like all the chrome." He looked both ways before pulling out, and then came to a full stop at the four-way.

Handsome kid, I noted, taking in his rich, olive skin tone and his bright, expressive eyes.

"Bubba and Daryl saved it from the garbage heap," he added, and in his exuberance, he pressed the gas a little too hard and we jerked forward a few times before heading straight. "How are you? I saw you fall on TV. I bet that hurt."

"Yeah, a little."

"I heard you and Meadow are kind of a thing now."

I chuckled, trying not to grip the seats, or cough, or blink my eyes in rapid succession. "I guess you could call it that."

He nodded, reflective, keeping his eyes on the road as he passed the post office on the left and then Lenny's hardware store next to it. "Yeah, I'm dating a few girls at school. Nothing serious though."

"Right. You've got plenty of time."

"I mean, I don't want to wait as long as you. How old are you anyway?"

"Well, I wouldn't recommend waiting as long as me either. I'm forty-four."

"Dang! Really? I thought Meadow was a lot younger than you but she's only a year younger. Wow." He bent his brows, glancing in the rear-view mirror before flicking his right blinker at Sacred Heart Catholic Church. "But she's like, pretty hot, so that's probably why she looks younger."

"Yeah, probably." The kid was merciless.

"Well, here we are. He's waiting for you." Fireman brought the car to a stop in front of a modest home behind the church.

When my phone rumbled with a text, I assumed it was from Father Patrick, but I was wrong. With dread, I clicked on the picture. A group picture this time. Me in the middle of all of them, my eyes dull and spiritless. She was there as well, her eyes vacant, listless, and strung-out. Old beyond her years.

Nausea swept through me then, what with the bleach, the stuffy car, and now, the photo. I could feel saliva building under my tongue. I gulped for air while fumbling with the door handle.

"Are you alright?"

"Yeah, I'm good." I freed myself from the Impala and took a deep breath. "Thanks for the ride, Fireman. Be careful. The sheriff has you in his sights." My teasing fell flat, and the boy looked at me strangely.

"Do you need some help?"

"I'm good." I managed a wave, staggered to the carport, and knocked on the door.

Father Patrick answered immediately as if he'd been waiting for me. After taking a look at me his eyes amplified. "Good heavens! Timothy!"

Hoping to regain my balance, and perhaps, my dignity, I leaned into the doorway. Only I missed the door frame entirely and cratered directly into the priest's chubby arms. My eyes fluttered uncontrollably, and the last thing I remembered before everything went black was the pristine kitchen in the background… and the overpowering smell of bleach and cleaning supplies.

Chapter Eight

Probably not a Donkey Though
Fireman

The fancy Kentucky preacher wasn't nearly as fancy as he looked on TV. Especially now, slumped on Father Patrick's freshly mopped floor—thank you very much—and trembling like a poorly treated, frightened dog.

"Shall we…can you…?" Father Patrick struggled for words. Well over two hundred pounds, the priest was out of breath and flustered, his upper lip beaded with sweat.

"I'll get him to the couch. Why don't you get him a glass of water?" I nodded in the direction of the sink. "Clean ones in the drainer. Fresh ice in the freezer."

"Splendid." He teetered in that general direction. "Simply brilliant."

I hooked my elbows under Timothy's armpits and lifted him to his feet. Then I positioned my right leg between his legs, grabbed his right hand with my left hand, and draped it over my shoulder. I'd never been able to use my training on a real live person before, so I was psyched to see that the technique actually worked. After taking his right hand into mine, I easily transported him to the couch. Worked like a charm.

As I admired my handiwork, Father Patrick huffed over, still breathless, but now with a glass of ice water in his hand. "Is that a Cheshire grin, I see? I'm not sure we're out of the woods yet. Should we call 911? Maybe Quietdove or Max could come do CPR—"

"Father, where do you think your call would go?" I planted my hands on my hips, a little peeved. "To the fire station. To me. Which is where I'd have been today if I hadn't been here deep cleaning your house." When he started to protest, I went on. "What is it they say about cleanliness is godliness or something like that?"

"Well," he stuttered, "you're quite right, of course, but there's no need to get cheeky."

I felt like a punk then, even though we'd always had a playful bantering-back-and-forth kind of relationship. "I'm sorry." We both turned our attention to Timothy. "All I'm saying is that I know CPR." *Although I'd never actually done it on a real, live person.*

Father Patrick perched his massive frame on the chair adjacent to the couch. "I suspect his ailment is rooted in something spiritual anyway. Possibly psychological. That's what we're going to work on."

"We?"

"Me. We. Meaning Timothy and me. Unless you'd like to expand on your godliness lecture…" He raised his bushy red eyebrow. "Possibly you have something beneficial to offer…"

"No, I'm good. Not really my field of expertise." But as my gaze swept between the two of them, I had concerns. There was Father Patrick, unsteadily clutching a glass of water, and Timothy, clumsily groping the couch. "It looks like he's coming to anyway."

Father Patrick and I watched as Timothy's bright blue eyes searched for something familiar to settle on.

"I say, jolly good." Father Patrick genuflected and made the sign of the cross.

As we helped Timothy sit up on the couch, I tried not to stare at the tattoos lining his arms, although I did catch a fragment of scripture from Philippians. "Try a sip," Father encouraged, carefully placing the glass in Timothy's shaky hands. We held our breath as he drank the water down to the very last drop.

"Want some more?" I asked.

"Yes, thank you. I guess I'm dehydrated. Probably from the plane."

I took the glass and padded to the kitchen, refilling the water as the two of them whispered together in the living room. Father Patrick bent his head toward Timothy and spoke in a low tone as I dallied with the ice. Struck by the sudden emergence of Father's confidence, a flash of pride sparked through me as I watched him handle Timothy's collapse with surprising poise.

I opened the refrigerator and removed the cheese tray I'd prepared earlier, adding a handful of crackers and arranging them accordion style. "Here y'all go."

As I placed Timothy's water and the cheese tray on the coffee table, I secretly studied the fascinating megachurch preacher. I had to admit that even I, a bona fide skeptic when it came to religion, found his condition unsettling. Occasionally, I'd watch his sermons online to please Wolfheart, and sometimes the charismatic pastor offered a nugget that lingered, a scripture or a way of looking at things that I could apply throughout the week. In my exchanges with Granny, for instance, or my encounters with the kids at school. Admittedly, it helped. So to see him in such a fragile state now, sniffling, wiping his eyes, and unable to focus, was not only disturbing but downright discouraging.

Father Patrick, on the other hand, sat up straighter, his eyes newly bright with purpose. "Now, where did my—?"

I handed him his Bible, which had been sitting on the freshly dusted end table next to the recliner. I slipped out then, and while Timothy barely noticed my exit, Father Patrick nodded his appreciation.

Just as I'd settled into the comfort and privacy of my own personal space, aka my Chevy Impala, I received both a text and a notification that my phone's battery was low. Since I'd just made it to the four-way stop, I decided to pull into Luke's Auto Body Shop. That way I could safely check the message—in case the sheriff was lying in wait to arrest me for texting-and-driving-while-driving-without-an-adult—and get Daryl or Bubba to buff out a new scratch I'd discovered on my right door.

While tapping in my security code, I glanced at Violet's fenced pasture across the road to see if there were any new additions. Two new goats, both black and white, a couple of lethargic calves, and a miniature gray donkey with long eyelashes. He or she watched me as I got out of my car and read the text from Desi. As usual, there were a lot of emojis involved. Hearts, party hats, big wide eyes, and my personal favorite, a fireman followed by big strong muscles.

I chuckled out loud. The lady was a riot, and she was even rowdier when Robin, her partner-in-crime, came to town.

```
Will you be here tonight? Now
that Sterling is here, Robin
and I want to let everyone in
on our plan. We may need backup.
```

I laughed again, amused as I meandered across the road to pet the donkey. It turned out to be a *he*, a sweet thing with giant brown eyes who liked to be petted.

"You're a good boy," I told him. "Next time I come, I'll bring carrots."

I fished in my pocket until I found an old butterscotch cracked inside the wrapper. After I fed it to him, he butted my hand in gratitude and stuck his snout between the rungs in the fence asking for more. As I gave him a good scratch, I thought about Father Patrick, and how, despite his current…challenges, he'd risen to the occasion when he'd seen a friend in need. Just as he'd done for me five years ago when I'd been in "fire" trouble, so to speak. And look at me now, driving a sweet ride, feeding donkeys butterscotch, and helping out the coolest ladies in Shady Gully.

```
You bet! It's going to
be awesome!
```

I texted, responding further in her preferred language, with an olive-skinned thumbs up, earphones, a microphone, and lots of stars in pinks and purples, and because Desi always had to get the last word, she dinged me back with a smiley face blowing a heart kiss.

After one last scratch for the expressive donkey, I crossed the road and entered the auto body shop, deciding right then and there that what Father Patrick needed was to have something to love, something to take care of…

Probably not a donkey though…

For once, Daryl and Bubba were actually working, so as they finished up with the paying customers, I chilled and perused the aisles of sellable goods. Now that I had my own car, most of the things I saw were interesting. Air fresheners, fancy keyrings, cupholders.

The kind of things you'd need on a date. I suddenly felt ashamed for lying to the fancy pastor about my dating status. I suppose I'd done it because I'd wanted to seem cool, something I certainly was not, at least not at Shady Gully High anyway. Ironically, the adults around town seemed to like me a lot, unlike my sophomore classmates who treated me like I was from another planet. The juniors and seniors ignored me altogether. Even though I had a cool car.

Actually, during an especially rough few months my freshman year, it had been Desi who'd offered the best advice. She'd been the new kid a long time ago, at Shady Gully High, in fact, and while she'd endured a lot of ridicule and nastiness, she'd come out of it just fine. She reminded me that people aren't always what they seem, and in high school especially, the ones who were the meanest usually were the ones who were hurting the most. She suggested I go my merry way and ignore any snubs or wickedness because the fight was not my own. She claimed that God had already taken care of it.

Naturally, when she veered into the God lane my head got muddled. I did perk up, however, when she insisted that above all else, no matter what, I was to absolutely stay away from Bouncy Girls. I wasn't sure what a Bouncy Girl was, but they sounded delightful. Nevertheless, my head got muddled with that one as well—but that was Desi. And with Robin by her side, they were *the* hot ticket.

"Yo, Fireman." Daryl sashayed over, his skeletal frame so light and easy it seemed to barely touch the floor. "What're you looking at there?"

"These carpet and vinyl floor kits are sweet."

"You want 'em? You can use my discount."

"Naw, that's not why I'm here. Bubba buffed out a scratch on my car a while back, and danged if I didn't find another one today. I was gonna see if he was here."

"He's in the shop. Finishing up a bumper replacement. I'll take a look at it for you." I followed Daryl as he gathered a rag, some solvent, and cutting polish from behind the cash register. Skinny, with sandy gray hair and a neatly trimmed beard, Daryl was dependable and as good as gold, and not nearly as excitable as Bubba.

Daryl had worked at Luke's Auto Body Shop for years, but with the incredible growth in Shady Gully recently, he'd leaned into his skills in construction, working part-time for Hoot Wheeler building houses and new businesses like Violet's Veterinary Hospital.

"How's she driving lately?" Squinting as we walked outside, Daryl popped the hood of the Impala and gave everything a good look-see, tinkering here and there. "Solid. Where's the scratch?"

I pointed to the offensive nick just as Bubba trooped out of the shop with his usual bluster. "Somebody ding you in a parking lot?"

"I don't think so. I got it somewhere though."

Bubba scrunched up his face. "I don't see a thing." He bent closer.

Daryl tapped the spot for Bubba and then provided an instructional exercise for my benefit. "First thing you gotta do is rub a gentle solvent around the scratch."

"That gets rid of bug and tar deposits," his co-star and sidekick added.

"Then dab a clean cloth into this here cutting polish, and you just rub nice and gently. In a circle. Like this." Daryl cocked his head, inspecting his work. Pleased. "See there."

"Nice." I grinned, grateful. "How much does that cutting solution cost?"

Daryl shrugged. "I was about to open some more anyway."

As Daryl put the cloth and cutting solution on the floorboard of the Impala, I asked Bubba, "How's Pierre?"

He huffed markedly. "Not good. I may have to take him back to see Violet. He just ain't right."

"He's in love." Daryl snorted. "Bubba, not the snake, and he thinks that creepy serpent is gonna win him a younger chick."

"Who?"

Bubba's jowly face blushed pink. "Nobody. It's nothing."

But Daryl tipped his head in the direction of Violet's Vet, past Dolly's Diva Dome, and finally, landed on Nails & Thread, Sigourney Sky's seamstress shop.

"Sigourney?" I howled. "But she's young."

"She's forty-three," Bubba countered.

"I mean, younger than you."

"By ten years," Daryl emphasized. "And she doesn't even know he exists. Nor is she the least bit interested in snakes, as far as I know."

I circled toward the driver's side of my car, knowing that this shtick could go on for a while. "Maybe she'll be at Desi's tonight," I offered hopefully to Bubba. Although that was one love match I couldn't see happening.

"Better not drive by yourself," Bubba said solemnly. "The sheriff is back in town."

✝✝✝

Jazzed because my car was once again perfect, I maintained a steady speed on the way to The Creek. Something about crossing the Unity Bridge lifted my spirits every time, and today was no exception, even though Petey flagged me down only one hundred yards from the bridge. "Shoot," I said under my breath, as I was eager to get home to Granny and anxious because my phone had lost all its battery.

But the sight of Petey's lopsided smile forced a chuckle out of me. He and Bluejay, a Creek elder who'd recently been diagnosed with cancer, stood outside the Unity Christian Church and waved. I slowed to a stop in the church's parking lot and got out as they moseyed over. While the structure of the church was basic, its high-pitched gable roof and tall white steeple added character, and Petey's idea to plant big white columns on either side of the small gable overhang at the entrance was spot on. The windows were plentiful, all framed in white, which made the deep red bricks of the church look even bolder.

"Man, oh man," Petey reeled, "we could see that hot rod coming a mile away. Ain't it nice, Bluejay?" He curled his arm around the old man affectionately. "I never had wheels like that when I was his age. Did you?"

"Can't say that I did," Bluejay half tittered, half coughed. "Nice color." After he and Petey exchanged a heartfelt hug, Bluejay waved his goodbye and walked gingerly to his old truck. Petey and I watched as the old beater chugged across the bridge toward The Creek.

When my gaze shifted back to Petey, he continued to stare in the direction of Bluejay's exhaust, using his hand to shield his eyes from the sun. I could see the black cross glistening on his wrist, the stark tattoo he'd come home with after interning with Timothy for a long summer.

A dart of concern skimmed across my mind, worrying that Petey might end up as tormented as Timothy someday. It was a heady and depressing notion.

After a moment he snapped out of his trance and turned his high-energy smile on me. Nothing like his dull, older brother, Luke, who incidentally, had stolen Bella from me, Petey was hilarious and fun. Far from buttoned up, Petey had shaggy hair and hazel eyes and an easy, kind, and enjoyable way about him. He'd brought two communities together when no one thought it possible, and his enthusiasm continued to solidify that unity today. And his faith, I suppose, but I didn't know much about all of that.

"Where ya headed, man?"

"Home. Going to check on Granny and then get ready for the shindig at your mama's tonight."

"How's your granny? She made me some zucchini bread a while back and it was…"

I laughed, Petey's tone cheering me. "Crappy, huh? Be honest, Petey. You're a man of God and all that now."

"That I am." He grinned. "So, I'll just say the bread was well-intentioned and made with love. How's that?" He glanced at the bridge. "Wolfheart passed through a few hours ago. He said he was going to check on your granny as well." He patted the top of my car. "Hopefully I can drag my bride away from all the critters, and we can join the fun later."

"She had a new little donkey in her pasture today."

"His name is Tom Petty." Petey inched his shoulders higher. "Don't ask me. Micah named him. Somebody found him tied up and abandoned. Somewhere in Azalealand, I think."

"Violet will get him fixed up," I said, glad that Petey and Violet had made their home here.

"You and Wolfheart oughta ride together tonight," he kidded. "I hear Magnum PI is back in town."

I scoffed. "I don't think he looks like Sam Elliott or Tom Selleck, just for the record."

I hopped into my car feeling lighter, suddenly looking forward to the festivities. Out of habit, I rolled slowly over the bridge, harking back to the dangerous, duct-taped contraption that had existed for years before Luke, Petey, and Sheriff Rick had spearheaded the building of the modern, state-of-the-art bridge it was now.

After I passed Meadow's shanty, which had also been spiffed up thanks to her Uncle Wolfheart, I drove slowly toward his place. While Wolfheart's home was simple and modest, his shop—where he kept his herbs for processing—was extensive. Housed with an assortment of supplies and equipment ranging from large herbal tools like measuring scales and grinders, to smaller necessities like pliers and cutting boards, Wolfheart provided an array of medicinal herbs for The Creek's citizens and Shady Gullians alike. Horehound for congestion. Rose yarrow for bleeding. Comfrey to ease soreness. Lavender for calming, and cat's claw and ginger as anti-inflammatories.

His sister, Peony, had taught him the skill, but as people had started coming from surrounding towns like Naryville, Toulouse, Azalealand, and Belle Maison, I suspected he'd expanded her legacy and was building one all his own.

As fancy as his shop was, however, nothing compared to the garden itself. Massive, professionally irrigated, and revered by everyone who saw it, images of his garden had been sought after by gardening magazines all over the south. Naturally, Wolfheart wanted no part of that as he treasured his privacy.

Although his ancient black truck wasn't in the dirt driveway, I was met by a collection of dogs, cats, chickens, and even a few rabbits. I roughhoused with two of my favorite dogs, Black and Blue, who chased sticks until their tongues lolled. "Good boys." I rubbed their bellies before refreshing their water and tossing kibble to one and all.

Finally, I hit the road for home. While I'd hoped to pick up Granny's herbs so I could get her comfy and settled before going off to the party, I was hopeful that Wolfheart had brought them as Petey suggested.

As I curved along Big Island Loop, I slowed, doing my best to avoid the ruts and potholes along the gravel road. Perhaps road improvement would be next on the taskmasters' agenda. Maybe I'd talk to them about it tonight…

But a strong feeling of foreboding filled me as I brought my car to a stop outside of my and Granny's home. Wolfheart's old truck sat in the driveway, and while there was nothing unusual about that, per se, a feeling of dread made my steps leaden as I approached the porch.

The screen door squeaked as Brad Wolfheart's tall frame came into view. Thin and wiry, olive-skinned, with a dark mass of thick hair sprayed with gray, Wolfheart had the piercing green eyes of most of the Creeks.

"Fireman." His voice cracked.

A hundred jets of stabbing pain shot through me as my head shook from side to side. "No," I choked as I stepped onto the porch to face Wolfheart. "No." I refused to accept what his face said, what his tear-stained eyes said. "No!"

When I attempted to rush past him, he stopped me with a firm hand. Surprised that a man of sixty-one had the strength to stop a boy my age, I pushed back angrily. "Let me…" I gritted my teeth, enraged. "I need to see…my…granny…" And just like that, I collapsed, sobbing at his feet…like the boy I truly was.

He folded me into his arms then, cradling me in his strong embrace.

Chapter Nine

Stuff
Sterling

Bubba and Daryl—well, Bubba mostly—were holding court with Uncle Lenny and Ricky in the living room while I helped Micah and Quietdove cut up boudin and sausage in the kitchen. When Quietdove nipped a piece of the boudin, Micah made a face.

"Gross."

"Gross?" Horrified, Quietdove stuck a toothpick in one of the Louisiana delicacies and handed it to me. "That's sacrilegious," he told Micah. "And you were born and raised in Louisiana."

"I agree," I added around a mouthful. "It's a Louisiana staple. You should be ashamed." Boudin was made by cooking down peppers and onions with seasoned pork and rice, and then stuffing the delicious, mouthwatering concoction into sausage casings. "What's wrong with you?"

"I had some somewhere that was cooked with liver." Micah's upper lip curled in distaste. "It scarred me."

"Was it on The Creek?" Quietdove grinned. "Lots of the old timers still use liver."

Micah thought as she carefully positioned the boudin on a party platter. "It may have been from Fireman's grandmother—"

"Well, there you have it," Quietdove teased. "Lacey could have added her own special ingredients like powdered coffee cream or baking soda. You know her eyesight is bad, don't you?"

"I'd take it with liver, coffee cream, or baking soda," I stated with conviction. "If only I could find it in Kentucky."

"I'll ship you some," Quietdove offered. "Or better yet, I'll make a trip." He cut a glance at Micah, clearly hoping for a response, but she sliced and diced, completely distracted. I sensed an effort by the normally reserved Quietdove to inject himself into conversations more than usual—certainly more than he felt comfortable with—all in a desperate attempt to gain Micah's attention.

"How do you like living at Luke's duplex? Is it weird having your brother as a landlord?" I asked, throwing Quietdove a bone—and another chance—to lure her into conversation.

"It's okay. It's fun having Bella there. And the dogs. Although the sheriff's nightly patrols are annoying." Micah shrugged. "But it beats living with Mama and Daddy."

"It's cheap and it comes with free security," Quietdove teased. "You can't beat that."

"Sure, I can," she quipped dismissively.

A sudden roar of laughter echoed from the living room where Bubba reenacted the moment when Fireman hopped on the scale and slung Pierre around his shoulders. His theatrical knee-buckling move prompted a wide range of giggles, even from Quietdove and me. Thanks to Uncle Lenny and Aunt Desi's ranch-style home's open floor plan, we were able to trade barbs and participate in all the wrangling.

"And then Daryl's buddy, Hoot Wheeler, comes in—"

"He's not my buddy," insisted Daryl. "I just work with him sometimes."

"Whatever. Mr. Macho comes in with this tiny little carrier that had pink flowers and frilly bonnets all over it—"

"It did not, Bubba," Micah called out in objection. "If you're going to tell a story, tell it right."

"I'll have you know, I'm a very good storyteller." Bubba frowned. "Why are you sticking up for him anyway?"

Naturally, everyone swiveled toward Micah, as well as Quietdove, whose formidable stature seemed to shrink as Micah grew defiant. "I'm not," she said. "I'm just saying the carrier didn't have pink flowers or bonnets on it. That's ridiculous."

Bubba's barnstorming performance and Micah's curious defense of Hoot Wheeler were put on hold as a staccato rap sounded at the front door. Petey and Violet made their entrance in a way that encapsulated their unique relationship. Petey danced and jived his way in while my sister's face smiled pink. My heart leapt inside my chest to see her happy and in love with her life in Shady Gully. My mom felt the same; I know because her contented expression found mine from across the room.

"Anyway," Bubba eventually continued with his story, "Hoot was acting all squirrelly, like he was embarrassed to reveal what was in the carrier. But Micah"—he cut his eyes at her as if to gauge her approval of his narrative— "told him straight up whatever it was had to be weighed and checked in."

"What was it?" my mom asked. "I'm dying to know."

"Was it a bird? A tarantula?" Aunt Desi prodded. "A spider?"

Petey smothered his mama's cheek with a wet kiss. "I think a tarantula *is* a spider, Mama." He looked over his shoulder at Violet, who walked toward us in the kitchen with a bag filled with party favors. "Isn't that right, Violet?"

"Well, technically," Violet answered, "they're in the spider family, but…"

Violet's voice was drowned out by Bubba's punchline. "To answer your question, Desi, Hoot Wheeler's pet of choice is a teeny-tiny girly dog." Bubba shook his head. "A pompom or something. As far as I'm concerned, he lost his man-card."

While everyone laughed, the sheriff remarked, "Bubba, I have an orange cat." He casually popped a taffy into his mustached mouth. "Her name is Gerty. Since you're divvying up man-cards, just wondering if mine is gonna be revoked."

"No. You're good, Ricky," Bubba managed above the laughter. "But only because it's orange."

Violet shook her head, bewildered as she set the grocery bag on the bar. "Hoot's dog is a Pomeranian," she informed the entire group, "and Tootsie *is* a very sick little pup. I'm keeping her for a few days and pumping her full of antibiotics and fluids." She pulled a bottle of wine out of the bag, murmuring to Micah, Quietdove, and me. "I think I need a glass. Stat."

Micah turned to Quietdove with a tablecloth and a basket full of paper plates, napkins, and plastic utensils. "Would you—"

"Sure." His green eyes softened as he gave her his full attention. "I'm here to serve."

Finally, Micah responded with an appreciative smile. "Would you go put these on the outside table? I'm sorry I'm grumpy. I'm just a little stressed because everything is falling on me since Mama wanted to play with Aunt Robin tonight."

Petey, who'd trailed Violet into the kitchen, made a face. "Big girl responsibilities suck, huh?" When Micah's expression fired daggers at her brother, Petey made a show of hiding behind Violet. While laughing at my cousins' antics, I kept one eye on Quietdove as he slipped out the door. I could see the earnest deputy through the giant floor-to-ceiling window in the living room. He carefully spread the checked tablecloth across the picnic table and then began setting out the utensils and napkins with great concentration.

Meanwhile, Petey crossed the bar in one stride and wrapped me in an enthusiastic man hug. "Cousin time. At the Cozy Corner. You, me, and Luke."

"Sounds good. Rumor is the menu is…elevated."

When the doorbell rang, we all turned to see my mom's brother, Max, and his wife, Danielle, file into the party. As I watched their warm embrace, I couldn't help thinking of my mom's other brother, Ernie, who for reasons unbeknownst to me, made little effort to visit when we came to Louisiana, even though he only lived thirty miles away in Belle Maison.

The volume in the house kicked up a few notches as the crowd grew bigger and more cocktails were poured. Violet handed Petey a glass of wine, and after they clinked glasses, they gravitated toward the lively, chattering guests.

"Where are Luke and Bella?" I handed Micah another tray. "And Meadow?"

She arranged andouille sausage in rows, placing a shot glass of toothpicks in the center. "Luke and Bella should be on their way. Meadow might come with them, but I think she was going to wait for Timothy."

"And he is?" I reached for a piece of sausage.

"Visiting with Father Patrick." She slapped my hand. "Honestly, how can you eat so much? I'd be as big as a barn if I snacked like you, Sterling."

I impulsively put my arm around her and squeezed her shoulder. We were two peas in a pod, she and I. While everyone else seemed to have a place, a purpose, and a future with a partner and a path—whether the path was a little fuzzy or paved in yellow bricks—Micah and I had always seemed to flounder. And while I wasn't nearly as dramatic about it as she was, I certainly felt an affinity for her struggles.

"So," I whispered as I took the knife and thus the job of slicing sausage. "What are you going to do about this love triangle of yours?"

"What in the world are you going on about, Sterling?" But her cheeks dimpled. "And speaking of love, what happened with you and Tammy Jo? Last I heard, she was doing contract nursing at hospitals all over the state."

Well, that's news to me, I thought.

"And who's this chick you met in Santa Fe? Aunt Robin was telling Mama about it earlier. Petra? Piper? Something with a P."

"What? No," I scoffed. "It's Pippa, but it's not like that. She's just a writer, kind of a critique partner, but definitely not…anything." I refocused my attention on Micah, refusing to fall for her diversionary tactics. "You know, Quietdove is a good guy, and he's had a thing for you for years. But you already know that, don't you?"

"We're just friends," she stated emphatically before glancing outside to consider Quietdove as he started a fire in the firepit.

"I like him. He's solid." I wanted to make my preference known, to get my vote in early, so to speak.

"That he is." Her voice turned husky as she watched him unfold lawn chairs and set them around the firepit. "Did you know Sheriff Rick is grooming him for sheriff?"

"I did. And he said we're supposed to call him Ricky."

She giggled. "Or maybe for you, it will be Daddy soon."

I cringed, unintentionally, but there it was.

Micah embraced me then, tugging me around the waist even as I stoically continued to cut sausage. "You're just doing that because I have a knife in my hand."

"No. I just feel mean tonight. I don't know why. Do you ever feel like that?"

I peered at her, intrigued. "No, Micah. I don't. You're weird." I tipped my head at the wine Violet brought. "See what kind of wine she's got there. I need a glass now."

"And Tammy Jo?" She set two wine glasses on the bar and poured us both some red. "After the way y'all hit it off at Luke and Bella's wedding, I thought for sure that was going somewhere."

"So did I, but apparently not."

Micah and I clinked glasses and drank heavily from the cabernet. "They're just so different." It took me a moment to realize she was talking about Quietdove and Hoot again. "Hoot is funny, and honestly, kind of annoying, but Quietdove is—"

"—steady. Dependable."

"Right." She grew irritated. "He has"—she made air quotes—"substance, as Mama says over and over and over again."

"Yikes." I drank more.

"She never stops. I mean, isn't that really just code for boring?"

"I don't think so. And your mama wouldn't steer you wrong. She loves you. Everybody loves you." I winked. "You're adorable."

We turned as the crowd cheered as Luke and Bella had finally arrived, and within minutes the grand exodus outside began as the sky darkened and Quietdove had coaxed his fire to a steady roar. Micah found another wine glass and poured from the cabernet bottle. "Can you finish the party platter?" she asked as she picked up both glasses of wine. "I need to go talk to Bella."

The house quieted in waves as the last of the stragglers drifted outside. I watched from the window as Micah pulled up a chair next to Bella, but not before handing the wine to Quietdove who lit up with a pleased smile when she did.

Once I finished with the sausage and arranged them on the platter, I moved to the sink window and watched and listened to the scene outside. Loud guffaws, laughter, intimate conversations. Years of history existed between these people, going as far back as when my parents and Micah's parents—and Bubba and Daryl and the whole lot of them—were all in junior high. I thought about Micah's angst, and mine as well, and wondered if the generation before ours had the same sort of worries that we have today.

It was hard to imagine that they did as they seemed so joyful now. Aunt Desi and Uncle Lenny smiled at one another across the fire, enjoying their time with their friends, but always aware of one another. I noticed Luke cut his eyes at Bella as she bent her head into Micah's, and Petey cast his gaze wide, then wider, clearly looking for Violet. His brows bent in concern.

It was then I realized my sister had come inside, and finally, it seemed, we were to have a moment alone. She set an empty platter beside my sliced sausage. "Those folks are a heart attack waiting to happen."

"Probably," I snorted, spearing a slice of andouille with a toothpick. "But what a way to go." I stabbed one for her, and she chewed. Swooned. "You seem happy," I told her.

"I am. It took me a long and twisted road to get here, but finally, everything has come together." Tears unexpectedly sprung from her eyes, and she gave me an impromptu hug, much like Micah had only minutes before. "Now you, Sterling, tell me everything."

Everything? I experienced a flash of anger. Perhaps similar to what Micah had described. Irrational, but sharp, mulish. "Well, you tell me, Violet? Did you read the story I sent you?"

She swiveled to the tray, considering the sausage. "Yes, I did. It was fabulous."

I waited as she stacked sausage. Tooth-picked it. Rearranged it. Finally, I caved. "And?"

"And it just was, Sterling. You're an excellent writer."

I felt the heat bloom in my face, my lips reflexively tightening. "What made it fabulous and excellent? Tell me. I can take criticism." *But could I?*

"I…I loved the characters. And it was just…cheery. I really, really liked it."

"Thanks," I said tightly, quickly placing the rest of the sausage in the tray. "That means a lot." I glanced at my phone, making a show of bending my brows. "Hey, I need to return this, and you better get out there with that sausage."

"I know, right?" She hugged me again, and it took everything in me not to recoil. Once she was gone and the house was mercifully quiet, I washed my hands and roamed. I found a quiet spot in Aunt Desi's office and sat in front of her computer. I couldn't help but smile when I saw all of her Post-its and her "Talk to Robin" list. She had lists for everyone, including me and Fireman.

Why couldn't I just be happy? Why couldn't I let those earlier sounds of humanity roll over me and fill me with cheerfulness? Why did I need this so badly? And what was *this* exactly? My writing? Tammy Jo? Or was it nothing more than vanity and lust?

Whatever it was, I deserved more than an out-and-out lie from my sister. I expected more from her, and I was irate. *So yes, Micah, I suppose I do feel angry and mean at times.*

The short story I'd entrusted my sister with had been far from *cheery.* It had, in fact, been an emotionally shattering story about our father's death.

✝✝✝

I sipped wine in the quiet of Aunt Desi's office, toying with Tammy Jo's name in the To Box of a text message. What could I possibly say to her at this point? If she had even an ounce of feeling for me, she would have responded to at least one of my pathetic, plaintive texts.

But anger and self-pity married and gave birth to a passive-aggressive text that even I found effective and satisfying.

```
In Shady Gully now, having a
blast with all the people you
used to care about. Perhaps
some more than others. They
send their best. Cheers!
```

I was busy trying to find an appropriate emoji, other than the wine and smirk ones, when I heard the door to Aunt Desi's office open. Before I knew it, the whole bunch of them had descended on me. Noisy, and a little drunk, their flushed faces and loopy grins flashed on me like a bunch of squirrels eager for a nut.

"We can't wait for Fireman anymore," my mom pronounced. "It's time to share our news." She and Aunt Desi held hands. "We're going to start a podcast."

"A what?" asked Daryl.

"What in the world about?" Micah looked appalled.

"Oh brother." Max took a swig of his beer. "Whatever y'all do, don't use my name."

"You can use my name," Bubba offered magnanimously.

Uncle Lenny beamed at his wife. "I think it's a great idea."

Ricky smartly agreed, although he'd probably never listened to a podcast in his life. "Sounds fun. Bravo."

"How will you manage it?" Bella asked, her enthusiasm growing. "Since y'all live in two different states."

"Well, that's where Sterling and Fireman come in. They're going to help us with all that"—an expression of distaste flooded Aunt Desi's face—"stuff. They'll be like our producers, our directors." She was happy once again now that that distasteful *stuff* had been covered.

I gladly took the handoff. "It's done all the time," I explained around a gulp of wine. "Most podcasts are co-hosted. Having multiple points of view makes for more engaging conversation.

I'll help them with the technical parts. The editing, the audio cleanup, how to publish the episodes, choosing the music—"

"Oh, music! Oh, my goodness, yes!" Mom shrieked, clutching Aunt Desi's hand. "We have to have a theme song."

"Something catchy, but not cheesy. We don't want it to sound like a commercial." Aunt Desi contemplated. "Something modern. And cool."

I chimed in a little wickedly, "Definitely cool, and maybe even a little edgy."

They cheered. "Fireman is going to help us with the equipment and all, and he and Sterling are going to coordinate the…" Mom looked at Aunt Desi, and together they said, "Stuff."

"Fantastic!" Petey clapped his hands. "I'm ready." His keenness was interrupted as his phone went off. "Hold that thought," he said.

The room grew quiet, and all eyes were on Petey as he spoke softly into the phone. He turned away from us, nodding, murmuring in a way that made his words impossible to understand… but reflected the graveness of the conversation.

Finally, he hung up, his face pale and drawn as he turned to face us. "That was Wolfheart. It's about Fireman."

"Oh no, what's happened?" Everyone leaned in, concerned.

"That blasted car," Ricky grunted, his voice thick with worry.

"No, no, it's not that," Petey said. "It's his Granny Lacey. She passed away."

Chapter Ten

Unfathomable
Timothy

I stared at the cheese as it congealed on the tray on Father Patrick's coffee table. Downtrodden, like me, the dairy snack sulked uselessly, aware that its value diminished with each passing second. Knowing that its window was closing, it clung to the soggy cracker, hoping against hope that it could salvage what remained of its potential.

"You should eat something." The demonstrative priest offered me the tray. "Or perhaps a hot cup of tea would help?"

"I'm fine, Father." I watched as he nipped a few of the crackers, nodding his approval before turning his blue-eyed gaze on me. At least my eyes had stopped watering, and I could inhale without choking on piquant gusts of bleach and astringent. "Your home is lovely. Thank you for seeing me."

"The notion that I could help you, Timothy, is unfathomable to me, but I'm ready to listen, to offer counsel, and always, to pray with you." And then, like a good spiritual advisor, he perched on the edge of his recliner, tilted his head with interest, and waited for me to begin.

Well played, I thought, only a little surprised that he'd set the tone so quickly. While he came off as jovial and more than a little befuddled on the outside, Father Patrick was the real deal. There would be no dodging questions, no half-truths, and no ambiguity.

In fact, I owed him as much. "When I counsel people," I began, "particularly those with…troublesome pasts…I remind them that just because they've removed themselves from the situation, or their circumstances have changed, their pain doesn't just go away. The wounds are still there, and if not dealt with, they tend to emerge later and present in negative ways."

Since Father Patrick's expression gave nothing away, I had no choice but to continue. "Usually, at that point in the counseling session, whoever I'm speaking with wholeheartedly agrees. Most people are hopeful about their futures, or they want to be, so even as I warn them about those pesky reoccurring wounds their eyes remain fixed on the door. They're simply glad to be free of their toxic environment or of their plight, and they can't—or don't want to—think that far ahead." I fumbled for my glass of water, determined not to look at the gooey cheese and water-logged crackers. "So I think I need to stress that part more in my counseling."

I massaged my temples, avoiding his gaze, hoping he'd accept my volley while I gathered myself.

He decisively cranked the levers on his recliner. "Problem solved then. Brilliant idea to revamp your counseling sessions to emphasize the hidden pitfalls of trauma. Splendid." He scooted out of the massive recliner and waddled to the kitchen. "Are you sure you don't want some tea?" He glanced out the window as the darkness of late fall had now obliterated the sun entirely.

Panic welled inside me as I realized I was now late to meet Meadow at Desi's party.

"Or perhaps a glass of pinot noir since it's legal now that the sun is over the yardarm?" As he fluttered about the kitchen, I recognized that he'd outwitted me. I waited with dread until he spoke. "As much as I love discussing counseling strategies, Timothy, perhaps we could have done this over the phone? Or on one of those Zoom thingys? I've been dying to try one for myself—"

"Father—"

"—and I'm sure the lad, Fireman, could have arranged it. He's quite tech savvy—"

"Father Patrick." While I had barely spoken the words aloud, he'd been listening.

And was ready and waiting. He returned immediately to the recliner. No tea. No wine. No distractions. "What is it, son?"

"It's catching up to me now. The wounds. The pain. The repercussions." *The consequences.* I gulped the water. "It's all coming for me."

Because he took so long to respond, I wasn't sure he'd heard. And then a flash of compassion and genuine hurt flashed across his eyes, but only for a moment. "So if I'm hearing you correctly, your past has come back to haunt you and your soul is a mess."

"Precisely." Again, he waited me out, this time so long my forehead began to bead with sweat. Eventually, I asked, "Do you want to hear about my past?"

"No. Not yet. First, I'd like to know, why now?"

I frowned, my heart pounding.

"Most people have troublesome, regretful, and even sordid pasts, Timothy, and as you know, it's quite common—and these days even fashionable—for people to lament publicly about the iniquities they've endured, but in my experience, when one starts to suffer physically"—he opened his beefy palm in my direction— "with panic attacks, fainting, and the likes, there is a reason. So I need to know one thing before we begin."

"And what's that?"

"What is the catalyst to your predicament? What has happened to suddenly raise the stakes in such a way?"

Have mercy, the endearing, old charmer was shrewd…

"I'm being blackmailed."

He didn't even flinch. "Are you wealthy? Do you have money in the Cayman Islands?"

I snorted. "I drive a Corolla and live in a small house in a modest part of town, Father. Contrary to what people think, all megachurches aren't corrupt. I don't have money."

Father Patrick leaned back in his recliner, thoughtful. Finally, he said, "So. It's your reputation you're worried about then. It would be sullied, yes?"

I nodded. "Yes, but it's more than that. Sure, failing my community would be horrible, and disappointing believers all over the country, and in Haiti and Uganda, would be devastating." I blew out a big sigh and met his eyes. "But that's not the worst of it."

"And what is?"

"Losing Meadow."

"Well, that's not a given. Perhaps you aren't giving her enough credit."

"No, you don't understand. In order to save her, to protect her, I have to end it. I have no choice."

A lengthy moment passed. "Alright. Let's have your past now then, shall we?"

✝✝✝

How to begin? What could I possibly say? There were simply no words. And then I remembered the word Father Patrick had used earlier. *Unfathomable.* Such a beautiful word, especially when written in cursive. Not easy on the tongue though. Its meaning? It had a few, but the one that came to mind now was *incomprehensible.*

Exactly. But words didn't make sense now. So with shaking fingers, I unlocked my phone, found the unseemly photo, and handed it to him without a word.

"Good Lord," he gasped.

Finally, I'd succeeded in shocking the spirited priest. "You can zoom in."

He fumbled for his glasses on the end table next to his recliner. "Is that you? The young boy?"

"Yes."

"And the woman?"

"My mother."

"And the rest?"

"No idea. I have very little memory of that time."

"*Humph.*" Father Patrick managed a grunt even as his eyes remained glued to the picture.

"My earliest memories are from Missouri, and I know it was Missouri because I remember being fascinated with the arch. I learned later it was called the Gateway. It became a landmark for me, so when I ran—or wandered—off, I could see it from anywhere. I could always find my way back…"

"Back to where?"

"To her." I met his eyes. "Where else?"

"You look quite young," he said hoarsely, narrowing his eyes at the picture. "What? Maybe three? Four?"

I shrugged. "It's the world's tallest arch. Clad in stainless steel." Talking about the arch soothed me, even now.

"This looks to be some kind of…heroin den." The priest lowered his spectacles further down his nose.

"It was designed by a Finnish-American architect. It cost over thirteen million at the time of its construction in 1963, which would be well over that now. Can you imagine?"

"Your mother, Timothy, she doesn't look well in this picture. Is your…father one of these men?"

"The arch was dedicated to the people of the United States. At least that's what the plaque says. I think I'd like to go back sometime and see it. Maybe."

"Timothy. Your father—"

"No, he's not in the photo. My mother always told me he died in a car accident, but I was never sure whether to believe her or not. She was a drug addict, after all." After seeing the sickly pallor on Father Patrick's face, I asked, "Would you like me to get you that glass of wine?"

"No, no," he said throatily, brushing his fleshy finger against the image on my phone. "The original photo looks to be a Polaroid. I can see the edges here."

I nodded. "Same with the others."

"Others?"

"All you have to do is swipe." When I saw his hand move, I warned him. "Brace yourself."

But he didn't, and when his eyes widened in horror, I knew

exactly which one he'd seen. "*Guh*," he croaked, genuflecting and calling out to God. "My heavens…the depravity!"

I offered him my water and watched as he drank greedily while holding the glass with both hands.

"Where in the world was your mother when this…" he looked away from the phone, "when this happened?"

I thought about the Gateway Arch, about how the observation windows were located near the apex, and how incredible it would be to take a riverboat cruise on the Mississippi and view it from the water. "Strung out. As usual. Especially toward the end." Unable to stand the look of horror—and pity—on his face, I turned away.

"Gracious, Timothy, you were just a boy."

"Father, have you ever counseled an actual heroin addict?"

"Of course." He set my phone on the end table. "Granted, we don't have many here in Shady Gully, but in Dublin, certainly." He sighed. "I suppose it's been a while though." He studied me for a long time. "You said toward the end? Is your mother dead?"

"Yes."

"Are you sure? I mean, perhaps she's the one sending you these repulsive photos. Or maybe it's one of these…men."

"She's dead, Father." I reached for my phone. "Trust me. I was with her when she died. ODed. Killed herself. Whatever." I rubbed my hands along the length of my thighs, dampening my jeans with sweat marks. "There are more though, if you want to see—"

"No. I do not. I need a break. A moment to decompress—" He jumped at the sound of his own phone ringing. He cast his eyes from side to side, a little agitated. "Where did that blasted thing get off to?"

Blasted? That was practically a curse word for the saintly priest. For a second it seemed I was counseling him as I hurriedly retrieved his phone from the bar. "It's Mr. Wolf," I read, amused by the moniker he'd tagged Brad Wolfheart with on his phone.

"Oh, heavens." After Father Patrick punched a button, he spoke softly to his friend.

I took the opportunity to wander into the kitchen and refill my water. While staring out the darkened window over the sink, with only a few random night lights from the church to see, I acknowledged that I'd fully committed now. By telling Father Patrick, I'd officially set things in motion.

Now I had much more to worry about than merely standing Meadow up for the party. My heart pounded feverishly inside my chest as I considered what was to come. I turned when I realized Father's call had ended and he'd stopped speaking altogether.

He rocked on the edge of his recliner, unseeing, his gaze fixed blankly ahead.

"Father Patrick?" I asked tentatively. "What's wrong?"

"I'm sorry, Timothy…I just need a minute." When he bowed his head, I realized he was praying. I took a seat on the edge of the couch adjacent to his recliner and prayed a silent prayer of my own. When he eventually raised his head, Father Patrick's eyes were bright with tears.

"What's happened?" I put my hand on his knee. "Please tell me."

"The most dreadful news. The young man who was here and was so helpful…"

"Fireman? Yes. I know him. I met him at Luke and Bella's wedding three years ago. Back when Meadow was carting him around everywhere."

Father Patrick nodded. "Such a good lad, and he's had a rough go of it." He swiveled to me. "Much like you, in a way. He never knew his parents. His grandmother has raised him since he was a young boy."

"What's happened? Is he alright? Was it…a wreck?"

"No, he's physically fine, but his grandmother died." His pupils seemed to dilate as his thoughts drifted again. "And now he has no one."

"That's not true." I gripped Father Patrick's knee. "He has

you. He has Wolfheart. He has…" my voice cracked, "…he has Meadow. Bella. Petey. He has all of Shady Gully, Father."

"Yes." Father Patrick buried his head in his hands. "Yes, yes he does."

I stood. "Let's go to him now." I helped him to his feet. "I'll drive the church van if that's all you have."

"The keys are in the ashtray on the bar. Along with my chargers. Just the way the lad arranged them earlier."

Chapter Eleven

Butterfly Kisses
Fireman

The shanty I shared with my Granny was dark except for a dim bulb over the kitchen sink, a lamp next to Granny's bed, and the random candles Wolfheart had started. The place smelled like a combination of pumpkin spice and lavender, which wasn't as unpleasant as it sounded.

Wolfheart placed himself at the foot of her bed, leaving me time with Granny at the head, where I repeatedly nuzzled her forehead, cheeks, and eyes. Her once fierce, green eyes were now closed and would never again brush against my face with butterfly kisses. Oddly, it was that random thought that nearly did me in.

As I swept her thick, gray hair away from her face with my clumsy fingers, I was startled by the waxy gray sheen of her olive skin. Automatically, I reached for her Jergens hand lotion on her bedside table, which had always been a staple in her skincare routine. I squirted some into my hands and then massaged her fingers, working around her gnarly knuckles and swollen joints as I'd done most nights for the past five years.

I sniffed the lotion, breathing in its cherry-almond scent greedily, realizing I'd forever associate the distinctive smell with my granny.

"Her hands won't hurt her anymore," Wolfheart said solemnly, pulling me out of my trance. Naturally, the subject of her arthritis would be upfront in his mind as he'd been devoted to her pain management. His special blend of cat's claw, turmeric, burdock root, and ginger had eased her agony many times.

In fact, we'd officially met on a night five years ago when I'd trekked through the swamp desperately seeking a remedy to her suffering. Wolfheart's sister, Peony, had just been murdered, and since she'd assisted Creek people for years with her herbal potions, I'd had no choice but to hope her brother was as gifted.

Turned out he was more than gifted.

That was also the night I'd met Meadow and fallen in love with Bella, setting in motion a series of events that had put each of us in the crosshairs of Peony's killer. Before it was finished, two churches had burned, Bella had nearly died when the raggedy old bridge dividing The Creek and Shady Gully had collapsed, and Wolfheart had been wrongly accused and thrown in jail.

A lot had changed since then.

"Was she…?" I couldn't meet his eyes, but I had to know. "Was she like this when you got here?"

Wolfheart stood, then rolled his chair next to mine. Despite my best intentions to be strong, to be a proper man, I leaned deeply into his embrace. "No. She was still alive," he said as the murmur of sirens echoed off the shanty's thin walls. "And we can talk about that now, or later, but you should know that she didn't suffer in the end. Instead, she…"

I looked at him sharply, and our faces were so close I could feel his breath, see the stains of his tears. "She spoke of you. Of how much she loved you." The siren grew louder. "She wanted you to have her cookbooks."

My lips turned up in a grin even as tears sprung from my eyes. "I bet she did."

A tap at the door forced us to turn, and in walked Quietdove, looking very different in his street clothes. He reminded me of the sort of guy you'd see in a commercial for cologne or athletic shoes, or both.

Wolfheart rose, embraced Quietdove, and then offered him his chair.

Quietdove glanced at me, lowering his voice as he spoke to Wolfheart. "The paramedics and the coroner are right behind me."

"I'll go talk to them." Wolfheart winked at me before he disappeared.

Quietdove blanched when he saw Granny. I'd never realized until recently that Granny thought much of him one way or the other, except for the obvious reason that we were all Creeks and tended to look out for one another. Then one day I found two glasses in the sink with lemonade sugar caked at the bottom. When I asked Granny about it, she casually informed me that she and QD—that's what she'd called him—had had their bi-monthly gossip session. I reckon my mouth dropped because she got feisty then, going on a tirade about how she had a life and all. Eventually, she confessed that mostly they talked about me, although she confided that occasionally he talked about his love life. Funny. I didn't know Quietdove even had a love life unless you counted his crush on Micah, and since that crush had gone on for a while without anything happening, I figured it was a lost cause.

Anyway, it now seemed that those "gossip sessions" had meant something to the deputy. I watched as his lips moved in a short prayer and then as he lowered himself into the seat beside me. Although he said nothing, somehow his very presence comforted me. We sat like that, just the two of us, for several minutes before he patted me on the knee. And then there was another tap at the door.

"Hey, kid." Patty, the lead paramedic, mussed my hair. Because of my job at the fire station, we knew each other fairly well. She'd always been nice to me. "You okay?" But now she took it to another level as she buried my head into her bosom and patted me like an infant. "You're gonna be alright."

My response came back muffled. "Taaaaaaaannnnks."

"We're going to need to get in here for a bit." She released me. "Why don't you go with QD, here, alright? He'll take you to the others."

I must have looked confused because Quietdove explained as he led me to the porch. "We got word at the party. I was able to discourage most of them, but you're gonna have your hard-liners."

"Dan." Quietdove shook the coroner's hand as our paths crossed.

"QD," he responded. The coroner looked at me with kind eyes and patted me on the shoulder. "Son."

The bombardment of compassion was beginning to overwhelm me, and I almost wished someone would be flippant or sarcastic or mean or—

And then I saw Meadow, who was in her Uncle Wolf's arms. He gently placed his hands on her shoulders and turned her in my direction. "Oh, sweet baby," she said, tears sliding down her face as she rushed to hug me. "I'm so, so sorry, Fireman." She sobbed. "I'm really going to miss her."

And once again, I was smushed into a bosom, but this time, I broke down and cried.

†††

Flashing lights rose and sank with the contours of The Creek's potholed roads, until eventually, Sheriff Rick's vehicle came to a stop in front of our shanty. He carried an Igloo in one hand and what appeared to be blankets in the other. The passenger door opened and Petey's shaggy head popped out. He carried a giant paper bag with handles and judging by the smell as he drew closer, the bag contained food.

Everyone had gathered on the porch while the coroner and the paramedics did whatever they do when their patient had already passed. The mood became increasingly somber as we waited, and soon my head began to pound with terrifying thoughts like, *What happens now?*

Sheriff Rick set the Igloo in front of me and wrapped one of the blankets around my shoulders. "It's heated," he said. "Something money can apparently buy because Robin sent one for everybody." He gestured to the rest of the blankets. Meadow immediately found one to her liking and wrapped it around her shoulders and then offered one to Wolfheart. While he took it, draping it over his shoulders, Quietdove declined.

The sheriff then removed a bottled water from the Igloo and

handed it to me. He watched as I drank steadily, angling his head this way and that as if to take measure of me. When I was done, he extended his long arm and pulled me into his chest.

I fought the tears that threatened because I had a reputation of irreverence and sassiness to uphold in front of the sheriff. Petey approached me then, setting the food on the porch while eyeing me just as the sheriff had. "Daddy sent food. Sausage, boudin, ribs. And Mama sent dessert. Hummingbird cake, blueberry pie." With that out of the way, he sat on the steps, patting the seat next to him.

I joined him because he made it so easy. That was the way with Petey.

He sipped his water, slowly screwing the top back on. "This really sucks," he said to me. "And we were just talking about her earlier, about her zucchini bread and all." He stared into the swampy marsh surrounding our shanty as if searching for answers.

"It really does suck." I reached into the bag, peeled foil from a large paper plate, and grabbed a rib. "Want one?"

He did. We ate quietly together on the steps as the rest of them stood around murmuring. I caught Meadow's eye a few times but refused to engage. It was easier Petey's way, focusing on the food and acknowledging how unfair it was. At some point he found some napkins, offering me a handful. They were ribs, after all.

"You got my number?" Petey asked. When I nodded, he said, "Good. Because there's gonna come a point, when all of this"—he indicated the ambulance and the flashing lights and the worried faces— "will fade, and I just want you to know, I really, really want to talk to you."

I focused on my napkin, swallowing hard so I wouldn't cry. "Okay."

"And little man," he leaned in, "this isn't the end. You're gonna see your granny again. I promise."

The way he said it made it almost seem true. *I wanted it to be true.* And while there were a lot of godly men in my life, like Wolfheart and Father Patrick, who were always ready to talk to me about Jesus, I'd love to hear Petey's take.

Speaking of the ever-muddled priest, Sacred Heart's church van ground its way up the dirt road, braking to a stop just beyond the sheriff's vehicle. The tall, blue-eyed pastor from Kentucky looked more composed now as he lowered himself from the driver's seat. All eyes were on him as he walked around to the passenger side and helped Father Patrick out.

A tickle behind my eyes started at the sight of the priest. I watched as he searched the crowd through the darkness, clearly looking for me and having a tough time of it as the glare of the blue and red emergency headlights made the shadows even murkier.

For some inexplicable reason, it made my heart hurt to see him so anxious to lay eyes on me. Usually, at this time of night, he was slumped in his recliner tearing into a giant bowl of pasta, and yet here he was, vulnerable and disoriented, braving the big ole' world so he could tend to me.

When I raised my arm and waved, his face lit up. "Heavens." I recognized the word from the way his eyebrows and beard moved. He charged across the yard as fast as his chubby legs allowed him.

Conversely, Timothy stopped to speak to Meadow, who suddenly seemed more interested in her heating blanket than in him. I couldn't tell what he was saying, but by the way the fancy pastor dug his hands into his pockets and shuffled his feet, it appeared he was apologizing.

Everyone swiveled suddenly as Dan the coroner came out of the shanty, followed by a couple of paramedics carrying a stretcher. And a body bag, just like you saw on TV. And there was a small lump that used to be my granny.

"We'll take good care of her." Patty brushed against my shoulder as she made her way to the vehicle. I watched, uncomprehending, as she climbed in and took Granny away.

What now? I thought.

And in answer, Father Patrick had finally made his way over to me, breathless and flushed, but wholly present. "Son," he said, holding me upright…just as my legs gave way.

✝✝✝

Shortly after Father Patrick's surprisingly quick reaction saved me from face-planting, I found myself leaning against the window of Wolfheart's ancient black truck, staring blankly as cypress trees flitted past me in the cavernous night.

"You can roll the window down if you need some air."

"Roll? How old is this truck?" I asked. "Even my Impala has automatic windows."

"Almost as old as me," he harumphed.

"Archaic then," I said, but my mockery fell flat. "I don't need a babysitter, you know."

"Of course, you don't, but you could use some hot soup and a warm bed." When he turned into his driveway, countless pairs of eyes glowed in the dark. "And a good night's sleep couldn't hurt."

After he unfolded himself from his truck, he grabbed a backpack from under his seat, tossing it to me as he picked up a huge yellow cat that was either fat or—

"This is Aurora. She's pregnant." He flipped on the kitchen and living room lights as he carried Aurora inside. "She bunks in here at night. Just to be safe."

I noticed that a few other cats and at least one dog slipped in before the door flapped shut. "You can take the first room on the right when you go up the stairs. And if you want a hot shower, the bathroom is just to the left."

"Bella's room? Really?"

Despite himself, Wolfheart chuckled. "You know she doesn't live here anymore. Since she got *married.*" He pulled Tupperware from the fridge and placed a saucepan on the stove. "And she's what? Thirteen years older than you? You really need to move on."

I shrugged. "She'll come to her senses one day."

As I set the backpack on the table, a wave of horror swept through me. "Who packed this?" I unzipped the pack, rifling through it. "It's got my underwear and everything in it."

"Meadow did."

I dropped my head into my hands, mortified.

"She's seen underwear before, Fireman." I could tell he found me amusing, although he was probably just relieved that I wasn't rolling on the ground bawling hysterically. "We'll go tomorrow and get you some more things. We weren't sure where everything was and didn't want to get…too personal."

"A little late now, don't you think?" I reached for the bowl he set on the table. It felt warm around my fingers. "Is this gumbo?"

"Yep." He handed me a spoon. "Not as good as ribs, but it'll do the job."

"Yeah, Lenny makes some mean ribs, but…I really couldn't… enjoy them earlier." I slurped, the spicy juices making my mouth water the more I ate. Wolfheart set a plate of French bread on the table, cutting several slices. Before he even offered, I stuffed one in my mouth. "I don't really need any more clothes. I can stay by myself tomorrow night at…Granny's. At home."

"Fireman—"

"I'm a man," I stressed. "I can take care of myself."

"You are, and you can, but let's just let the next few days play out. Okay?" He sipped his tea. And because he looked meditative, I braced myself. "There is something we have to talk about now though."

I waited, focusing on the yellow cat as it tried to balance its massive frame on Wolfheart's narrow lap. "And what would that be?"

"You know I don't abide with a lot of the old school Creek thinking, but we do need to have a funeral and get her buried. I know it's difficult to talk about, but…" He sipped and stroked the cat. "Do you have any ideas?"

"What do you mean?" I picked up my bowl, angling it to pour the last of the gumbo juice down my gullet.

"Well, I figured you'd want to bury her in The Creek's cemetery, and since y'all didn't have any…immediate family, what do you think about laying her to rest next to Peony, my sister?"

My stomach felt fluttery all of a sudden. "She really liked Miss Peony. I think Granny would…" I finished hoarsely, "I think she would like it there."

Wolfheart nodded, and I could tell he was mentally calculating, like a computer when the setting cog spins and spins. "And who would you want to officiate? Or speak?"

"Well, you could talk," I told him. "She loved you a lot." More butterflies playing in my tummy. "And, I don't know, what about Father Patrick?"

"Good choice."

I thought. "And Petey. How's that?"

"Excellent choices."

"I mean, I like Timothy, like when we watch on Sundays, and sometimes the stuff he says really sticks, but I don't know if he's up to it lately. And he didn't really know Granny like Petey and Father Patrick did."

While I could no longer see the cat, I could hear satisfied purring rising up from Wolfheart's lap. "I think that all sounds good, Fireman," he said thickly. "And then there are flowers and music—"

"Can you? Would you…do all of that?" When he nodded, I picked up my bowl and took it to the sink. The cat jumped off Wolfheart's lap and rubbed a figure eight between my legs. All at once I became utterly exhausted. I literally couldn't hold my eyes open.

"Absolutely, I can, and I will." Wolfheart rose, brushing his hand along my shoulder. "Why don't you go to bed now? Get some sleep. Rest assured that I'll take care of everything."

I hugged him then. A hard, clingy squeeze that kept me grounded for another minute or two. "Good night," I mumbled.

"Sleep well, son."

✝✝✝

Within minutes, I'd brushed my teeth and slipped into bed in my underwear. My breathing was heavy as exhaustion surrounded me, and my eyes became slits as I watched lightning reflect from the window and dance against Bella's pink wall.

Bella's room, I thought, *Wolfheart's home.*

Where was Granny? Where was she now? Was she watching over me? Was she in heaven like the believers claimed? Or was she floating in…nothingness?

Such heavy thoughts. Such hard questions. All I knew was that Granny was gone, and I was alone…

My eyes popped open sometime later. Still heavy, still tired, but open enough to see that it was still dark. I heard purring at the foot of my bed and could see Aurora's shadow rising and falling as she slept.

And then another head popped up. Followed by another. Black and Blue padded to the head of the bed to nestle beside me. They bookended me, guarding me against the night.

And I slept.

Chapter Twelve

The Very Definition of Extra
Sterling

Luke, Petey, and I sat at a picnic table at the Cozy Corner, while Duke and Duchess stretched the limits of their ten-foot leashes. "Duchess," Luke pleaded, "stick within the boundary here." The fox-faced troublemaker cocked her head and continued to tug the leash. "Duke," he sighed, "will you…?"

Petey shook his head in disbelief. "Dude, I'm a little concerned about your parenting skills."

Duke obediently distracted Duchess in a playful tussle, eventually pinning her down under Luke's feet. We watched as the dogs pranced, danced, and pawed each other in play. "Actually," Luke smacked, "I think our strategy works just fine. As long as there aren't any squirrels around."

Charlie Wayne, who had traded in his Cozy Corner BOSS T-shirt for a button-down shirt and blazer today, brought three cups of coffee over in a paper tray. "Those mutts better not trip me. I got places to go."

"Nice duds." Petey grinned, flapping the opening of his own blazer. "We match."

"You wish." Charlie Wayne smirked. "What'll you have?" He pulled out a pad and snapped his pencil impatiently. "We only got a couple of hours before the funeral, and I ain't gonna be late. That would be low class."

"I agree. I'll have a sausage biscuit." Petey slid his menu to me across the table.

"Same here," Luke echoed. "Can I get some jam to go with it?"

When Charlie Wayne made a face, he added, "Please?"

The curmudgeon turned to me, and I decided not to challenge the system. "Sounds good." After smushing his coke bottle glasses higher up his nose, Charlie Wayne carried his short, paunchy frame toward the kitchen, orneriness falling off him in waves. "I wonder if he'll let JJ Wheeler off for the funeral."

"He might. He's mellowed a bit." Luke swigged his coffee. "If you can imagine that." He turned to his brother. "How are folks holding up on The Creek?"

Petey sighed heavily. "Pretty rough. Wolfheart took it hard. Meadow too. I think Quietdove and Fireman are still in shock, to tell you the truth." Petey swirled his cup against the wooden picnic table. "And Fireman can't stay at that house by himself. Ricky's already warned everybody about it."

"He seems like a responsible kid," I spoke up. "Pretty self-sufficient for a fifteen-year-old."

"He is. But he'll have to have a legal guardian for a few more years," Luke pointed out. "According to the law, anyway."

"What about you?" Petey asked me. "How have things been at Mom and Dad's?"

"Good. Fine." I hesitated to say anything, but I'd sensed some uneasiness at Aunt Desi and Uncle Lenny's, and although I couldn't put my finger on it, I knew it was unrelated to Granny Lacey's passing.

"They seem pretty excited about their podcast," Luke said just as Charlie Wayne dropped three wrapped biscuits onto the table, the grease fragrant as it seeped through the paper wrapper. Without a word, he tossed us each a plastic tab of jam. "Thanks, Charlie Wayne." Luke smiled. "You're the best."

"Yeah, yeah." He hustled away.

"They're excited about the podcast, yes…" I caved and confessed to my cousins, "but there was something else. I mean, they're always weird and secretive, but whatever this was, your dad seemed to be in on it. I got the feeling that he and my mom were comforting Aunt Desi about something."

"What?" Luke and Petey glanced at one another, concerned.

"I don't know." When I bit into the biscuit, I let out an involuntary groan of pleasure. "I may go to the lake house tonight just to get away from them all."

"Man, Bluejay told me yesterday the white perch have been biting out there on Lake Osprey," Petey said. "You should go, Sterling."

"Yeah, I took Bella and the dogs out there last weekend," Luke put in. "It was beautiful. We enjoyed the lake view and the fresh air."

"I'm glad it's being used. Y'all should go often and enjoy." Years ago, when my family had begun to move from state to state for my dad's career, my parents decided they wanted a home base in Shady Gully, so they invested in a beautiful lot on Lake Osprey and eventually built the lake house.

"We should all go," Luke suggested. "Enjoy some fishing together while Sterling is here."

Petey chewed. "We'll see how things go today." He dipped his biscuit in jam, turning to me. "I didn't get to chat much with Timothy last night. What's the scoop? Is he alright?"

I thought about the episode at the airport. "I don't know," I answered honestly.

"The Unity Christian Church Revival is coming up. I was hoping I could persuade him to preach at least once. The community would love it. You know how they adore him."

"You should ask him." I reached quickly for my phone as it buzzed with a text, thinking it might be Tammy Jo. But no, it was Pippa.

```
Sorry to text, but can we talk
a minute?
```

Good grief.

Petey flashed a conspiratorial wink at Luke before harassing me. "Who's that? Somebody from your fan club?"

"Hardly," I mumbled, disappointed.

"Are you kidding? With that handsome mug flashing across

the TV screen every Sunday?" Luke chuckled as he scratched Duchess under the chin.

"I'm a guy, and your cousin and all," Petey piled on, "but you look really hot up there playing your guitar. Especially when you sweat a little bit up here on your temples." He tweaked me beside the head.

I snorted, wadding up the greasy biscuit wrapper and miming a pitch at him.

"Watch out," Luke jibed. "You-know-who is watching."

"I'm aware, trust me." Charlie Wayne's garbage can spray painted with *Garbage Goes Here, Moron!* was legendary.

"You want to ride with me and Violet?" Petey asked. "I'm headed over there now to pick her up."

I glanced at my watch. "I'm supposed to be waiting for Micah. We're going to ride together."

"Good luck, she's always late."

✝✝✝

I held my breath as Micah teetered precariously from the gravel parking lot to the grassy gravesite in three-inch heels and a skintight pencil skirt. I shouldn't have worried, however, because at the first sight of her, Quietdove strategically placed himself in her path so he could escort her to her seat.

My mom and Aunt Desi waved, signaling me over to join them, but I figured I'd linger on the outskirts a moment to make sure the women got their seats first. To say attendance was huge would be an understatement. Granny Lacey was loved throughout Shady Gully and The Creek, even if her baking was not. She'd been feisty, irreverent, and bold on the outside, but the turnout suggested that many knew her on the inside. There were tears. There were shared memories, most told in raucous tones and accompanied by the sound of misty laughter.

I saw a lot of people I hadn't seen since Luke and Bella's wedding, which had been an event of grand proportions with an enormous crowd. A wedding fit for a mayor, in other words.

Conversely, Violet and Petey's wedding had been a quick, low-key event. Quick to suit Petey's eagerness to be married and low-key to suit my sister's shy disposition. Though it had been an awesome, festive event on Osprey Lake, Violet had had to leave a week after the wedding to start school in Baton Rouge. While she commuted on the weekends, Petey filled his time with practical, brick-and-mortar plans and purposefully began building a life for them here in Shady Gully.

The two of them looked cozy now, chatting quietly with Sigourney Sky, a Creek woman who was a talented seamstress and sharp entrepreneur. Nails and Thread, Sigourney's business, sat right next to Dolly's Diva Dome. While they were technically competitors, I noted the two exchanged pleasantries as Dolly and Adam—who were surprisingly still an item—searched for a seat. Dolly, who according to all accounts had been the quint-essential mean girl at Shady Gully High back in the day, and Adam, a carousing, would-be country music star who'd left a trail of broken marriages in his wake, had apparently turned over a new leaf. As a couple at least. Go figure.

Naturally, Bubba and Daryl were in attendance as they loved Granny Lacey to the core. When Wolfheart's sister, Peony, had been alive, she and Lacey had run together, and Bubba and Daryl had done their best to make sure they had wheels. Not an easy task as the vehicles they drove were even older than they were.

The Creek community had assembled in great numbers as I spotted Redflyer, Youngdeer, Moonpipe, and even Bluejay, who I'd heard had cancer. And sure enough, Charlie Wayne strutted in with JJ Wheeler in tow, followed by Big Al and Thaddeus. Even Sprite from the Quick Stop had come to pay his respects, all ninety-nine pounds of him. Patty the paramedic and her friend, Denise, who'd gone to school with my parents, filed through the crowd and found a seat. Not surprisingly, Cruella Claire from the post office was in attendance along with her buddy and fellow pot stirrer, ole man Chester.

I searched the crowd for Fireman and finally caught a glimpse of him with Father Patrick, Timothy, and Uncle Lenny. Struck by his good looks and how tall he'd grown since I'd last seen him, I was relieved that he seemed fairly composed, for now anyway.

All of the seats had filled up by this point, except for those reserved in the front, so I resigned myself to standing in the rear, which was fine by me. While I stood my mind flapped, searching for the right words to capture the sentiment of the event, or Granny Lacey, for that matter. What an unconventional firecracker of a lady she'd been!

Unconventional. Firecracker. I should run those words by Pippa as she had a knack for clever descriptions.

While I was struggling to compose the right words, I spied Meadow, Wolfheart, and an elegant Creek woman I'd never seen before talking a distance from the memorial. The woman wore a fluid skirt that seemed to shift in time with her long, grayish-black hair. Their heads were bent together in serious discussion, and shockingly, I could tell Meadow was trying to be friendly.

Again, go figure.

As Luke began to make moves around the microphone up front, tapping it and introducing himself as mayor, etc., Meadow and her uncle bid the woman farewell. After she handed Meadow a bouquet of flowers, the woman slipped away so inconspicuously I wondered if I'd hallucinated the whole scene.

As the gathering quieted down, I noticed that Meadow placed herself right next to Fireman and tended to him in a way that was almost maternal. The service itself was both gut-wrenching and magnificent. Each speaker brought his own memories of Granny Lacey, some touching and some hilarious, like when Wolfheart quoted an old Navajo saying that was reminiscent of Granny Lacey's personality. "There is nothing quite so eloquent as a rattlesnake's tail."

The attendees roared with laughter, some guffawing with, "Yep, that was her alright."

Petey's contribution was conversational, as he recollected his many meaningful conversations with Granny Lacey about Jesus. "She'd become very active at Unity, attending Sunday school and Bible Studies and always, *always* wanting to contribute to the potluck dinners."

After a bit of laughter, everyone held their breath in anticipation, and Petey didn't fail them—or her. "During the planning of one particular potluck dinner, there was quite a bit of talk about the need to prepare dishes that were vegetarian. I'd been sitting next to Granny Lacey that day, and I'll never forget the way she leaned into me and asked if I knew what the Indian word for vegetarian was. When I told her I didn't, she said, and I quote—"

The audience bowed forward in anticipation.

"—bad hunter."

"Ha!" I laughed out loud along with the rest of the congregation, and to my surprise, there was even a bit of clapping. *What a funeral*, I thought, so *full of...*

I struggled for just the right words to describe it. And then it hit me!

Brevity and veneration.

When Father Patrick closed the sermon, tears flowed as he quoted another Indian saying, this time one Granny had read to him when she'd spoken about her treasured grandson, Fireman. The priest cleared his throat and swallowed deeply before reading the Blackfoot quote. "What is life? It is the flash of a firefly in the night. It is the breath of a buffalo in the wintertime. It is the little shadow which runs across the grass and loses itself in the sunset." He surveyed the crowd for a long moment and then settled his blue-eyed gaze on Fireman. "*That* is my boy, Granny Lacey told me. *That* is my little man."

"Whoa," I mumbled, absorbing the words along with the heartened crowd.

And then my phone rang. Loud enough for everyone to hear and turn around in their seats.

Embarrassed, I desperately rooted for the off switch. "Sorry," I mumbled, my eyes cast downward.

When I saw the caller ID, annoyance flared, and I struggled to tame my temper.

Pippa.

What was her problem?

††††

After the funeral, Unity Christian Church hosted a grand feast that Granny Lacey would have been proud of, including a variety of salads, casseroles, and jambalayas, and because Petey knew his community, he'd had the foresight to incorporate a large outside pavilion where the star of the show currently roasted on a pit of hot coals.

A pig roast was the very epitome of a grand feast—at least in Louisiana.

High heels were abandoned, shirts came untucked, and kids squealed with glee as they ran in every direction. High-octane, sugar-filled sodas flowed freely, and by the way some of the grownups carried on, I suspected a flask or two provided an additional kick.

As I trolled the church grounds, still reeling with humiliation, I passed the time by keeping a running tab on the reactions to my excruciating faux pas. They ranged from, *oh man, don't worry about it,* to, *bro, you should have turned your phone off,* and my personal favorite from a five-year-old Creek boy, *you are a total loser and should jump off the Unity Bridge.*

Meanwhile, Mom and Aunt Desi were chatting up the oh-so-dazzling Hoot Wheeler, and I wondered, did he just appear dazzling because he'd dialed up the charm for the benefit of two middle-aged ladies? Or was there something *there?* Something beyond the gelled hair and the in-vogue trimmed beard.

I decided to mosey over a little closer and judge for myself.

As I approached, the matriarchs of Shady Gully gazed up at Hoot with cool fascination, all as Micah perused the appetizer and snack tables feigning indifference. She couldn't fool me though. I marked the heightened flush on her cheeks.

"Well, I just think it's impressive for a man, especially such a good-looking man like yourself, to be so sensitive about his pets," my mother oozed.

Hoot nodded, perhaps agreeing with her on the subject of his sensitivity and handsomeness. "Thank you, Miss Robin. It's been difficult not having her home, especially when she's…fighting for her life." Was that a tear in his eye?

Meanwhile, Aunt Desi looked on with thinly veiled skepticism. "Oh, I'm sure she'll be alright. Violet is an excellent vet. What was your dog's name again?"

Hoot battled through a pained response. "Tootsie."

I decided it was time to make my move. "Hey, Hoot, how've you been?" I inched into the conversation, offering my hand.

"Good." He had a firm handshake, good eye contact, and a pleasant smile. "It's Sterling, right? What's it been? Three years?"

"Yeah. We met at Luke and Bella's wedding."

"That's right." He switched his gaze to Aunt Desi. "And what a beautiful wedding it was." His tone dripped with flattery. "The venue, the decorations, and the food, all amazing."

"Well," Desi said, "your daddy came through with the barbecue in the end. We're all glad he and Charlie Wayne are getting along these days."

"Isn't that the truth?" Hoot flashed his pearly whites. "They work well together, and I think their cooking styles complement one another's."

Wow, laying it on thick now.

Finally, Micah joined the conversation, which was clearly what Hoot had been waiting for as he ramped up his playful sarcasm. "Are you gonna eat all that?" He motioned toward the heaping plate of pralines and divinity in her hands. "You're gonna get fat," he joked.

"No. I was bringing something sweet to Fireman." She skewered him with a rigid look. "And Quietdove."

Well played, cuz!

But Hoot quickly recovered, excusing himself to say a word

to his father and Charlie Wayne who chatted with Sigourney Sky near the rotisserie fire. Once he was out of sight, Aunt Desi boomed with vindication. "He's all flair. No substance whatsoever." She implored Micah. "Can't you see that, honey?"

"Oh, here we go again." Micah, the queen of the eye roll.

"I'm serious. You want a nice young man who is steady, who proves himself with his actions."

"But fun," Mom chimed. "You want someone who makes you laugh."

"That one is too flashy," Aunt Desi emphasized her point. "He's insincere."

"You don't know that, Mama, and anyway, I can't deal with this now. I'm out of here." We watched as she teetered off in her bare feet, heading in the direction of Fireman, and by association, Quietdove. But not before sneaking a glance toward the fire, where Hoot chuckled loudly at something Sigourney had said.

"Oh, how I worry about that one," Aunt Desi bemoaned, and almost on cue, Uncle Lenny appeared with a plate of chips heaped with Cajun cheese dip.

"Thank you." She stood on her tippy toes to kiss him. "*My man of substance.*"

Ricky wasn't far behind as he always seemed to keep tabs on Mom as well. She cut a jaunty expression at his mustached mouth, and for a minute I panicked, thinking they were going to kiss.

Thankfully, they didn't, but the victory was short-lived as Claire ambled over sporting a new hairdo with pink highlights and her signature cat-eye spectacles. Her nose ring was conservative today, no doubt in honor of the funeral, but her dangling mailbox earrings made up for it.

I noticed Meadow scouting out the snack table, thinking I'd make my way over to chat with her when I heard my mom quip, "Cool earrings, Claire. How've you been?"

"Well, the bigger question, Robin, is how have *you* been?" She cut her eyes at the sheriff. "And you, Ricky? How was your sabbatical in Lexington?"

"It was a week, Claire. Hardly a sabbatical. More like a little vacation." He made a frown with his mustache, which even I had to admit was pretty impressive.

Meanwhile, the bouncing mailboxes on Claire's ears bobbed in rhythm with her nodding head. "At least y'all were there in Lexington when Timothy had his breakdown."

"Breakdown?" Meadow piped from the snack table, her paper plate unsteady in her hands. "What are you going on about?"

But Claire wasn't done. She turned her attention to Aunt Desi, who suddenly looked like a deer caught in headlights. "And you? You must be so upset about Tom."

"Tom?" Ricky traded urgent glances with Lenny, who had drawn closer to Desi protectively. "Tom's been in a nursing home in Belle Maison for years now. What's going on? Did he pass?"

"Not yet," Claire nearly swooned, her cat-eyes never leaving Desi. "Word is Desi's stepdad is hanging on, and he's not giving up the ghost until he talks to her."

It was my sweet Aunt Desi who looked like a ghost now. Her normally rosy complexion had turned pasty, transforming my mom into a bulldog and Uncle Lenny into something even more fierce. He steered Aunt Desi away from Claire, sneering, "That's about enough, Claire, don't you think?"

What the devil was going on? Could this be what the carefully masked tension had been about lately?

But I wasn't to find out anytime soon because my phone rang, and naturally, it was Pippa with her no-good, horrible, bad timing. I stepped away, far enough to raise my voice and private enough to say my piece. "Hey," I said irritably as I leaned against a giant cypress tree facing the parking lot. "What is so urgent that you have to keep calling while I'm at a funeral?"

"What? How would I know you were at a funeral? You didn't return any of my calls."

"That's because…" I groaned, exasperated. "What's going on?"

"Well, you know I'm working on my cozy mystery novel, right?" She went on, oblivious to the fact that I'd just said I was at a funeral. "And remember I told you that I was going to stage the murder at an art gallery?"

"No, I don't remember that." *She was completely maddening.*

"Well, I did, and I'm in New Orleans now. There was a cool conference at the Hyatt. Oh my gosh, Sterling, you would have loved it. I took lots of notes though, and I emailed them to you."

"Pippa. I'm at a funeral. Can you get to the point?" She was truly the most exasperating person I'd ever met.

"Yes. Oh, and I want to talk to you about the funeral. It's not like family or anything, is it?"

"No."

"Well, that's good. Thank goodness."

"Pippa, I really have to go."

"Okay. Okay. I'll get to the point," she gushed. "I'm just so excited because the idea hit me, and the plot came together. All at once, like pieces in a puzzle. You know how that happens?" *Not lately,* I thought forlornly, *I don't.* "Anyway, I remembered your mom and aunt are prominent in the art world, and I thought since I'm right here in Louisiana, I could come to Shady Gully and interview them!"

Unbelievable, I thought. She truly was the very definition of extra. I mean, who imposes that way? Outrageous!

"I could meet all the people you're always talking about. Like that ornery Charlie guy at the local eatery…"

At some point, I just quit listening. She wouldn't stop until she got it out of her system. That was Pippa. *Exasperating and extra and maddening.*

My eyes rolled up in my head and I watched, in a trance, as a random Ford Bronco pulled into the parking lot. I glimpsed a pair of high-heeled shoes as they dismounted from the bronco. Then I lifted my gaze higher…to see a mane of raven hair.

And then a curvy body…

A curvy body I recognized at once. A curvy body that looked— and felt—all at once known to me. A curvy body that sent familiar, sharp pangs of hunger throughout my body.

My God, she was beautiful.

Tammy Jo shut the door of the Bronco and slipped her sunglasses off as she moved like a cat toward the Unity Church grounds. When she spotted me leaning against the tree, she smiled. Then waved.

But I had to stop playing the fool. I was done being a doormat.

"…and your mom and sister." Pippa continued to drone on. "I'd love to meet them. Sterling, are you there?"

"Yeah," I grunted, never taking my eyes off Tammy Jo as she got closer.

"So, is it okay if I come?" Pippa wanted to know. "Since I'm kind of…already in Louisiana?"

I smiled at Tammy Jo as I pushed myself away from the tree.

"Sure. Yeah," I told Pippa. "Come." And I gave her the address.

Chapter Thirteen

Pesky Blackmail Business
Timothy

As Meadow and I sat side by side on the biggest, bluest rocking chair I'd ever seen, the bottom of my shoes rustled a lazy rhythm against the porch of Lenny's Tool Shed. I could smell the first pot of coffee brewing somewhere inside the store, its aroma so potent I could practically feel hair growing on my teeth. The sun, painted orange and gold, rose just beyond Shady Gully's cemetery and overlooked the convalescing animals in Violet's pasture on the four-way stop.

"Quite the setting, huh?" I shot Meadow a goofy grin beneath the brim of my new Lenny's Tool Shed ball cap.

She dangled her feet. Relaxed, content. I watched as she giggled, thinking how far she'd come from the shattered woman I'd met three years ago. She was still hard, sarcastic, and decidedly unamused most of the time, but beside me now in the ridiculously large chair sat a woman with…hope.

Guilt stabbed me then, the pain so visceral it parked in the bottom of my stomach, robbing me of the picturesque sunrise in Shady Gully. "What are you doing today?"

She cocked her head and looked at me funny as if she'd known I needed a diversion from my thoughts. "Uncle Wolf and I are going to talk to Anjulie, the artist I was telling you about."

"The pottery lady, who also paints hawks and raccoons and woodsy critters."

"Yes. She was at the funeral."

"She brought flowers."

Meadow cut her eyes at me, surprised. "She did, which says a lot about Granny Lacey because the woman really is something of a hermit. She lives way back in the swamp, like *way* back. Uncle Wolf is going to have to load his four-wheeler into his truck just to get us to her place."

"Wow. I've seen his truck." I raised my eyebrow. "You think it'll make it?"

She chuckled. "I enjoyed hanging out with Petey and Violet last night. Did you?"

"I did." After yesterday's celebration of Granny Lacey, Petey had wanted to talk church, so Meadow and I huddled around the fire with them and toasted marshmallows late into the evening. Admittedly, presenting a good front while maintaining my reputation as an approachable, confident man of faith was challenging. I felt none of those things of late, but Petey, so animated and enthusiastic about the community's growing faith, needed my attention, and fortunately—for now, at least—my calling trumped my feelings.

"He reminds me of you." Meadow tilted her head again, her expression searching. "He has fire in his eyes. Were you like that at thirty?"

I lowered my gaze, playing the part, much as I had done last night. "Absolutely. My faith was strong. I couldn't write my sermons fast enough. I was always on the lookout for lost sheep." All at once, a grotesque, haunting image clouded my mind.

"And now?"

"Sometimes it's hard to tell the difference between a lost lamb and a wolf."

Had I said that aloud? Please God, no. No, no, no.

Meadow pursed her lips, her dark eyebrows angling in confusion. Before she could respond, I asked, "You and Violet seem to get along well."

I registered the flash of resolve as it traveled through her, her posture indicating she'd decided to yield this one. "We hit it off when Luke and Bella married. We're both…odd ducks, I suppose.

Neither of us really fit in, and we refuse to conform. Or we're unable to, I don't know. We just clicked." And just like that, her wounded smile disarmed me, which is why I wasn't prepared for the directness of her next comment. "You don't have to be weird about seeing Father Patrick for counseling. If that's what it is."

Taken aback, my response was more defensive than I intended. "It's just a recharge. It's what we do for one another. Like with Petey last night."

"I don't know. I think Petey lives fully charged, and I suspect he mostly wanted to ask you about preaching at the revival."

Finally, safer territory. "I made notes before I went to bed. I'd love to."

"Timothy, you shouldn't feel pressure, you know? Especially if you're feeling"—she lifted her shoulder—"wounded."

"I'm fine."

"There's talk about you having a breakdown."

"What? Even here in Shady Gully?"

"Especially in Shady Gully. Small towns, you know? Well, and Cruella Claire."

Just then, the squeaky hardware store door pulled our attention away from one another as Lenny scampered out with two smoking mugs of java in his hands. "Here you go." He handed me a coffee. "How do you like those rockers? Some crazy scheme of Micah's to get followers on social media or some such nonsense."

As he turned to offer Meadow a coffee, I wiped the sweat off my brow. *Have mercy. Even Shady Gully wasn't safe.*

I heard Meadow declining Lenny's offer of coffee and his quick response that he'd known she'd refuse so the second mug was actually for him. It all sounded like mumbo-jumbo beneath the roaring in my ears.

"Ricky is bringing you a sweet tea," Lenny explained as the tall, mustached sheriff rolled his Ford F-150—with the department's logo and the word "Sheriff" displayed across the sides—into the parking lot of Lenny's Tool Shed. After he parked, Ricky moseyed up the store's quaint front porch steps and handed

Meadow a bottle of sweet tea. Lenny leaned toward Meadow and whispered conspiratorially, "He said y'all are pals now after hanging out in Lexington."

As they all snorted with laughter, my hearing slowly began to come back. I pressed a grin on my face as Meadow unscrewed the cap on the tea.

Lenny squinted. "That's a good brand. Maybe I ought to carry it here. What's in the bag?" He referred to the paper bag Ricky carried—the one that smelled a lot like cinnamon rolls.

Ricky opened it, teasing all of us with a good whiff. "They're from Sprite's Quick Stop. Apparently, he's got a new vendor. You better watch it, Lenny, or he'll steal your business."

"When he gets pressure washers and PVC pipe I'll start to worry." Lenny reached for the warm pastry and took a hungry bite.

"Are you supposed to be eating that?" Meadow asked him. "I thought Desi had you on a diet?"

"Aw, come on, Meadow," I joshed as I reached for my own cinnamon roll. "You know how it works. What happens at Lenny's Tool Shed…"

"Exactly." Ricky winked, turning to Lenny. "Where's Micah today? Isn't she the one who does the ordering and keeps you current on what's trending?"

"She's at Violet's Vet today. She divides her time, as you know, but you're right, she's got an instinct for retail, even if she's a bit indecisive in other ways…" His sudden stare drew everyone's attention toward Hoot Wheeler, who steered his oversized dark blue truck toward the rear of the store.

"I'll say," Meadow quipped.

Hoot stuck his tanned, muscular arm out the window, lowering his shades just enough to make eye contact with Lenny. "I need some 2 x 4s. I'll get them loaded and then come in to settle up."

Lenny nodded, and they all waited until they heard the truck's big engine quiet to a stop in the back. When Lenny let out a big sigh, Ricky asked him directly, "How's Desi doing?"

"About like you'd expect." Lenny glanced at me; his expression unsettled. "Tom's probably wanting her forgiveness for what he did to her when she was in high school, but it's easier said than done."

"It's the hardest thing to do," I told Lenny, thinking I was a shameless hypocrite, "but once Tom passes, it'll be too late, and she might regret it later."

"Well, it's up to her. I'll support whatever she decides." Lenny wadded up the pastry wrapper. "But I won't be doing any forgiving, I'll tell you that."

"Think hard, Lenny," Meadow said softly. "I'm here to tell you it's the first step in letting go of a bad thing that happened to you."

There was a sharp smack of silence as everyone on the porch knew Meadow's past, the bad thing that had been done to her, and how she'd held that hostility so close for nearly three decades it nearly destroyed her.

The moment was interrupted by an intense, almost guttural huffing and puffing, followed by a gasp and a heave as Father Patrick *walked* into the parking lot of Lenny's Tool Shed.

"Good grief," Ricky exclaimed. "Did you walk all the way from the church, Father?"

Meadow grimaced. "Even more concerning is that warm-up suit you're wearing."

I stood, moving to give the luminous priest my seat next to Meadow. "I remember those. They're from the eighties."

"It looks like foil." Sheriff Rick slipped his shades on, bewildered. "You want a taffy? I got a banana one right here."

"No, thank you, Sheriff." Father Patrick lowered himself into the giant rocking chair with a ragged breath. "And that's the point of these suits. They're supposed to make you sweat." When Meadow offered him her tea, he passed. "I can't have sugar, my dear, so unfortunately, no taffy or tea for me, but thank you."

As Lenny hopped up to get a bottled water from inside the store, Ricky eyed Father Patrick and me. "I heard the two of you were having a little powwow today." After Meadow's revelation that Shady Gully was chin-wagging about my supposed break-down, I tugged my cap lower on my forehead.

"That we are," Father Patrick stated matter-of-factly. "Nothing quite like swapping pastor stories."

"Sounds like fun," Ricky said dubiously. "Y'all ought to take a ride to Lake Osprey. Robin said she had the lake house all cleaned up and y'all are welcome."

"That sounds divine." Father Patrick glanced at me. "Perhaps tomorrow? Since I already have big plans for us at Sacred Heart today."

"Sure." I shrugged obligingly, even as my coffee dipped like a tilt-a-world inside my belly.

"I think it would be good for you." Meadow glinted at me. "It's a nice place to unwind. You should spend the night there tonight. Especially if Robin had it specially cleaned."

Meadow was worried about me. Maybe she'd even begun to doubt me, to see me as weak. It seemed my hard-earned façade was wearing off.

As soon as Lenny brought the bottled water, Father Patrick heaved himself out of the massive blue rocking chair. "Mind if we walk?" he asked me. "I need to get my steps in."

✝✝✝

Even though his reddish-gray hair was plastered to the side of his bulbous head with sweat, Father Patrick pushed on, some-how (miraculously?) pumping his chubby legs one in front of the other at a brisk, determined pace.

"Slow down, Padre," I teased. "I can't keep up with you."

He flicked his wristband. "Half a mile to go, Timothy. We can do it, come on."

Genetics had made me tall, skinny, and slightly uncoordinated, but still, I should be better at keeping up with an overweight, aging priest. But the old rascal had the heart of a champion and the faith of a mustard seed, and my bony legs wobbled like rubber.

"Hurry along, Timothy. We're almost there now." He lifted

his thumb toward a country road we'd just zipped past. "That's Opry Lane. It leads to a nice, established subdivision with cleverly named roads like Waylon, Willie, and my personal favorite, The Boys."

"That's…that's…cute," I gasped. "Geez man, are you on diet pills?" I leaned over, dropping my lanky arms to rest on my thighs in an attempt to catch my breath.

"No. Are you?" He stopped, his eyes brightening. "Do they work?"

I managed a weak chuckle. "I have no idea. How old are you?"

"Never mind. Pills are just another crutch. They won't solve anything. And to answer your question, I'm sixty-three."

"What's going on with you?" I managed to stand and place my hands on my hips. "Is this part of my counseling? Your plan is to tear me down and build me back up? Like boot camp?"

"Oh heavens, no. I'm just trying to get myself in shape. I've let myself go, grown complacent, lazy even." He patted my back, urging me on.

As we walked at a more leisurely pace, my breathing returned to normal.

"I did decide to come clean with you, though," he said. "To expose myself, sins and all, in hopes that you'd find it easier to share your story with me." When I looked at him curiously, he explained. "Gluttony is a sin, and I'm a sinner."

"As am I."

"It took a pint-sized boy with the weight of the world on him to show me how I'd been living, and he did it…" Father Patrick's voice grew thick "…because he cared. Because he's good." He tapped his heart with his fist. "In here."

"I'm guessing you're talking about young Fireman."

"The one and only. And my goal is to honor his act of kindness and not squander the good I can do for others. I simply must get myself together."

"I've always thought you were the very epitome of together, Father." I cleared my throat as a swell of emotion pulsed through my suddenly very exhausted and uncomfortable body. "Of all the Godly people I've met, including ministers, clergymen, and saved sinners alike, you're the one I called when things became… untenable."

As we closed in on Sacred Heart Catholic Church, he nodded his appreciation. "Let's get to work then." Fortitude glinted in his eyes. "What say you?"

✝✝✝

Twenty minutes later, after Father Patrick had poured us each a Thermos of water and prepared a dish of carrot sticks, celery, and broccoli served with low-fat Ranch dressing and hummus, we settled into the front pew of Sacred Heart Catholic Church. I watched solemnly as he murmured a prayer and genuflected, and then turned to me with a celery stalk tucked into the corner of his mouth. He reminded me at that moment of an Irish gangster, skulking around a smoky card table and looking particularly smug as he had a royal flush tucked into his chubby hand. "How did you get to this point, Timothy?"

Okay. Not at all what I expected. When he handed me a carrot stick, I surprised myself by taking a bite.

"You told me a little about your troubled beginning, which is tragic, sordid, and heartbreaking, but what would lead someone to use it as fodder for blackmail? Clearly, you were a child, a victim, for heaven's sake, and bear no blame."

I chewed my carrot. "You know how they say, it's not the crime, but the cover-up?"

"Ah."

"I've never talked publicly about my…childhood, for lack of a better term. I've managed to keep my past vague, because I eventually made it out of that heroin den—"

"—when your mother died."

"Yes, and I hitchhiked my way out of Saint Louis and never looked back. Eventually, I ended up at College of the Ozarks in Point Lookout, Missouri, and the rest, as they say, is history."

The amused priest laughed and brushed his vegetable fingers along the leg of his shiny warmups. And then he nodded. "I see." But I could see that he was no longer amused, and perhaps, never had been.

"Yes," I said flatly, reaching for some broccoli.

"So, whoever is blackmailing you could be anyone with a Polaroid from that godforsaken drug den, or someone you encountered between then and College of the Ozarks, where I presume you blossomed into the charismatic preacher you are today." He smirked, his expression wry. Definitely *not* amused.

"It's free, you know. At COFO. They don't charge tuition for full-time students. They have the—"

"The student work program. I'm aware. They don't call it Hard Work U for nothing." He studied me for a long moment, forcing me to look away. "I have so many questions. Like, how old were you when you…er…hitchhiked your way to freedom?"

"Ten or eleven. I don't remember exactly."

"And did you live on the streets?" When I didn't respond he dragged a ragged breath from his barrel chest. "Timothy, how can I help you if you won't talk to me?"

"I *am* talking to you."

"You're answering direct questions as if this were an interrogation. I want you to really talk to me. It's just us. I'm on your side."

I folded the uneaten broccoli into a napkin and drank heavily from the Thermos.

"Let's start at the beginning. At the arch. Where you ended up with your mother."

I took my time screwing the lid back onto the Thermos. "I remember being hungry. *Ravenously* hungry. I lived with—or endured—an insatiable appetite that couldn't be quenched. I honestly think that was my first childhood memory." I locked eyes with the priest. "My mother had a ravenous appetite as well."

"For drugs."

"Yes, painkillers like Percocet or Vicodin at first, and then crack and heroin later. Whatever she could get, really. And then she graduated to morphine at some point. At the end."

"How did she maintain her habit?"

Anger sparked inside me then as I realized he was going to make me say it. "How do you think?" I sighed, frustration building to a crescendo inside me. I sat back in the pew, folded my arms, and focused on Jesus, crucified on the cross at the head of the church. "She prostituted herself, Father. She did whatever she had to do to get her next fix and trust me, her fix was always more important than me—"

"Timothy—"

"No, you wanted me to talk," I barked testily. "Now I'm going to talk."

"Okay." He looked contrite, but also a little victorious.

"I saw her debase herself over and over, just so she could get enough of the drug to obliterate her reality. It was…all-consuming for her. It was her god."

"She was an—"

"She was *weak*," I emphasized, my voice thick with disgust, devoid of even a shred of compassion. "Besides the arch and the hunger, I also remember—very clearly—the horrible, sinking moment when I realized I was totally alone. Because of her weakness, *everything* was on *me*. That's an unbearable concept for a little kid to grasp…"

I despised the resentment filling my spirit, the heaviness pushing at the corners of my eyes. I was upset with Father Patrick for making me revisit the past. I hated having to think about it, to voice it aloud. The words themselves taunted me. The telling cloyed at me. Threatened to drag me back into the depths of that nightmare.

I clenched my fists, suddenly desperate to strike out at something. Anything.

Although fury drove my tears, my hands remained impotent, and I sat…paralyzed in my rage. "Completely alone, I was left to fight off predators of all kinds, and sometimes, I felt that my mother was one of them. Perhaps the worst of them."

Visibly shaken, Father Patrick handed me a tissue, then took one for himself.

From some twisted corner of my psyche, I took pleasure in his faltering. *He asked for it,* I thought, the victory making me salty. "But it's all in the past now."

"It is, yes, other than that pesky blackmail business, of course," he said gruffly. "But yes, look at you now. You're one of the country's most successful pastors."

I said nothing, suspicious of where he was leading.

He bent his eyebrows, deep in contemplation. "Or do you relate more with that scared, hungry little boy?"

I winced.

The sly priest pressed. "The boy? Or the pastor?"

I studied him for several seconds, trying to intuit his angle. "I'm the pastor of Northlake Christian Church in Kentucky. That's who I am."

Father Patrick focused on the vegetables and toyed with the hummus before switching gears. "I understand Petey asked you to speak at Unity Christian Church's revival this weekend."

"He did." Suddenly ravenous, I used a piece of celery like a spoon, digging it into the hummus like a bulldozer.

"I know you're angry with me right now, but I would urge you not to do it. I don't think it would be…helpful."

I chewed noisily. "I've already made notes. The sermon is practically written." Once again, he held my gaze for so long I was forced to lower my eyes. Eventually, I shrugged. "You can read my notes if you want. I'll email them to you."

Like a swinging pendulum, my phone vibrated in my pocket. I didn't even have to look. *I just knew.* After reading the text, I matched Father Patrick's sharp gaze, then handed him my phone.

Tick-Tock. What will you do?

Fiery at Best, Explosive at Worst
Fireman

When the crazy hermit lady arrived at Granny's, I wanted to raise my hands in the air like the Christians and shout, *Praise the Lord!* Finally, I had a moment to myself without Wolfheart hovering over me asking if I wanted to talk, or if I needed anything, or if I wanted to go toss a fishing line in the creek. I didn't want any of those things. I simply wanted to be left alone to soak up some peace and quiet.

If I'd known he and Meadow were going to set up camp here at Granny's I'd have gone to school. At least there I could have tuned everyone out and remained invisible as usual.

Thankfully, my two bodyguards were on the porch now sipping tea with Anjulie, the odd bird who lived in the Black Lands, an isolated area even deeper in the swamp than The Creek. The reclusive woman had probably never received so much attention and was likely spinning with confusion and uncertainty. And clearly fear, as she was practically curled into herself on the rocking chair, her long hair hiding much of her face.

"Your work is exquisite," Wolfheart said in a voice I didn't recognize. "Why not share it with the world?"

Since the window was open, I could hear their entire conversation, which was fine because I didn't have to answer back or participate in any way, and the screen allowed the crisp, fall air into Granny's house.

My house. Hard to believe I was a homeowner now. Didn't matter that it was a mere shanty. It had plumbing, gas, electric, and window units for AC. Of course, Wolfheart was chomping at the bit to get me to move in with him permanently, but I wasn't going to do it. Not that I didn't like him more than most, I just valued my independence.

I had a car. I had a job. And now, I had a house. I would be fine on my own.

"Perhaps, I could agree to that," Anjulie said in a flowy voice that matched her skirt and blouse. "But I wouldn't want to be… on site. Or to travel."

"Robin and Desi are fine with that." The sound of tea being poured drifted through the window. And what was up with Meadow's voice? She actually sounded…agreeable. "While we'd love for you to be there occasionally and meet the patrons, we certainly understand your reticence about travel."

"And later, if you wanted to try to attend a showing, perhaps I could go with you?" It was Wolfheart again. "We could drive if you didn't want to fly." *Was he flirting?* Curious what a flirty Wolfheart looked like, I risked a peek out the window, and sure enough, he was a little googly-eyed. *Whoa.* I blinked several times, trying to get the picture out of my head.

Eventually, I tuned their boring conversation out, focusing instead on another of Granny's storage boxes. I used to think Granny was a packrat, but now I was convinced she was a hoarder. Some of the boxes I'd gone through had nothing in them except used Kleenex, broken hangers, and ancient, rotary style telephones. When I'd shown them to Wolfheart, he suggested I keep the phones, *for nostalgia's sake.* Whatever that meant. Looked like junk to me.

Finally, I opened a box full of cookbooks, some dating back years ago. I recognized my own childhood doodles sketched onto the pages alongside Granny's illegible scrawl. Actual ingredients had been scratched out in many cases, replaced with Granny's own interpretation of the recipe. Phrases like, "add lots of sugar" or "bake until six o'clock" were dotted throughout the pages, as were my drawings of Granny. Granny with her hair sticking out in all directions. Granny with a soiled apron. Granny with her glasses askew. Granny confused. Granny smiling. Granny on a horse. Granny on a treadmill.

I snorted, chuckling at the images, at the way my world had always revolved around Granny. As far back as I could remember, it had always been me and Granny. I'd never known my parents, and since she'd refused to talk about them, I assumed they were dead. I had a feeling my father was her son, but didn't know for sure, and never pressed, because truly I didn't care. As long as I had Granny, they were irrelevant. I wanted for nothing, and no one—other than her.

As I traced my finger along an especially creative sketch of Granny, my vision grew hazy. Granny wore a straw hat as she paddled a boat through the kitchen on her way to the stove. I'd greatly exaggerated her arthritic hands as well as the size of the catfish dangling from her fishing pole. Apparently, I'd had a flair for smoke and heat even then because the cast iron pot waiting on the stove looked fiery at best, explosive at worst.

Squinting, I tried to read what she'd written above my drawing.

The screen *rat-tat-tatted* against the frame of the door as Meadow and Wolfheart meandered inside. "What are you looking at?" Wolfheart asked. *Here we go again*, I thought, already missing my quiet time.

"Nothing. I found Granny's cookbooks. Or some of them anyway." I shook my head. "But her handwriting was as bad as her cooking."

"Let's see." He pulled his glasses from the collar of his long-sleeved cotton shirt and held the cookbook at a distance. And then closer. Closer still. "It's a scripture. Looks like Matthew 4:19."

Losing interest, I mumbled, "I suppose you know what that means right off the top of your head."

"It's when Jesus tells Peter and Andrew to follow Him, and he'd make them fishers of men."

"That doesn't even make sense."

"Sure, it does. He's calling them to discipleship. And they have so much faith in him they—"

"—throw away their nets and give up their businesses." When Meadow piped up to finish his sentence, something passed between them I didn't recognize. Wolfheart looked pleased, and surprisingly Meadow seemed pleased that he was pleased.

Great. I inwardly rolled my eyes, deciding right then and there that if Meadow turned into a Bible Thumper, I'd give it all up. "Where's your boyfriend?"

She shrugged, trying a little too hard to appear indifferent. "Hanging out with Father Patrick." The way she and Wolfheart exchanged glances made me wonder about the pastor, who was one righteous dude despite the way I'd picked on him when I drove him to Father Patrick's house. Even though he was old, his tattoos were cool, and heck, everybody fainted once in a while, right?

"So how did it go with the hermit lady?"

"Don't call her that," Meadow snipped.

"She's actually a very nice woman." Wolfheart inspected some of the cookbooks in Granny's box. "And an amazing artist."

As I studied the most beloved and honorable man on The Creek, I detected a little masking on his part as well. And these two were worried about *me?* "I think you like her, which is good since she's old like you."

"You think everyone is old." He ignored me, flipping through pages in Granny's recipe book. "But yeah, sixty-one is a long ways from being a spring chicken." When his eyes skewered me with green devils, guilt puddled in my gut.

"Oh, there's plenty of time for love," Meadow chipped. "And still lots of available ladies out there. *Available* being the key-word." She arched a brow at her uncle. "I wonder if Anjulie has ever been married."

"She hasn't," I said as I returned a cookbook to the box. When they looked at me curiously, I explained. "Remember the brushfires a couple of years ago? I do because I'd just started volunteering at the fire stations and we had to drive around and warn people in the surrounding areas. Miss Anjulie wouldn't even let Redflyer or Moonpipe in, but she let me in. And she gave me a cookie."

Wolfheart considered me, all in now.

"She had this big building in the back of her place, and I helped her move some of her jars and stuff while they were putting out the fire down the road. She seemed more worried about those jars—"

"Pottery," Meadow corrected.

"—than with her house. Anyway, she had a few pictures of some old people, like, older than her, and some dogs and cats and stuff. She said they were her parents, and she didn't have a husband. Anything else y'all want to know?"

"Nope, I'm good." Meadow winked at me, making me feel included in the fun of baiting Wolfheart. When he didn't bite, she moved into the kitchen and went about setting the tea paraphernalia in its proper place. She opened the refrigerator. "I think I'm going to clean this stuff out."

"Why?"

"Because it's spoiling." Her upper lip slanted in disgust when she sniffed a gallon of milk. "And you can't stay here by yourself," she said over her shoulder as she washed the milk down the sink.

"Why can't I? I'd be fine."

Wolfheart let out an exaggerated sigh. "It's not that simple. There are legalities involved, Fireman, and you're underage."

"About that," I started. "I have a plan." I sat on the couch, gesturing for him to join me.

"Let's hear it." Wolfheart smiled like a coyote coaxing an old dog to come out and play.

I cleared my throat, deepening my voice to sound more assertive. "Let's be reasonable. I mean, we all know I'm capable of taking care of myself. How about I check in with you every morning and every night?"

"That could work, and I think it's a step in the right direction, but how are you going to keep the lights on?" I didn't like where this was going. "Do you have a checking account?"

"No, you know I don't, but I have lots of money saved up. And I know there's more than just electricity. There's water. Gas." I tapped them out on my fingers but got stuck when I couldn't think of any others off the top of my head. "And other stuff."

"Fireman." Wolfheart finally sat, perching on the coffee table with his elbows resting on his thighs. "It's not the money. I will take care of all of that. We'll keep your Granny's house up—"

"My house."

"Your house. That's right." He glanced at Meadow as she came to sit on a chair adjacent to the couch. *Great, now they are going to double-team me.* "We'll keep it up and it will be ready for you when you're eighteen. I was even thinking we could make some improvements. Maybe add a carport to keep your Impala out of the weather. Fix the roof. Some new paint. Put in some new flooring."

"It's not fair," I said through gritted teeth, even as tears pushed at the corners of my eyes. "I can do all of that. I do stuff for everybody all the time. Who do you think did everything around here? Who do you think kept Granny from burning the house down?"

"You did. I know that, son."

"You're the best kid I know," Meadow added, "and very capable, but it's just not safe for you to be out here alone."

"I'm a man! I can take care of myself!" But even as I shouted the words, the wetness on my cheeks betrayed me.

"You *are* a man. One of the best I've ever known." Wolfheart spoke with emotion. "I mean that sincerely, Fireman. But I'd really, really like you to come live with me. That way you could keep saving your money. Just think of what you could do with it when you graduate from high school. You could go to college. You could go to trade school. You could build a brand-new house in Shady Gully."

"I'm going to live on The Creek."

"Well, you could build one here. As you said, you own this

land." He squeezed my knee. "It just makes sense. And besides, I could use the company."

"I don't want charity."

Meadow glanced at her uncle. "Oh, I'm sure he could find things for you to do. To earn your keep, if that's what you're worried about."

"I could definitely use help feeding my tribe of critters." Wolfheart grinned, the lines rising like half-moons around his eyes. "And think how happy Black and Blue would be."

I swiped at a tear, my heart pounding with anger and… something else…

Tears gradually rolled down my cheeks, and when my vision blurred to the point I couldn't see, I dropped my head and covered my cries by folding into myself. I was aware of Meadow's body moving alongside me on the couch and Wolfheart's increased pressure on my knee. Even though I felt cared for and protected, I was angry. I wanted to scream…but all I could do was cry.

Where was Granny now? Was she in the ground? In some pit of never-ending darkness? Could she see me? If she could see me, couldn't she come back?

Why couldn't she come back?

I wanted my old life with my Granny! Everything had changed. Nothing was the same. The roads and the trees looked different. The sun and the moon looked different. The feelings in my tummy felt different. Looking in the mirror felt different.

I didn't like it! It was all wrong!

My body suddenly went limp, and I surrendered to my grief. Meadow and Wolfheart stayed with me like that on the couch for a long time, where I at last broke down and wept unashamedly.

Sometime later, with my eyes swollen into slits and my body weary from the somewhat cathartic crying jag, a vibration from my pocket drew the three of us back to real-time. "It's Micah," I mumbled. "I'd better take it."

"I'll say," Meadow remarked. "Talk about inventing drama." Wolfheart gave her a stark look as I answered my phone.

"Fireman, I'm sorry to bother you," she huffed. "I know it's a bad time, but…I'm freaking out!"

"What's wrong?" I eyed Wolfheart and Meadow, who undoubtedly could hear Micah's frantic words through the phone.

"It's Bubba and that blasted monster snake of his! Violet is off campus today birthing a calf, and when Bubba brought that danged python in…" she panted, "I was super busy at the front desk. I told him…" Her voice faded as her panic mounted.

"Micah," I said, my voice still hoarse from crying, "take a breath. You remember how I taught you?" I found myself breathing in and out along with her. "One more time. Now, tell me what happened."

"It's gone, Fireman!" She squealed as the sudden CRASH of the phone brought us all up short. "Oh my gosh, I just thought I felt it slither across my leg, but no…thank God." She gulped. "Anyway, I told Bubba to go put him in the back with the other patients, and he said he did, and then he left. But…I just went back there…and the tote is empty. The lid is off, and I can't find the snake anywhere! Not that I want to. Violet is going to kill me. And what if the beast…eats someone? I don't know what to do! I called Daddy, but he didn't answer. I think he and Sterling went fishing and are out of range. Max and Quietdove are on the way, but they were in Toulouse so it will be forty-five minutes or longer."

I skirted from around Meadow and Wolfheart's protective sphere. "I'm on my way."

"Thank you! Oh gosh, I think I'm going to lose my job, Fireman. Hurry."

Meadow stood, her eyes flitting in a wicked dance as I disconnected the call. "Well, this will be fun."

Wolfheart snorted, hauling himself up as well. "I guess we are all on our way."

"I'm driving." I grabbed my keys from Granny's beloved

green ashtray, the one she'd bought not because she smoked but because she liked its peanut shape. "And I don't want to hear y'all telling me to slow down. This is an emergency. And remember," I cut my eyes at Wolfheart, "I haven't said yes yet."

A wide grin spread across Meadow's face. "Oh, and let me tell you, there's a long list of people who've reached out. Everybody wants you, kid. You are Mr. Popular around Shady Gully." She pumped her thumb at Wolfheart, encouraging me. "You should definitely make him work for it." She searched for her purse. "I'm kind of excited to see the snake. I hope we find it."

I'd already made it to my car and into the driver's seat before the two of them finally puttered out of the house with their water bottles, phones, and whatnot. I honked. "Come on!"

Meadow stretched out in the backseat while Wolfheart rode shotgun. Thankfully, neither offered a running commentary on my driving, so the trip went smoothly. Right up until we got to the Unity Bridge and passed Unity Christian Church.

"Do you think Violet would really fire her own sister-in-law?" Meadow wondered.

"Doubtful," Wolfheart replied. "But she'll light a fire under her. I doubt it ever happens again."

"Violet's pretty serious." I nodded in agreement. "I wouldn't put it past her. Besides, it's not like Micah doesn't have other jobs."

"I love her. Violet, I mean." Meadow stared out the window, her lips curving upward. "She's my kind of gal."

"I think I'm going to talk to her about getting extra hours helping out at the vet." I glanced at Wolfheart for a reaction, but he was reading from his phone, a grim line set on his face. "So," I eyed Meadow through the rear-view mirror, "who all invited me to live with them?"

"Everybody. Let's see. How about Bella and Luke?"

"Nah. I kinda still have a crush on Bella, so that would be awkward." Wolfheart, amused, lifted his gaze from his phone. "But on the other hand, I'd get to hang out with Duke and Duchess, so that would be awesome. Who else?"

"Petey and Violet?"

"They're a little intense. Next?"

"Quietdove?"

"Too boring."

"Desi and Lenny have really campaigned."

"They're too old." When Wolfheart grunted in response, I added, "But they're in the top tier."

"Sigourney Sky?"

"The dress lady? Pass."

Meadow leaned across her seat, poking her head between Wolfheart and me. "How about me?"

"No way. You're too grumpy."

We all laughed as the gravel converted to black top and we entered Shady Gully proper. "Father Patrick asked about it as well."

I nodded, saying nothing at first. "He might make me go to church."

"Well, that would be horrible, wouldn't it?" Wolfheart said sarcastically.

Meadow popped her head over Wolfheart's shoulder. "Who are you texting?"

"Desi." He brooded, unsettled. "The nursing home called. They're telling her that Tom isn't going to make it too much longer. They want her to come soon."

"Where's Lenny?" Meadow's tone was gruff. "What's he say?"

"I guess he's at the lake with Sterling, like Micah said."

I focused squarely on the road, trying to make myself invisible. Over the years I'd been privy to more than my fair share of Shady Gully's biggest secrets and scandals, mostly because adults tended to think of me as one of them—or else they felt so comfortable they dismissed my presence entirely. Either way, I'd gleaned enough to know that Desi's stepdad, Tom, had taken liberties with her when she was in high school. Obviously Wolfheart, as her friend, was agitated because she was having to revisit the nasty ordeal at this stage in her life.

Theirs had to be one of the most unlikely friendships ever, as by all accounts, Wolfheart had been a hoodlum back in the day. But as he liked to say, he got right with the Lord and mellowed as he got older, and now he was quite close with Robin, Lenny, and Desi. But especially Desi.

"What are you telling her?" asked Meadow.

"I'm not. It's not my place."

"What *would* you tell her if it were your place?"

Tension ricocheted within the confines of my Impala as Wolfheart considered his answer. "I'd tell her she should go. She should forgive him because that would be the right thing to do."

As we approached the four-way stop, it was clear that total chaos had erupted at Violet's Vet.

"But I wouldn't mean a word of it," Wolfheart muttered.

Chapter Fifteen

Bench of Shame
Sterling

Osprey Lake in November was as soothing as a rolling hill-side in Kentucky and as mesmerizing as a sunset in Santa Fe. While each contained a singular beauty all its own, combined they were a testament to God's infinite works of art.

Moving quietly, Uncle Lenny baited his hook with a cricket and launched a long, pointed cast off the dock behind the lake house.

"Nice," I whispered.

"Did you see that white perch pop over there?"

"Yup. Luke told me they were biting."

"It's the cool weather. They like that." He grinned, joy meeting his eyes.

I'd never had a better fishing partner than Uncle Lenny. Mom thought it gross; Micah thought it cruel; and Dad had, frankly, been terrible at it. I chuckled in memory of his haphazard casts and the way they repeatedly got caught in the limbs of cypress trees.

"I miss him too." Uncle Lenny tugged a little on his line. *How did he know?* "It's hard not to think about him whenever I'm out here. He built this place. Well, not physically, but you know what I mean."

We laughed as I recollected. "He wasn't coordinated enough to ever build a house himself, and he wasn't athletic, but he was determined to eventually catch a fish."

"I don't think he ever did." Uncle Lenny's fishing line faced a little resistance when he tugged again. "Truth be told, I don't think he really cared, but he enjoyed the process. And the kidding."

"We used to pick on him about how clumsy he was."

"He was probably the most ungraceful person I ever knew." Uncle Lenny laughed. "That's why in school he opted to keep the stats while Ricky and I were out on the football field. But your dad had many other talents." He wound his reel in, securing a nice sized white perch on the line. "Not bad."

I watched as Uncle Lenny gently removed the hook from the fish's mouth and tossed it back into the lake, sending it on its way.

"You ever catch the same one twice?"

He hee-hawed. "I usually put 'em in the ice chest and bring 'em home for Desi to fry." He bent his brows together. "You reckon we ought to save 'em for Timothy? Robin said he was going to stay here tonight."

"I can't imagine Timothy frying up a batch of fish, even if he was in top form."

I twined my reel in tight, pulling in a decent white perch of my own. Uncle Lenny grabbed the fishing string, unhooked the fish, and then returned it to Lake Osprey. "Wouldn't want you to get your writing fingers bitten off."

"By a perch?"

"Probably not. But a catfish? You'd better get 911 on speed dial."

We laughed easily together, leaning back in our lawn chairs and fishing, but not *really* fishing. I was as relaxed as I'd been in ages. The funny thing about Shady Gully was the way it felt more like home than anywhere else. I was born in Texas, enjoyed a fun childhood in Kentucky, attended college in North Carolina, and traveled all over the country as an adult…but Shady Gully was home to me. Every time I was here, I wondered why I didn't just settle down, but then I'd leave and get busy with the labor of living, and those feelings would wane. How was it possible that such strong feelings could fade so easily?

Then I'd find myself another year later on a floating dock on a beautiful lake, setting fish free with one of my favorite people. What was I doing? I was twenty-eight years old, for crying out loud, I really needed to figure myself out.

"You oughta come down here by yourself sometime, Sterling. You could sit up there on the porch of that nice lake house and write the next great American novel."

If only it were that easy. "It feels like you're reading my mind sometimes, Uncle Lenny. It's kind of creepy."

He chuckled, amused as he cast leisurely into the lake. "I hate to tell you this, son, but you have tells." He side-eyed me. "That and your mama is worried about you. You know what your mama and Desi do when they get together, huh? They talk all day long, pausing only long enough to stretch, go to the bathroom, eat a bite, and then they simply move to another room and repeat the process. All. Day. Long."

"It's baffling, isn't it?"

"The damnedest thing I've ever seen." He tugged, reeled in. "Point being, I can't help hearing some of their chitchat, even if I don't want to. You look great, sharp as ever, but I gotta know, are you happy?"

I used my foot to drag the ice chest closer. Pulled out two beers and handed him one. "Have one, I won't tell Aunt Desi." I lifted my eyebrows playfully. "What do you know? I can read minds too."

He snorted, then popped the top and took a long sip.

"I'm okay, Uncle Lenny. I've got my paying job at Northlake, and that's swell, but I'm trying to…I don't know…make something of myself. I have a lot to say." I tapped my chest. "I want so badly to express myself. That's what Mom always says." I took a swig of beer. "And Dad always said I had a great imagination. You put those two together and—"

"—you have a writer."

"I'm trying." I flashed him a wolfish smile. "Like a hamster on a wheel."

"You can do it, son. Hang around here long enough…" He *tsked.*

"You can't make this kind of crazy up." His big breath seemed to draw the oxygen out of the air. "You've got plenty of time to find your place, Sterling. Same thing I tell Micah. But your mama and Desi, they worry about all of us. It's what they do."

"How is Aunt Desi? I heard her stepdad isn't doing well. Were they close?"

Uncle Lenny bit down hard on his lip. "A lot of people around Shady Gully assume things. Very few people know the truth. But I can tell you for sure that they were *not* close. At all."

I said nothing. Waited.

"He molested her when she was a young girl. But it was way more than that really. He stole her innocence. He killed her spirit. Caused a lifelong kerfuffle with her mama." Uncle Lenny shrugged, his face reddening. "Heck, you could even say he was the reason Sunny overdosed. Or committed suicide." He jerked his shoulders. "Either way. He was—*he is*—a monster, and now that he's about to meet his maker he wants to summon her to the foot of his bed so he can impress the Lord. The gall."

"Whoa." I set my beer on the dock because my hands were unsteady. "I had no idea. Does my mom know?"

"She does, but Desi didn't tell her until years later after your daddy died."

"Wow. Poor Aunt Desi." I cocked my head. "And poor you. That must have been hard."

"There's not a day that goes by that I don't want to throttle that pervert, Sterling. I know that's wrong, but I truly feel that everything that hurts Desi's heart stems from that trauma. Now that I've got some years on me, I can see it more clearly, and it angers me in a deeper way than it did when I was young."

The revelation staggered me. It was like finding out you were adopted, or you had a sibling you never knew about, or some other shocking discovery about the one thing you were an expert on—yourself.

"What are you going to do?"

"I'll do whatever Desi wants to do—physically. If she wants

to go and talk to him, I'll go through the motions, be by her side, but…" He trailed off. "We're supposed to talk to the Holy Men tomorrow—about forgiveness—so maybe that will help."

"The Holy Men?"

"That's what your mama and Desi are calling Father Patrick and Timothy these days. Something to do with their podcast." Uncle Lenny sighed in bemusement. "Anyway, I reckon there's power in numbers, so I'll go and have a listen to what they have to say."

After a few moments, I admitted, "I'm embarrassed to even confess this now, but I had almost convinced myself that your generation had it made and that it was mine and Micah's generation who were especially burdened. I arrogantly presumed the trials and pressures we suffered were unique and so much more complex than yours…" I ducked my head in humiliation. "When I say it out loud it reeks of arrogance and self-importance."

"I think every generation feels that way. I felt the same about my parents." Classic Uncle Lenny, quick to let me off the hook. *That's why it was always so easy being honest with him.*

"Well, I'm ashamed." I picked up my beer. "Y'all seem so happy when you get together with your classmates. The way you cut up and laugh with one another, it's just hard to imagine y'all ever had a bad day. Like you, Uncle Lenny. Did you struggle with anything then?"

"You bet I did. Lots of things. But I reckon my biggest trouble was fighting for Desi. Quite literally, sometimes."

"What? I can't imagine Aunt Desi ever loving anybody but you."

"Oh, there was one. He's still around. Bee-bops around town. Big belt buckle. Cowboy hat. Currently dating Dolly of the Diva Dome."

I thought. "The singer guy with the boots? Adam?" Shock and disbelief rippled through me for the second time in a span of five minutes.

"That's the one." He turned to me. "You know, your own mama wasn't immune to hardships either. You should be aware of that, tuck it away for when you get annoyed with her."

"Tell me. Please."

Uncle Lenny had pretty much given up on fishing at this point. He leaned back and took a long pull from his beer. "Robin was fragile in a way that Desi was tough. She had insecurities. Big ones. It was…tough for women then. In the eighties, anything less than perfect was unacceptable, and I guess, to hear them talk about it, the bar kept moving. Anyway, I don't think she ever felt worthy."

Stricken, I let that wash over me, sad suddenly for the young girl who felt ostracized at school, for the young woman who raised twins alone while her executive husband traveled, and for the grown woman who lost both parents in a car accident. *What more didn't I know?* All this time I'd thought my mother had led a pampered life of affluence.

Self-important much?

When Uncle Lenny hauled himself up and started rattling around, I followed suit. As he finished his beer and stuffed the can into the garbage, I packed up the rods and reels and set the remaining crickets free at the foot of a cypress tree in front of the house.

Patting me on the shoulder, Uncle Lenny suggested with a playful smile, "After that conversation, I propose a ride around Shady Gully."

"Your favorite pastime." I nudged him mischievously. "I'm in."

"We'll go the long way, what do you say? We'll drive along the lake and circle back through The Creek, make our way into Shady Gully proper, and have a cheeseburger at the Cozy Corner."

"Sounds like a plan."

†††

We'd just crossed through the drivable part of the Black Lands and entered the outskirts of The Creek when Uncle Lenny surprised me for the third time that day.

"So, what's with this girl coming to talk to your mama and Desi? What's her name? Piper? Penny?" Uncle Lenny's cap was on backwards, the windows were open, and his arm rested comfortably on the door frame of his truck. He was in his happy place. And he was comfortable in his own skin, despite the fact that much to my sadness, his middle-aged paunch had expanded, his once bright hazel eyes had dulled a tad, and his hairline had thinned.

"It's Pippa. And she's…" I shook my head, searching for the right words. "She's exasperating."

Uncle Lenny processed, his face unreadable.

"I met her at a writer's conference a while back. She lives in Santa Fe, New Mexico."

"Really? That's where Desi's originally from, you know? Her dad lived there until he died."

"Yeah, that's right." I'd actually forgotten that nugget. "Well, Pippa"—I shook my head again—"she goes to all of the conferences. She is the quintessential networker. She makes friends everywhere."

"You say that like it's a bad thing."

"She's just…a lot. She's always sending me pages, wanting to know what I think. She's always after me to send her my stuff."

"Have you ever done that?"

"Actually, I have, and she's pretty good at spotting things, offering constructive ideas on what's not working."

"Again, you say that like it's a bad thing."

As we crossed the Unity Bridge and passed Unity Christian Church, Uncle Lenny waved at Thaddeus and Youngdeer who milled about the parking lot. The two grinned broadly as they returned my uncle's customary wave.

"We do well work-wise," I continued, "but she has a lot of energy and is kind of all over the place. She drives me crazy." I flipped my hat backwards like Uncle Lenny's and rested my arm on the rim of my door. "For example, she'll text late at night and want to know if I'm up for a spitball session."

"Okay. That's weird."

I sniggered, my mood lightening by the second. "That's what

writers do, Uncle Lenny. It's like where you bounce ideas off each other and stuff."

"Oh." He cut his eyes at me, clearly fighting back a smile. "So, what does Pippa look like?"

"It's not like that. We're not…"

"Just asking."

"She's petite, like Mom and Aunt Desi, and she's got wavy hair, about to here." I moved my hands below my chin. "Kind of an auburn shade. She has hazel eyes. Dimples."

"*Humph*," he remarked, practically trembling with restraint. "That's a lot of detail for—"

"It's really not like that, Uncle Lenny." I thought about Tammy Jo, and how she was the exact opposite of Pippa in every way. Tammy Jo was tall and curvy, while Pippa was pint-sized and delicate. Tammy Jo had long, dark hair, and Pippa's hair was wild and curly. "Did you see Tammy Jo at the funeral?"

"I did. She didn't say much. Not to me anyway. You?"

"Not much." I sighed. "She's always been reserved though. You know, careful with her words. Actually, that's a good example. Pippa is a talker. She has absolutely no boundaries and is always painfully chatty and overly effusive. She'll strike up conversations with random people on the street. About the weather. About the dog they're walking. It doesn't matter, she'll just gab away."

"That's what we call friendly here in Shady Gully."

"She's…just a lot."

"You said that."

"She's really hard to explain. You'll see when you meet her."

"I'm looking forward to it."

All at once, our phones started blasting with text messages we'd missed while at Lake Osprey. Lenny's alerted with Led Zepplin's "Stairway to Heaven" and mine chirped with a polite chime. "Wow," I muttered, thumbing through all the messages.

"Check mine." Uncle Lenny handed me his phone.

"Looks like we're getting similar messages. You've got one from Aunt Desi but most of them are from Micah."

"Is something wrong?"

"Hard to say, but we need to head to Violet's Vet ASAP. It seems there's a python on the loose."

†††

The scene at the four-way stop was far from the small-town utopia I'd conjured up a few hours ago. Flashing police car lights outlined the corners of the four-way as each vehicle was stopped with dire words from either fire or law enforcement. When we slowed to a stop, Deputy Max, who was my mom's brother and my actual uncle, propped his arm on the opened truck window.

"Heard y'all been at the lake? Catch anything?"

"A few." Uncle Lenny surveyed the scene at Violet's Vet. "What's going on, Max?"

"Bubba brought that dang snake to the vet but didn't secure him. Now he's on the loose." Uncle Max brushed his hand against his gun while surveying the perimeter.

I bit back a smile. "Is he dangerous? The way Bubba talks, he's a teddy bear."

"He's a python, Sterling. What do you think?" He sighed deeply, the weight of the world on his small-town shoulders. "We're telling everybody to lock their doors, secure their pets, kids, and small livestock, because we got us a hundred-pound killer slithering around Shady Gully." He told Lenny in a cloak-and-dagger tone, "I'd keep your gun handy."

"Where's Bubba?" Uncle Lenny wanted to know.

"With Violet." He made a face. "It ain't pretty either. She's ticked."

"I bet," I mumbled, knowing my sister's temperament.

Uncle Lenny tucked his chin then, took a right at the four-way and steered his truck into the parking lot of Violet's Vet. Just as Uncle Max described, amid the mayhem stood an angry Violet berating a contrite Bubba who sat on a bench near the entrance. Hands planted on her hips, feet shoulder width apart, my sister's mouth spawned a furious slash.

Luke and Petey walked over to the truck along with Wolfheart, who as usual appeared calm and maybe even slightly amused. "Nice day at the lake?" he asked.

"Awesome." I couldn't help but grin because Wolfheart truly was one of the coolest dudes I'd ever met. "But we didn't run across a python, sorry to say."

He nudged Uncle Lenny's arm playfully. "Micah's a little upset. She's filing a police report with QD."

"Of course, she is." He frowned. "What for?"

Wolfheart shrugged. "Missing snake. Bad day. Who knows?"

"I guess I'd better go check on her."

"Watch your step, Dad," Luke offered as Uncle Lenny extricated himself from his truck and plodded toward Micah, who watched like a hawk as Quietdove recorded every single word in her statement. When Uncle Lenny reached her, she threw herself in his arms and buried her head in his chest.

"She's so spoiled," Petey said wryly. "And you," he turned to Luke, "way to calm the town down, Mr. Mayor." Petey explained to me, "When he got here the first thing he did was herd Bella and the dogs into his truck and get them tucked away at home."

"That's what Violet said to do," Luke argued. "We don't want anyone getting hurt. Small animals—and kids—are most at risk."

"If you put Pierre the snake and Duchess the Shiba Inu in a room together, I guarantee you the dog would come out victorious." Petey chuckled. "She'd come out dragging that python by the tail, wearing her cheesy smile. Besides, Bubba feeds that snake all the time. I doubt he's very hungry."

"Whatever. There's a reason Violet's anxious to get to her little veterinary pasture. She's worried about her goats and small animals. They're sick, remember? Easy prey for Pierre."

"Are we going to form an official search party?" I asked.

"Heck yeah!" Petey fist bumped me while Luke gestured. "Look. Violet's fixing to talk now."

A flat-sounding beep got everyone's attention as Violet took the megaphone Redflyer handed her. "Listen up, everybody. First, make sure your own home and small pets are secure, and then if you want to help find the snake—"

A forlorn Bubba offered from the Bench of Shame. "He has a name. It's Pierre."

"—there are things you need to know. First of all, do not approach…Pierre. That's key. You are to call Bubba or me immediately. We have the tools to retrieve him." She tapped a giant snake hook like a cane and patted her fanny pack which contained God knew what. "We will secure him, and this time, Bubba is going to make sure he has zip ties for his tote." A splatter of laughter and boos shuttered through the crowd. "We're also going to be setting traps in the vicinity."

"Traps?" Bubba rose from the bench.

"Flour and cornstarch traps." Violet settled Bubba. "If he's close, he'll slither across it and leave a trail. A line of pennies will work as well." She glanced across the road to the Cozy Corner.

Petey whispered, "Charlie Wayne and JJ were the first to close shop and split."

"We need to check the Cozy Corner," Violet instructed, "because it's warm and toasty. Pierre will likely seek out a cozy, tepid spot. Also, keep in mind that even though he's big, he can crawl up into very small places. Now, I need to go check on my livestock pasture ASAP."

"He ain't at the Cozy Corner," Bubba quipped. "Don't you reckon somebody would have seen a hundred-pound python puttering across the road? And he ain't mean or nothing," Bubba said plaintively. "Pet snakes rarely bite, and he don't feel good, so remember that."

"Poor Bubba," Wolfheart muttered. "He's really shook up."

Violet shook her head, all business. "Bubba is right. Pierre can't be far, and he's probably not a threat, but let's proceed with caution, nonetheless. Y'all have our numbers?"

Shouts of *yes, 10-4,* and *copy that* rose from the crowd. Within seconds groups started to form and peel off in different directions.

The firetrucks backed out and headed on their way while the flashing lights of the deputies' cruisers pushed off as well.

I noticed young Fireman flash Wolfheart a thumbs up as he took up a position with Moonpipe and Big Al, part of his fire station posse.

"How's he doing?" I asked him.

"I think he's going to be alright," Wolfheart answered. "This is actually good for him. The kid is at his best when he's helping others." There was affection, and even pride, in his tone.

When Lenny and Micah walked over with Quietdove and Meadow, I winked at Micah, whose mascara had left trails of tears on her rosy face. "Rough day, cousin?" I hugged her, much like Uncle Lenny had done.

"I think I'd rather work at Daddy's hardware store. This is too stressful."

We all turned as a blue monster truck turned into the parking lot. Hoot Wheeler removed his shades and stepped out of the truck. "What's going on?"

Quietdove stood straighter, presenting a more authoritative demeanor. "We've had a little emergency. We're dealing with it."

Hoot ignored Quietdove and instead looked at Micah. "Are you alright?" He stroked his fingers along his cheeks, miming tears. When Micah scoffed at him, he shrugged. "Whatever. I just came to pick up Tootsie. I got a call this morning that she was ready."

Micah paled. "What?"

"Yeah, I'm late, but I've been in Belle Maison working on a spec house all day."

"Uh…" Micah wheeled and then made a B-line inside the veterinary hospital.

Because she seemed agitated, we all followed as she skittered past the bench and into the office lobby, cutting a quick path to the back room where the patients were contained. When she shut the door behind her, we waited.

A sharp, panicked squeal emanated from the room. After a beat, I cracked the door open and Petey, Luke, Wolfheart, and I joined her inside. She pointed to an empty cage, its door swinging open ominously.

"Oh no," Petey breathed. "Don't tell me."

Micah's voice was as slight as she was when she said, "Tootsie is gone."

We all jumped when my phone chimed. I reacted when I read the text.

"What is it?" Micah cried. "Did somebody find…*them?*"

"No," I mumbled just as Uncle Lenny walked into the room with his phone in his hand. "Did you get that text? Pippa has arrived. She's at the house with Desi and Robin now." He beamed like the cat who ate the canary.

Or, uh, the snake who ate the small dog.

"Whose Pippa?" asked Luke.

"I didn't know you had a girlfriend," mused Petey.

"Gotta go," I breathed, thinking that for once, Pippa had actually saved me.

✝✝✝

We heard laughter as soon as we walked into the house. Ginger and Mary Ann dashed to the door as if they hadn't seen us in weeks. They dived and jumped, and Uncle Lenny, the old softy, picked up Ginger, the papillon, and nuzzled her.

Mary Ann, the black and white cocker spaniel, trailed me into the kitchen where Mom, Aunt Desi, and Pippa sat around the table drinking margaritas.

What the…?

"Sterling!" Pippa jumped up and nearly took me down with a rambunctious hug. "We're having so much fun!" She looked over my head. "Uncle Lenny!" She pounced on him with an enthusiastic introduction. "I'm Pippa. I've heard so much about you. You're just like I pictured. You want a margarita?"

"They're so good. It's a special mix Pippa brought from home." Desi grinned, a blush of pink coloring her cheeks. "Lenny, did you know Pippa is from Santa Fe?"

"We've had the best time talking about all the interesting characters in the City Different. Oh, and the restaurants there," Mom put in, eyeing me. "How come we haven't met this darling girl before?"

Uncle Lenny and I exchanged glances.

Aunt Desi gushed at Pippa. "Have you ever been to the Bull Ring? They used to have the best steaks in town."

"They still do," Pippa said. "I have the recipe for their secret seasoning. You know the stuff they sear the steaks with? I've got it on my phone right here."

Aunt Desi gleamed.

"I think I will have one of those margaritas." Uncle Lenny took a jaunty step over to Aunt Desi and kissed her on the lips.

"Coming right up," piped Pippa. "And I'm making one for you, Sterling, so sit your booty down and get ready to have fun." While Pippa bounced around the kitchen like she'd been there a million times, I shook my head in wonder. But Uncle Lenny was happy, and Aunt Desi was smiling, so I went with it.

We were in Shady Gully, after all, and like Uncle Lenny said, you just couldn't make this stuff up.

Chapter Sixteen

Heaven
Timothy

I savored my little slice of heaven. A perfect cup of coffee, a comfy rocking chair, and a darling tree frog looking over my shoulder as I read my morning devotionals on the front porch of a gorgeous lake house. *Amen,* I thanked God for the incredible beauty on Lake Osprey, complete with egrets side-stepping through the shallow water as they perused the breakfast buffet.

As I reflected, I thought about young Fireman and wondered how his morning was going. Grief had a way of tainting everything, tilting the world to immeasurable degrees, making it impossible to imagine how the rest of humanity carried on as usual while you floundered numbly from the sidelines.

I prayed for Desi and Lenny as well, who Father Patrick and I would meet later in the day. A wrong had been done to Desi in childhood and the repercussions resonated today. They'd mushroomed, in fact, beckoning long-dormant hurts to the surface once again.

Once more, immeasurable degrees. God knew I could relate. I flinched as I considered the way Father Patrick was slowly peeling away the layers of trauma I'd buried for years. Back then, suppressing the woe hadn't been that difficult, as I'd been swept up at College of the Ozarks, flourishing in God's glory and in His word. Specifically, Philippians 4:8.

Finally, brothers and sisters, whatever is true, whatever is noble, whatever is right, whatever is pure, whatever is

*lovely, whatever is admirable—if anything is excellent
or praiseworthy—think about such things.*

And I had. I'd focused on the right, the noble, the lovely…
and most of all, on the way God had rescued me. Spiritually,
figuratively, and perhaps even literally. I'd dwelled on the good,
as instructed in Philippians, and refused to think about my
beginnings, about the debasement, the hunger, and the grief…

Until now. Because someone was *forcing* me to remember.
And what? Go public? *What good would come of that*, I wondered.

I thanked God for Father Patrick, a true shepherd in every
sense of the word, as he was leading me to a better place, to
safety, and maybe even to freedom.

A text from Meadow lit up my phone. Another slice of heaven.
If only I didn't lose her on the way to freedom. I felt the tree
frog tickle my ear as I read Meadow's message.

```
Hope you had a good night's
sleep. If you and the Padre
see a python out there, send up
a flare. Shady Gully is losing
their minds because Bubba's
snake hasn't turned up yet.
```

As I sent a quick text in return, I heard a vehicle door slam
in the carport below. The houses were built up high on Lake
Osprey, so I didn't know who the unexpected guest was until I
plodded down the stairs.

The Sacred Heart Catholic Church van took up half the carport, not because it was big but because Father Patrick parked
without method. He waved. "Cheerio, Timothy! I decided it
best to get an early start today, what with Desi and Lenny
joining us later."

Oh, how the sly priest loved to disarm me. Throwing me off
my game was part of his strategy, and admittedly, after enjoying
my little slice of heaven, I wasn't quite ready to revisit hell yet.

Surprised by his vigorous pace as he climbed the steps, I must
have looked dumbfounded when he reached the porch up top.

He narrowed his eyes as he took measure of me. "My word, Timothy, did you sleep at all last night?"

"Uh, I think so."

His eyes knitted with doubt. "I see. Well, let's get to it. We have a lot of ground to cover."

"Coffee?"

"I've got all the fuel I need right here." He took his seat in the rocker next to mine and unloaded a stack of books, a thick folder, a Bible, and a yellow legal pad decorated with copious notes. The staggering amount of reference material he'd brought matched the wise, clear-sighted look on his face.

"I think I'll grab another cup."

"I think I know the answer to this question, but I'm going to ask it anyway," Father Patrick began. "Have you ever received counseling? Formally, I mean."

I extended an ambiguous nod. "At COFO we were always encouraged to share everything. Our fears, our shortcomings, our aspirations, our hang-ups—"

"What about past traumas?"

"Well, sure." I took a swig of coffee, which soured the instant it hit my stomach. "But I never spoke about anything… of substance."

"Just as I thought. I'll adjust accordingly." After he slashed several lines across the legal pad in vivid fashion, he stared across the lake, fixating on a small islet bursting with trees and foliage. "Even on the cusp of winter, there is growth."

I hesitated, unsure if—or how—I was meant to respond to his pensive introspection.

"We're going to eventually dive into the trauma, so don't you worry, but now I believe it prudent to focus on more pressing matters. Such as what this blackmailer wants from you. You said you don't have money. So what, pray tell, could it be?" Determination met his eyes. "A personal vendetta?"

"I don't know. I can't imagine, but maybe."

"When did the texts start?"

"About two or three months ago. I'd get one about once a week, and I didn't think too much about it until a couple of weeks ago when they became more frequent…and included pictures. I knew then it was personal."

"And he or she texted you directly? Did you find that a little curious?"

I felt a flush of heat spread across my face as I processed this reality.

"Did you ever respond?" After I shook my head in the negative Father Patrick contemplated. "Maybe you're too close to the situation, Timothy. Perhaps I could intuit more if I looked at the texts. Do you mind?"

Without a word, I handed him my phone, my fate and pride tagging along for the ride. As Father Patrick scrolled, his thumb flicked up and down. I resisted the temptation to conjure the images of the photos in his line of vision.

"Did you teach about anything specific during this time?" His tone was matter of fact, mercifully replacing my embarrassment with a measure of dignity. "Northlake is worldwide, it's possible you said something that rankled this individual somehow."

"It's possible. We do occasionally ruffle some feathers, but those missives usually show up on social media or via email on the church's website. I can't think of anything specific. We had a summer prayer festival, which would be like Petey's revival at Unity." I paused, recollecting. "We would have been through a few series at that point." I extended my hand for my phone and after Father Patrick returned it, I pulled up Northlake's website, scrolling through the recent teaching sermons. "Heredity vs. Environment. Sins of Our Fathers. You can look at the series' videos online, but I can't recall anything especially provocative."

"I'll do that." He wiggled his chunky fingers, wanting my phone back. When I handed it to him, he scribbled something on that ominous yellow pad of his. "I'm going to make a suggestion."

I waited.

"Why not have the authorities run a search on the phone number of the sender? I've watched enough NCIS to know it can be done."

"I don't know." A wave of dizziness made my eyes flicker erratically.

"You're in Shady Gully, Timothy. Not Lexington, and we have relationships with people in law enforcement. People who would be discreet. Think of Sheriff Rick or Quietdove. You can trust them."

Reluctantly, I consented.

"Very well," he said as he returned my phone for good. I hoped. "Let's move on then. Shall we talk about your early years with your mother or the period after you escaped the depraved drug den?"

I chortled because, despite it all, I found Father Patrick's straightforwardness refreshing. "Just for the record, there was more than one heroin den, as well as a spell in the crumbling projects. Not far from the arch actually. I remember because it was in an industrial area, and there were lots of old, abandoned apartment buildings. But maybe let's skip that part for now." I was afraid I wouldn't be able to give Desi and Lenny my best if we went too far down that rabbit hole.

Father Patrick deferred to my wishes while maintaining a firm hold on his pen and yellow legal pad. "You were around twelve then, right?"

"Around that. I don't recall exactly."

"Right. Right." But all the while he wrote furiously on his yellow legal pad. "Okay, let's pick up *after* your mom died then, if you're more comfortable with that. So young Timothy is eleven or twelve when he's liberated and reenters civilization. What did that look like? Did you simply burst through the forsaken projects with the Rocky theme playing in the background?"

I guffawed.

"I apologize. Just going for a little levity, son." Father Patrick drank greedily from a Thermos he'd brought with him. "Seriously, how did a young boy from such sordid, meager beginnings end up at College of the Ozarks and rise to lead one of the most powerful megachurches in America?"

"It's simple really." I eyeballed him. "God."

Finally, Father Patrick put his legal pad away and glinted at me with expectation. "Tell me more."

Since my coffee had long since gone cold, I placed the cup on the end table between our rocking chairs. After one quick glance at the last egret loitering in the shallows of Lake Osprey, I began, "After my mother died, I sneaked out in the dead of night while all the junkies were passed out, and I can assure you there wasn't any triumphant music playing in my head at all. I was emaciated, dirty, and had fleas and bug bites all over me from the rotting mattresses. I also had lice and nasty, oozing, infected sores. A truck driver picked me up."

"Have mercy," Father Patrick muttered, aggrieved.

"Thankfully, he was a kind man. His name was Philip, and he was from Nebraska, which I'd never heard of before. I got my first geography lesson from him. Since he was ending a shift, we checked into a motel, and I got a shower, a shampoo, and a very amateurish haircut. I thought I was in heaven."

"Did he…try anything improper?"

"No. After I'd been cleaned up, we walked over to the diner next door, and he introduced me to all of his trucker buddies. Apparently, this was a meeting point in the middle of the country for these guys. While they were catching up, I ate a hot meal of meatloaf, mashed potatoes, and corn. I wanted dessert but Philip suggested I let that settle before choosing a piece of pie. Philip asked his buddies if they'd seen Paul, who seemed to be a fan favorite within the group. Before we left, he asked the cook, who told him Paul would likely be rolling through the next day. So we stayed another day."

"My word. This man delayed his trip to meet with this Paul person?"

"He did, and that meant I got to sleep in. Even better, he let me shower again, which was astonishing to me. By the time we made it to the diner at lunch time, Paul had arrived."

"Splendid."

"Not so much. Paul didn't react well to the sight of me. In fact, he found my presence disturbing. I don't know why he found the sight of me so excruciating, other than the sores and the bug bites, of course, but I got to eat ice cream while he and Philip talked privately."

"What happened?"

"They talked most of the day. They drank a lot of coffee. And before the evening crowd came in, Philip said, 'Kid, I gotta hit the road, but you're in good hands with Paul here.'"

"What? He left you with this Paul person?! That seems irresponsible."

"Not really." I sighed. "Think about it. I wasn't Philip's responsibility. He'd done more for me in one day than anyone had in my whole life. Besides, I saw him again, the next time he came through town."

"But what happened in the meantime?"

"Well, after he ordered another coffee, Paul slid into the booth across from me, pulled out a deck of cards, and taught me how to play gin rummy."

"Consider me intrigued, Timothy. I'm literally on the edge of my seat." He actually was, and for a minute I worried about his bulk tilting the rocking chair over the wrong way.

"That night Paul took me to the home of a lady named Lydia. Again, I thought I was in heaven because she had a bunch of stray cats and dogs."

"She sounds like Mr. Wolf."

"She was exactly like Brad Wolfheart. Quiet. Dutiful. Content. Anyway, she made me a hot meal and spread me a nice bed. The next day she dropped me off at the diner before she went to work. I remember feeling a little scared, thinking it was all too good to be true, and here was the proverbial brick about to fall, you know? But the cook at the diner handed me a menu and told me to order whatever I wanted." I grinned. "I ordered pancakes." I looked across Lake Osprey, to the islet that had preoccupied Father Patrick earlier. Perhaps he was right, and even a scarce, rare weed could find its way out of the longest and weariest of winters.

"And did you ever see Paul again?" Father Patrick asked.

"Oh, yeah. He came in later that day and taught me how to play Spades. And then Poker. And the following day, he told me about Jesus."

†††

When I heard Lenny's truck pull up downstairs, I excused myself to the bathroom long enough to splash cold water on my face. Reassessing the past had weakened me. I could see the strain in my eyes as I looked in the mirror, and I could feel it in my listless stride as I paced back into the living room. I only hoped Desi and Lenny couldn't read it in my smile as I greeted them, because I genuinely cared for these people.

"Desi." I lowered my upper body to embrace her fully. "Lenny." I shook his hand and patted him on the shoulder. Truly, it was hard to distinguish who looked wearier. Desi's eyes were sunken into her already small face, while Lenny's coloring was off, and his breathing was labored. "Are you okay?" I asked him.

"Fine. Just those stairs." He patted his paunch. "Guess I'll soon be wearing aluminum foil suits and walking around Shady Gully along with our favorite priest."

As Desi gazed at the bright yellow walls around the house, she seemed especially melancholy. While she revisited pictures of her and Robin's families, she zeroed in on a painting over the fireplace. Clearly painted by her mother, Sunny, it depicted a spirited group of kids gathered around a bonfire. Although painted nearly three decades ago, the enraptured faces of Desi and Robin were clear.

Although she said nothing, Desi's expression was rueful as she moved away.

"You wanna sit down, honey?" Lenny took a seat, patting the cushion next to him. Desi sat as Father Patrick appeared with a pitcher of sweet tea and glasses.

"I've been privileged to occasionally retreat here myself," Father Patrick said, "so I have a general idea where all the important stuff is." He placed the setting on the coffee table, said a short prayer, and genuflected. Lenny poured several glasses and passed them out before raising his own. "Cheers," he said. After we clinked glasses, Lenny downed most of his tea in one gulp. Comfortable in a matching recliner, I decided to sit back and let the capable priest take the lead. "Desi," he asked, "what's the latest on Tom's condition?"

"I believe his end is near. I got a call from Wanda, his wife, just before we left to come here." She glanced at Lenny. "She pleaded with me to come and let him say his piece. She said it would mean a lot to her."

"A cheap shot," Lenny grumbled. "I mean, Wanda's a nice lady and all, but this has nothing to do with her, and her putting pressure on Desi is just wrong." He poured himself another glass of tea. "In my opinion."

Father Patrick and I traded glances. He started, "Lenny, I understand you're angry—"

"I'm beyond angry, Father. You don't just get to do something like that, scar a person for life, and get away with it. It's wrong and I'm madder than hell." He clutched Desi's hand, raging on as tears glided steadily down his face. "Truth is I've been holding back all this time. Just over three decades now, and I've done nothing but lay low and take care of Desi, help her through all the sick things he did to her, but I'm so damn angry still—"

"Lenny." Desi caressed his hand. "Please don't upset yourself."

"Too late for that," he grunted. "Who is he to summon her like that anyway? Wanda said he wants to say his piece, well"—he balled his hands into fists—"when do I get to say *my* piece? Huh?"

"The same time as Desi," said Father Patrick. "You have every right to have a word with him." He turned to Desi, who dabbed a Kleenex to her dull eyes. "What do you think, Desi? How do you feel about seeing Tom again?"

"I feel…nothing." When Lenny looked at her oddly, she shrugged her shoulders. "It damaged me at the time. I kept it a secret from my best friend, and even from my husband—"

"I guessed," remarked Lenny. "I knew."

"—but when I finally did tell them—and this was long after the kids were born—I started to heal. Isn't that strange?"

"You felt heard," I spoke up, glancing at Father Patrick. When he encouraged me to go on, I explained, "People tend to think that sharing their traumatic experiences is just about getting support, but it's much more than that. Sometimes it helps to make sense of it. By that I mean, it becomes more than just a jumble of reactions and emotions. When you tell someone, you are also processing and reassessing it." I looked directly at Father Patrick, caught in the realization that, in fact, this very thing was happening between us now.

I gulped my sweet tea much like Lenny had done earlier. "Also, it's important to remember that you are more than your trauma. Seriously, what happened doesn't define who you are, Desi. Do you understand what I mean?"

While Lenny frowned, Desi nodded. "Yes. It did define me for a long time, but not anymore." She looked at Lenny. "Look at us. We have so much to be thankful for. We have our kids, Lenny, and we get to see them flourishing and happy. Isn't that amazing?" She inched her shoulders up. "I really don't think about the wrongness of what happened anymore, except in terms of the young me, because that version of me was too young to know what to do with all the confusion and self-loathing and worse—the shame. Like you said, Timothy, it was all a jumble of emotions, and I couldn't make sense of it. My heart breaks for her, the young me, but not for the me now."

Thoroughly impacted by Desi's words, I grunted incoherently when everyone swiveled in my direction. I'd lost complete track of my narrative! As I struggled mightily to fill my lungs with air, Father Patrick poured more tea into my glass and inched it closer to my hand. "God's healing is miraculous, isn't it?" He diverted Lenny's and Desi's attention as my heart pulsed with Desi's revelation: *The young me didn't know what to do with the confusion, the self-loathing, and the shame...*

"In fact," Father Patrick continued, "He'll use the painful experiences in our lives to mold us into the person He wants us to be."

Although Lenny still looked doubtful, Desi nodded in agreement.

"It's never easy to let go of anger," Father Patrick directed his comments to Lenny, "especially after someone has hurt you or someone you love, but if you trust God and go through the process of forgiveness, healing will come, and you'll come out the other side better for it."

Desi linked her arm into her husband's, tugging him closer on the cushy couch. "I think we should go, and just see what he has to say." Lenny's lips tightened in a straight line, still unconvinced. "Lenny, if you want to say your piece, this will be your last chance to do it."

I awkwardly cleared my throat, doing my darnedest to open an air passage. After a few deep breaths, I offered, "Perhaps Father Patrick and I could go with you. Would that—"

"Yeah," Lenny chirped. "I'd like that."

"It's decided then." Father Patrick rubbed his thighs, looking pleased with the victory. "Set it up with the nursing home, and we'll meet you there." He spread his arms wide, indicating that we should form a circle and pray.

After we said the Lord's Prayer, Father Patrick genuflected and then offered one last bit of wisdom as he looked pointedly at me. "Just remember that there is freedom in forgiveness. As the brilliant Lewis B. Smedes said, 'To forgive is to set a prisoner free and discover that the prisoner is you.'"

Desi and Lenny had gone, and Father Patrick and I walked

down to the floating dock behind Robin's lake house. He held his arms parallel to his shoulders. "Incredible how this thing moves along with the water, isn't it?"

"It is." I closed my eyes, listening to the sound of the waves and breathing in the fresh air. "I love it out here."

"How's your balance? I know it's been a trying day for you."

"I'm fine. I feel good about Desi and Lenny. I feel like they'll get where they need to be."

Leaning on the railing of the dock, Father Patrick took in the vast landscape. "I agree. Surprisingly, Desi's already there, and she'll see to it that Lenny gets there as well." He turned to me, his expression suddenly serious. "There is one timely issue we need to talk about, Timothy, and I've worried about how to approach it with you."

"Go for it." I was trying for a cavalier tone but could tell I'd missed the mark.

"It's about your sermon for Unity's revival. I read your notes."

I fought back a swirl of defensiveness.

"The theme, *betrayal,* is very strong in it, and I'll give you marks for that…but it's a little on the nose, don't you think?"

"I'm not sure what you mean."

"Well, you talk about how in several of the Gospels, Peter repeatedly denies Jesus, and specifically how *betrayed* Jesus must have felt. Now, we can quibble about the semantics another time—"

"Yes, of course, but—"

"Just hear me out. What concerns me is the personal—and slightly plaintive—tone in the sermon. For instance, and I'm paraphrasing here, you say, 'imagine if it were your best friend or someone you deeply loved, and think how it would feel for them to hurt you, to deny your very presence over and over—'"

"But that's what Peter did."

"Yes, but the obvious parallel concerns me."

"Parallel? I don't understand—"

"I feel it would be risky for you to deliver this sermon. It would be a setback, Timothy, and I'm afraid it would wreak havoc with your already frayed emotions. You, of course, may do what you wish, but I would strongly advise against preaching at the revival at all."

Unable to meet his eyes, I turned to face the water.

"And the burning question I have now is, who betrayed you, Timothy? And who do you need to forgive?" He dipped his head, his eyes locking into mine. "I assume the inspiration for the sermon was your mother, yes?"

Chapter Seventeen

Open Auditions
Fireman

I was probably on my fourth dream when a howl and a screech combined to make an unusually terrifying sound that drummed with fright. Both Black's and Blue's heads rose in panic as they mistakenly looked at me to save them.

"What is that?" I asked the dogs, but they didn't answer. Instead, they pawed dolefully at the sheets, aiming to join me under the covers. "It sounds close."

I grunted as I crawled out of bed and dropped to my knees. When I lifted the bedspread, two terrified orange eyes glowed back at me. "Aurora!" The enormous cat let out a wretched cry. "Oh no!"

My bare feet hurriedly padded across the hall to Wolfheart's room, and we nearly crashed into one another as he charged toward mine. Or Bella's. Either way, it was temporary.

Wolfheart carried a towel and a heat lamp, and as we entered the room, he shooed the dogs away. "Off you go, boys." He knelt on the floor, cooing to the massively pregnant cat. "She's queening," he said. "I had a feeling she was getting close. She didn't eat yesterday and was unusually needy and affectionate earlier. How long has she been like this?"

"I don't know. Her crying just woke me up." *And what the heck was queening?*

Carefully spreading the blanket on the floor, Wolfheart set the heat lamp near the bed and turned it on. "She's a first-time mama, so we need to be calm, keep her settled, and talk to her in a soothing voice." He squinted as he tried to get a read on Aurora's condition.

"Do you need a flashlight?

"Yes. Go look in the junk drawer in the kitchen."

I quickly scurried off, a little dismayed that I instinctively knew which drawer contained random whatnots. On my return, as I maneuvered past Black and Blue who lurked outside the closed door, I noted a new, especially harrowing cry emanating from under the bed. Wolfheart took the light and shined it in the direction of the distressed cat.

"Uh-oh," he muttered. "It's hard to see, but I think she's having difficulty. It looks like—"

I grabbed the flashlight and crawled on my belly to get a closer look. I groaned when I saw that the floor was slick with blood and even more worrisome…

"I think I see a kitten's head." I pointed. "Down there."

"Okay. Okay." Wolfheart spoke in a gentle tone as he tried to ease Aurora closer, but when she let out a hair-raising bellow, it left us only one choice.

"I'm calling Violet."

"It's three in the morning, Fireman. Come on. We can do this."

But I was already on my phone, sending an SOS. "She'll come," I said with certainty.

✝✝✝

Six hours later, Violet had successfully delivered all three of Aurora's kittens.

Petey and Wolfheart sat on the floor, looking a little green around the gills as they leaned against the wall of Bella's room.

"Y'all did the right thing," she said, glancing back at Wolfheart even though I was the one who'd called. "There were definite signs of dystocia."

"What does that mean?" I asked, petting the mama cat as she nursed her babies.

"It just means a difficult pregnancy. I think she was straining hard for a long time, and the kitten got stuck because she was weak and tired." She winked at me, whispering so that Petey and Wolfheart wouldn't hear. "They're such babies."

Super jazzed from the whole experience, I asked, "What do we need to do now?"

"I can take them to the vet clinic with me in the morning if you want." She glanced at her watch. "Well, in a few hours. But you know what? I think you'd do a great job looking after Aurora and her kittens. You just need to keep her warm and comfortable and make sure she's nursing all of them. Sometimes the little ones get pushed aside, so you have to pay close attention."

"I want to keep them here." I glanced at Wolfheart, who after slowly pulling himself off the floor, offered Petey a hand up. "Is that one a boy or a girl?" I asked Violet, eyeing the tiniest one, who was orange with white paws and a slash of white across the nose.

"That's a girl, and she's the smallest so you'll have to watch that her brothers don't push her off her mama's teat."

"Anybody want some tea? Or coffee?" Wolfheart asked, looking over the kittens with a look of amazement. "Interesting coloring, and it looks like you've even got a male calico in the mix. They're very rare, you know?"

"Yep," Petey said from behind him. "But my favorite is the black and orange one."

"They're all sweet," Violet mused in a dreamy voice. "You should take some pictures to take to the revival today, Fireman, in case some little girl or boy wants a new kitten."

"That's a great idea." Wolfheart raised his brow. "We've got plenty of critters around here as it is."

"Okay, but I've got dibs on the little orange and white one." I flashed a plotting smile. "I have an idea for her."

As Petey and Wolfheart left to go make coffee, I scratched the female kitten under the chin. "It's pretty neat, what you did," I told Violet. "What you do every day."

"Thanks. And I agree. It's fun. Especially when it has a happy ending like this."

As Violet tidied up, wiping down her instruments and placing everything just so in her medical bag, I watched with interest. Pretty in an odd way, Violet was extremely tall with blonde hair and pale coloring. While her demeanor presented as shy and delicate, she was anything but, having flipped Shady Gully on its head a few years ago when she decided to ditch medical school and become a veterinarian. Bold move, for sure, and one which began her transformation from shy waif to no-nonsense business owner.

It was kind of cool to see her expression soften around the kittens and call her job fun.

"Any news on Hoot Wheeler's dog? Or Bubba's snake?"

She sighed, no doubt worrying about the type of ending looming for Pierre and Tootsie.

"No. We have flyers all over town about the pup, and I plan to bring some to the revival later today. I'm a little worried about Pierre as well. He suffered second-degree burns, and the affected area was fairly large. Being lost in unfamiliar surroundings isn't ideal for a sick snake, and it's getting cold—which snakes hate—so he's probably distressed."

I couldn't believe it. She seemed to care about a python as much as a kitten! "Do you like snakes or cats better?"

She actually giggled. "Both. All animals are God's creatures, so I hope we find Pierre soon, and I hope we find homes for these sweet kitties."

"I'll come help you this week. We'll find him—*them*," I offered, in case Tootsie hadn't become a meal. "I know good places to look."

She smiled at me, her eyes going all misty like Meadow's did sometimes. "You're better than a good kid, Fireman. You're an exceptional boy with a big heart." She leaned in, lowering her voice. "I know what it's like to be different and to feel like nobody gets you or even sees the real you. The you in here." Her long, slender fingers lightly tapped my chest. "Continue to do good and be your unique and special self, and if anybody ever pushes you to conform," she pronounced as she snapped her medical bag shut, "resist."

†††

I'd be long gone by the time the preaching part of the Unity Christian Church Revival started this evening, but for now, the sun was out, the air was crisp, and the aroma of hot dogs and hamburgers seasoned the atmosphere with merriment.

After helping Violet with the missing dog and snake flyers, I used social media and the biggest mouth in Shady Gully to spread the word about Aurora's kittens. Cruella Claire was more than happy to talk it up from behind her throne at the post office, as well as to gossip about how *that "odd duck" Violet had rushed to The Creek with her preacher husband Petey in the middle of the night to birth some kittens. Cute ones at that, come have a look.'*

With any luck, I'd find homes for the kittens before noon.

I'd just slipped off to the stocked pond behind the church with my burger, hot dog, pork rinds, and soda, and was about to enjoy a quiet moment on the outskirts of the festivities with my fishing pole when a swirly-swish sounded behind me.

Admittedly, I jolted at the possibility of coming face to face with Pierre the Python, not so much because I didn't want to, but because I really wanted to eat first. When I turned, I realized the swish and the swirl had come from Sigourney Sky, who no doubt was wearing one of her wild, wispy creations.

"Hey, Fireman," the dress lady said. "I didn't mean to startle you."

She hadn't, but her dress sure had. Long, with green and blue layers at the bottom, the garment seemed to spin every time the lady took a breath. "Nice dress." *Where had I seen it before?*

"Thanks. It's one of my most recent designs. It's not for sale at the shop yet, although I did sell one to an eccentric artist on The Creek." She made the shushing gesture. "Don't tell anyone."

Because Granny had taught me to be polite, I offered Sigourney a pork rind. "Want to sit down? I was just going to eat and throw a line into the pond."

"No. I just…well, we don't really know each other well, but I wanted to tell you personally how sorry I am about Granny Lacey. She visited me in the shop frequently, and although she never purchased anything, she told me a lot about you."

"Oh." I forced down a bite of hamburger. "Thank you. For telling me."

"I live alone on The Creek," she said, "and I have plenty of room at my home if you ever need anything. A hot meal. A warm bed. Company." She raised her shoulders uncomfortably. "I really liked Lacey, and I just wanted you to know you're welcome."

"Thanks," I said awkwardly. And then, because I was desperate to change the subject, I asked impulsively, "Have you seen Bubba lately?"

"No," she blushed, "but I heard about Pierre." *Whoa. She actually blushed! Color me shocked.* "I don't see him around today," she put in casually. "I guess he's pretty sad."

"We're gonna find his snake. He'll be alright." I took a bite of my hot dog, thinking I couldn't wait to see Bubba!

She seemed on the verge of saying something else when a flash of red, black, white, and tan raced past us toward a towering oak tree that bent over the pond like an umbrella. I caught a glimpse of their perky grins as Duke and Duchess surrounded the tree and gave the barking squirrel the what for. Fragments of fluffy tail baited them as the squirrel shimmied to the top of the tree and celebrated its victory.

Bella and Sigourney exchanged greetings and essentially traded places for my attention. As Luke hung back to chat with the dress lady, I was thrilled to have Bella all to myself for a moment. She sashayed over with a ginormous smile and flopped on the dirt beside me. "Catch anything?" She reached for a pork rind.

"Not yet." I dipped my chin toward the dogs. "I see, as usual, you have your psycho dogs under control."

Bella huffed, her brows bending in frustration. "I thought Duke was going to calm Duchess down, but I think she's just making him wild." My heart flipped inside my chest as her lower lip plumped in an adorable pout. "So, what's up with you? Are you doing okay?"

"Yeah," I said, finding it impossible not to stare at her, as she was the very essence of perfection. Shocking blue eyes, shiny dark hair—currently tossed in a messy bun at the nape of her exquisitely angled neck—Bella was beautiful like her mother, Meadow, but softer, happier, and quicker with a smile.

"And look at him now," she groused, watching as Duke, unflinching, stared at the squirrel like a sentry. "He'll stay like that until the squirrel gives itself up or Luke manhandles him into the truck."

Our laughter intensified as even Duchess had grown bored, having moved on to sniff around the edges of the pond.

Much to my chagrin, Luke plodded over, all fastened up in his khakis and button-down shirt. "Hey, Fireman. How are you?"

"Hey, Mayor. I'm good." *Already bored.*

A quick, silent exchange passed between them, at which point Bella opened in a husky voice. "I know it's early, and you're still reeling from losing your granny, but we, Luke and I, wanted to extend our invitation for you to come live with us. You've been to our place, and we have plenty of room. Oh, and guess what?" Bella brushed my thigh excitedly. "Luke is going to put in a pool at the duplex this summer. Won't that be fun?"

"Yeah," I managed.

"We'd love to be your legal guardians, and have you stay with us..."

"I've already looked into a college fund," stated Luke, looking hopeful, "and we can put something into it every month, so you wouldn't have to work so many jobs. Unless you wanted to, of course."

Bella beamed. "Duke and Duchess would be so excited."

I realized I should say something. "Thanks."

"And we have some more news," Bella cut her eyes at Luke, "but you can't tell anyone. You'll be the first one to know." She shifted. "We're going to have a baby! I'm pregnant!" She giggled as Luke crouched on the ground next to her, shushing her with a giggle of his own.

"Can you believe it, Fireman?" Luke said. "It's going to be awesome, and we'd love for you to be a part of it."

Whoa!

Speechless, I looked at Luke and then Bella. She was having *his* baby. It looked like things between Bella and me were finally over. While I was a lot of things, I drew the line at being a homewrecker.

✝✝✝

Finally, after countless platitudes and several diplomatic hugs, Bella, Luke, and Duchess peeled away, leaving me, Duke, and the squirrel to contemplate our current predicament.

As I numbly cast into the pond, hoping to catch a bream, a white perch, or maybe even a python, I regarded the crowd milling around the church grounds. There were lots of squealing kids pulling kites. The band was tuning up their instruments. Dogs, and even a few cats, meandered in and out of attendees' legs hoping for scraps. A small group of old men played checkers under a cypress tree. Women sat in a circle of chairs with their Bibles on their laps. Teenagers wearing jeans with holes in them scowled at one another.

I got a nibble on my fishing line, but whatever it was skittered away. I let out an exaggerated sigh and turned again to the activities, thinking it might be time for me to head home, which meant to Granny's until dark and then to Wolfheart's. That was our deal—for now.

As I packed up my gear, I noticed Timothy playing basketball with a group of kids on the marked court Petey had set up. And there was Sterling, laughing at something a really hot girl with reddish hair said. I also noted the serious conversation Lenny, Desi, and Wolfheart were having with Robin and Sheriff Rick. Meanwhile, Violet was engaged in an animated conversation with Sprite and Charlie Wayne, while pointing at a flyer tacked onto a tree. And all the while, Micah sulked on a bench with Quietdove, while he glared at Hoot Wheeler a distance away.

A day in the life of Shady Gully.

"Hey, squirt." Her salty tone easily recognizable, I turned to Meadow as a smile slipped from my lips. "Where do you think you're going?" she said. "Don't think you're leaving me here with all these yahoos."

"You know you love it, especially with your boyfriend over there shooting baskets in his shorty shorts."

Meadow cackled, twisting her head to get a load of Timothy. "He's such a dork. Who wears shorts like that anymore?"

"Shows off his tattoos, at least." I eyed the ink lining Timothy's arms and the strangely unreadable one on his back calf. "I think I'll chill at Granny's for a while. You know this church stuff isn't really my thing."

"I get it. It didn't used to be my thing either, but I'm coming around to the realization that it is *the* thing. Like the *only* thing that really matters."

I tilted my head, genuinely confounded.

Meadow squinted toward the pond. "What's with Duke pledging his loyalty to that tree over there?"

"Squirrel."

"Of course." Her green eyes swiveled as she spotted the squirrel. "Uncle Wolf sent me over here to tell you not to let the sheriff catch you driving alone. He'd tell you himself but right now he's deeply invested in Desi's current drama." We both pivoted to see him tug Desi into an affectionate hug. Meadow turned back to me with an ornery expression. "Are you having fun at Uncle Wolf's? I heard y'all gained three more mouths to feed."

I reached for my phone in my back pocket, showing her photos of the kittens. "If you want one, you'd better say now, because Cruella is on a mission."

Meadow harumphed, surveying the Shady Gullians at length.

"How are you?" I felt compelled to ask, strangely unsettled by something in her demeanor. "Is Timothy improving any?" When she looked at me curiously, I hesitated. "He seemed a little better at Granny's funeral…"

"Better than when? What are you saying?"

"I…I just meant…" Any attempt at evasion was squashed after one stern look from the Ice Queen. "Well, he fainted when I dropped him at Father Patrick's the other day. He was kind of babbling nonsense and…seemed in a bad way."

There was a look of surprise followed by a sharp catch in her breath. It was hard to witness. *Stupid. Stupid. Stupid.*

Eventually, she appeared to regain her composure. "Uh-oh," she said in a distracted voice. "Two o'clock, chubby red-headed priest, headed your way."

When I turned to look, Meadow drifted away without another word.

†††

"You seem peppy," I told Father Patrick as he approached.

"It's a gorgeous day and the band is about to key up the worship songs. Plus," he gushed, "Big Al and JJ Wheeler both told me I looked as if I'd lost weight."

I stood back, craning my neck to give him the once over. "You actually do. I'm proud of you. I bet you feel better, don't you?"

"I do indeed. Although," he patted my shoulder, "my dogs are barking. Is there a bench over there?"

I led him to a bench adjacent to the pond. "Just watch out for the python. Something big was nibbling at my hook earlier."

He let out a groan of relief as he settled on the bench. "Ahhhh." He asked, "What on earth is that dog doing?"

"Waiting out a squirrel. My money is on the dog."

"Rightly so." He laughed. And then, "How are you?"

"If I had a dollar for every time somebody asked me that, I'd be rich."

"Doubtful. The buck doesn't go as far as it used to." Angling his head to get a better read on me, he pushed, "Are you settling in with Wolfheart?"

"I'm staying there at night, but I'm not *settling* in *anywhere*." I glanced at my phone. "I'm probably going to head out soon. Go to Granny's until this evening. Or maybe go look for the missing dog and python."

Father Patrick scoffed. "This is exactly why people worry about you. Why not stay for the music and worship?"

"Is Timothy preaching?" I asked, suddenly curious about his progress.

"No, he isn't, but the charismatic Petey is, and then a dodgy ole priest you know will say a word as well."

I clucked. "Hate to miss that, but to be honest, I could use a little space right now. It's been like open auditions around here today."

A roll of laughter tumbled from the colorful priest. After recovering from the cough that followed, he patted my leg. "You can't blame folks for wanting to look out for you, Fireman. Not only are you an honorable and fine young man, but James 1:27 encourages us to…'look after orphans and widows'…so you see, all the kind gestures you've received are not only a tribute to you but an act of worshipping God."

"Well, number one, I'm not an orphan, and number two, you look out for me just fine."

He shot me a brief flick of surprise. "Funny. I see it the other way around."

Saved by the music which keyed up just as I grew embarrassed, I stood. "Well, I'm out of here."

"Help me up." Father Patrick extended his hand. "Meanwhile, what on earth are we to do about that dog?"

Chapter Eighteen

Wholeheartedly Endorse
Sterling

I doled out countless introductions as Pippa and I strolled the grounds of the revival. Since everyone was curious about the "sociable cutie" with the "big smile" I didn't have to work too hard. Most folks came to us, and a number of impromptu receiving lines sprung up organically.

The whole spectacle was utterly embarrassing.

Even Violet made her way over, which was surprising as she had a bit of a crisis on her hands with the missing snake and dog. Shocked that she spent more than a courteous allotment of time chatting with Pippa, I fought a measure of jealousy as she'd hardly taken that much time showing an interest in *my* work.

But now it was all, "Cozy mysteries? I really enjoy them! Have you heard of Michelle Bennington's *Small Batch* series set in Kentucky?"

"Of course," oozed Pippa. "Horses, bourbon, and murder. It doesn't get any better than that!"

Meanwhile, Mom and Aunt Desi were fit to be tied. Clearly, Pippa had won them over with her spirited personality, but their whispers and side-eyes were painfully over the top. Unfortunately, it wasn't just them. Uncle Lenny was smitten, Sheriff Rick had given her a whole handful of taffy, and even the mysterious, reserved Brad Wolfheart lingered with a smile and a story or two.

I considered slipping away as all the profuse fawning was insufferable at best, nauseating at worst, but once Tammy Jo made her appearance in a tight, fall-toned sweater, high-heeled boots, and jeans, I was all in.

Admittedly, I was pleased that Tammy Jo was there to witness Pippa's smashing debut. And I might have even placed my hand strategically on Pippa's shoulder or brushed it along her waist when I was sure Tammy Jo was looking.

As I steered Pippa toward the refreshment table, she mooned enthusiastically, "These people, Sterling. They're fabulous! I have one very important question though."

Since the band had taken the stage in preparation for their sets, I lowered my head so I could hear. "What's that?"

"The guy, Sprite? From the Quick Stop place?" When she stood on her tippy-toes I was blindsided by two explosive discoveries. The first was how incredibly nice she smelled and the second was the pleasing way her breath felt lightly brushing against my ear. "Does everybody call him that because he's petite?"

"They do." I chuckled. "And because he siphons sodas by the gallon. He's kind of a sugar addict." Enjoying the sound of her laughter, I added, "He has this super tall stool he sits on in the front window of his store. That way he can see the gas pumps, and because the stool swivels, he can also engage the customers in the store. He's got a lot of energy and is very talkative because of the—"

"—sugar!" She giggled. "I knew you were going to say that." When she spontaneously entwined her arm into mine, it caught me off guard. But I didn't hate it.

Just then, Dolly from the Diva Dome moseyed over with her boyfriend, Adam, Shady Gully's very own country crooner. "Hey, Sterling," Dolly asked, "who's your friend?"

I introduced them to Pippa as Adam shook my hand. "Sterling, I really love your vibe on Sunday mornings. You sure can shred on that guitar, my man. Props."

It was hard to look at Adam the same way after what Uncle Lenny had shared with me. By all accounts he was—or had been—a womanizer and a rogue, and the notion that he'd come between Aunt Desi and Uncle Lenny was impossible to comprehend. Nevertheless, according to the grapevine, he and Dolly had been hanging out pretty regularly, and they seemed pleasant enough now. I wondered, could two baddies actually make a goodie? Dolly certainly seemed to have changed. Perhaps she'd finally escaped the shadow of her unseemly twin brothers, whose nasty rivalry had set the whole community at odds for a time. Jesse's and James's dueling churches had not only ended in flames but had sent Jesse into perpetual rehab and prompted James to move to Arkansas to start a new church.

Good riddance, I thought rather unkindly, only half listening as Pippa and Dolly talked about hair. I risked a glance over my shoulder and found Tammy Jo staring directly at me. By the time I turned back, Dolly was brushing her fingers through Pippa's curls while Adam looked on in fascination.

I figured it was as good a time as any to drift away for a minute. "I'll be right back," I whispered to Pippa.

"Okay, have fun." She never took her eyes off Dolly. Nor did Adam take his eyes off the two of them. I experienced a sharp moment of doubt as I worried that Shady Gully's villainous couple would corrupt naïve little Pippa.

But I headed over to Tammy Jo anyway.

✝✝✝

Despite clearly signaling me over, Tammy Jo seemed preoccupied by the time I made it to the other end of the venue to say hello. She watched Petey as he stood near the makeshift stage and chatted with Daryl, who appeared gloomy and out of sorts without his sidekick, Bubba.

"Hey." She finally dragged her gaze away from my sister's husband to acknowledge my presence. "What's up?"

What's up? Really? "I'm surprised to see you here," I told her. "All the way from Naryville."

"I'm working in Belle Maison these days, so it wasn't such a long haul. Besides, my mom heard the legendary Timothy from

Northlake would be speaking at the revival, so she wanted me to get a picture with him."

"Oh." I searched the grounds for Timothy, finally spotting him on the opposite side of the venue, sweating on the basketball court with a bunch of ten-year-old boys. "He doesn't look like he's getting ready to take the stage. Maybe he's only here to listen, learn, and worship like the rest of us."

She hitched her shoulders up. "Oh well, I bet he'll still take a photo with me at some point. Especially since we met in Kentucky while I was there." Her attention seemed to wane again.

"What's going on, Tammy Jo?" I pressed. "What are we doing?"

"Who's the cute girl?" she asked finally, looking past me to where Pippa was engaged in an animated discussion with Dolly and Adam.

"It doesn't matter. Let's talk about us, and whatever this is, because I need to know if we're done or if there's still a scrap of something left."

She shrugged and shook her head, neither gesture giving me anything hopeful to cling to. "I don't know, Sterling. I really don't."

"You keep coming around, giving me these mixed signals, and I…I need to know, Tammy Jo, what went wrong with us? Is what we had salvageable? Because I really cared—care—about you."

Once again with the head shake, but this time it definitely ticked in the negative. "I just couldn't handle your dark moods. They wore me down over time."

Funny, I'd always felt the same about her affection. It had either sparked hot or cold, never consistent, never reliable, and never feeling true one way or the other. It was as if she'd been biding her time until something shinier came along.

I agonized over my response, stretching for the right words, and struggling over how to arrange them in a perfect counter—just as I did when I was trying to write. It wasn't a pleasant experience, so I stopped trying. After a marked breath, one in and one out, I said flatly, "Okay then. Let's just move on."

Finally, I had her full attention, not the distracted gaze that switched from Petey, me, and even Timothy's game of horse with the kids. "So, who is she? Really?"

"She's a friend. A writer. Her name is Pippa, and she's…"This time, I didn't have to scramble for the right words. I watched the animated conversation taking place across the church grounds, wondering what in the world Pippa could possibly be saying to entertain—and tame—the disreputable Adam and Dolly. "She's different from you."

I acknowledged the sudden lightness in my soul, realizing I'd rather be there, listening to whatever goofy, unfiltered tale Pippa was spinning, than here, listening to someone I used to care about tell me I was dark, moody, and not good enough.

"And you know what? That's okay," I said as I turned and headed back, a feeling of great resolve shifting over me in transformative waves.

✝✝✝

Before I reached Pippa, she'd peeled off from Dolly and Adam and moved to join Micah and Quietdove who were seated on a bench in the sun. One of the things that had always struck me about Pippa was her ability to approach people so freely, whether she knew them or not. Awed by her boldness, I'd asked her about it at a recent conference. She'd been utterly confused by my question and had responded quizzically. "How else are you supposed to approach people, Sterling? They're either going to like you or they're not, and it's good to know that upfront."

Perhaps she was right, as I could see that she'd somehow coaxed a giggle out of Micah who up until then had been sulking on the bench all day, no doubt brooding over the lost dog and snake. Meanwhile, Quietdove, whose emotions were dictated by the woman he longed for, sat loyally by her side.

"What'd I miss?" I asked as I joined them.

Micah raised her chin in Pippa's direction. "I wholeheartedly endorse."

I could feel the heat rising on my face, and apparently

Quietdove noted it as well because he helped a brother out by changing the subject. "Hoot doesn't seem too broken up about his lost dog—"

"Tootsie," Micah put in, wavering once again at the sound of the dog's name.

"Couldn't tell it the way he's over there chatting up those gals from Toulouse."

"Toulouse? What an adorable name." Pippa's eyes widened. "Is that an actual city? Or is it from *The Aristocats*?"

"It's more like a small community," explained Quietdove.

"Pippa's right though. Toulouse *is* a kitty from *The Aristocats* movie." Micah's mouth formed an "O" as Pippa started shimmying her shoulders to the tune of, "Everybody Wants to Be A Cat."

Quietdove and I exchanged an amused glance as Pippa and Micah struck up their own interpretation, and because we were so absorbed in their performance, we didn't notice when Hoot Wheeler marched over to confront Micah.

"So nice that you can sing and dance while my dog is missing." Although Hoot's expression contained a hint of coy playfulness, his words caused Micah's face to fall with regret.

"I'm sorry." She looked up with sad eyes at the strapping Hoot Wheeler.

When he seemed on the verge of smiling, Quietdove let out an aggravated groan. "It's not your fault, Micah. If anybody is to blame, it's Bubba." Quietdove stood and faced Hoot toe-to-toe. "Bottom line is there's no point in making her feel worse than she already does."

Obviously more annoyed with Quietdove now than he'd ever been with Micah, Hoot backed off, but not without a parting shot. "I'd better not find out that snake ate my dog. If I do, you can tell your boss"—he cut his eyes my way—"and your sister, that there will be a lawsuit."

As Hoot stalked off, I couldn't tell if he was serious or not, but Pippa offered her impression. "Well. That was mean."

"It really was," muttered Quietdove.

"And wrong," Pippa said. "Technically, the snake wouldn't eat the dog." When we all looked at her in confusion, she explained, "It would be more like a smothering thing."

I sucked in my breath, once again cursing Pippa's unrestrained personality.

And then Micah's shoulders began to shake. "You're outrageous, Pippa." She laughed, pivoting to me. "Have I told you that I wholeheartedly endorse?"

†††

Pippa and I wandered toward the pond, perching on a bench by the water's edge where Fireman and Father Patrick had previously been sitting. "What a cute dog," she said in puzzlement, her head dipping back to investigate the large tree. "What's he looking at?"

"That's Duke. Evidently, he treed a squirrel. He's very, very patient."

"He did what to a squirrel?"

"He chased a squirrel up a tree." I grinned. "It's Bella's and my cousin Luke's dog—"

"Luke's the mayor, right?"

"Yep. I think you've got all the characters straight now."

"Talk about," she gushed. "And how about the sexual tension between Micah and the hot deputy?" She fanned herself. "And that gossipy post office lady. Wasn't she something?"

"We call her Cruella Claire."

She shook her head, crowing. "This place is golden, Sterling. *This* is what you should be writing about. These people. This place. It's overflowing with humanity at its best—and most ridiculous. The characters alone…" She gazed out over the pond as a fish popped.

"I don't know." I shrugged my shoulders. "I enjoy thrillers. Mysteries."

"You enjoy reading them or you enjoy writing them?" She cocked her head at me. "Because I enjoy reading romance novels but couldn't write one if my life depended on it. All the bodice-ripping, yearning, and pulsing desire is not in my skill set."

While I did my best to shake off the image of her saying *yearning* and *pulsing*, I quipped, "You could write anything, Pippa."

"No, I really couldn't, and I'm serious, Sterling. I've read your work. You have a knack for heart-wrenching moments of consequence."

"I don't even know what that means."

She nudged me. "Yes, you do. And even if you don't know what it's called, I can assure you it's in everything you write. Like your story about the little girl who was homeschooled. Remember that? Her house backed up to an older couple's, and one day the man finds what he thinks is trash caught up in the fence they share, but upon closer inspection, it's a letter tied with a ribbon. It's from the little girl."

"It's for his wife. I remember, but—"

"The lonely little girl had drawn a picture for his wife and written in the note that she wanted to be her friend. So the husband goes in and brings the note to his wife, and they share a sweet moment because you see, they're lonely too, and sad because they'd just lost their dog of sixteen years. Anyway, the lady thinks and thinks, and she decides to bake some cookies and include them along with a bag of oranges in her note back to the little girl, which of course, she's written on her very best stationery."

"Right, but the story is really about the other neighbor who is embezzling money at his company and ends up murdering his secretary because she discovered the crime and—"

"No, Sterling. The story is about the friendship between a lonely little girl and a grieving woman and the beautiful way it sustains them both."

I realized Pippa was trying to give me a compliment, but somehow, it felt like criticism. Discouraged, I said, "But that wasn't the story."

"Well, maybe it should have been because that's where your

writing shines. You have an affinity for those kinds of moments. That's your gift."

I shrugged, unconvinced. "If you say so."

"I do." She linked her arm into mine and tugged me closer. "I really think you're writing in the wrong genre."

I looked sharply at her, her comments eerily echoing my mom's almost word for word. "Have you been talking to my mom?" The thought was unsettling. As unsettling as the realization that I wasn't even sure I *enjoyed* writing anymore. In fact, my lack of confidence had digressed to the point that any attempt at writing resulted in my dragging my knuckles through my hair in frustration or writhing in anxiety and misery at my cursed inability.

"Well, yes, I talked to your mom, but not about this. By the way, she and your Aunt Desi were incredibly helpful with my research. After chatting with them about the nuts and bolts of art galleries, I've decided to go a completely different direction with my novel. I'm absolutely psyched!"

"That's fantastic," I said, a little envious. When the music keyed up on stage, I nudged her. "Are you ready to go listen to some worship music? Maybe meet a few more cantankerous characters?"

She hopped up. "Let's do it."

As we trudged through the crowd toward the stage, I marveled at Pippa's boundless enthusiasm for…well, everything. "You don't seem miserable," I said mostly to myself.

She looked at me oddly.

I hesitated, and then decided to confide in her. "Sometimes it just seems that writers as a whole are the most miserable people on earth. Think about it. A lot of them end up killing themselves. Ernest Hemingway. Virginia Woolf."

"What in the world are you talking about?"

"Think about the writing conferences we go to, for instance. Have you ever seen so much doom and gloom? Everyone's frustrated because they can't get an agent, because they're convinced that that's what will get them to the next level. Or they're complaining about their publisher if they're lucky enough to have one." I raised my voice as we drew closer to the stage. "Or they're miserable because they're stuck creatively, or they're resentful because other writers are more successful. Just in general, they're miserable, you know?"

"I think you're weird," she said into my ear, "and taking it way too seriously."

As we closed in on the band, I was astounded to see Tammy Jo, once again with her clutches set on Petey as he tried to move toward the stage. I scanned the grounds for Violet, finally spotting her as she talked to Youngdeer and Charlie Wayne with a flyer in her hand. My passionate, earnest sister, who drove me crazy and hurt my feelings, but who I'd fight for and protect no matter what. Even though I knew Petey was only being polite, a flare of anger sparked inside me because Tammy Jo's motives were proving dodgy.

The vibe of the revival took a further dive when my sightline intersected with an upset Meadow confronting a sweaty, defeated-looking Timothy. They obviously thought they were hidden behind a giant oak tree, but the sudden flash of black, tan, and white flitting in my peripheral had given them away.

And proved Duke's patience had finally paid off as he gave the squirrel chase.

"Also," Pippa went on, "you have to focus on the good stuff. Like when the pieces of your work in progress fall into place and you know with absolute certainty that this is what God wants you to do."

"God?" I looked down at her, surprised. "I didn't know you were religious."

"Neither did I." Her dimples puckered when she smiled. "But I've been in Shady Gully a few days."

Chapter Nineteen

The First Strike
Timothy

"I need to know what's going on. Does this have something to do with me? Am I doing something wrong?"

"Of course not." I inched toward her cautiously. "Why would you think that?" While I was used to Meadow's ornery nature, this fresh burst of impatience made me wary.

"Because you used to be a fine, well-adjusted, faith-filled man, and suddenly, now that you're dating me, you're having a breakdown."

"I'm not having a breakdown."

"Fireman said you fainted again and that you were speaking incoherently. That sounds like a stroke or—"

"It wasn't a stroke. I'm just going through some stuff. Emotionally."

"Okay, I get that, and I understand that's why you're here—to get help from Father Patrick." She folded her arms.

"And to be with you," I added with a wobbly smile.

"We're not teenagers, Timothy." She watched as Duke dashed off to chase a squirrel, nearly knocking over a table with sodas in the process. "If we can't talk about whatever is going on with you, I just don't know how this is going to work."

And there it was. The first strike. The indication that she was willing to end it.

"We're too old for this. And I…" She swallowed deeply, a sign that whatever came next would be significant. "I've been through too much. Lost a good chunk of my life marinating in my misery." Her flickering green and gold eyes captured mine and held them in an insistent expression.

"I can't…I won't…go through this again. You need to figure this out."

"I will," I breathed, overcome with guilt. "Please don't give up on me."

"Is it me?" she asked spontaneously. "Is it because of what happened to me? Do you see me as tainted in some way?"

"What? Of course not!"

"Am I not faithful enough? Is that it? Because I'm really trying." Her eyes drifted closed, and her lips tightened in frustration.

Because I knew it would infuriate her for me to see her tears, I looked away. "You're perfect, Meadow."

"I'm not." She swiped angrily at a traitorous tear. "But because of you, and what I've learned from you, I'm starting to believe that God loves me."

"Meadow…" I reached for her, but she brushed me back.

"No, I mean like *really* believe He loves me. Even if things don't work out for us, you need to know that you helped me realize that."

She turned away from me then and stalked toward the sound of worship music blasting from the stage. I stared at her until she eventually blended into a swarm of people. So lost in my cluster of disturbing emotions, I barely registered when a text rattled in my pocket.

With dread, I tapped my phone, reassured to see it was Father Patrick.

```
Lenny and Desi plan to leave
early in a.m. to speak to Tom.
So to get an early start, I sug-
gest you stay with me tonight
rather than going all the way
to Lake Osprey.
```

I responded with a thumbs-up emoji, grateful, as marshaling others through difficulty always seemed to assuage my own.

✝✝✝

Despite how miserable I felt about my current circumstances, I volunteered—insisted—that I drive the church van to Belle Maison early the next morning. Not only were Father Patrick's eyes questionable at the crack of dawn, but he tended to lose focus when engaged in serious discussion.

"Take a left there." He pointed at the upcoming highway that intersected the little haven otherwise known as Shady Gully. "And then you'll go straight for twenty miles before you get to Belle Maison." He put his spectacles on and removed his yellow legal pad from his modest backpack. "Lucky for us, we have plenty of time to talk."

Unsure I was ready for whatever the ole spiritual drill sergeant had in store for me today, I clicked my left blinker. "How's the coffee?" I asked. We'd stopped at Lenny's Tool Shed and grabbed a cup, but since Micah was working and had obviously made the coffee, it appeared a little suspect.

"If you like bland, flavorless water, you'll love it," he said. "Now then. Why so gloomy this morning? Other than the obvious, of course."

I passed a slow-going stock trailer, returned the driver's wave, and released a deep sigh. "Meadow. She's unhappy with me." I glanced at the priest. "Your boy Fireman squealed about my fainting spell and generally poor condition the other day."

"My word. I'm going to have to speak to him about discretion."

"Well, knowing Meadow, she probably beat it out of him."

Father Patrick looked amused. "I imagine she's looking for some honesty about now. Some truth. And frankly, she deserves it."

"Despite her hard exterior, she's very fragile."

"Timothy, don't forget that she's been abused…as well." I felt the perceptive priest's scrutiny.

I didn't bite, choosing to clarify instead. "I don't mean fragile in that way. She can handle my past. I mean in terms of her

201

faith. She's a new believer, Father. She's trusting. Hopeful." I swallowed. "And vulnerable. That's another reason I'm struggling with ending our relationship. It seems I'm going to betray her no matter what I do." Since his misunderstanding was palpable, I elaborated further. "I'm deeply in love with her and quite honestly, I'd given up on ever having someone in life, but I'm also weak, Father. I'm a shameless, barefaced sinner."

"As we all are. We've already covered that."

"I have an ego," I continued, ignoring his remark, "one that is padded every day by a community who thinks they know me intimately, who treat me as if I have a hotline to God himself."

"Your point?"

"I'm not proud of this, but part of me worries that some measure of my initial affection for Meadow was rooted in the challenge of saving her—spiritually, I mean. When I first met her, she was a mess. She was lost, broken, and so damn magnificent." I blew out a massive breath, greatly relieved by the confession. "How could I resist the invitation? Clearly I couldn't," I went on, answering my own question, "because since then I've been haunted with this image of myself as a predator, a wolf disguised as a shepherd…and Meadow, an innocent lamb, lost and vulnerable…" I let out a guttural sigh. "I've had many variations of that same ghastly nightmare for weeks now."

"So, let me get this straight," Father Patrick eventually said as he twisted his generous frame in the seat. "The handsome, greatly revered mega-preacher deems himself responsible for saving the reluctant, exploited beauty? Do I have that right?"

"Pretty much."

When he burst out laughing, I felt my face flush with heat. "I'm sorry, Timothy, but what you're describing isn't original. I suspect a few navy seals have felt the same way about saving damsels in distress."

I frowned.

"But you're missing one very important truth. And that is this: you're not God. Meadow isn't and has never been yours to save.

She's God's, and however faulty your motivation for guiding her spiritually is, He's always been in charge. So while your ego definitely needs to be checked, your incentive is a very human one." He pointed. "Turn left, and then take a right."

I followed his direction, passing a sign that read, *Welcome to Belle Maison, Louisiana.*

"Here's another consideration. Perhaps, since you're genuinely in love with Meadow, it's time to invite her into *your* mess. Share with her *your* brokenness. Confide in her. Trust her. Perhaps she can rescue you." He winked. "Especially if there may be wedding bells in your future."

I said nothing, although I could feel myself blushing.

"As I always say to the young couples I counsel, you never want your marriage to be based on a lie, because these things have a way of coming out. And in your case, Timothy, because you're a public figure, it might be good to get in front of the narrative, as they say."

I nodded, my momentary glow fading.

"Speaking of which," Father Patrick said, "I took the opportunity at the revival yesterday to give the sheriff the black-mailer's number."

My breath hitched with the reality of that. "Okay."

"And here we are." Father Patrick hummed as I turned into the nursing home's parking lot. "Park there, next to Lenny's truck. And the sheriff's—"

"Is that Robin and Ricky?" I squinted. The two were sitting in the cab of his truck, Robin's diminutive figure comically childlike compared to the tall, brooding sheriff's.

"They're here for moral support, no doubt. Now," he said as he carefully climbed out of the van, "let's get in quickly, lest we're too late."

As we trooped into the facility, I couldn't shake Father Patrick's words: *you're not God.* It wasn't until we reached the entrance that I remembered that Luther had said the exact same thing to me in Lexington.

†††

We weren't too late for Desi and Lenny, but Tom's last minutes in this world were coming to a finish. As we crept into his room, we did our best to remain unobtrusive and reflect the reverence of the moment. Desi and Lenny, and a woman with red-dyed hair, perched beside his bed. A few of the nursing home staff safeguarded the door, while a nurse monitored the beeping and swishing of medical equipment inside the room.

The redhead turned, her eyes widening at the sight of me. I bowed my head, whispering my condolences, while she cracked an almost sheepish smile. "I'm Wanda, Tom's wife, and he'd like the fact that you're here, Timothy. We've been watching Northlake's services for a few years now."

I never knew quite how to handle moments like this. "Good," I said, "I hope it's provided some level of comfort for you." As Father Patrick lowered his head and murmured soothingly to the woman, I moved toward Desi and Lenny—and Tom. The man looked ashen and unresponsive for the most part, while Desi appeared resolved and surprisingly unhurried. Lenny, meanwhile, fidgeted, clearly uncomfortable with the scene.

Father Patrick genuflected and said a private prayer over Tom, and then Wanda asked if I'd say a few words. I took Desi's warm hand in mine and lightly brushed Tom's cold, limp hand as it rested on the sheet of the bed. "Let us pray. Lord God, heavenly Father, look with favor upon your child, Tom. Forgive him for all his sins, and comfort him with the promise of the resurrection to life everlasting through your son, Jesus Christ, our Lord, who lives and reigns with You and the Holy Spirit, one God, now and forever. Amen."

Everyone mumbled a solemn amen, and then Desi, astoundingly, spoke to the man who'd violated her when she was a teenager. "Tom, I don't know if you can hear me." She tentatively touched his hand. "Wanda told me about the talks y'all had, and how you told her about…the thing you did to me."

I glanced at Father Patrick and then Lenny, who was as pale as the bed sheet.

"I was glad to hear that because it would be harder to forgive you if you hadn't felt some remorse for what you did. I struggled for a long time. I felt ashamed and dirty and angry. Angry not just because of what you did to me but because of what you did to my mama. Bit by bit you smothered her fun-loving personality. You stole her joy and her vibrant…color. All the things that made her…Sunny."

Desi paused, resolved and calm. "And when you did what you did to me, you broke us. Both individually and as a mother and a daughter. You destroyed her. But guess what? You didn't destroy me. I'm alright. I let it go years ago, around the time I found Jesus. I hope, I truly do, that you know Him like I do. I'm happy now." She looked at Lenny. "I have my husband, my kids, and hopefully, maybe soon some grandkids. Anyway, I'm having a great life, and I…well, I just want you to know…" She wavered, then swallowed deeply and finished with conviction, "I forgive you."

A poignant silence filled the room, making it easy to spot the exact moment Tom's hand twitched next to Desi's. She gasped in shock, then seemed to gather her strength as she deliberately picked up his hand and squeezed. Lenny inched closer to her, assuring her of his presence.

Compelled at that moment to recite Psalm twenty-three, I began, "The Lord is my Shepherd; I shall not want. He maketh me to lie down in green pastures; He leadeth me beside the still waters. He restoreth my soul—'"

The beeps of the monitor interrupted the psalm, and after several minutes the nurse looked at Wanda and offered a solemn, "He's gone."

✝✝✝

Robin jumped out of Ricky's Ford F-150 the minute she saw Desi file out of the nursing home. The two embraced, clinging to one another for a prolonged moment, no doubt murmuring in a wordless language that traveled the span of their youth and into their adulthood right up to the present moment.

"I'm okay," we heard Desi finally say. "Actually, I feel a great burden lifted." She turned to Lenny, reaching for his hand. "Father Patrick was right. I feel liberated."

I studied her for an extended moment, surprised, but encouraged by her honesty.

"So…uh…y'all want to go to the Cozy Corner?" Ricky suggested tentatively.

A cascade of relieved exhales spread between us then, and after I felt the grumble of my stomach, I thought a greasy cheeseburger served with a sprinkle of Charlie Wayne's cussedness sounded good about now, but unfortunately, my spiritual drill sergeant had other ideas.

"Timothy is helping me with a little project," Father Patrick said, "so that's a no for us."

"Oh, phooey." Desi glanced at Robin. "We wanted to talk to our favorite Holy Men about our podcast. We have a little proposal for you."

Robin chimed. "Sterling and Fireman are going to help us with the technical bits, but our show, our podcast, I mean, is going to be spiritual in nature, so if we occasionally get stumped, we might need to"—she made air quotes with her fingers—"call a friend."

I chuckled. *These two…*

"Consider me intrigued." Father Patrick's eyes twinkled. "I can't wait to hear more."

Lenny patted his truck a few times. "I could use a spin around God's country. Any takers?"

"Oh, me!" Desi grinned.

"I'm in." Ricky winked. "I'll send Max and QD back for my truck."

Father Patrick and I watched as they all piled into Lenny's truck, rolled the windows down, and took off out of the nursing home's parking lot like a group of teenagers. We glanced at one another, the sound of their laughter lingering behind.

"Do you hear that, Timothy?" he asked softly. "That's the sound of freedom. That's what forgiveness brings."

†††

Because I couldn't sit another minute, I agreed to answer all of Father Patrick's questions if he allowed me to clean out his fireplace and start a fire. "Brilliant idea," he exclaimed. "I don't believe I've done that for years. If ever."

While he made tea, I hauled in a load of firewood and dragged the vacuum and some tools across the living room floor. After removing the andirons and grate, I set them on a towel and then swept up the ashes with a broom and a dustpan.

"My word, it looks brand new!" Father Patrick marveled. "I'll set your tea over here." He placed the mug on a coaster on the end table.

I scrutinized him, suddenly looking at him with fresh eyes. "Have you lost weight? Just since I've been here?"

"I thought you'd never notice!" He sipped herbal tea. "This is delicious, by the way. It's a wonderful chai Wolfheart suggested."

"Can't wait," I said over my shoulder as I attached the hose to the vacuum cleaner.

After a healthy slurp of his chai, he said benignly, "So, tell me more about Philip and Paul."

I started the vacuum. "Huh?" And sucked up a few spider webs and dust bunnies along with the last remnants of ashes. "I can't hear you." Once I had the inside looking sharp, I returned the grates and added some kindling, then topped that with some small logs. "How's that?"

He shook his head. "Stop stalling and come drink your tea."

Using matches I lit the fire, picked up a probably never used poker, and stoked a little. "I'm going to teach you how to do this because trust me, you're going to love it. You won't be able to drink tea again without a nice, roaring fire."

On the way to my chair, I picked up a crocheted throw and placed it on his lap. "You're probably cold now that you're so skinny." I took a healthy sip of the chai, longing for a burst of soothing warmth right about now. "I didn't see Philip too often. He had a wife, and of course, his trucking job."

"And Paul?"

"He saved me. Or," I considered, then reworded in light of our earlier conversation, "he introduced me to Jesus. Used the Bible to teach me to read. He led me on my journey of faith, and in the figurative sense, he saved me from a life on the streets."

"My word," Father Patrick breathed. "A guardian angel. Go on."

"Paul had an RV at a local campground, so whenever he was in town, I'd stay with him. He divided my lessons between history, reading, writing, and of course, poker, gin rummy, and spades." I stared at the fire, lost in memories. "Lydia taught me math and social skills."

"You divided your time between the two?" When I nodded, he said, "They both did a fine job."

"They did. And they were also the ones who helped me get a proper birth certificate. Become legit, so to speak. After years of falling off the Department of Social Services' radar, I didn't see much point, but they said I'd need one for school and for lots of important things when I grew up."

"And?"

"It was quite the process, but with a little help from Public Health and Vital Records, as well as Ancestry.com, they were able to confirm my birth." I tried for a chuckle. "And I am indeed forty-four years old."

"And your father?"

"I got a name, yes, and apparently my mother told me the truth about him dying in a car wreck. He died in Kentucky, so I imagine his death served as the catalyst for her exodus to Saint Louis."

"I wonder if he had family. Your father, I mean." Father Patrick considered. "Have you thought about that?" He leaned forward with newfound zeal. "You may have living relatives, Timothy. On both sides."

I massaged my temples, frustration rising. "Father, I can't think about that now. Right now, all I want is to keep my life from imploding." He graciously backed off, allowing me to continue. "Anyway, eventually I tested and got into regular school, and thanks to their tutoring, I tested well."

"And College of the Ozarks?"

"Paul had connections and was able to pull some strings. And Lydia knew people as well." I inched my shoulders up in wonder. "I scored a thirty-three on my ACT and maintained a GPA of 3.9, so that helped. COFO required a legal guardian the first year, so they fit the bill."

"And you worked."

"My tail off. It was worth it to get the free tuition. I had a good experience there. I made friends. I felt normal. I fit in."

"Of that, I have no doubt. If it were possible to teach personality, Timothy, yours would be the model."

"Thanks." I swallowed thickly, lost in good remembrances, but Father Patrick swiped them all away like an eraser on a chalkboard with his next question.

"Did they enjoy your success? Are you in touch with them now?"

I set the mug down, leaned forward, and burrowed my elbows onto my thighs. "They never knew. Lydia died in a car accident the year before I graduated, and Paul…" I rubbed my temples. "He got pancreatic cancer before I got my first pastoral job. I was in Haiti on a mission trip when I got word that he'd passed."

Father Patrick clicked the lever on his recliner and heaved himself forward. "That's tragic. I'm terribly sorry." He looked absently toward the kitchen, and after a moment asked, "Would you like another cup of tea?"

"No, thanks."

"Well then, how about a glass of cabernet?"

The sun had set, the fire was toasty, and the cab was delicious. I leaned back in my chair and lazily tracked the flames shimmering in the fireplace.

"I say, Timothy, it does have a nice ambiance doesn't it?"

"The fire or the cab?"

"Both," he said pleasantly. "And you're right, I simply must learn how to build one of these splendid fires."

"I'll teach you." We clinked glasses, signing the deal.

And then, "Would you tell me a little about your mother?"

I closed my eyes, pretending not to hear, but he waited me out. "Why?"

"I think it's important," he said in an impossibly sober voice.

"I don't remember much about her except that she was scrawny and had dull, flat eyes." I met his shocked expression head-on. "She dragged me from place to place. Drug dens, sketchy areas beneath the overpasses, the abandoned projects. Every time she'd tell me it was going to be better, and she'd promise to buy me a hamburger, and I always believed her. Until I didn't. It was never better. And I never got a hamburger. It got worse every time. At some point, I could barely see her face because of all the sores. She looked like a…monster."

"Sores from…?"

"Burns from the drug pipes. From scratching herself raw because she felt like she had bugs crawling all over her. I'd tell her, 'Mom, there are no bugs,' and she'd call me a liar, and force me to scratch her harder and harder…until I drew blood. Somehow that satisfied her. Everywhere we went, crack pipes and needles littered the floor. The mattresses were gross, but it beat the concrete or the hard ground. It never got better though. Only worse."

I stood and made my way to the bar for the bottle of cabernet. After refilling my glass, I brought it to top Father Patrick's off, but his glass was still full. Sighing with exasperation, I returned to my chair, missing the fire as it had now dwindled to meager, sporadic embers. "All I can tell you about my mother is that she didn't give two flips about me. She didn't care."

"She was an addict."

I snorted. "Oh, okay. Well, thanks. All better now."

"I'm not saying it's okay, I'm just saying—"

"I cared about her once, at the arch. When we first got to St. Louis, I remember standing there with her, and we were looking up at the arch, and I thought she was pretty. And the arch was pretty. And I felt happy. That one time."

He paused, swirling his glass. "Tell me about the abuse." When I didn't respond, he prodded, "The pictures. From your phone."

I slanted my eyes at Father Patrick, this fine man I'd come to care for and trust.

"Drifters were always coming in, seeking shelter sometimes, selling drugs other times, just enjoying their crappy, useless lives, I suppose." I glanced at him. "That's where the pictures came from, the Polaroids, I'm sure of it. Although I couldn't tell you who or when. As you can see from the group photo, the dens were a revolving door for the dregs of society."

Father Patrick didn't push, instead, he intuitively waited as I processed all the horrific memories bouncing around my psyche. Finally, I told him, "They made me do things in exchange for drugs for my mother, maybe a hamburger for me."

"She condoned this?"

An ugly sound croaked out of my throat. "Hell, Father, she talked me into it." When he looked genuinely aggrieved, I felt sad.

†††

The wine had made me drowsy, and the memories had scraped my soul raw. Father Patrick led me to the spare room and pulled the covers down. "Get comfortable. You need to rest." When he disappeared, I leaned on the pillow, still sitting, but very relaxed.

When he returned with a glass of water and an aspirin, I did as he asked, agreeable, pliable, numb. He dimmed the lamp and read scripture to me for several minutes until my eyes grew heavy.

Sleep didn't come, but tears did. Silent, without expression, they just flowed down my face one after the other. Father

Patrick continued to read, pausing only to dab my cheeks with an old-fashioned handkerchief.

"Was it difficult when she died?" he asked gently.

"Yes, believe it or not. As horrible as she was, she wanted me right there with her at the end. I never left her side. I sponged her face when she was hot. I covered her up when she was cold. I listened to her weep when she was in pain. I listened to her beg…" I hesitated.

"What did she beg for, Timothy?"

"I think you know," I muttered ruefully. "She wanted me to forgive her."

"And did you?"

"I told her I did. I promised her even. Because that's what she wanted to hear." I let out a guttural growl, unleashing nearly three decades worth of remorse. "But no." I twisted so he could see the back side of my calf. "I got a tattoo on my leg though."

Father Patrick pushed his spectacles higher up his nose, reading, "Forgive."

"I know I should, that I *need* to, but I can't."

"That's alright," he said without judgment, and I loved him for allowing me—for now anyway—that small act of defiance.

"Remember when you asked me if I identified more as the successful pastor or the scared little boy?"

"Yes."

I closed my eyes, inadvertently sending another fresh wave of tears down my cheeks. "I definitely feel like that little boy tonight."

He closed the Bible, and lightly brushed the tears from my face with his handkerchief. "You're safe now, Timothy. I promise, you're safe."

Chapter Twenty

Just the One
Fireman

The idea struck me as I watched Aurora's kittens latch on and single-mindedly suckle their breakfast. Remembering what Violet told me about making sure the runt got her fill, I nudged the bully of the group, Mr. Black and Orange, away from Mr. Calico's favorite nipple, thus opening a spot for the petite orange kitten with the white slash across her nose. Little Ms. Slash was going to have a great life if only I could successfully navigate all the moving parts of my plan.

Since it was only a matter of time before Wolfheart or Meadow or Father Patrick started dropping subtle hints about my returning to school, time was of the essence. I picked up my phone and texted Sterling.

```
What time do Desi and Robin want
to meet about their podcast?
```
He quickly texted back.
```
        Whenever is good for you.
```
I replied.
```
Let's do it this afternoon. If
you're free now, meet me at
Violet's Vet. I have an idea
about catching the snake.
```
He responded with a thumbs up, two perky women, and an exploding head. Translation: Desi and Robin were driving him crazy, and he'd meet me at the vet, pronto. Now, I just needed to text Bubba.

✝✝✝

I shared my hunch with Sterling and Bubba as we gathered on the back porch of Violet's Vet. "I think Pierre might be closer than we think. I got to thinking that Opry Lane subdivision is only about a half mile from here, if that. It literally backs up to the cemetery and Violet's pasture. The problem is there are woods in between, which is probably why nobody looked there."

"That's right," Bubba agreed. "So far we've mostly been focusing on this end, around the houses in the four-way stop area."

Sterling nodded. "So let's work our way in the opposite direction. Do you have the tote?" he asked Bubba.

"Yep. And zip ties."

"Okay, Bubba," I posed a question, "if you were Pierre, what would you be hungry for? And please don't say a small dog."

Bubba scrunched up his face. "My cousin brings his chihuahua, Charlie, to the house all the time and Pierre could care less. He doesn't have a taste for it."

Sterling and I traded looks.

"But I'll tell you what he does like." Bubba grinned. "Roosters."

The screen on the porch door made a slapping sound as Violet appeared, wearing scrubs and her usual curt expression. "So what's the plan?"

"Who has chickens around Opry Lane?" I asked her.

"Mrs. Shanna May brings me fresh eggs sometimes," Violet mused. "And I think somebody has a chicken coop on Waylon Road, near Mrs. Guidry's place."

"Let's start there." I brought my hands together.

"Copy that." Sterling winked at his sister. "Operation Recover Pierre is officially underway."

"Don't forget about Tootsie," she added.

We armed ourselves with tools to swath a path if necessary—and Bubba—because he was our biggest asset. "I want you to call out to him like you normally would," I suggested. "Like when it's dinner time."

"Snakes don't really react to that," he said, already breathing heavily as we trooped toward the woods. "Pierre responds more to movement and scent. Especially mine. Hey, maybe we should look over yonder, past Dolly's Diva Dome—"

"You mean around Nails and Thread? Your girlfriend's shop?" I joked.

"What?" Sterling stopped short. "Are you serious?" He looked at Bubba with fresh eyes. "Nice."

"Well, it ain't real serious or nothing…"

"Nothing being the key word," I piped. "Although she did ask about you at the revival."

"Are you serious? What'd she say?" Bubba's mouth quivered hopefully.

Since I didn't want him to lose focus, I turned to Sterling, who was most assuredly not out of breath. Tall, in excellent shape, and good-looking in that all-American way, Sterling had dark hair and eyes, a strong chin line, and an easy smile. "Who was the hot girl you were hanging around with at the revival?"

Baffled, he asked, "Tammy Jo?"

"No. The happy one with red hair."

"Oh. That was Pippa. She's a writer friend."

"If you say so," I joked. We'd just passed the cemetery and were angling west toward the backside of the subdivision when we heard a rooster. "Whoa…" I breathed.

"It's coming from over there." Sterling pointed, eyeing a makeshift trail. "Somebody's been through here. See how packed and smooth the ground is."

"Sure," Bubba chipped. "If you live in Opry Lane subdivision, it's a lot quicker to get on your four-wheeler and drive through here instead of getting in your car and driving all the way out of the neighborhood, then onto the main road, and then to the four-way stop."

I removed a large Ziploc bag from my backpack, sprinkling a trail of flour behind us. "If we don't find him, let's be careful not to track through this on the way back."

As Bubba waved his arms with big, wide motions, the trail faded, and several houses appeared. Remember to look up," Bubba said. "Pythons love to climb trees. And with the sun out, he could be up there sunning himself to keep warm."

"The rooster," Sterling pointed. "It's coming from over there." Sure enough, there was a neat little barn, painted red and white to match the red brick house in front.

"That must be Mrs. Shanna May's house," I mumbled. "Maybe we should go knock on her door."

"Y'all go ahead while I take a look in the barn. Oh, and be sure and tell her you're with me." Bubba added for Sterling's benefit, "She was the school secretary when me and your mama was at Shady Gully High." He grinned mischievously. "I spent a lot of time in the office."

As Bubba disappeared into the barn, Sterling and I circled to the front of the house. We were just about to knock on the door when a chorus of barks erupted at the house next door. Two little dogs raced across the front porch, shoved their snouts through the slats, and barked in enthusiastic outrage. We both watched as a heavy-set woman padded onto the porch. "Juliet!" she fussed, "stop that!" When she saw us, she halted and planted her hands on her enormous hips. "Who's that?"

Sterling followed as I trotted down Mrs. Shanna May's steps and walked the short distance to her neighbor's house. "Fireman and Sterling. We're looking for—" I stopped. First, because I didn't want the woman to have a heart attack upon hearing the word *snake,* but also because one of the dogs looked an awful lot like—

"Tootsie?" Sterling said from behind me. "Is that…?" The mop of fur passing itself off as a dog trembled in elation.

"Who? Who did you say you were?"

"Are you Mrs. Guidry?" Sterling asked. "I'm Sterling, Robin's son. Remember she and Desi were—"

"Oh, my gracious, yes! Oh, what dolls! I do hope they both get on the homecoming court this year. How sweet that would be, them being friends and all. I saw them at the ballgame just last night. Canoodling with their beaus, of course. Dean is my favorite. That boy is going places."

I cleared my throat, squatting next to the dogs. "Cute pups. What are their names?"

"Oh, well, there's just the one. It's my darling Juliet." She frowned. "Has she run off again?"

"No, ma'am." I cut my eyes at Sterling, who had turned reflective at the mention of his deceased father. "It's just that there is another pup here." I checked the collar on the prancing furball.

I turned to Sterling. "Tootsie."

Unfortunately, Bubba had no such luck finding Pierre. "I looked everywhere," he complained. "All around the bales of hay. Underneath the coops. Nothing." He tried to hide his disappointment as he watched me struggling to balance the overly hyper and very squiggly Tootsie. "At least we got the mutt. Hoot'll be happy."

"Violet's thrilled," Sterling said. "I just texted to let her know."

When Tootsie began to squirm anxiously in my arms, I nearly lost my grip. "I wish we'd brought a carrier…"

"Stop," Sterling said in a serious tone. "Look." He indicated the flour trail I'd dropped on the way. "Bubba, do that hand thing again. Pierre's definitely been here."

Sure enough, the flour track exposed the long, heavy imprint of a reptile.

"In the last hour," I breathed, holding tight to Tootsie. We'd spent about that amount of time or more having a coke on the porch with Mrs. Guidry, who'd gone on and on about her past, which in her mind, was very much her present.

Bubba cut a path in and out of the surrounding brush, even marching in circles as he tried to follow the tracks in the tussled flour. We watched as he bent his head way back, carefully searching in the tall loblolly pine trees above. As we followed him, small flakes of pine bark suddenly rained down on us.

"I see him!" Bubba shrilled. "He's there! Pierre!"

"Awesome." Sterling and I breathed with relief, but when we reached Bubba, Sterling's mouth hung open. He pointed up into the tall pine.

"Pierre." I craned my neck, using my hand to shield the sun from my face. The hundred-pound reticulated python was twined around the trunk of the tall loblolly pine tree, his massive frame leisurely basking in the sun—thirty to thirty-five feet high.

"Look at my boy," Bubba said almost proudly, even as thick flakes of pine bark dust continued to float onto his head. "Say, Fireman, I reckon we're gonna need a ladder."

✝✝✝

By the time Big Al, Redflyer, and Moonpipe arrived in Shady Gully's famed big red fire truck, they'd acquired quite the following. Even Charlie Wayne and JJ Wheeler, it seemed, had managed to stop service at the Cozy Corner long enough to join the other looky-loos with their phones.

Meanwhile, Tootsie, alarmed by the sirens and the spectacle the sight was quickly becoming, twisted and churned in my arms like a greased pig.

"I'll take her." Sterling secured the squirmy pup. "I think they're going to need help." He indicated the fire crew who stood with their arms folded tightly against their chests as they gazed at the massive snake sprawling in the tree.

"I'm not climbing up there," Moonpipe stated emphatically. "And no way am I touching that snake."

"Me either," echoed Big Al.

"Aw, come on," urged Redflyer.

"Are you crazy? Who do you think we are? Bare Hands Beran?"

Redflyer looked thoughtful. "How long ya think it would take him to get here? He's just in Missouri." He poked his thumb upward like it was just up the road a ways.

By this time, Bubba's sidekick, Daryl, had arrived to offer his support, while Violet had tracked out of her office along with

Sigourney Sky of Nails and Thread and even Dolly of the Diva Dome. Dolly took photos; Sigourney grinned at Bubba; and Violet scowled at Shady Gully's finest. "What? Am I going to have to climb up that tree and get him?"

"No…uh…we'll get him," Big Al said with a total lack of confidence.

"Save Pierre!" Someone in the crowd started chanting. "Save Pierre!" The rhythmic cadence hastily picked up, growing into a battle cry of sorts. "Save Pierre!"

Quietdove and Max rolled in, followed by the sheriff, and their lights flashed in tandem with the firetruck's to create an ironic light show. "What in Sam Hill is going on here?" the sheriff growled.

"Everybody just chill," Bubba said resolutely. "I'm gonna go up there and get him. Just roll out the ladder." Sterling and I caught Bubba's subtle glance in Sigourney's direction. Unfortunately, after climbing a total of three steps, Bubba slipped and landed heavily on the ground.

"Okay," I muttered, stalking over to the tree. "Let's get this bad boy down. Y'all hold the ladder." Despite the pulsating beat of the crowd's increased chanting, I made my way up the ladder fairly quickly. "Now what?"

"Well, uh…" Bubba had apparently recovered. "You just need to let him wrap himself around you, Fireman. And then y'all come on down the ladder."

Oh, okay. No problem.

Eventually, I was able to move my arms in a way that attracted Pierre, and he latched onto my torso with curiosity. Or hunger, but I tried not to think about that. I concentrated more on maintaining my composure as he twined, coiled, and leaned into me. "Yeah, that's it," Bubba encouraged me. "Nice job."

It took some patience and finagling, but finally I—we—made our way down the ladder. By the time my shivering, shaky foot landed on firm ground, I was panting for breath and my legs and arms were shaking with strain.

The crowd cheered as Bubba carefully coiled Pierre safely into the tote, all with Violet watching over his shoulder as he secured the zip ties.

The crowd was jubilant. Charlie Wayne offered free sweet tea at the Cozy Corner and vowed to add a chili dog to his menu and name it after Pierre. "Make sure it's a footlong," someone joked, and off they all went.

By the time we got to Desi's house, word of our special operations victory had already traveled throughout Shady Gully. She and Robin had rigged up balloons and prepared banana splits in celebration and treat.

"These are delicious," I said through a garble of scrumptious sugar and dairy, wishing I could tell Granny about it when I got home.

"You deserve it," Robin gushed. "You singlehandedly saved Violet from a lawsuit."

Sterling frowned. "I helped."

"Yeah." I scooped a large spoonful of ice cream into my mouth. "He carried the teeny tiny dog while I helped wrestle the python back to the vet with Bubba."

"No appreciation," returned Sterling, swiveling comfortably in the office chair behind Desi's desk.

A sudden rush of paws, tails, and attitudes sprinted past us sounding very much like a herd of galloping horses. Eventually, Mary Ann and Ginger—the cocker spaniel and papillon respectively—caught up with Buford and Gerty—their very presumptuous feline houseguests—and proceeded to resolve their differences in a feisty tussle that ended in a huddle at the end of the hall.

"Whoa," I mumbled in exclamation, even as a tickle in my throat grew into a laugh.

"They're all psycho." Sterling shook his head in bewilderment. "You sure can't have all that rowdiness going on when we record."

Robin put her hands on her hip and skewered Sterling with a look. "Of course not. We'll take the kitties to Ricky's on recording day."

"Yes, ma'am." He absorbed a grin. "Okay then. Let's get down to it. I've ordered some microphones, and I'm uploading the software now—"

"What will that do?" Desi asked.

"It'll take care of audio cleanup, will let you add music, and even piece together your audio segments."

"How about direct publishing of episodes?" I asked Sterling.

"It does that as well." He switched his gaze to Desi and Robin. "So, all y'all will need to do is upload your recordings and the podcast editor will take out the big mistakes."

"Uh…" Robin appeared alarmed. "I thought y'all were going to do all those techy things for us."

"We will," I said, eager to master the program myself. "Sterling will take care of it on the Kentucky end, and I'll help Desi on this end, and we'll make a template that y'all can use every time."

"Right, I think y'all will eventually find it easy, but like Fireman said, we're here until you get the hang of it." Sterling scraped his spoon against his bowl, setting it aside.

"Okay, then." After a telepathic powwow, the two friends decided they could get on board with the plan. "Let's do it."

"Alright, the first thing y'all need to do is make some decisions." Sterling tapped the keyboard. "Your topic."

"Prayer and encouragement for women," Robin said decisively. "And we'll have special guests and talk about issues that matter to women. And we're not going to sugarcoat anything either."

"That's right." Desi bobbed her head in agreement. "And we've already got commitments from Petey, Father Patrick, and Timothy. They'll be our Holy Men on Call in case we need help."

"I like that." I grinned, warming to the idea, even though I wasn't religious. "Father Patrick could recite the alphabet and be entertaining. Plus, it will keep him busy."

"Great." Sterling jumped on the bandwagon. "Pippa has a

friend who does graphic art. We'll get you a couple of visuals to pick from, something that fits your theme. Because you'll want to promote via social media and email."

"What about length?" I asked. "The average drive time for commuters is twenty-eight minutes, but y'all will want it a little longer in case you occasionally go off topic."

"Yeah." Sterling made a face. "They'll definitely need to account for that."

After a round of joshing and mock outrage, Desi said, "We think we can talk for at least forty-five minutes. How does that sound?"

"Perfect," I said, looking over Sterling's shoulders as he flipped through music and graphics. "What about a name?"

Sterling glanced at me. "That was my next question." He turned to his mom and Desi. "Any thoughts?"

"I don't know," Robin sighed. "We're just two hardheaded southern gals who want to talk about things that matter to women—"

"—and how they can apply scripture to ease all matters of the heart." Desi returned Robin's sigh. "But I don't know how to say that in a title."

Clearly not my bailiwick, I observed Sterling as he spun the office chair in circles. After a long moment, he said, "How about Heart Headed? A podcast for strong women with gentle hearts."

Even before Desi and Robin started squealing, my heart jumped. The dude totally nailed it.

We were on our way.

✝✝✝

Even though it was still light outside, I decided to go straight to Wolfheart's rather than sit at Granny's. Although I hated to admit it, I was super psyched about working on the podcast—in essence, developing it from the ground up—and I couldn't wait to share my excitement with someone. And since I knew Wolfheart would be especially interested, I relished the idea of giving him the scoop.

When I parked in the dirt driveway of his yard, half a dozen critters surrounded my car. "Hey, boy." I ruffled Blue's ears, squawked playfully at a random chicken, and picked up Aurora, who nuzzled my neck, no doubt glad to have a break from her demanding litter.

"Well, there he is." Wolfheart whistled as he poked his head up from the garden. "The man of the hour. I heard you snagged a python today."

"Yeah, and a little dog too."

He chuckled. "I suppose Bubba and Hoot Wheeler are relieved."

"Bubba almost cried." I took the water hose from him and proceeded to give the mustard and collard greens a sprinkle. "It's probably best to skip the beets, huh?" I made a face.

"Nope, douse them, they're good for you." When Black came over to investigate, Wolfheart scratched him under the chin. "And Desi? Did you and Sterling get her and Robin squared away on their podcast?"

"It's going to be awesome! Sterling came up with this great name for their show, and we decided the first episode is going to be an introductory episode, you know, where they'll talk about who they are and where they live and yada, yada."

"Yada, yada?" Wolfheart took back the hose to give the cabbage and beets a proper drink. "I think they'll enjoy themselves, and it sounds like you're enthused about it as well."

"I'm interested in learning more about that kind of stuff, and Sterling is wicked smart, so yeah, it'll be fun. Oh, and get this, they're going to do a special segment when they call up a holy man for guidance or advice or whatever. Either Father Patrick, Petey, or Timothy."

He turned off the hose, flashing me a goofy smile. "That could be dangerous."

"I know, right?" I laughed. "Hey, what's for dinner? I'm starving?"

We sat on the porch with a pitcher of iced tea between us, our legs propped on the railing and heaping bowls of chicken and sausage gumbo cradled on our laps. "Desi made banana splits today," I said with a mouth full of gumbo. "I think I got a little high from the sugar. I've been buzzing ever since."

"You'll sleep well tonight." Wolfheart cocked his head. "Has the sheriff caught you zipping around town by yourself?"

"I haven't been zipping, and I'm wearing my seatbelt and following all the rules." I lifted my shoulders. "I don't know if he's seen me or not. Max did. He waved." I changed the subject. "Where's Meadow?"

Wolfheart made a show of scraping his bowl, which I knew meant he was thinking of a careful way to answer. "She's at her place."

"I hope she doesn't blow it with Timothy."

Wolfheart's expressive green eyes turned downward. "I hope *he* doesn't blow it with her."

I scraped my bowl, copying Wolfheart's method of thinking before speaking. "Yeah, I suppose it goes both ways. Timothy hasn't been his usual self lately. Do you think he'll be okay?"

"I do. God will get him through whatever he's struggling with, and he'll come out the other side spiritually and emotionally stronger." Wolfheart stared up at the moon, its light holding his face gently as night fell. "Our histories can haunt us, Fireman, damage us even, but God is bigger than our pasts, our futures, and our pain."

I said nothing for a long beat, as I was used to Wolfheart going on about his faith. "And Meadow? Will she be alright?"

A pensive smile spread across his lips. "Most definitely."

"Good, because even though she's still grumpy, she's way nicer than she used to be."

He murmured his agreement. "She's happier than I've seen her in…well, years."

"When what happened to her…happened, you mean?"

He nodded but didn't elaborate, so we sat in silence for several minutes, watching as Black and Blue meandered aimlessly about the yard, gently herding errant chickens and stray cats before finally settling into comfortable curls at our feet.

"Did you know your parents?" I asked spontaneously.

"Not really," he answered, his face settling on mine. "Peony and I were very young when they disappeared—or died. We never really knew what happened. We were passed around on The Creek and raised in different homes according to the seasons or who was available. We were looked after fairly well, all things considered."

I did some moon studying of my own. "Guess that'll be me too."

"Hardly. You will be cherished and tenderly looked after no matter what. This, I know with certainty."

"I never knew my parents. Granny wouldn't talk about them." I strained my eyes to see him in the dim light. "Did you know them?"

"No, sadly, I didn't. They would have been much younger than me. And Granny Lacey was always pretty tight-lipped about it with everyone."

"Probably because they were awful." I sighed.

"Not necessarily. But perhaps it's healthier to look forward."

"Yeah. Granny raised me from a baby. There are pictures of her feeding me with a bottle." I hiccupped. "She looked different then."

"So did you, I bet." When I started giggling, he got tickled, and soon we were rolling with laughter, causing the dogs to lift their heads in wonder. Eventually, we recovered and turned once again to the moon for answers.

"You're going to be fine," Wolfheart said in a gruff voice. "And so is Meadow. No matter what happens with Timothy."

"I hope so."

"You know, Meadow's recent peace and serenity aren't entirely because of Timothy."

"Oh, you're talking about God again. I see what you did there."

"Without God, there is nothing, Fireman. Everything that's

good in the world comes from Him, and once you realize that He knows you and loves you—"

"He doesn't know me." I blurted, perhaps a little too indignantly.

Wolfheart *tsked.* "That's where you're wrong. He knew you from the beginning, when you were in your mother's womb, and He'll be the one with you at the very end."

The notion that God knew me even before I was born shook me. Even more astounding was the idea that He knew my mother. "I don't understand. I have questions."

"I can explain. If you want. Your Granny had questions as well, and she came to know Jesus. We prayed together many times, and I read to her from the Bible."

"Yeah, Petey said something like that at her funeral."

"It's true. She became very faithful."

I wouldn't have believed that if I hadn't seen the scripture she'd scrawled in her recipe book. "She didn't say anything about it to me."

"She wanted to, son. She told me as much, but she…took a bad turn and never had the opportunity. But it was very important to her."

"Okay," I eventually muttered in a voice I didn't recognize. "I'm listening."

Chapter Twenty-One

Talking Points
Sterling

"How'd Hoot Wheeler take the news?"

"He was relieved," Violet answered. "Although not as much as me, especially when I heard he was talking about suing me." She took a generous gulp of coffee. "Of course, he'll hold it over Micah's head from here to eternity. Or until they get married."

I balked. "Please God, no."

"Crazier things have happened. For instance, did you know Sigourney Sky has a thing for Bubba?" She swirled her Lenny's Tool Shed mug, swigging again. "Boggles the mind."

"That's fully leaded coffee, by the way. Uncle Lenny made it. Said to tell you hi."

"I love Uncle Lenny's fully leaded coffee." She grinned. "It's always my first stop in the mornings."

My mind filled with images of my sister's daily routine. "Must be nice living so close to everyone. Seems like a good life."

"It is," she said wistfully. "But seriously though, Bubba and Sigourney? I don't see it."

"Could be a rumor. Possibly even started by Bubba himself."

Violet snorted with laughter, and then we fell into an easy silence slurping our coffee and contemplating the view outside the screened porch beside Violet's veterinary office. Not for the first time I considered Petey's careful and intentional planning when constructing my sister's dream facility.

Absorbed in melancholy, I watched the recovering animals graze in the pasture that met the four-way stop. "The donkey is cute." A little guy, gray, with soulful eyes, he seemed to match our gazes as if he knew he was part of the conversation.

"His name is Tom Petty, and he's doing great now. Some jerk abandoned him at a trailer park in Azalealand, left him tied to a post to starve." My sister's tone grew edgy with passion. "He'll be fine. I've got to decide now whether to send him to the humane society or keep him here as a mascot."

"Keep Tom Petty. No need for him to live like a refugee."

She cackled at my joke, even before the words came out of my mouth. "We'll see how he does. Some donkeys have attitudes."

As I took measure of my sister, lingering over coffee and pondering the abused animals in her care, I saw no trace of the aloof, painfully reserved Violet of old. Instead, I saw a serene woman, a woman who was content as she faced the day. "Are you happy?" I pushed for confirmation. "You look great. At ease and very tranquil."

"I am, brother." She shot me a rare—but singularly colorful smile—the very one I'd known and treasured all my life. "The ride was bumpy, the route was skewed, but I arrived right where I wanted to be. Where God intended me to be."

"You sound like your husband now," I teased.

"It's hard not to pick up some of his talking points." She ducked her head, regarded me under a veil of pale eyelashes. "And you? Mama has been worried."

"I heard."

"She's currently preoccupied with what Daddy would say, how he would advise you and encourage you on your journey."

"Y'all act like I'm a nutcase."

"She just wants you to be happy." She sipped. "And you *do* have a tendency to mope."

I bit back an aggravated sigh.

"I really like Pippa, by the way." Violet tipped her head back, draining the last of her coffee. "And not just because I'm a little jealous of Tammy Jo, but because you're different around her. More playful, less uptight."

"You shouldn't be jealous of Tammy Jo—"

"She's gorgeous."

"—because Petey is deeply in love with you and would never, ever, in a million years be unfaithful. He's utterly smitten. I've never seen him so settled and happy."

She blushed.

"Gross," I teased.

"But she is gorgeous. Tammy Jo."

I twisted in the porch chair so I could see her fully. "So? That only goes so far."

"Pippa is also beautiful. Just in a different way. She's like Micah. She's got that alluring, perky thing going on."

Realizing how much I'd missed having a candid conversation with my sister, I took a risk. "You don't understand. Things have been…difficult."

She glanced at her watch. "So tell me. I've got time. I pushed back my appointments today so we could visit. I thought we could go tidy up Daddy's grave. I brought some mums from the house. They're blooming bright purple this time of the year."

"That sounds good. And you know…"

Sheriff Rick—Ricky—had asked if we'd meet him at the Cozy Corner for lunch.

"Don't remind me. I'm trying not to think about it." Violet met my dread and raised it with her own doubt. "What do you think he wants?"

I raised my eyebrows and told my sister honestly, "I think he's going to ask for permission to marry Mom."

✝✝✝

Violet carried a vase of brightly colored lavender and purple mums while I carried a rake and a garbage bag to collect weeds. As we walked the short distance to Shady Gully's cemetery, I tried to explain to my sister the agony of being a writer.

"It's not just me, this is what you have to realize. If you could be a fly on the wall at a writer's meeting or conference, you'd see that I'm not alone in my angst. We are truly some of the most doomed people on earth."

"For heaven's sake, Sterling, don't you think you're being a tad melodramatic?"

"Now you sound like Pippa." I used my hands to emphasize my point. "We are filled with self-doubt. Seriously, at my last conference, we divided up into groups to critique one another's work, to spitball ideas, and to vent and share with people who could truly relate. Anyway, not one of the authors there had any confidence in their work. They truly believed no one would want to read what they'd written and that they were absolute and total frauds."

"What a bunch of self-involved losers," Violet remarked.

"That's mean," I scoffed. "Have some compassion, Queen Maleficent. Here's the thing, these writers…their work is golden. Some of these people are bestselling authors."

"Like who?"

"Whom. And I can't tell you. I'd be breaking the "doomed artists" code. What we lack in confidence we make up for in loyalty. Anyway, all this to say, it was disheartening to see that such talented people seemed better at *creating* worlds than weathering their own."

"Wow, that's deep. And depressing." She shoved me playfully, which inexplicably cheered me tremendously. "Get away from me." She giggled. "You're killing my vibe."

As we jostled easily together, I marveled at the way my sister could anchor me like no other.

"Look," she said as we closed in on Dad's gravesite. "Someone's already been here."

The grave was immaculate, the obelisk pristine, and fresh flowers had been perfectly placed around his stately gravestone. "Mom," I said. "It has to be."

"Yep," Violet said thickly. "Pink roses. That was his thing. Remember?"

"I do. Instead of red roses, he'd always get her pink ones. He said they suited her better."

"And they do. And they're hard to find. Mama probably special-ordered these."

I squatted, running my hands through the grass along my father's resting place. I felt Violet's hand brush the top of my shoulder. It was supportive, concurring. Being children of Dean and Robin was a club of only two—and would remain that way until the end of time.

"I wonder what he would tell me," I stuttered, "about my current course in life. Maybe he'd tell me I should quit writing since it makes me so miserable."

"I don't think he'd tell you that, Sterling. You're a great writer."

I stood, my gaze landing firmly on my beautiful twin sister. "How would you know? Seriously, Violet, would it kill you to read my work? I know you're busy doing important things, but…" I trailed off, turning my gaze toward my father's name on the headstone. "Do you know what it's like when the people you love the most, the very people you're writing for and trying to impress, when they won't even make an effort—or don't care enough—"

"Sterling, I read your story." She dragged her hand across her face and pinched her nose. "I could tell you were mad at me the other night, so I—"

"You said it was *cheery*, Violet."

"I'm sorry, and you're right, I need to make a better effort." She sighed. "But I finally read it and…I just couldn't…I couldn't handle it. It broke my heart."

I cleared my throat, hardly believing what I was hearing.

"The way you wrote about him. The man in the story. Derek. You captured him to a tee. And it wrecked me."

"Because Derek was Dad?"

"No, not just because Derek was Dad, but because of the immersive, emotional way you write. Your storytelling is provocative, Sterling."

"Why didn't you tell me?"

"I don't know." With tears staining her cheeks, she waved her hand to indicate her face. "Because of this probably." She turned away from me then, her shoulders shaking as she dimly watched the goats nibbling in the pasture while the donkey mimicked their actions ten feet away. "You're truly gifted, Sterling." She wept. "Please don't give up. Daddy wouldn't want you to." Her thick-throated sobs rose as she wheeled and burrowed her head into my chest. "And neither do I."

I held her tightly, my eyes never leaving my dad's grave, or the pink roses my mom left. The four of us—a family, forever and always linked—no matter how the seasons of our lives changed.

†††

When we walked over to the Cozy Corner, Ricky was already there, perched on the bench of a picnic table facing in the direction of Violet's Vet. With his long, blue jean-clad legs stretched out before him, he studied his steel-toed boots as if they were tarot cards. He stood the moment he saw us, his mustache curving in his quirky version of a smile.

"There y'all are. How's your day going?" he rambled nervously. "Apparently, Charlie Wayne is in a good mood because he offered this new menu." He tapped the laminated sheet, handing it to Violet hopefully. "Have a look-see."

I scanned over my sister's shoulder as she read. Sure enough, Charlie Wayne was featuring—only for today—a whole wheat grilled chicken wrap with avocado, onions, and peppers. *Oh yeah, this was definitely happening.* Violet and I exchanged a glance before joining Ricky at the table, which had been set with cloth napkins and actual silverware.

"Wow," Violet muttered as JJ Wheeler appeared out of nowhere. "This is…quite nice, Sheriff." Her eyes widened as JJ ceremoniously—and with great pomp—snapped her napkin and placed it on her lap.

"Ricky," he urged Violet, "call me Ricky. I've almost got Sterling trained—" He glanced nervously at me. "I didn't mean anything bad by that—"

"No worries, Ricky." I felt for the guy. "I'll have the chicken wrap, JJ. It looks fabulous."

Wheeler kissed his fingers when Violet chose the same, letting us know we were in for a treat. "We have iced tea, soda, sparkling water, or," he added proudly, "chilled chardonnay from the Monterey County vineyard."

"Oh my." Violet grinned. "Well, as much as I'd love a glass of white wine, I don't think my afternoon patients would appreciate it, so I'll just have tea."

After we ordered our food and Ricky offered us a taffy, I asked in a conversational tone, "Have you talked to Mom today?"

"Oh yeah, she and Desi are like dogs with a bone. They're busy building their podcast, or whatever you call it. You and Fireman done lit a fire underneath 'em and they are champing at the bit."

While the sheriff deserved points for his imagery and generous play on words, his obvious discomfort was painful to watch. I decided to throw him a rope, so to speak. "Well, I guess the citizens of Shady Gully can rest easy today knowing there's no longer a hundred-pound python skulking around their gardens."

"No doubt. 'Course, I got you and Fireman to thank for that. And I reckon, Bubba, but since it was kinda his fault to start with, he doesn't count." The sheriff pondered as he smacked a taffy.

Charlie Wayne followed JJ Wheeler to the picnic table, observing critically as he presented our food with exaggerated spectacle—and on actual plates. "I think Bubba learned his lesson," Violet said, appearing utterly delighted with her wrap. "Thanks, guys, these smell delicious."

Charlie Wayne winked at the sheriff and then dragged JJ Wheeler away before he could utter the word *elevated*.

To his credit, the wraps were exquisite. He'd enhanced them with fire-roasted chili peppers from New Mexico. Just as I was digging in, Ricky took a deep breath and "went there."

"Shady Gully is in good hands though, especially with Quietdove on deck, should I retire…which, I'll probably do…soon."

"Oh? What in the world will you do with yourself?" *I couldn't resist.* "You're pretty young for retirement."

"Well, now that you mention it, Sterling, that's one of the reasons I invited y'all here today. You're right, I'm only fifty-three years old, which I reckon sounds ancient to y'all, but anyway, I got a nice pension built up, and I figure it's time to live a little."

"Good for you," Violet mumbled between bites of avocado, shrugging when I looked at her in astonishment.

"Y'all know how I feel about your mama," the sheriff went on awkwardly, "or maybe y'all don't, so I'm here to tell you that I love her more than I've ever loved anyone. More than I've ever loved, period." The man looked sincere as he eyed each of us for a long, palpable moment. "Here's the other thing. I loved your daddy too. He was my best friend. Me, him, and Lenny, the three of us…" He cleared his throat. Drank some sparkling water—perhaps a little too quickly as he sputtered with a series of coughs afterward. When he recovered, he said, "There's not a day that goes by that I don't think about him and miss him. That's something else that connects me to your mama, and to y'all, if you'll let it."

I glanced at Violet as the sheriff took another, more deliberate sip of water.

"I'm not trying to—nor could I ever—take the place of your daddy. I guess what I'm asking is just to be a part of the family." He dug in the pocket of his jeans and pulled out a black jeweler's box. He set it on the table, next to Violet's half-eaten chicken wrap. "I'm hoping y'all will allow me to propose to your mama."

He opened the box, revealing a small diamond set in a gold band, which had probably cost him a significant portion of that law enforcement pension he'd spoken of. "I love her and will do everything in my power to make her happy. And y'all too, if you'll allow me."

Violet picked up the black velveteen box and looked at the ring. "It's very pretty." She cast her eyes at me, as we both knew what had to be done.

I shook Ricky's hand and told him sincerely, "You have our blessing."

When we parted, Violet went to see her patients—completely sober—while Ricky, I assumed, went about his sheriff's duties with a hop in his step, no doubt planning his proposal to my mom. I hung back, taking some time to amble out to the cemetery alone. I strolled past my grandparents' grave, Gene and Mabel, who had died over twenty years ago on their way to the church's bake sale. According to my mom, my grandmother Mabel had been quite the baker. Unfortunately, I'd never had a chance to taste any of her delicacies myself, although Mom attempted to imitate them at family gatherings and holidays.

Not far away rested Desi's mother, Sunny, whose art was displayed at our homes in Lexington and Osprey Lake, as well as Mom and Aunt Desi's art galleries. Her reputation suggested a life of color, fervor, and struggle.

As I shuffled to my father's grave, I wondered about them and the others whose earthly bodies rested in this cemetery. Surely their lives had been filled with self-doubt and private longings, as well as their share of joy and good news. How utterly ridiculous—and narcissistic—I'd been to think that my battles were in any way unique.

As I settled at the foot of my father's grave, I pondered the range of emotions I'd experienced in the span of only a few hours. With my sister alone I'd run the gamut of happiness, hurt, surprise, and finally, a renewed connection and a fresh interpretation. As to the exchange with Ricky, it had transformed long anticipated dread into absolute certainty, and finally, a begrudging kind of acceptance.

And here I sat with my father, whose presence felt all at once intimate, and very, very distant.

So many emotions, all of them impossible to put into words.

And that very thought prompted me to pick up my phone.

I shook my head, more than a little surprised when my finger tapped the avatar of her very *extra* face.

Chapter Twenty-Two

Rattled the Curse
Timothy

I stumbled into Father Patrick's kitchen the next morning—or early afternoon—mostly because I smelled the heavenly aroma of bacon. I observed the chipper priest as he bebopped around his cooking space, pulling biscuits out of the oven and stoking bacon on the stove, all to the sound of Mel McDaniel's "Louisiana Saturday Night."

"And here I thought your choice of dance music would be a little ditty from the hymnal book at Sacred Heart. Silly me."

"Timothy!" He wheeled, his bright smile coinciding with his sprightly movements. "How did you sleep?"

"Great." I moved in the direction of the table, obeyed when he motioned me to sit, and swigged orange juice when he set a glass in front of me. "I can't believe I crashed so long."

"You needed the rest, son. And there's nothing better than having eggs and bacon after noon. How do you take your eggs?"

"Sunny side up, of course."

"Brilliant. Just as I suspected."

After he forked the bacon onto a plate lined with a paper towel, I watched as he cracked eggs, again thinking he was slimmer and more energetic than when I'd first arrived in Shady Gully. "Coffee?"

"The orange juice is fine. And delicious. How long have you been awake?"

"Oh, with the roosters, I'm afraid. Now,"—he looked over his shoulder—"any bad dreams?"

I rubbed my hands along my whiskers, thinking I needed

a shave. "No wolves disguised as sheep. No lambs morphing into…" Dismayed suddenly, I stopped.

"Excellent. Glad the animal kingdom represented itself appropriately. Now then, what about Meadow? Did you let her know you were alright?"

"No." I reached for the plate of eggs, bacon, and toast, said a quick prayer of thanks, and dove in hungrily. "I'm not really sure what to say at this point." I glanced hopelessly at my phone on the table. "But I feel better. I can't thank you enough…"

"Nonsense. As a shepherd, my job is to protect the lambs and shoot the wolves, and right now, Timothy, you are a lost lamb, a better-rested one, certainly, but a wayward lamb nonetheless."

I scraped my toast against the dregs of the eggs, just as my phone vibrated on the table. Immediately, the scrumptious food I'd just devoured turned to rock inside my stomach. I tucked my head toward my phone, inviting Father Patrick to do the honors. "Tell me. What's it say?" I watched numbly as he screwed up his eyes to read. "Is it…him?" I asked.

"Yes."

"Are there pictures?"

"No. Just a message." His expression grew pinched. "It says, *Do the right thing*." Father Patrick peered at me. "You said you never responded, isn't that right?"

"Right. I've been afraid to engage him. Or her."

"Perhaps it's time." He studied me over the top of his glasses. "Do you mind?"

I didn't. After the emotional torment of last night, I was weary, numb, and ready to yield. "Text away."

Father Patrick pecked slowly, his hands awkward, but hardly hesitant. "I'd like to know exactly what the right thing is. Wouldn't you?"

"Yeah, I would. I'm done, I surrender." I drained my orange juice. "I'm ready to find out who the wolf is."

"Indeed." Just as he circled his pointer finger theatrically and readied himself to hit send, a car door sounded outside. Carefully setting my phone back on the table, he glided to the kitchen window. Upon seeing the driver, he hastily opened the door, catching the sheriff's hand mid-knock. "What divine timing, Sheriff. Please come in."

"Timothy." Obviously shocked by my disheveled appearance, the sheriff tipped his hat politely. Evidently, my unruly carriage bore out my suffering, but fortunately, Father Patrick kept the sheriff distracted with offers of a biscuit, bacon, and coffee.

Patting his non-existent belly, the sheriff begged off. "I just had a fine meal with Sterling and Violet. A rather…productive one, you might say."

"Oh?" Father Patrick glinted expectantly.

"Charlie Wayne and JJ prepared a right nice meal." He winked conspiratorially. "Heightened, you might say." Something was different about him. He didn't seem as antsy as usual. "I reckon I'm on my way to Osprey Lake to meet Lenny. He said the women were driving him crazy with their podcast planning, and I figured it was a good day to take the afternoon off. Speaking of which"—he eyed us accordingly— "they want to introduce y'all and Petey on their first show."

"We'll be there with bells on," Father Patrick chirped.

The sheriff nodded as he handed a folder to Father Patrick. "Here's the information you asked for. A perfect match." He glanced at me. "There's no question who's been hassling you."

"Thanks," I said hoarsely, my heart pounding inside my chest.

"It's almost impossible to keep crazies from tracking down somebody's phone number these days. Especially when they're in the public eye." He added, "Regardless, I've got contacts in Missouri, so if you need me to light a fire under 'em to pick up this guy, let me know."

Missouri? Guy? My legs trembled under the table.

"We'll let you know, Sheriff." Father Patrick lightly skimmed his arm. "Thank you for your help. And please tell Lenny hello for us." Thankfully, Ricky was so bemused he didn't linger, and after another tip of the hat, he was off.

Father Patrick looked solemn as he sat down at the table with the folder. "Are you ready?"

"I think so. I mean, yes." I swallowed deeply. "You read it."

I tried to gauge Father Patrick's reaction as he opened the folder and scanned the information. He blinked more than once, looked over his spectacles, and then under them. As I was just about to snatch the folder away from him, his eyes widened. He gasped.

"What?" I huffed.

"My word…"

"Father?"

"It's Philip…"

✝✝✝

"But how? Why?" I gabbled incoherently. "I don't understand."

"Let's find out, shall we?" Before I could object, the priest took my phone and pulled the trigger on his earlier text. While we waited, he speculated. "I just don't understand how he got his hands on the pictures."

"I can't imagine."

The sudden *Ding!* caused us both to jump in our seats. Because my hands were shaky, no doubt in cohesion with my trembling legs, I was grateful when Father Patrick took the lead and read the text.

```
The right thing to do is to
tell your story. ALL OF IT.
```

My heart skipped.

"That's rather cryptic, don't you think?" Father Patrick actually rolled his eyes in exasperation before turning to me. "How would you feel about a phone call? Or better yet? Facetime?" Before I could react, he was texting, and within seconds, he got a *Ding!* "Game on," Father Patrick breathed. "He's going to call. Do you know how to work the Facetime? I could text Fireman—"

When the phone rang, my first and only thought was: *I wish I'd shaved.*

But then I threw myself into gear and hit the Facetime button on my phone. The face that filled the screen was unrecognizable to me.

"Well, well. There he is. Our pride and joy. You don't look so good, kid."

But the voice was spot on. And the "kid" had been Philip's endearment for me.

"Philip," I mumbled, emotionally stirred. Father Patrick moved his chair closer but remained off-screen. He patted my thigh, reassuring me of his support, and for this, I was glad. "How... how are you? I'm sorry we've lost touch."

"I'm okay. My trucking days are over, and my Dottie passed away in July. So, it's just me and the dogs now. We watch you every Sunday."

"I'm sorry to hear about your wife." I resisted the urge to glance at Father Patrick as I was utterly clueless how to proceed. The chatty, congenial tone of the conversation was not at all what I expected.

"Got nobody left. You heard about Lydia. And then Paul." When I noted the catch in his throat, I found myself responding emotionally, the way I would with anyone who was grief-stricken and lonely. "And most of my other trucking buddies passed. Or retired. They live all over, as you might remember."

"I do. Maybe we could get together. Maybe I could visit you sometime. I'm so grateful for what you and Paul did—"

"Don't give me that, kid." Suddenly angry, Philip leaned closer to his phone, causing the upper half of his face to disappear. "When my Dottie died, I suddenly had all this time alone and it got me to thinking about the folks that mattered and made a difference in my life. And then every Sunday, I'd see you up on that stage in Kentucky, up there on your pedestal, ignoring the truth and denying your, let's just say, humble beginnings, and I'd get to stewing something awful. You act like you never even met us. Like we never happened—"

"That's not true—" I objected, even as Father Patrick squeezed my leg, urging restraint.

"I don't care for me, you understand," Philip snapped, "but Paul, that's another matter." He swiped the bottom of his nose, turning emotional now. "He did everything for you. He taught you how to read, for crying out loud. He taught you the Bible. He steered you to the Lord. He got you into COFO. He was your mentor—"

"He was," I insisted. "I loved him. I was in Haiti when he passed or else I would have come—"

"Don't matter none about you coming to the funeral, kid. This is about you recognizing how generous that man was. How good he was." Now Philip jerked the phone, apparently digging for a handkerchief as he came back into view rubbing his red nose. "You remember that day you met him? At the diner?"

"Of course."

"How he was so upset at the sight of you. You ever think about that, kid? You ever wonder why that was?" I waited as my heart pounded wildly in my chest. "That's because he was *there*. He's the one who took those pictures. He was an addict. Yeah, that's right. He was caught up in that life for years till it nearly killed him. Do you know how he got out of it? Do you know what finally gave him the strength to step away from it?"

I shook my head, as I didn't trust my voice.

"*You*. He couldn't bear the thought of a helpless little boy being dragged all over, not being looked after, being used and abused and neglected and disrespected by his own mama. That's what rattled the curse out of him. That's what drove him to get treatment."

I dropped my head into my hands, distraught.

"And let me tell you, he suffered. Getting clean nearly done him in, but he kept those pictures, and he looked at 'em every night. To motivate him. To keep him strong."

"I didn't know." I teared up. "I never knew."

"I didn't either. Not until that day. That day I brought you in there to meet him. I'd never seen him like that before. It was like he'd seen a ghost." He swiped his eyes. "That's when he told me the truth about his past."

"Why didn't y'all tell me?"

"He didn't want you to know. That wasn't who he was anymore, and he accomplished a lot after he got clean. He was on fire to turn people toward the Lord. He sponsored other addicts. He taught Sunday school. He was an honorable man." Philip's gaze drifted off camera, his eyes blank as he lost himself in another lifetime. "You know, when he got that poison out of his system, he went back to that godforsaken place and tried to find you, but there wasn't nothing left but cruddy needles and human waste." Philip blew his nose, his rage tempered now, turning weak and pliable. "But then I brought you into the diner that day and he just knew, he knew that after all you'd gone through—and the fact that God led you right back to him—he knew that you were destined for great things. And even better, he knew he could play a part in it. He was so proud of you."

Beside me, Father Patrick quietly succumbed to his own wrought emotions.

Philip went on, "Paul was thankful that, in spite of your trauma, you turned out to be a fine young man, a strong Christian, and like him, was called to share the word of God." After a long pause, he mumbled, "Truth is, I don't think I coulda brought myself to release those photos, but I did want to shake you up." And then, almost pleadingly, "All I'm saying, kid, is that you wouldn't be where you are without him, and even if it hurts your pride a little, you need to tell the truth about your past. About Paul."

His breath crackled as he let out a beleaguered sigh. "It would help folks who're going through treatment. People who are barely hanging on. Paul's story matters. And when you think on it, it's kinda your story too."

✝✝✝

After we finally said goodbye to Philip, Father Patrick and I talked late into the afternoon. Profoundly moved by Philip—and ultimately Paul's—story, Father Patrick praised the good nature of the majority of mankind. "Despite the horrible things that happened to you, Timothy, God led you to Philip, Lydia, and Paul, who ultimately set you on a path to serve others. Isn't it amazing how one act of kindness can ripple and swell into perpetuity?"

"It is. And Philip is right. I should be using my platform to celebrate that fundamental truth."

"Ditto." He nodded robustly. "Consider me inspired. I've already been thinking of ways to incorporate that theme into next Sunday's Mass."

I side-eyed him, measuring his stamina as we rounded the church's parking lot for the second time. "Are we going another lap?" I questioned whether the newly vigorous priest was up for another fast-walk around the grounds of Sacred Heart Catholic Church. "Or is two enough for you?"

"I've got another one in me." He led the way. "Plus, I've got to get my steps. We'll stop off at the church and finish with a prayer after this last one." He suddenly cut his steely eyes at me. "What's this?"

"What?" I avoided his sharp gaze.

"I'm sensing some inner turmoil lingering just below the surface. Shock? PTSD? Exhaustion?"

"Honestly?" I almost stopped short but for his exercise routine. "I'm conflicted, Father, about what's been in my own heart all these years. I mean, why *didn't* I talk about it? Philip is right. What he, Paul, and Lydia did for me was nothing short of—"

"Inspired. Miraculous. Selfless. Divine. Yes, quite."

"So why didn't I preach it from the rooftop? Why didn't I keep in touch with Philip? I should have done better. I should have *been* better."

He walked on without a word, letting me stew in my guilt.

I huffed, more winded now than the sprightly priest. "I suppose there was an element of vanity there," I admitted. "I guess, after what I'd been through, I felt I was due. That my success was my reward…" A guttural wince rose from deep within me. "Or that it would taint my image. Ah, how shameful. How utterly wrong!"

"Quite." He patted me on the back. "But I think we've already covered the part about us all being sinners."

"Yes…" I sighed, once again amazed by this unassuming man who'd just led me through the depths of the proverbial valley.

After a long moment of silence, except for the sound of Father Patrick's light breathing in rhythm with our steps, I ventured. "You know, you should count yourself among those who have blessed me with precious and valuable acts of kindness. I can't thank you enough—"

"Ah, no need for that. It's a two-way street." He appeared thoughtful. "And since you were so honest with me, I suppose it's only fair to be honest with you. Your need came at just the right time. When I received your message, I confess, I wasn't in a good way."

"What?" I stopped, immediately concerned.

He urged me along, picking up his pace and trying to show me up. "I'm not proud to say I'd fallen into a dreadful pattern of gluttony, Timothy. Drinking too much wine. Second helpings at dinner. Huge desserts. Not to mention I was living like a slovenly old goat because I was too lazy to clean up after myself. But"— he emphasized with a dramatic finger in the air— "fortunately, there was a pint-sized shepherd in my life at just the right time. Much like Paul and his friends were for you."

"You mean Fireman." I grinned.

"Indeed. Such a good boy. A giver if there ever was one." He slowed as we approached the sanctuary. "Now, let's talk about Meadow."

"Wait. I want to hear more about you."

"You will. Let's just say you owe me a counseling session, and you can trust I'll come collecting it one day." He patted me on the back. "Have you spoken to her?"

"Texted. I'll see her tomorrow morning. Early." I glanced at my watch. "I figured it was too late today, and I could probably use another good night's sleep for this conversation."

"Splendid." When he sat on the wrought iron bench outside

the sanctuary, I took it to mean that our exercise session was over. "Now then," he began, "two important things. First, I think it imperative that you continue with trauma therapy upon your return to Lexington. Just as you told me at the beginning, even though your circumstances have changed, the wounds are still there and if not dealt with they'll emerge later in negative ways."

I nodded in agreement.

"And finally, I have one more question for you to consider." When he patted the seat next to him, insistent that I join him on the bench, I sat. "At one point in our talks, you related to the scared little boy of your childhood. At another point, you saw yourself more as the accomplished pastor you are today. I ask you now, Timothy, which are you?"

"Is this a trick question?" I asked nervously.

"Not at all."

I shrugged my shoulders. "I'm both."

"Yes." The cagey old priest beamed. "That you are. And that's what you need to bring to every sermon you preach and offer to every person you counsel. You, me—all of us—are the sum of our own experiences, good and bad, virtuous and sinful, and no matter how traumatic our pasts, God can heal us, but just as *He* shows *us* mercy and grace—and forgiveness—we should offer that to others.

I rolled out a long, begrudging sigh. "You're talking about my mother."

"Mercy, grace, and forgiveness cover a lot of territory."

"I'm getting there."

✝✝✝

Although the Sacred Heart Catholic Church's van provided a bumpy ride to The Creek, I made it to Meadow's shanty precisely at sunrise. I patted my pocket before trudging to the front door and swept my hand across my face as I waited for her to answer.

I waited long enough to discover I'd nicked myself shaving and missed a spot under my left ear. Still, no Meadow. I knocked again, louder this time. Eventually, she stumbled to the door, threw it open, and blinked at me as if I'd woken her up, which apparently, I had. Her eyes were puffy, her hair was plastered to her left side, and there was a faint imprint of a crocheted quilt hugging the side of her neck.

Most women would have been up an hour early and presented at the door in full make-up with a cup of coffee on the ready. Meadow wasn't most women, which was another reason I loved her madly. She took my breath away. And I was struck with the overwhelming desire to run my lips across the imprint of the quilt.

Without a word she turned, moving back into the shanty. I followed obediently. When she clicked on the coffee pot, I was pleased to see that she'd set out two coffee cups. Something to hang my hat on, at least.

"Sorry I woke you," I said.

"No, you're not." Her face softened a tad. "But I'm assuming you're sorry for something, and that's why you're here."

"It is—" Since the coffee pot's gurgling drowned me out, I poured us each a cup of coffee and brought them to the table where she waited. "I'm sorry for a lot of things. For withdrawing when we got to Shady Gully. For not being honest about the extent of my…issues. God, I hate that word—" I stopped, not liking the direction of this one-sided conversation. "Are you hungry? How about I make you an omelet?" I hopped up, removing a bell pepper, onion, and some ham from the refrigerator.

"Eggs are at the top," she said, a peculiar look planted on her face.

I found a skillet and set about whisking and cutting, somehow finding it easier to talk while in action. "You told me to figure it out." I lifted my eyes from slicing a bell pepper. "And I realize now the part I needed to figure out wasn't the *it* of what happened but the *why* I couldn't tell you part."

"Okay. I'm trying really hard to follow. Maybe I need more coffee."

I stopped to fill her cup and then returned to my slicing and dicing. "When I met you, Meadow, your trauma was up front and center—and I was completely captivated by you—but I've spent the majority of my life trying to hide my trauma—my truth—from the world. And I'm sorry to say that includes from you these last three years. My past, particularly the early years, is swamped in unseemliness…and while I eventually escaped the situation, I…well, let's just say there's a lot you don't know."

When I risked a look at her, I found her staring oddly at the pantry. She turned at the sound of my silence. "I don't have mushrooms."

"Oh." I gaped, completely baffled. "It's okay. I hate mushrooms."

"You do?" All at once she smiled, and somehow, I sensed this had nothing to do with mushrooms.

So I went with it and took it as a sign to continue. "As things got more serious between us, I should have confided in you, but I was afraid it would tarnish my image and that you wouldn't see me the same way. And then the situation escalated when someone from my early years popped up out of nowhere and threatened me."

"Physically?"

"No, not really, and it turned out fine. Father Patrick helped me, and it's resolved now, but I should have shared it with you like you wanted me to—"

"Timothy." She stood.

"—because I love you, Meadow." I set the knife down. "I'm deeply in love with you, and I want us to have a life together, but what I've learned is that figuring it out means coming clean and telling you everything because I don't want our marriage to be based on a lie."

"Marriage?" Her eyes popped a few sizes larger.

I covered my face with my hands. *I'm such a doofus. I blew it.*

"What are you saying?" she pressed.

I removed my hands, revealing my embarrassed face, and took a chance, deciding right then and there that it was worth it. That she was worth it. "I have a complicated past, one that is so far removed from the upstanding, moral, and pristine 'Timothy from Northlake' that the world thinks I am. I'm ready to share it with you, and I hope and pray you'll stand by me because it's possible the world might reject me when I confess my sad, sordid history."

She grabbed my belt loops and yanked me closer, her head craned way back so she could look up at me. "I'll stand by you, just like you've stood by me. And for the record, I love you too."

I cupped the lower half of her body and pulled her into me, and the kiss we shared swirled and lingered, and all that was unjust, wrong, and bothersome seemed to fade away. When we finally moved apart, I shoved my hand into my pocket and started to lower myself on one knee.

"What are you doing? Is that a toy?" Her face was shiny with laughter.

"Actually, it is. I got it from Sprite's Quick Stop, but it's really cute. See, it's a little unicorn." When she threw her head back, fully surrendering to giggles, I hugged her playfully. "Hey, it was either that or a bread tie from Father Patrick's. I had to improvise." I kissed her spontaneously. "We're going to go shopping when we get home and you can pick something you like, but for now, this unicorn symbolizes my profound love for you and—" I stopped, as her laughter had become contagious.

"Yes." She eventually presented her hand for me to adorn with said unicorn. "I'll marry you, but…"

"What? Please don't break my heart, Meadow."

"I just want to talk a little bit about what home looks like."

"So while you've been off with Father Patrick fighting your demons, I got some amazing news." We'd moved into the living room with our coffee and omelets, and Meadow looked adorable with her feet tucked underneath her on the couch while speaking animatedly about something that was going to be "life changing."

"Tell me." I set my cup on the coffee table in anticipation.

"I'm going to be a grandmama."

I offered her a gigantic smile. "Are you serious? Bella and Luke are getting *another* Shiba Inu?"

"No, Bella is pregnant," she breathed as if she could barely say the words. "We're talking a real live baby. I can barely process it."

An image of Meadow rocking a newborn baby flashed before me. "You're going to be a terrific grandmama."

"I hope so," she said almost pensively. "Bella and I have had our issues—I know you don't like the word." Her breath hitched as she brushed a tear from her cheek. "But I feel different ever since she told me. Nervous inside, all fluttery and…changed somehow."

"This is amazing news." I squeezed her thigh. "Do Desi and Lenny know? This will be their first grandchild as well."

"No, I think she and Luke are telling them tonight. So far, only I know. And Fireman. And now, you."

"Fireman? That guy is everywhere." I chuckled. "He's the most popular kid in Shady Gully."

"He is that, but I think Bella and Luke told him hoping it would sweeten the pot when they offered to be his legal guardian."

I lifted my shoulders. "Good strategy. Diabolical even."

She grinned, acknowledging my silliness, and then started seriously, "I understand you're firmly rooted in Lexington, and as your wife"—she blushed—"I want to be supportive, but it's important to me to be there for Bella and the baby. She and I have struggled. We wasted some important years and significant life events because of misunderstandings, false perceptions, and the inability to communicate, so this is my chance to do better." She glinted at me imploringly. "I simply have to get it right this time."

"Absolutely. And you will. *We* will."

"But how? Where is home?"

"Anywhere. Everywhere. As long as we're together and firmly rooted in God's word." I shrugged. "Look, right now my base is in Lexington, but who knows what's going to happen to my flock in the next couple of months."

"Your flock will remain loyal to you, no matter what."

"If you say so."

"I do. But everything is remote nowadays, right? Perhaps it's time to switch your focus, concentrate more on places that are full of need." She gripped my hand in both of hers. "A place that's full of nonbelievers and skeptics like me."

I nodded, warming to the idea. "You're not wrong. And I admit, after the last few months, my thinking has shifted. Maybe we could divide our time. Robin is always wanting someone to use the lake house on Osprey. Maybe we could stay there, and then dash off to Kentucky when necessary." I squeezed her hands decisively. "We'll make it work. We will, and we'll be here for Bella and the baby. And even Luke."

Meadow grunted in amusement. "It's all so fantastic, Timothy. A few years ago, I couldn't have imagined this—me, Meadow from The Creek, living like a jetsetter."

"Stick with me, babe," I joked. "We're just getting started."

"One more thing. I've been thinking about Fireman. About his future." She wiped a new swell of tears. "Even though he says I'm a grouch, I know he really loves me. And now that we're getting married, maybe we could provide a big life for him…"

God, this woman. She continues to surprise and amaze me. I can't wait to marry her! "So you want to throw your name in the hat as well?"

"It's worth a shot."

"I'm all in. Although, I think the kid is gonna end up with a bidding war before it's over."

I Choose...
Fireman

Father Patrick rode shotgun while I steered my Blue Velvet Mystique Impala toward The Creek. It was mid-afternoon and since Timothy had apparently ditched the priest to go make amends with Meadow that morning, I decided it was the perfect time to enact my plan.

However, if I'd known he was going to babble non-stop all the way to The Creek I'd have dropped him off at the post office with Cruella Claire. The busybody had flagged us down when we passed, her hands gesturing in such a wild way we assumed the post office was on fire. Turned out she only wanted to butter Padre up in hopes of getting the scoop on Timothy's supposed breakdown—scandal—firing—arrest—

Pick one, any one. She wanted to dish.

"I did something I never thought I'd do," Father Patrick went on, making himself at home in my passenger seat. "Though you have to promise not to tattle on me or I'll be kicked out of Shady Gully. Anyway, I found the recipe online, and normally I wouldn't try something willy-nilly, but the picture made it look absolutely gorgeous."

"I think Cruella is calling you. Shall I take you back?"

"Avocado toast! Imagine that, Fireman. Did you ever think you'd see the day that I devoured such a trendy treat? It was absolutely divine."

"Hear that?"

"What?" He frowned. "I don't hear a thing."

"Exactly." I bumped up my jam, listened to Taylor Swift sing about karma being a cat. "You like that?" I asked. "Isn't that great?"

Now he clutched the side of the door as if I were driving like a maniac when in reality I was only going ten miles per hour—the speed limit—across the Unity Bridge. "It has a nice melody, but I can't understand a word of it."

I pointed to his ear. "You need hearing aids."

He scoffed, but I noticed he was tapping his foot.

When we arrived, Wolfheart was sitting on the porch with Meadow and Timothy.

The dogs pounded their tails in the dirt when they saw me drive up and park. I razzed their fur in greeting and traipsed up the porch steps behind Father Patrick. I stuck my thumb in his direction. "I needed a passenger, and he was bored."

"Tea?" Wolfheart asked, ever the host.

"Oh, I'd love some. Maybe some of that delightful new blend of yours?" As Wolfheart jumped up to accommodate his guest, Timothy and Father Patrick did the man hug thing. Afterward, he turned to Meadow. "Meadow, my dear." He greeted her warmly, his eyes zeroing in on her left hand. "What a unique piece of jewelry."

I flashed at Meadow's finger, not really surprised that she was wearing an engagement ring, but very surprised that it was in the shape of a unicorn. Sounded like a Taylor Swift song in the making.

"Actually, Fireman," Meadow said, "Timothy and I came to chat with you."

I raised my eyebrows at Wolfheart when he returned with Father's tea, hoping for a hint as to what was going on, but he barely made eye contact. *Oh boy.* As I waited for them to spring the latest whammy on me, I sprawled on the steps with Black and Blue, allowing the old folks to have the chairs.

When Meadow repeated, "So…uh…we just wanted to talk to you," I detected a covert note in the atmosphere. "Well, first of all, have you made any decisions about your future? As to who you want to be your legal guardian?"

"I'm narrowing it down."

"Okay, well then, in that case…" Meadow floundered, eventually thrusting her hand in the air. "We're engaged."

"Cool." I figured the less I said the better, but when they all stared at me, I added, "Congrats."

"And well, we're still trying to work out the logistics, of course, but we figure we'll divide our time between Louisiana and Kentucky." She waited.

"Nice." *Did they want my approval?*

"Timothy and I thought that if you wanted to live with us, it might be the perfect opportunity for you to see a little more of the world. There are a lot of fun things to do in Kentucky—"

"Basketball, horses," Timothy ticked enthusiastically. "I was going to say bourbon but maybe not that, but there is hiking—" He stopped. "Look, can I be straight with you?" When I nodded, he sprawled on the steps beside me. "You're an amazing young man, very independent and self-sufficient, and the truth is you probably don't need anybody hovering over you, keeping tabs on you, and all that boloney, right?" While I wholeheartedly agreed, I thought it wise to remain quiet. "I get it, I really do. Look, you probably know I've been going through some stuff, right?"

"Yeah."

"Right. Well, for a long time, I thought I could handle it on my own, and I did okay for a while, just like you would do okay on your own, but what I've learned is that it's so much nicer when you have someone to lean on." He switched his eyes on Father Patrick before turning them back to me. "I promise you, Fireman, knowing there's someone you're accountable to makes all the difference. And it's more fun." He smiled in his uniquely goofy way. "Seriously. Someone to come home to at night. Someone to share a hot meal with…" He hitched his shoulders up. "It's a sweet deal, trust me."

Meadow did a weird sniffling thing before she shored up his

argument. "We want to be that for you. We really care about you, and we'd be happy to have you—"

I never thought I'd see Meadow grovel, and sadly, it wasn't nearly as fun as I thought it'd be. I had to put a stop to this now. "Thanks, Meadow." I looked at her famous fiancé. "And Timothy. I really appreciate the offer, but I've actually made my decision."

Everyone's heads swiveled in my direction. Even Black and Blue cocked their snouts in expectation. I took a giant breath.

"I choose Wolfheart."

The man's mug of tea froze midway to his mouth, and his green Creek eyes expanded. Of course, he said nothing, because that was his way, but Father Patrick reacted enthusiastically. "Lovely! What splendid news!"

Despite Meadow and Timothy's powerful, over-the-top pitch, neither of them seemed particularly broken up, which was a relief. Nevertheless, I figured I'd better set them all straight, ASAP. "Just until I'm eighteen though, and I get to go stay at Father Patrick's sometimes in case he needs my help. And Granny's to check on the place during the day." I looked squarely at Wolfheart. "And if you start dating somebody like that Anjulie lady, or anybody, I'm out. How's that?"

"Sounds good," Wolfheart stated serenely before casually returning to his chai.

"I really appreciate the offer," I told Timothy and Meadow, "and Kentucky does sound pretty cool, but this is my home. Folks depend on me around here. Staying with Wolfheart makes the most sense."

As they all bobbed their heads in understanding, I shot Wolfheart a charged look. Our relationship had been founded years ago, and since then it had been filled with intense moments of loyalty, significant acts of trust, and meaningful examples of love. I chose him for the countless gestures, illustrations, and kindnesses that had fortified me time and time again.

I really hoped that he'd get all that from the expression on my face because there was no way I could ever put it into words.

"Plus," I did say, "I've never had a grandpa before so it might be kinda fun."

"Grandpa?" He raised a terse eyebrow, sipping his tea as he returned my look.

He understood.

†††

To my great frustration, it took Father Patrick a good hour before finishing his tea and excusing himself to sneak off to the "little boy's room." When he did, I followed him inside and waited.

"My word!" He exclaimed when he met me hovering at the door on his way out. "Do you have to go too?"

"No. But I have a surprise for you." I flashed my teeth sheepishly. "Follow me." I led him to the utility room at the rear of Wolfheart's house. "Wait right there." When I ducked into the room, Aurora was sprawled on her side as the kittens dozed in mid-suckle. Upon seeing me, the calico stirred, picking up where he'd left off.

The little orange and white kitten with the white slash across her face flashed blurrily at me. When I picked her up and held her inside my jacket, she purred. I padded out of the room, shutting the door behind me.

"What on earth are you doing?" Father Patrick worried. "Have you changed your mind about Kentucky? Because truly, I think Wolfheart would be devastated if you moved away."

"I'm not going anywhere. Who would look after you if I left?"

"I'm doing much better, thank you very much, and I would never hold you back. Also, I'll have you know, I made an appointment with a physician. A real, live physician."

"Really? Not another veterinarian?"

"No need to get cheeky—" He stopped. "My word, your chest is moving."

I let out a silky chuckle. "I have a surprise for you." I opened my jacket, revealing first an orange ear starting to unfold and then a small head bursting with unfocused, searching eyes. "I thought that since Timothy would be leaving soon, you could use something to take care of. Something all your own to look after."

"My heavens…"

"She's just a baby, so her eyesight is still unfocused, and her sense of hearing and smell are starting to develop. She'll need to be with her mama for several more weeks, but I wanted you to meet her."

"I…I don't know what to say, Fireman. What do I know about taking care of a kitten? I've never had a pet in my life. What does she even eat and drink?" Despite his reluctance, I could see his lips inching upwards in interest. "You did say she's a she, right?"

"Yep. The only one in the litter, which is why I figured you'd like her. And no need to overthink all the details. I'll help you with that, and so will Violet."

"This is part of the litter that Violet delivered the morning of the revival, yes?"

I nodded, lowering myself onto a mud bench outside of the utility room. "She's much nicer than her brothers. And she's orange. Y'all match!" I chipped. "How's that for chutzpah?"

"Oh my." Bubbling over with amusement Father Patrick sat down, brushing his titan finger against the top of her head. "What would I even name her? She's so tiny. She could fit in the palm of my hand." He puffed up with pleasure when she purred loudly. "My gracious."

Got him.

"I really think she would be good for you." I handed him the kitten and watched as he gently held her and nuzzled her downy fur. "You've done so much better with Timothy here. I mean, look at you, you have more energy, you've lost weight, and you're eating avocado toast, which sounds gross, by the way."

When Father Patrick's belly shook with amusement, the kitten blinked and amped up her purring.

I stroked the ball of orange fluff. "She's in good hands. Although you *will* have to come up with a name."

"Flana is a lovely name for a female. Its derivation is Irish and

Gaelic, and it means russet hair." He thought, his expression doting as he rubbed his finger beneath the kitten's chin. "But something about the name Scarlet speaks to me as well."

The kitten had fallen asleep in Father Patrick's hand when Wolfheart came looking for us. "I figured," he said, delighted. "So, you've decided on Slash, eh?"

"Now that's an intriguing choice." Father Patrick considered. "But a little too masculine. I'm considering Scarlet, Ruby, or Flana."

Wolfheart joined us on the mud bench. "Lovely names, and all appropriately red." He glanced at Father Patrick. "Just be ready to drag your head from the clouds tomorrow for Desi and Robin's podcast."

"I can hardly wait." Padre bobbed with gusto. "Although I will have to polish up my introductory speech. Being lumped in with two superstars like Timothy and Petey is a tad daunting."

"I'm confident you can hold your own." Wolfheart cast Father Patrick an encouraging wink before changing the subject. "Meadow and Timothy are getting ready to leave. They wanted to know if you wanted to hitch a ride?"

"Oh goodness, how time flies." Father Patrick looked down at the kitten then, as if he wasn't quite sure how it came to nestle against his chest and drift into a deep, contented sleep.

"What? They're leaving now?" I squeaked. "But they can't leave yet!"

Both Wolfheart and Father Patrick traded mystified looks before swiveling to me in question.

It was now or never, I decided. "There's something else," I told them. "Something I'd like to do."

When I was sure I had their undivided attention, I explained, "I want to do that thing. That thing when you introduce yourself to Jesus." I looked quickly at Wolfheart. "Even though I know He already knows who I am."

Only slightly aware of Timothy and Meadow entering the room, I went on, totally committed. "I want to tell Him I'm sorry that I ignored Him and that I haven't been around, but that deep down I knew He was there. I understand now," I again sought Wolfheart's eyes, "that Jesus died on the cross for me, and that He wants good things for me, and that He's the best friend I'll ever have, but I feel like I want to say it out loud to Him, in front of everybody, because I'm kind of excited about my new life.

"I miss Granny a lot. Every night I think about her before I fall asleep and sometimes it hurts so bad, but then sometimes thinking about her makes me laugh too. Anyway, I've been feeling fresh lately, different somehow, especially when I read for myself what it says in the Bible about Jesus loving me." I felt my lips tremble as I smiled at them all, not even embarrassed if I looked like a baby with tears in my eyes. "Even though I never got to meet my parents, a lot of good stuff has happened to me." I glanced at each of them. "That's why I want to do that thing."

"You know," Meadow said in a small but steady voice, "I want to do that thing as well."

Timothy pressed his lips together, visibly moved, while Father Patrick covered his mouth with his fist and coughed in a thick-throated way.

Wolfheart, meanwhile, grinned like he'd won the lottery. "It'll be cold," he said, "but we can baptize you in that small gully near the Unity Bridge, where Timothy baptized me a few years ago."

"How lovely." Father Patrick looked at his watch. "If we hurry, we can make it for sunset. Now that would be a heavenly scene indeed." He raised his hands dismissively. "While this isn't quite the way we do it in the Catholic Church, I'd love to come along and add my joyous prayers to the mix."

I stood up, my excitement growing. "Yes! That's why I wanted you all here." I moved toward Meadow, hugging her in my overflow of excitement. "I guess we have to find some shorts."

Somehow Wolfheart found old T-shirts and ragged shorts for

all of us, except Father Patrick who opted for comfy warmups and a heavy sweatshirt. While we were waiting for him to finish dressing, I showed Meadow and Timothy the kittens. They seemed to share a significant moment as they watched Aurora lick her paw leisurely as her little ones suckled. Timothy, in particular, seemed reflective.

"Do you want one?" I asked him. "The solid orange one and the calico are still unspoken for."

"Maybe," Meadow said, winking at me as she tugged Timothy along. She too seemed eager to start her new life.

We enjoyed a moment of hilarity as we all piled into the church van. After a big to-do about who would drive and where everyone would sit, Timothy selflessly offered to seat Meadow on his lap while Wolfheart drove. Eventually, after a ceaseless amount of teasing, we headed toward the small gully Wolfheart had mentioned.

Once we arrived, Father Patrick pulled out his Rosary and watched as we waded into the gully a few feet away. I heard Timothy whisper to him on his way into the water. "I think I will take your advice and try to find some of my relatives. Who knows, maybe I'll find a straggler or two." I sensed an undercurrent of significance in that exchange but figured I'd learn more eventually.

As the sun set over Shady Gully that day, and especially over a small gully near the Unity Bridge, I committed my life to Jesus. I said the words: "I believe with all my heart that Jesus is the Christ, the son of the living God. He's my savior, and my friend." And I meant them.

I may not have known my parents, but that day I was surrounded by people I loved. With Wolfheart and Timothy on either side of me, the water washing over me felt *heavy*, but the *knowing* that came when I rose out of it was nothing short of divine. I felt triumphant, joyous, and *new*.

It was a little like when I sat in my Impala for the first time… but way better.

Chapter Twenty-Four

That's a Wrap
Sterling

Fireman and I had hauled a large round table into Desi's office and placed a notepad, pens, and a set of earphones in each host's and guest's spot. A pot of coffee and a pitcher of water sat in the center of the table along with peppermints, fruit, and caffeinated sodas.

All three of the guest speakers were here—Father Patrick, Petey, and Timothy—as well as the hosts' most devoted fanbase, Lenny, Wolfheart, and Ricky. As they all chatted easily on the office couch, Meadow mulled around the workspace looking cranky, but as always, beautiful. Today she sported a particularly interesting bubblegum ring from Sprite's prime collection. Worn on her left hand, it featured a colorful unicorn on top. I resisted the urge to ask about it, at least for now, as Fireman and I were navigating some minor technical difficulties.

We'd been in the process of setting up the brand-new micro-phones when we realized the internet wasn't working. "It's been spotty all morning," I complained. "Now I can't get a signal at all."

"It's always spotty." Uncle Lenny exhaled ruefully. "Let me go reboot the modem. Sometimes that helps."

"I'll go." Petey hastened in that direction before his dad could protest. "I've gotta up my game if I'm gonna maintain my posi-tion as the favorite child." A hearty sequence of guffaws rose in reaction to his reference to Luke and Bella's baby news. "Don't laugh," Petey told them over his shoulder, "a set of twins is all Violet and I need to stay in the game."

"Is Desi excited?" Wolfheart asked Uncle Lenny playfully.

"Are you kidding?" he answered. "She's been dropping hints about a grandbaby ever since they got married. And she'd love a set of twins. The more the merrier."

"Speaking of Desi," Fireman piped up, "where are she and Robin?"

"Here," Petey shrilled as he returned to the office. "Everyone, the divas…have arrived."

I wheeled at the sound of high heels clicking on the hickory floor. Sure enough, they were in full hair and makeup with attitudes to boot. Aunt Desi wore a black pencil skirt with a white turtleneck that glittered—yes, glittered—and Mom presented in a chic red pantsuit with a matching spectator hat. Well, that would have to come off, I thought as I continued to fiddle with the microphone. I managed a covert glance at my mother's ring finger, shamefully relieved to see that it was still bare. Knowing her though, she might have forgone the announcement in order to give Meadow and Timothy their moment.

Hovering somewhere between amusement and astonishment, I shook my head at the two of them. "Y'all know the audience isn't going to see you, right?"

"Well, that's their loss." Aunt Desi chuckled, turning to admire Mom. "Because we look fabulous."

While Wolfheart, Uncle Lenny, Father Patrick, and Timothy were busy fawning over the podcast divas, Ricky approached me with concern, as apparently his instinct for snafus had been alerted. "Problem?" he asked.

"Hey." Fireman pushed in as well. "How are we going to do this without the internet? We can't even get these mics hooked up, much less do any editing."

"Um," I said to Uncle Lenny, who rubbed Aunt Desi's shoulder lovingly, "maybe we should call your internet provider."

"Huh? Well yeah," he said, reaching for his phone. "Okay."

"We got to get this going for them," Ricky stated emphatically, as clearly his sheriff's keen sense of urgency had been rattled. "They got their guests here. And they're all gussied up."

As Father Patrick and Timothy chatted privately, their heads bowed in serious conversation, Wolfheart joined our trouble-shooting circle. "What's going on?"

"I'm on hold with SPEED, the internet provider," Uncle Lenny explained with an all-encompassing hand wave over the equipment. "They said the wait to even speak to an associate would be at least thirty minutes."

"Ridiculous," the sheriff muttered.

"What's ridiculous?" Mom asked as she joined us, nestling affectionately into Ricky's side. "Is something wrong with the internet? I had to switch my phone off Wi-Fi earlier to get a signal."

"Kind of," Fireman mumbled. "We're trying to get ahold of SPEED now."

"Oh no, Ricky." She tugged his sleeve, highly agitated. "You have to do something."

When the sheriff tipped his cowboy hat down to look at her, his expression turned dogged. With renewed determination, he bobbed his head. "I'll make a few calls."

Once Timothy and Father Patrick concluded their conversation, they became aware of the problem. As usual, Timothy remained unflappable, finding a deck of cards in a bowl in Aunt Desi's office and challenging everyone to a game of gin rummy. Wolfheart, meanwhile, had slipped out of the office to make a few calls of his own.

After a rambunctious hour of gin rummy, Fireman was proclaimed the winner, raking in a sizable pot of three dollars and twenty-two cents, Uncle Lenny was still on hold with SPEED—while simultaneously holding his own in gin rummy—and Sheriff Rick had reached a dead end and become frustrated with his "lack of results."

Since my back-and-forth texts with Pippa had grown to novel length in the span of an hour, I was on my way to call her when

Aunt Desi pointed out her office window. "Look!" To our surprise, a SPEED van rolled down the driveway.

"It's a miracle!" Mom and Aunt Desi collapsed in giggles, as they always found the Lord's hand in everything.

Wolfheart moved his wiry, quiet-as-a-panther frame toward the front door. "May I?" To the sound of rambunctious cheers, he let a young SPEED technician inside and shook his hand. "Everyone, this is Rising Owl, he's Redflyer's nephew. He'd be happy to take a look."

Aunt Desi and Mom rushed Wolfheart in a wildly demonstrative hug, and just like that, the *Heart Headed* podcast was back on.

✝✝✝

After we got the microphones set up, we gathered everyone to the table with their notes and reference material. While Timothy and Petey opted for their laptops, Father Patrick clung to the notepads we'd provided. "I'll be old school until the day I die," he quipped.

Both the hosts and the guests had a cup of coffee or a glass of water in front of them, and when Fireman addressed the power of muting, I was impressed. "Sterling and I can fix a lot in editing later," he explained, "but don't be afraid to hit mute if you have to get a drink or need to cough."

"Great point, Fireman. Now, let's talk about microphones. Everyone make a fist." Even though Timothy had done his share of podcasts, I appreciated his humility as he made a fist with the newbies. "That's the ideal distance you want between your mouth and the mic."

"And don't put your mic too high or you'll sound nasally," Fireman added, his confidence growing. "Speaking down to the mic adds a warmer tone."

"Got it." Petey grinned, squeezing his mama's hand. "This is gonna be fun!"

Before Fireman and I took our place behind the computer

on Aunt Desi's desk, I signaled to the participants that it was time to put their earphones on. I got a little resistance from Mom, who really wanted to keep her hat on, but she eventually acquiesced.

I raised my eyebrows at Fireman, and then at Meadow, Wolfheart, Uncle Lenny, and Ricky as they huddled on the couch in anticipation. After a "let's do this" look, Fireman and I bumped fists.

"Okay. Let's cue the music," I said in a low voice, watching as Fireman selected the music track Aunt Desi and Mom had decided on, an inspiring combination of Chris Stapleton meets Elevation Worship. "Are y'all ready?"

After they traded their own version of the fist bump, Fireman hit the music, and I said into the microphone, "*Heart Headed, a Podcast for Strong Women with Gentle Hearts. Episode one.*"

"I'm Desi."

"And I'm Robin."

"And we're just two southern gals who want to chat about the things that really matter to women."

"So we won't be talking about makeup or baking. Well," Mom chuckled, "sometimes we might because Desi makes an out-of-this-world hummingbird cake." I grinned as she and Aunt Desi dissolved in laughter, recovered, and then nailed the sound bite. "Mostly though we're going to talk about real struggles in women's lives. Things like loneliness, feelings of inadequacy, complicated family dynamics, and the repercussions of abuse."

"And we're not going to sugar coat it either," Aunt Desi put in, her voice thick with knowing, "but we will show you how you can apply scripture to ease all matters of the heart."

"And we *will* celebrate the unfailing love of Christ."

And they were off and running. Naturals, the both of them. It was as if the rest of us—the audience—were privy to a private conversation, as their manner was relaxed, funny, affectionate, and genuine. For those of us who knew and loved them, it was a lovely glimpse into their lifelong friendship.

I couldn't help but think of my dad, of how proud he'd be of my previously insecure, frail, and passive mother, by the way she'd triumphed over loss and shined now with the zeal of someone who'd been awarded a second chance.

During their conversation, she and Aunt Desi discussed everything from recklessness and dishonorable behavior to substance versus flair. Fortunately, Micah was covering at Lenny's Tool Shed today, or she'd have been mortified.

Eventually, they got around to introducing their Holy Men, as they liked to tag them. Petey boldly played the son card, telling humorous stories about his mama and insisting that he was his parents' favorite and that they loved him way better than his older brother Luke, who happened to be the Mayor of Shady Gully. His personality shined through as he spoke about his wife, Shady Gully's very own veterinarian, and then of Unity Christian Church, the raising of which had been a pivotal part of his spiritual growth.

Father Patrick, whose temperament belied the usually austere image most people had when they thought of priests, was a hands-down hit. Hilarious, to be sure, but also humble, endearing, and very approachable. I was certain listeners would respond to him like an uncle or a grandfather, someone they could pour their heart out to in front of a roaring fire.

"And now," Aunt Desi began, her eagerness bursting through in the tone of her voice, "Robin and I are thrilled to welcome the one and only Timothy from Northlake Christian Church in Lexington, Kentucky." And with that, the gifted and charismatic pastor revered across the country, cleared his throat.

When Petey spontaneously whistled and clapped, it created a ripple effect of celebratory applause throughout the room. Even the fan club from the couch enthusiastically echoed the cheers. Thinking the impulsive splash of emotion would actually be good to include, I let it go on for a few moments, which is when I caught the subtle exchange between Father Patrick and Aunt Desi.

The priest had covertly slipped her a note, and after reading it she looked at him in shock. When he nodded his insistence, she appeared to concede.

What in the world?

"Thanks for having me, Desi," Timothy said pleasantly. "I'm a big fan of yours and Robin's."

"Ha! Well, thanks." She hesitated. "Timothy, most of us have the pleasure of watching you on Sundays, and of course, there are those lucky folks in Lexington who get to see your teachings in person, but I think what would be interesting for our listeners… is to get a feel for how you got where you are. Tell us a little about the beginnings of your faith journey."

A quick exchange between him and Father Patrick revealed that Timothy was very much in on whatever was about to happen.

"Actually, Desi, I'm glad you asked that. For those at Northlake, as well as the viewers who saw me collapse on stage recently, I know there's been a lot of concern. And rightly so. My faith journey, as you put it, has been weighing on me lately. Particularly the early stages, when I didn't believe in God at all. I didn't believe in Him because I didn't know Him, and it's those years and the things that happened in that period of my life that I've hidden from my congregation, my colleagues, and even my close friends. I've been carrying around a lot of shame…" He trailed off for a brief moment, then seemed to rally with fresh resolve. "So I figure why not use this wonderful platform to tell the truth?"

I held my breath, because surely if I let it out, its echo would roar in the quiet of the room. I glanced at the supporters on the couch, who all exuded shock, concern, and curiosity. All except Meadow.

"Although I was born in Kentucky, my first memories are of Saint Louis, Missouri, at the foot of the arch. I was there with my mother." He cleared his throat, and for the first time, I saw a wrinkling of strain across his forehead. "My mother was a drug addict. I spent the first ten to twelve years of my life living in and out of derelict projects, under overpasses, and in heroin dens."

Naturally, it would be my mother who gasped aloud—*sorry, Fireman*—forgetting all about the power of muting. You could hardly blame her though, as even Petey's expression had seized up, his breathing coming in heavy bursts through his mouth. I glanced at Fireman, who while clearly surprised, seemed remarkably composed.

"I never had a formal education until I was a young teenager, nor did we ever escape that life. The truth is my mother never got clean. In fact, she overdosed and died in my arms."

A pall of shock swept through the office. Finally, Aunt Desi said, "I'm so sorry, Timothy."

"Here's another truth." Timothy swallowed, glancing quickly at Father Patrick before letting loose with another truth. "I know it sounds terrible, but part of me was relieved when my mother died. While I loved her, her addiction, up until then, defined my life. I suffered from neglect, malnutrition, and as you can imagine, a fair amount of abuse. So for a battered, sullied, and illiterate kid, I looked at her death as a means to freedom."

"But you were so young," my mom said lightly, "so vulnerable. What did you do? Where did you go?"

"I truly believe that God had His way with me then. He gave me the courage to walk out of that drug den. He sent a truck driver who saw me wandering on the highway and kindly picked me up, fed me, and gave me shelter." Timothy stopped, lost in memory. "Can you imagine that? Isn't that simply astounding?" He reached for his water and drank deeply. "The truck driver's name was Philip, and he was the first in a series of, I believe, angels who shaped the rest of my life. He listened to me, and for the first time, I felt heard. Seen. And then he introduced me to another man named Paul." When Timothy faltered, Father Patrick reacted proactively and muted both of their microphones. As Father Patrick spoke softly to him, everyone around the table and in the room lowered their heads in respect until Timothy eventually picked up his story. "Paul had been through a similar kind of hell. But God saved him, and because Paul was a good, decent, and above all, a grateful man, he dedicated his life to the Lord. He was passionate about sharing the good news, and he took me under his wing. It was through him that I met Lydia, a woman gifted with an inherent and most gracious maternal instinct."

This time, Timothy muted the microphone himself, taking a moment to regain his composure. "Truly, I could cry now just thinking about her," he confessed after he clicked the mic back on. "She taught me how to do math and how to treat women." When Timothy glanced at Meadow, he nearly succumbed to the emotion bubbling below the surface.

"God provided for me," he continued. "He lovingly sent me these exemplary stewards who willingly invested their time, their love, and their resources to provide me with opportunities that wouldn't have been possible otherwise. Even more importantly, they led me out of darkness and into the beautiful, bright light that is Jesus." He took a giant breath before looking squarely at his hosts. "That's my faith journey, Desi, Robin. God restores. God provides. God loves. Everything is possible with God. Even forgiveness."

Beside me, it was young Fireman who had captured Timothy's attention, maintaining eye contact with the renowned preacher for several seconds. I noted the subtle, reciprocal nod they swapped.

"Amen," Petey breathed into the microphone.

"Indeed," Father Patrick echoed, genuflecting reverently.

Aunt Desi surprised everyone then, probably even herself, when she pressed with one more intuitive question. "So...you were able to forgive your mother?"

"Yes." Timothy glanced at Father Patrick. "You see, even when you think your faith journey has progressed and…matured, God never stops sending us champions, and what I recently learned is that sometimes even shepherds need shepherds. After what happened to me on the stage of Northlake Christian Church recently, God provided me with another giver, a nurturer, a noble guide at just the right time in my life." He gripped Father Patrick's shoulder. "This fine priest helped me find my way, and because of his counsel I've been able to recognize the significance of the troubling, reoccurring nightmares that robbed me of sleep leading up to my collapse."

My mother asked, "Can you tell us about them?" While part of me wanted to cringe, the other part wanted to cheer her boldness. *How about that, Dad?*

"It was the same dream, night after night, with only the slightest deviation. In essence, I was safe in God's kingdom. Protected, surrounded by beauty. I had everything I needed to be joyful and content. And yet, when I heard the sound of frightened, lost lambs beyond the gates, I couldn't resist the temptation. Pride convinced me that I was the only one who could save them. Vanity drew me out, and of course, once I reached the sheep, they morphed into frothing wolves that turned on me. In their ghastly faces, I recognized my mother who represented someone I'd cared for and trusted. Someone who'd betrayed me. Someone who'd let me down."

"That's awful." Petey grunted, visibly shaken.

Aunt Desi muted her microphone, struggling to maintain her composure as she swiped back tears. I couldn't help but wonder if she was thinking about her own mother. Or her stepfather, Tom.

"It *was* awful," Timothy said, "but with Father Patrick's help, I realized the only way to fully move on from the past, to free myself, was to forgive her." He and Father Patrick traded meaningful looks. "It really is true what they say. There *is* freedom in forgiveness."

Aunt Desi grazed Timothy's hand supportively. Uncle Lenny, who up until then had been sitting quietly on the couch, stood on the ready—just in case she needed him.

"The other thing that dream taught me," Timothy finished, "which is also profound, is that we have to stop chasing that *thing*—whatever it might be—that thing that keeps us up at night with want. That thing we think we need that'll surely make us happy, lovable, beautiful, prosperous…"

Timothy paused for a moment, reflective. "That dreaded thing that makes us discount ourselves. Makes us feel less than…and unworthy. The truth is, we already have everything we need. Our Father assures us of that. These silly battles we obsess over daily have already been fought, and guess what? God won. He wins every time."

The extended silence that followed startled me out of my daze. When I quickly swiveled to the computer, Timothy jumped in, perhaps covering for my lapse. "On a lighter note," he said, "I'd like to send a shout-out to my good friend, Grandma Tallulah, from Lexington. Hope you're feeling better. Looking forward to our next game of gin rummy. Heads up, there's someone I want you to meet." He switched his glance to Meadow, who actually blushed.

Relieved and thrilled because the upbeat note was a perfect way to end the podcast, I glanced at everyone as they waited expectantly for my direction. I signaled my mom, who'd been waiting for her prompt to do the closing.

I turned to Fireman, signaling that he should roll the closing music.

As the music played, I listened to my mom ease through the flash points of the show's conclusion, directing listeners to the *Heart Headed* website where they could sign up for the newsletter and find out about the next episode. She totally killed it.

"Four. Three. Two. One." I smiled at all the faces in the room. "That's a wrap."

Cheers went up and hugs were aplenty, with Wolfheart finding the sturdy hands of Petey and Father Patrick as everyone else had clinched their various mates in hearty embraces. He then made his way to Fireman and me, nodding his impression in his singularly understated way. "Nice job," he said.

"Y'all were fantastic," Aunt Desi gushed as she pounced over and wrapped Fireman and me in a hug. "Such fabulous direction."

"You did pretty good too." Fireman grinned, totally swept up in the spirit of it all. "Nice follow-up question to Timothy."

Aunt Desi threw her head back in laughter as she leaned into Wolfheart, impulsively pulling Fireman into their embrace. "You made a good choice in this guy," she told him. "He'll lead you well."

When Timothy ambled over, he shook Fireman's hand. "Is there anything you're not good at?"

Fireman blushed. Then shrugged. "I got what you said, you know? About God putting people in our lives who provide opportunity. And love."

"I knew you would. And if *Grandpa* here ever starts to drive you crazy, you know where to reach me. We'll ride a horse to a Wildcats game or something."

After a loud *POP!* prompted everyone to cover their heads and duck, my mom whooped from the kitchen. "The champagne is served!"

"Hey." I tugged Timothy before he headed that way. "I'm glad you told your story. It actually helped me…think of things a little differently."

He patted me on the back, pulling me into a man hug. "Then my work is done." His usually goofy grin was filled with relief. "Are you headed back to Lexington soon?"

"No, actually, I think I'm going to go to Santa Fe for a few days. I'll be back Monday."

"Take your time." He winked. "Meadow and I plan to."

"Congrats on that, by the way. The unicorn is classy."

After he drifted into the kitchen with the other celebrants, Fireman appeared and swiveled in an office chair. "Now what?"

"Now we get to work," I told him. "With any luck, we can get this thing edited and launched tonight."

Together we fine-tuned the intro and outro music, sliced, diced, and smoothed out the ambient noise and all the awkward moments, and after filling out the episode title, description, publish date, and episode number, we felt pretty good about getting it done before midnight. I tipped my head to indicate the upload button flashing on the computer screen. "You want to do the honors?"

"Absolutely." Fireman grinned. "So what do you think? Do we have a hit here?"

"Only one way to find out."

And with one click of the mouse, he sent Mom, Aunt Desi, and Timothy's truth out into the world.

Epilogue
Sterling

The *Heart Headed* podcast went viral twenty-four hours later.

I know because I was sitting in the Alexandria International Airport waiting for my flight to Dallas, where I'd hop another flight to Santa Fe, New Mexico. Two things happened simultaneously. A group of women sitting in the terminal behind me started buzzing about "that pastor at the megachurch in Kentucky" and Fireman texted with:

> Their website nearly crashed
> because of all the traffic! So
> far, they've got ten thou-
> sand newsletter sign-ups! And
> a reporter wants to interview
> them! SOS!

For dramatic effect, he added several emojis. The head exploding, the big, scary eyes, and the wink.

Lots of mixed signals there, but I knew he could handle it. However, I texted back:

> Get with Micah, she's always
> looking for a new job. Maybe
> she can do some of the PR stuff
> while you maintain the site.
> I'll be back soon.

I scrolled through my phone, more out of habit at this point than any burning desire to check for query responses or rejections.

As I was about to return my phone to my pocket, a new text came in from Fireman:

    Good luck with the hot girl!

He punctuated his text with the kissy face emoji.

I chuckled, continuously amazed by this remarkable kid who possessed an innate kindness and a desire to help others. Talk about a giver, despite his less-than-ideal circumstances, Fireman was a shepherd in his own right.

Since the podcast, I'd been consumed with the whole notion of shepherds. What had Timothy said? *Even shepherds need shepherds.* He'd been referring to Father Patrick, of course, another holy man who was also full of compassion and humanity and probably suffering with his own flaws and battling his own demons, and yet he'd charged in without hesitation to come to Timothy's rescue.

Just as Timothy had been doing for others prior to his breakdown.

Perhaps that's what shepherds did. No matter what, their job was to look after the lambs and protect them from the wolves. Wolves could represent anything from physical danger to anxiety to depression to addiction. Wolves never let up. They never slept. But fortunately, neither did shepherds.

It occurred to me that shepherds came in many different forms and could be any one of us at any time. We all had opportunities to be shepherds, to guide someone out of their own personal periods of darkness. Heck, my sister did it every day, whether it was comforting a pet owner or rushing across the creek to deliver kittens. So did her husband, Petey, who'd built a church to bring two communities together. Wolfheart continuously counseled people on The Creek, representing them personally as well as professionally as their councilman. Luke was another one who went about his mayoral duties with little fanfare, as did Quietdove and Max—and even Ricky, the sheriff of Shady Gully.

Heck, the town of Shady Gully itself had rallied to find a lost dog and a hundred-pound python. They'd also stood in line to offer a home to a young boy who needed a guardian. A tiny town chock-full of wisecrackers, eccentrics, and curmudgeons, and yet they'd all stormed in to answer the call.

And Pippa. Hadn't she, in fact, shepherded me? Certainly, her unwavering belief in my work had pushed me to consider changes, to explore new opportunities and fresh approaches rather than obsess over dead ends and closed doors. Her positivity had also shined a clear and bright light on my interactions with Tammy Jo, revealing the miserable note of desperation in my quest to win her affection. Sadly, I hadn't liked myself much in those moments.

Pippa was another story entirely. She was like the sunny side up to Tammy Jo's over easy. She brought out the best in me. She made me feel hopeful, and I liked who I was when I was with her. Her affection fortified me, and her encouragement caused me to look at everything with fresh eyes.

Not for the first time today I thought about Timothy's view that everything we needed was already in our possession. Specifically, God, and all that encompassed—His love, His light, and His care. Why then did we fight so hard pining for all the rest?

I reached for my phone, experiencing a hitch in my breath as I considered texting Pippa. As badly as I wanted to update her on the podcast news, I restrained myself as it was still very early in Santa Fe. Also, I could hardly wait to see her and tell her about a new idea I'd been toying with…

I realized I was smiling. Sitting in the airport all by myself—smiling.

"Attention passengers of Flight 1025 to Dallas. We've called in mechanics to have a look at a minor issue on the plane, so we're looking at about a forty-minute delay before boarding."

Naturally, groans erupted throughout the terminal, and phones lit up as folks scrambled to reschedule connecting flights. I instead returned my phone to my pocket and dragged my laptop from my backpack.

With thoughts of Pippa, shepherds, small towns, and moments

of consequence, I started a new Word Document. My fingers hesitated over the keyboard for several minutes. I closed my eyes as waves of doubt ebbed and flowed, and then rose and clawed at me with menace.

And then I pushed those thoughts away, dwelling instead on my renewal of faith. My belief that God would get me where He wanted me to be, and that He would complete His work in me.

In His time.

The Shepherds, I typed. *Chapter One...*

Note to Readers:

Thank you for spending time with me in Shady Gully.

If you enjoyed *Paint Me Fearless*, *Wolfheart*, *Shades of Violet*, and *The Shepherds*—and look forward to Book 5 in *The Shady Gully Series*, please take a few minutes to leave a review on Goodreads, Amazon, Barnes & Noble, Books-A-Million, BookBub, or wherever you purchase your books! Your reviews MATTER!

And everyone, please sign up for my blog and newsletter. When you become a FRIEND OF HALLIE, you'll get all my book news FIRST, including release dates, cover reveals, contests, giveaways, recipes, and more! www.hallielee.com

I'll see y'all back at the Cozy Corner in Book 5.

Until then …Stay Fearless!

https://linktr.ee/HallieLeeBooks
https://www.facebook.com/HallieLeeBooks
https://www.instagram.com/Hallie_Lee_Books
https://www.twitter.com/HallieLeeBooks
Hallie Lee (@hallie_lee_books) TikTok | Watch Hallie
Lee's Newest TikTok Videos

Acknowledgements
& Thanks:

This book is fiction. That means I made it all up. For real.

First and foremost, thank you to Mike Parker and Wordcrafts Press. I'm grateful for your encouragement and absolute faith in my work.

As for *The Shepherds*, so many people contributed to this story. Whether with editing, research, or just listening to me fret while laboring in the "writing" trenches.

Because I love animals, it was inevitable that one of my characters would become a veterinarian, and because Violet is way smarter than me, I depended on a lot of experts to get the facts, nuances, and veterinarian lingo correct. Thank you, Bonnie Massie, for sharing so many entertaining stories from the world of doctoring animals.

In the case of Pierre, I needed first-hand experience on pythons. Lucky for me, Michael Beran of Bare Hands Rescue at the Wildlife Command Center in Missouri, was a fellow classmate of mine in a small town very much like Shady Gully. Thanks Mike, for spit-balling ideas with me and giving Pierre some character. Your legend is bold and far reaching, as even the "fictional town of Shady Gully" refers to you in awed tones. ☺

Quite honestly, my editors make my world a better place. Jenn Jakes, thank you for editing my books and in this case, providing the inside scoop on all things Saint Louis. And Barbara Shoemaker, not only did you inspire Duke and Duchess, but you continue to be my #1 reference on all things Shiba Inu.

You've also become a most valuable safety net in my writing journey.

Kathy Fox Vancil, the esteemed narrator of the Shady Gully audiobooks, you're an eagle-eye editor in your own right, as well as a dear friend and confidante. I'm eternally grateful for your moral support. Oh, and thanks for making me laugh. A lot.

And then there are the people I call my "writer friends." Have mercy, what would I do without y'all? Janetta Fudge Messmer, I love you to the moon and back! And Charly Cox, the bestselling author of the Alyssa Wyatt series, you've taught me so much, not only about writing but about friendship and the blessing of finding the right person's hand to hold while in the trenches. #HGUS!

Michelle Bennington, I'm so glad you're here on Ground Zero with me in Kentucky. Our lunches, road trips, and venting sessions keep me going. And your multiple series—*Small Batch*, *Hazardous Hoarding*, and *Widows & Shadows*—inspire me, encourage me, and enchant me!

And finally, and most importantly, I'd be lost without my husband, Bruce, and my beautiful daughter, Bree. You are my people, and I love and adore you.

Who's Who in Shady Gully

The Matriarchs & Their Families

Desi – married to Lenny, best friends with Robin, mother of Luke, Petey, and Micah

Lenny – married to Desi, father of Luke, Petey, and Micah

Luke – Desi & Lenny's oldest son, mayor of Shady Gully, married to Bella

Petey – Desi & Lenny's son, charismatic, loved by all, spiritually driven, married to Violet

Micah – Desi & Lenny's daughter, baby of the family, works as a dental hygienist in Belle Maison as well as her dad's hardware store and at Violet's Vet

Robin – widow of Dean, best friends with Desi, mother of twins, Sterling and Violet

Sterling – Robin's son, handsome, creative, musically inclined

Violet – Robin's daughter, brilliant, driven, well educated, married to Petey

Shady Gullians

Sheriff Rick – the sheriff of Shady Gully, graduated with Desi, Lenny, and Robin. In love with Robin

Max – Robin's baby brother, deputy in Shady Gully

"Cruella" Claire – graduated with Desi and Robin, gossip, head of Shady Gully's post office

Charlie Wayne - ornery owner of The Cozy Corner, Shady Gully's favorite eatery

Sprite – owner of Sprite's Quick Stop, a gas station & general store at one of the corners of Shady Gully's fabled four-way stop

Bubba – graduated with Desi, Lenny, Robin, works at Luke's Auto Body Shop

Daryl – graduated with Desi, Lenny, Robin, works at Luke's Auto Body Shop, also does construction work

Patty – Shady Gully's favorite EMT, friends with Denise, a classmate of Desi and Robin's

Tammy Jo – Petey's ex-girlfriend, nurse

Jesse & James – twin sons of Brother Wyatt, who was a pillar in the Church community and brothers of Dolly

Dolly – daughter of Brother Wyatt, sister of Jesse and James, owns Dolly's Diva Dome, and once married to Mitch

Ole Man Chester – ornery old coot who hangs out with Claire at the Post Office

Big Al – outspoken resident of Shady Gully, works at the fire station

Thaddeus – Big Al's sidekick

JJ Wheeler – Hippie chef who hijacked the four-way stop in Book 3, now works at Cozy Corner

Hoot Wheeler – JJ's brawny son who owns Wheeler Construction, flirts with Micah

Across The Creek

Wolfheart – born & raised on The Creek, devoted to his niece, Meadow, and her daughter, Bella. Friends with Desi & Robin

Meadow – Lives on The Creek, delivers mail in Shady Gully, mother of Bella

Bella – daughter of Meadow, Wolfheart's great-niece, married to Luke

Quietdove – hails from The Creek, handsome, deputy sheriff in Shady Gully

Sigourney Sky – A Creek woman who opened Nails & Thread, a successful salon, at the four-way stop in Shady Gully

Redflyer – hails from across the creek, now heads the fire station there

Youngdeer – Redflyer's friend, works at The Creek's fire station

Moonpipe – Redflyer and Youngdeer's buddy, works at the fire station

Fireman – young Creek boy who accidentally set a church on fire, has a crush on Bella, and wants to be a fireman when he grows up

Granny Lacey – Fireman's elderly grandmother, notorious for her bad cooking

Bluejay – hails from across the creek, reserved, a staple in The Creek community

Rising Owl – Redflyer's nephew, works at SPEED, an internet service

The Shepherds

Father Patrick – popular priest at Sacred Heart Catholic Church, Irish ancestry, jolly, loves food and wine and the people of Shady Gully

Timothy – pastor of the mega church, North Lake Christian Church, in Lexington, Kentucky

Shady Characters

Mitch – graduated with Desi, Lenny, Robin, became guidance counselor at Shady Gully High. Briefly married to Dolly, but eventually left Shady Gully after scandal involving a young student

Tom – Desi's stepdad who sexually abused her

Adam – pursued Desi in high school, and even after she married Lenny, an aspiring country music singer, a womanizer

Deceased

Sunny – Desi's flamboyant mother, artist, loved by all

Dean – Lenny, Sheriff Rick's friend, brilliant businessman, was married to Robin, father to Sterling and Violet

284

About the Author
Hallie Lee

Born and raised in Louisiana, Hallie Lee's first novel, *Paint Me Fearless*, debuted at #1 on Amazon's Hot New Release List, was Bookfest 2022's #1 Contemporary Christian Fiction winner, and blossomed into the successful, bestselling Shady Gully series.

In between writing novels, she writes devotions for *Guidepost's All God's Creatures* magazine, a devotional that reveals all the miraculous ways God uses animals to nurture our faith. She currently lives in the hills of Kentucky with her family and new intern, Piper, the orange cat.

Connect with Hallie online at:

www.HallieLee.com

www.ingramcontent.com/pod-product-compliance
Lightning Source LLC
Chambersburg PA
CBHW031511010826
48973CB00012B/414